Intervention

ALSO BY ROBIN COOK

Intervention

Robin Cook

G. P. PUTNAM'S SONS
NEW YORK

PUTNAM

G. P. PUTNAM'S SONS
Publishers Since 1838
Published by the Penguin Group
Penguin Group (USA) Inc., 375 Hudson Street, New York, New York 10014, USA •
Penguin Group (Canada), 90 Eglinton Avenue East, Suite 700, Toronto, Ontario
M4P 2Y3, Canada (a division of Pearson Canada Inc.) • Penguin Books Ltd,
80 Strand, London WC2R 0RL, England • Penguin Ireland, 25 St Stephen's Green,
Dublin 2, Ireland (a division of Penguin Books Ltd) • Penguin Group (Australia),
250 Camberwell Road, Camberwell, Victoria 3124, Australia (a division of Pearson
Australia Group Pty Ltd) • Penguin Books India Pvt Ltd, 11 Community Centre,
Panchsheel Park, New Delhi–110 017, India • Penguin Group (NZ), 67 Apollo
Drive, Rosedale, North Shore 0632, New Zealand (a division of Pearson New
Zealand Ltd) • Penguin Books (South Africa) (Pty) Ltd, 24 Sturdee Avenue,
Rosebank, Johannesburg 2196, South Africa

Penguin Books Ltd, Registered Offices: 80 Strand, London WC2R 0RL, England

The Scripture quotations contained herein are from the New Revised Standard Version
Bible, copyright © 1989, Division of Christian Education of the National Council of
Churches of Christ in the U.S.A. All rights reserved.

Library of Congress Cataloging-in-Publication Data

Cook, Robin, date.
Intervention / Robin Cook.
p.   cm.
ISBN 978-0-399-15570-3
1. Biotechnology—Fiction.   I. Title.
PS3553.O5545I58   2009   2009017820
813'.54—dc22

Printed in the United States of America
1   3   5   7   9   10   8   6   4   2

BOOK DESIGN BY AMANDA DEWEY

This is a work of fiction. Names, characters, places, and incidents either are the product
of the author's imagination or are used fictitiously, and any resemblance to actual persons,
living or dead, businesses, companies, events, or locales is entirely coincidental.

While the author has made every effort to provide accurate telephone numbers and Internet addresses at the time of publication, neither the publisher nor the author assumes
any responsibility for errors, or for changes that occur after publication. Further, the publisher does not have any control over and does not assume any responsibility for author
or third-party websites or their content.

This book is dedicated to those families,
victims, and researchers who have
contributed to the extraordinary advances
in the treatment of childhood cancer.

Intervention

Now a certain man named Simon had previously practiced magic in the city and amazed the people of Samaria, saying that he was someone great. All of them, from the least to the greatest, listened to him eagerly, saying "This man is the power of God that is called Great." And they listened eagerly to him because for a long time he had amazed them with his magic. But when they believed Philip, who was proclaiming the good news about the Kingdom of God and the name of Jesus Christ, they were baptized, both men and women. Even Simon himself believed. After being baptized, he stayed constantly with Philip and was amazed when he saw the signs and great miracles that took place.

Now when the apostles at Jerusalem heard that Samaria had accepted the word of God, they sent Peter and John to them. The two went down and prayed for them that they might receive the Holy Spirit (for as yet the Spirit had not come upon any of them; they had only been baptized in the name of the Lord Jesus). Then Peter and John laid their hands on them, and they received the Holy Spirit. Now when Simon saw that the Spirit was given through the laying on of the apostles' hands, he offered them money, saying "Give me also this power so that anyone on whom I lay my hands may receive the Holy Spirit." But Peter said to him, "May your silver perish with you, because you thought you could obtain God's gift with money! You have no part or share in this, for your heart is not right before God."

Acts of the Apostles 8:9–21
New Revised Standard Version

1

J ack Stapleton's transition from restless sleep to fully awake was
instantaneous. He was in a runaway car plunging down a steep
city street, rapidly closing in on a line of preschoolers crossing in
pairs and holding hands, unaware of the calamity bearing down on
them. Jack had the vehicle's brake pedal pressed to the floor but
to no avail. If anything, the car's speed was increasing. He screamed
at the children to get out of the way but caught himself when he
realized he was staring up at the streetlight-dappled ceiling of his
bedroom in his house on West 106th Street in New York City.
There was no car, no hill, and no children. He'd had another one
of his nightmares.

Unsure if he'd cried out or not, Jack turned toward his wife,
Laurie. In the faint light of the bare window he could see she was
fast asleep, suggesting he'd managed to suppress his shriek of horror.
As he returned his attention to the ceiling, he shuddered at his
dream, a recurrent nightmare that always terrified him. It had begun
back in the early nineties, after Jack's first wife and his two young
daughters, aged ten and eleven, had been killed in a commuter

plane crash after visiting Jack in Chicago, where he'd been retraining in forensic pathology. Originally an eye surgeon, Jack had decided to switch his specialty to escape what he saw as the progressive intrusion of the four horsemen of the medical apocalypse: health insurance companies, managed care, unenlightened government, and a seemingly indifferent public. He had hoped that by fleeing clinical medicine he'd paradoxically be able to regain the sense of altruism and commitment that had attracted him to the study of medicine in the first place. Although he was ultimately successful in this regard, in the process he felt he had inadvertently wiped out his beloved family, plunging him into a spiral of guilt, depression, and cynicism. The runaway-car nightmare had been one of the symptoms. Though the dreams had disappeared entirely several years earlier, they'd returned again with a vengeance in the last few months.

Jack focused on the play of light on the ceiling from the streetlamp in front of his building and shuddered anew. On their way inside, its beams passed through the leafless limbs of the lonely tree planted between his house and the lamppost. As the night breezes blew the branches, it caused the light to flicker, projecting an undulating series of hypnotic Rorschach-like patterns. It made him feel alone in a cold, merciless universe.

Jack felt his forehead. He wasn't sweating, but then he felt his pulse. It was pounding and rapid, somewhere in the hundred-and-fifty per minute range, a sign that his sympathetic nervous system was in a full fight-or-flight reaction, typical after experiencing this brakeless-car dream.

What was unique about this particular dream scenario were the children. Usually the dreaded focus was purely personal, like a flimsy guardrail running along a precipice, a solid brick wall, or a fathomless body of water filled with sharks.

He turned his head to the clock. It was after four a.m. With his heart racing, he knew instinctively that there was no way he'd fall back to sleep. Instead, he gently tossed back the covers to avoid disturbing Laurie, and slipped out of bed. The oak flooring was as cold as marble.

He stood and stretched his stiff muscles. Despite being in his fifties, Jack still played street basketball whenever the weather and his schedule permitted. The evening before, in an attempt to harness his current anxieties, he played until he nearly dropped. He knew he'd pay a price in the morning, and he was right. He pushed himself through the pain and discomfort by bending over and holding his palms flat to the floor. Then he headed for the bathroom while musing about the children in his nightmare. He wasn't surprised by this fresh torture. The source of his current anguish, reawakened guilt, and threatening depression was a child: his own child, in fact, John Junior—JJ, as he and Laurie called him. The baby had arrived in August, a few weeks earlier than expected. But they'd been fully prepared, Laurie especially. She'd taken the whole experience in stride. In contrast, by the time the delivery was over some ten hours later, Jack was as exhausted as if he'd been the one who'd given birth. Though he'd assisted with his two daughters, he'd forgotten how emotionally difficult the experience was. He was relieved that both mother and child were fine and resting comfortably.

Things had gone reasonably well for the first month or so. Laurie was on maternity leave and enjoyed being a new mother despite JJ's nighttime fussiness. Jack's fears that the baby would be born with a genetic or congenital problem dissipated. He'd never admitted to Laurie that after the delivery and assurances that she was fine, he'd rushed to look over the pediatrician's shoulder.

Panicked, Jack had checked the child's facies and counted his fingers and toes. He wasn't sure if he could handle a handicapped child, as guilty as he felt at the fate of his two daughters. He had struggled with the idea of having another child, and whether he could risk the vulnerability and responsibility of parenthood, particularly if the child was disabled. He had even been reluctant to remarry. If not for Laurie's stalwart patience and unflagging support, he wouldn't have risked it. Deep down Jack couldn't rid himself of the feeling that he was somehow fated to bring disaster to those he loved.

He grabbed his bathrobe from the hook behind the bathroom door and padded down to JJ's room. Even in the darkness, Jack could appreciate the nursery's over-the-top décor, thanks to his mother-in-law, Dorothy Montgomery, who'd pulled out all the stops for the grandchild she'd worried she'd never have.

The baby's room was gently lit by several night-lights at baseboard level. Hesitantly, Jack approached the white eyelet–swathed bassinet. The last thing he wanted to do was wake the baby. Getting him back to sleep after the last feeding had been a struggle. With little of the night-lights' illumination reaching into the depths of the bassinet, Jack couldn't see much. The baby was on his back, hands splayed out to the sides at forty-five-degree angles. His fingers were clenched over each thumb. Some light glinted off the child's forehead. His eyes were lost in shadow, but Jack knew that beneath them were dark circles, one of the early symptoms of his problem. The dark skin had developed slowly over a period of weeks, and neither Jack nor Laurie had really noticed it. It was Dorothy who'd brought it to their attention. Other symptoms gradually made their presence known. What was initially termed "fussiness" by the unsuspecting pediatrician rapidly developed into sleepless nights for the entire Stapleton household.

When the diagnosis was finally made, Jack felt as if the wind had been knocked out of him, as if he'd been hit in the stomach with a baseball bat. The blood drained from his brain so dramatically that he'd had to grasp the arms of the chair he'd been sitting in to keep from falling to the floor. All his worst anxieties came true. His fear of a curse on his loved ones, particularly children, was alive and well. John Junior had been diagnosed with neuroblastoma, a disease responsible for fifteen percent of cancer deaths in children. Even worse, the cancer had widely metastasized, the malignancy spreading throughout JJ's body and into his bones and central nervous system. John Junior had what was termed *high-risk neuroblastoma*, the worst kind.

The next months had been pure hell for the new parents as the diagnosis grew more dire and a treatment plan was determined. Luckily for John Junior, Laurie had remained remarkably clearheaded during that time, particularly those first few crucial days, while Jack struggled to keep from falling into the same emotional and mental abyss he had years earlier. Knowing that John Junior and Laurie really needed him had saved the day. With great effort Jack fought off the overwhelming guilt and anger and was able to be a reasonably positive force.

It had not been easy, but the Stapletons were fortunate to be referred to the neuroblastoma program at the Memorial Sloan-Kettering Cancer Center, where they quickly came to rely on the professionalism, experience, and empathy of the talented staff. Over a several-month period, JJ underwent multiple courses of individualized chemotherapy, each requiring hospital admission, for troublesome side effects. When the chemotherapy had achieved what they thought was the desired result, JJ was started on a relatively new and promising treatment involving the intravenous injection of a mouse-generated monoclonal antibody to the neuroblastoma cells. The antibody, called 3F8, sought out the cancer cells and helped the patient's immune system destroy them. At least that was the theory.

The original treatment protocol had been to continue two-week cycles of daily infusions over a number of months, or perhaps a year, if possible. Unfortunately, after only a few cycles, the treatment had to be stopped. John Junior's immune system, despite the previous chemotherapy, had developed an allergy to the mouse protein, causing a dangerous side effect. The new plan was to wait a month or two, then recheck John Junior's sensitivity to the mouse protein. If it dropped low enough, treatment would start again. There was no other option. John Junior's disease was too widespread for autologous stem-cell therapy, surgery, or radiation.

"He's so darling when he's asleep and not crying," a voice said in the darkness.

Jack started. Caught up in his thoughts, he'd been unaware that Laurie had come up alongside him.

"I'm sorry to have startled you," Laurie added, looking up at her husband.

"I'm sorry to have awakened you," Jack said sympathetically. Given the demanding circumstances involving JJ's care, he knew she was chronically exhausted.

"I was already awake when you jolted yourself awake. I was afraid you were having another nightmare, with your rapid breathing."

"I was. It was my old runaway-car dream, only this time I was hurtling toward a group of preschool children. It was terrible."

"I can imagine. At least it's not hard to interpret."

"You think so," Jack said with a touch of sarcasm. He wasn't fond of being psychoanalyzed.

"Now, don't get your dander up," Laurie added. She reached out and grasped Jack's upper arm. "For the hundredth time, JJ's illness is not your fault. You have to stop beating up on yourself."

Jack took a deep breath and let it out noisily. He shook his head. "It's easy for you to say."

"But it's true!" Laurie insisted, giving Jack's arm an empathetic squeeze. "You know what the doctors at Memorial said when we pressured them for an etiology. Hell, it's more likely it was I, considering the chemicals we're exposed to as forensic pathologists. When I was pregnant, I tried to avoid all solvents, but it was impossible."

"Solvents as the cause of neuroblastoma has not been proven."

"It's not proven, but it's a hell of a lot more likely than the supernatural curse you keep torturing yourself with."

Jack reluctantly nodded. He was afraid of where the conversation was going. He didn't like to talk about his curse as he didn't believe in the supernatural, nor was he particularly religious, two beliefs he thought related. He preferred to keep to his immediate reality, things that he could touch and feel and generally appreciate with his own senses.

"What about my taking fertility drugs?" Laurie said. "That was another one of the doctor's suggestions. Do you remember?"

"Of course I remember," Jack admitted testily. He didn't want to talk about the issue.

"The truth is that the cause of neuroblastoma is not known, period! Listen, just come back to bed."

Jack shook his head. "I'd never fall back asleep. Besides, it's got to be close to five. I might as well shower and shave, and head in to work early. I need something to keep my mind busy."

"An excellent idea," Laurie agreed. "I wish I could do the same."

"We've talked about it, Laurie. You could go back to work. We'd hire nurses. Maybe it would be better for you."

Laurie shook her head. "You know me, Jack. I couldn't. I have to see this through, no matter what. I'd never forgive myself." She looked down at the seemingly peaceful sleeping baby, his slightly bulging eyes thankfully lost in shadow. She caught her breath as a sudden rush of emotion overtook her, as it unpredictably did on occasion. She'd wanted a child so much. She never imagined she'd have a child who'd suffer as much as JJ, and yet he was only four months old. She too struggled with guilt, but unlike Jack, she'd found at least some solace in religion. She'd been brought up a Catholic, now lapsed. Still, she wanted to believe in God, did so in a vague way, and managed to think of herself as a Christian. She secretly prayed for JJ, but at the same time, she couldn't understand how a supreme being would allow evil like children's cancer, particularly neuroblastoma, to exist.

Jack detected the change in Laurie's state of mind from the sound of her breathing. Choking back tears himself, he put his arm over his wife's shoulder and followed her line of sight back down to John Junior.

"The hardest thing for me at this point," Laurie managed, wiping away tears, "is the feeling that we are treading water. Right now, while we wait for his allergy to mouse protein to abate, we're not treating him. Orthodox medicine has, in a way, abandoned us. It's so frustrating! I felt so positive when we started the monoclonal antibody. It made so much more sense to me than the shotgun approach with chemotherapy, especially for a rapidly growing infant. Chemo goes after every growing cell, while the antibody goes after only the cancer cells."

Jack wanted to respond but couldn't. All he could do was agree with what Laurie had said by nodding his head. Besides, he knew that if he tried to talk at that point, he'd get choked up.

"The irony is that this is one of conventional medicine's failures," Laurie said, regaining some emotional control. "When evidence-based medicine runs into a snag, the patient suffers, as does the family, by being put out in the proverbial cold."

Jack nodded again. What Laurie was saying was unfortunately true.

"Have you ever thought of some sort of alternative or complementary medicine for JJ?" Laurie asked. "I mean, just while our hands are tied in relation to the monoclonal antibody treatment?"

Jack raised his eyebrows and gazed at Laurie in shocked surprise. "Are you serious?"

Laurie shrugged. "I don't know much about it, to be truthful. I've never tried it, unless you count vitamin supplements. Nor have I read much about it. As far as I know, it's all voodoo except for a few pharmacologically active plants."

"That's my sense as well. It's all based on the placebo effect, as far as I know. I've also never been interested to read about it, much less try it. I think it's for those people who have more hope than common sense, or for those people who are actively looking to be scammed. On top of that, I guess it's for those who are desperate."

"We're desperate," Laurie said.

Jack searched Laurie's face in the darkness. He couldn't tell if she was being serious or not. Yet they were desperate. That was clear. But were they that desperate?

"I don't expect an answer," Laurie added. "I'm just thinking out loud. I'd like to be doing something for our baby. I hate to think of those neuroblastoma cells having a free ride."

2

Shawn Daughtry had the Egyptian taxi driver stop at the al-Ghouri mausoleum, the tomb of the Mamluk leader who'd turned the rule of Egypt over to the Ottomans early in the sixteenth century. Shawn's last visit had been ten years earlier, with his third wife. He was now back with his fifth wife, the former Sana Martin, and enjoying the visit considerably more than his first. Sana had been invited to participate in an international conference on genealogical tracking. As a celebrated molecular biologist with a specialty in mitochondrial genetics, which had been the subject of her Ph.D. thesis, she was one of the conference's star speakers. Benefits included an all-expenses-paid trip for the two of them. Shawn had taken advantage of the opportunity by making arrangements to attend a concurrent archaeology conference. As it was the last day of the meeting, he'd skipped the concluding luncheon to accomplish a very specific errand.

Shawn stepped from the taxi and into the sweltering, dusty heat, crossing the bumper-to-bumper traffic on al-Azhar Street.

Every car, truck, bus, and taxi honked its horn while pushcarts and pedestrians threaded their way between the mostly stationary vehicles. Traffic in Cairo was a disaster. In the ten-year interval since Shawn's last visit, the population of metropolitan Cairo had swelled to a staggering 18.7 million people.

Shawn headed up al-Mukz li-Den Allah Street and into the depths of the narrow-laned Khan el-Khalili souk. The labyrinthian fourteenth-century bazaar sold everything from housewares, clothes, furniture, and foodstuffs to cheap souvenirs. Yet none of these interested him. He headed to the area that specialized in antiquities, searching out a shop he remembered from his previous visit called Antica Abdul.

Shawn was a trained archaeologist, and at fifty-four years old was at the peak of his career, heading the department of Near Eastern art at the Metropolitan Museum of Art in New York City. Although his main interest was biblical archaeology, he was an authority on the entire Middle East, from Asia Minor through Lebanon, Israel, Syria, Jordan, and Iran. Shawn had been dragged into the market on his last visit by his then wife, Gloria. Separated in the midst of the twisting lanes, Shawn had stumbled upon Antica Abdul. He'd been captivated by a stunning example in the shop's dusty window of a six-thousand-plus-year-old predynastic, unbroken piece of terra-cotta pottery decorated with a design of counterclockwise swirls. At that time there was an almost identical pot on prominent display in the ancient Egyptian section of the Metropolitan Museum, though the piece in Antica Abdul's window was in better shape. Not only was the painted design in superior condition, but the museum's pot had been found in pieces and had needed to be completely restored. Fascinated but also convinced Antica Abdul's pot was, like many other supposedly ancient antiquities in the bazaar, a clever fake, Shawn had entered the shop.

Although he had intended to make a cursory examination of the pot and then return to the hotel, he'd ended up staying for several hours. His furious wife, suspicious of his skulduggery and abandonment of her, had even beaten him back to the hotel. When he finally did return, she'd laid into him mercilessly, claiming she could have been kidnapped. As Shawn reminisced about the incident, he realized how auspicious such a denouement would have been. It would have made the divorce proceedings a year later that much easier.

What had kept Shawn in the shop for so long was essentially a free lesson in traditional Egyptian hospitality. And what started out as an argument with the proprietor over the authenticity of the pot ended up becoming a captivating discussion of the widespread market of cleverly made fake Egyptian antiquities over many cups of tea. Although Rahul, the owner of the shop, insisted the pot was a true antiquity, he was willing to share all the tricks of the trade, including the thriving scarab market, when he learned Shawn was an archaeologist. Scarabs, the carved talismans of the ancient Egyptian dung beetle, were considered to have the power of spontaneous regeneration. Using an inexhaustible source of bone from ancient cemeteries in Upper Egypt, talented carvers re-created the scarabs, then fed them to various domestic animals to impart a convincing patina. It was Rahul's contention that many of the pharaonic scarabs in the world's top museums were such forgeries.

After the long conversation, Shawn had bought the pot as a way of thanking Rahul for his hospitality. After some friendly haggling, Shawn paid half of what Rahul initially asked. Even so, Shawn thought that two hundred Egyptian pounds was more than double what he should have paid, at least until he got back to New York. Taking the pot to his colleague Angela Ditmar, head of the Egyptology department, Shawn was in for a shock. Angela determined that the pot was not a fake but instead a genuine relic and definitely more than six thousand years old. Shawn ended up donating the piece of pottery to the Egyptian department to replace the restored pot on permanent display to assuage the guilt he felt for having unknowingly spirited the valuable object out of Egypt.

Shawn walked deeper into the true depths of the bazaar. Stretching across the narrow lanes between the buildings were carpets and awnings effectively blotting out the sunlight. Passing butcher shops with hung lamb carcasses complete with skulls, eyeballs, and flies, Shawn was enveloped in the pungent aroma of offal, soon replaced by the smell of spices and then roasting Arabic coffee. The souk was an assault on the senses, both good and bad.

In the midst of converging alleyways, Shawn paused, lost, as he'd been ten years ago. Stopping in a tailor shop, he asked directions from an elderly Egyptian in a white skullcap and brown djellaba. A few minutes later he walked into Antica Abdul. Shawn was not at all surprised the shop was still there. On his previous visit, Rahul had said that the establishment had been in his family for more than a hundred years.

Except for the lack of the fantastic predynastic pot, the shop looked essentially the same. Since most of the so-called antiquities were fake, Rahul just kept on replacing them from his sources as they sold.

The shop appeared unattended as Shawn entered, the glass-beaded strings clacking into place behind him. For a moment Shawn wondered if Rahul would still be there, but any concern evaporated as the man quickly emerged through the dark drapes separating a pillow-strewn sitting area from the front part of the shop. Rahul motioned a greeting with a slight tilting of his head as he stepped behind an old glass-topped counter. He was a heavy-boned, full-lipped former fellahin who'd transitioned easily into an adroit businessman. Without a word, Shawn advanced a few steps and stared into the shopkeeper's dark, fathomless eyes. Almost immediately, Rahul's eyebrows knitted and then wrinkled upward with recognition.

"Dr. Daughtry?" Abdul questioned. He leaned slightly forward to get a better look.

"Rahul," Shawn replied, "I'm shocked that you remember me, much less my name after all these years."

"How could I not?" Rahul said, rushing from behind his counter and pumping Shawn's hand. "I remember all my clients, particularly those from famous museums."

"You have clients at other museums?" The shop was so modest it seemed farfetched.

"Of course, of course," Rahul intoned. "Whenever I get something special, which isn't too often, I communicate with whomever I think would be the most interested. It's so easy now with the Internet."

While Rahul hastened out into the alleyway by pushing through the beads and barking orders in Arabic, Shawn marveled at the speed of globalization. It seemed to him the Internet and the ancient Khan el-Khalili should have been worlds apart. Obviously, such was not the case.

A moment later, Rahul reentered the shop and gestured for Shawn to pass beyond into the seating area at the rear of the store. Oriental carpets covered the floor and the walls. Large, heavy brocade pillows dominated the space. A hookah stood to the side, along with a number of stacked, faded cardboard boxes. A bare lightbulb dangled from the ceiling. On a small wooden table were a few faded photographs, one of a large man in typical Egyptian dress who resembled Rahul. Rahul followed Shawn's line of sight.

"A photo of my uncle, given to me recently by my mother. Almost twenty years ago he owned this shop."

"He does look like family," Shawn commented. "Did you buy the shop from him?"

"No, from his wife. He was my mother's brother, but he got himself mixed up in an antiquities scandal involving a very important find: an intact tomb. His association cost him his life. He was killed here in the shop."

"My goodness," Shawn voiced. "I'm so sorry to have brought it up."

"In this business one cannot be too careful. Allah be praised that I have had no such trouble."

In the next instant the heavy curtain was drawn aside and a barefoot young boy appeared with a tray and two glasses in metal holders, each filled with steaming-hot tea. Without a word the boy placed the tray on the floor next to Shawn and Rahul, then retreated back through the curtains. All the while Rahul maintained a lively chatter about how pleased he was to enjoy a visit from Shawn.

"Actually, I had a specific reason," Shawn admitted.

"Oh?" Rahul replied questioningly.

"I have a confession to make. When I was last here in your shop, I bought a predynastic terra-cotta pot."

"I remember. It was one of my very best."

"We had a rather lengthy argument about its authenticity."

"You were reluctant to be convinced."

"Actually, I was never convinced. I bought it as a souvenir of our most interesting conversation, but when I got back to New York, I had it looked at by a knowledgeable colleague. She agreed with you. Not only was it real, but the pot is now on prominent display in the museum. It is truly a handsome piece."

"You are so kind to admit your error."

"Well, it has bothered me all these years."

"That is easy to remedy," Rahul responded. "If you would like to appease your conscience, all you need to do is pay me additional money."

Taken aback by the unexpected suggestion, Shawn stared at Rahul. For a moment he thought the man was serious. Then Rahul smiled, exposing his yellow, poorly maintained teeth. "I am joking, of course. I made a handsome profit with the pot from the children who found it, and I am satisfied."

Shawn smiled himself with obvious relief. He found Arabic humor as unexpected as Arabic hospitality.

"Your confession has brought to mind a most amazing piece I got only yesterday from a fellahin friend who is a farmer in Upper Egypt. It's something you might find of particular interest, given your biblical scholarship. With this particular object you will know more than I, so I trust you will not cheat me if you decide to buy it. Would you like to see it?"

Shawn shrugged. "Why not," he said. He didn't know what to expect, and he wasn't about to get his hopes up.

After rummaging in one of the cardboard boxes pushed against the wall, Rahul pulled out what looked to be a soiled cotton pillowcase. It wasn't until he'd sat back down that he removed the contents and placed them in Shawn's hands.

For several beats Shawn did not move while Rahul sat back and made himself comfortable against his large pillows. He wore an expectant, self-satisfied expression. He knew the archaeologist would soon guess what he was holding. The question was whether he'd be willing to buy it. The illegal cache needed the right person, one with relatively deep pockets.

Shawn quickly surmised what it was. Like most biblical scholars worth their salt, particularly those interested in New Testament studies or early Christian Church history, he'd seen and even handled the originals. The question was: Was what he was holding genuine, or was it a fake, like the scarabs and most of the other imitation antiquities that Rahul sold? Shawn had no idea, but given the unexpected authenticity of the predynastic bowl, he was willing to gamble and buy what he had in his lap. If by some chance it was real, it could be the biggest discovery of his life, and even if he eventually returned it to the Egyptian authorities, it was the kind of object whose story alone would set him apart from his contemporaries. Shawn didn't want one of Rahul's major museum contacts to get it—a distinct possibility, given his Internet contacts.

"Of course it is not real," Shawn began, in an attempt to start the haggling on the right foot. The problem was that despite the modest appearance of the shop, he knew he was dealing with a professional, business-savvy negotiator.

3

You're a doctor?" the uniformed policeman questioned with exaggerated surprise. The policeman's car was pulled to the curb behind them on the west side of Second Avenue as morning traffic streamed past on its way downtown. The cop's partner was still sitting in the passenger seat, drinking coffee. Jack's relatively new Trek bike was lying on its side on the pavement just in front of the cruiser. When Laurie had started her maternity leave, Jack had gone back to his old habit of commuting to the Office of the Chief Medical Examiner by bicycle.

Jack just nodded. Although he was calmer than he'd been, he was still irritated as hell at the taxi driver who'd cut him off by pulling across four lanes of traffic and stopping on a dime to pick up a fare. After managing to stop himself with just a minor jolt against the car's rear bumper, Jack had dashed around to the driver's side before the customer had gotten seated in the back. Jack had quickly inflicted several small but definite dents in the cabdriver's side door with his heel in hopes of encouraging the driver to climb out of the car so that a proper discussion could ensue. Lucky for everyone, the incident was brought to a rapid close by the arrival of the police. Apparently, the cops had witnessed at least some of the confrontation.

"I think you could use some anger-management classes," the policeman continued.

"I'll take that under advisement," Jack said sarcastically. He knew he was being provocative, but he couldn't help himself. The policeman had dismissed the cabdriver without even checking his license. It was as if the cop thought the incident was Jack's fault, since he was the one being detained.

"You're on a bike, for crying out loud," the cop complained. "What do you want to do, get yourself killed? If you are going to be crazy enough to ride a bike you have to expect the unexpected, particularly from cabbies."

"I've always felt New York City taxis and I could share the road."

With a final head shake and a roll of his eyes, the policeman handed back Jack's driver's license. "It's your funeral," he said, washing his hands of the affair.

Irritably, Jack picked up his bike, climbed on, started pumping, and rapidly pulled away from the police car even before the officer had climbed back into his cruiser. Soon the frenzy of the traffic, the icy wind, and the sustained exertion cooled his hot blood. Reaching the optimal speed of nearly twenty miles per hour, he was able to make the lights all the way to 42nd Street. As he waited for the green, panting for breath, he had to admit the policeman had been right. Hungry cabdrivers were always going to stop for a fare without regard for their surroundings. By failing to be a defensive rider, Jack was slipping into the pathologically destructive behavior that had put him at risk in the aftermath of his wife and daughters' deaths. Jack knew that he couldn't afford such selfishness. Laurie and John Junior needed him. If the family was going to beat the neuroblastoma, they had to do it as a team.

Arriving at the Office of the Chief Medical Examiner at the corner of First Avenue and 30th Street, Jack crossed the wide avenue and made his way to the building's driveway. Although the OCME building looked the same from First Avenue as it had when it was built in the sixties, changes had been made, particularly after 9/11. The old loading dock had been replaced by a larger parking area and a series of rollaway garage doors to accommodate the arrival of multiple vehicles with their corpses. Also gone was the herd of aged brown mortuary vans with HEALTH AND HOSPITAL CORP. stenciled on the sides parked helter-skelter all over 30th Street, replaced by an orderly fleet of new white vans. And instead of having to carry his bike into the morgue, Jack just rode it into one of the garages, where he could leave it safely in full view of a much better managed security office.

Inside the OCME were more changes. With the department's importance highlighted after 9/11, it was rewarded by the legislature with more personnel, equipment, and space. A brand-new building had been built a few blocks down First Avenue to house the expanded department of forensic biology, including, in particular, the DNA laboratory. Though the OCME of New York City had once fallen on hard times because of budget cuts, losing its famed countrywide leadership in the field of forensics, those days were past.

Jack now had more than thirty medical examiner, or M.D. forensic pathologist, colleagues across the city. The number of non-M.D. forensic investigators in the Manhattan office had been increased, their titles changed. No longer referred to as physician's assistants, they were now called medicolegal investigators, or MLIs. There were also eight new forensic anthropologists on staff, in addition to the forensic odontologists that Jack and the other MEs could tap for appropriate cases.

Jack had also personally benefited from all the growth and change. Along with the entire DNA and serology departments, other divisions including records, administration, legal, and human resources had moved to the new high-rise building, freeing space in the old building. All medical examiners now had their own, separate offices on the third floor. In addition to his desk, Jack now had his own lab bench, which meant he could leave out his microscope, slides, and paperwork without fear it would be disturbed.

Jack walked into the building, vowing to rise above his raw emotions and focus on his work. Feeling suddenly as if he were on a mission, he didn't wait for the back elevator but took the stairs. He quickly traversed the new sudden infant death syndrome offices and cut through the old medical records room, which now housed the warren of new investigator cubbies. The graveyard shift of medicolegal investigators was finishing up reports for the seven-thirty shift change. Jack gave a cursory wave to Janice Jaeger, the night-shift investigator he'd known since he'd started work at OCME, and with whom he frequently partnered.

He tossed his jacket into an aged leather club chair when he reached the ID office, where all the medical examiners eventually started their day. Stacked on the solitary desk were the records of the cases that had come in during the night and that fell within OCME jurisdiction, according to the medicolegal investigation team. These cases represented those deaths that had occurred in any unusual or suspicious manner, including suicide, accident, criminal violence, or merely suddenly when the victim was in apparent good health.

Jack sat down at the desk and began going through the cases. He liked to pick out the more challenging ones because they gave him the opportunity to learn. That was what he most enjoyed about forensics. The other medical examiners tolerated this behavior because Jack also did the most cases of anyone.

The normal morning process involved the medical examiner on first call for the week to come in early, usually about seven or slightly before, and go through the cases to determine which ones definitely needed postmortems, then assign them out on an equitable basis. Even Jack had the duty about a dozen times a year, which he never minded since he was invariably there anyway.

Within a couple of minutes Jack found an apparent meningitis case of a teenage boy from a private school on the Upper East Side. Since Jack was generally known as the infectious-disease guru after having made several lucky diagnoses in the past, he read the record slowly and put it aside. He thought that case might be good for him, since many of his colleagues shunned infectious cases. He truly didn't care.

Jack slowed down on his perusal of the next case as well. It was another relatively young individual, although this time it was a female. The victim was a twenty-seven-year-old woman who'd been brought into an emergency room with supposed rapid onset of confusion, spastic gait, and ultimately coma and death. There had been no fever or malaise, and according to her friends, she was an avid health enthusiast, shunning drugs and alcohol. Although her friends had been enjoying cocktails at the time of her collapse, they claimed the victim had consumed only soft drinks.

"Oh, shit!" a voice lamented, loud enough to snap Jack's head up.

Standing in the opened doorway leading out into the empty ID room was Vinnie Amendola, one of the mortuary technicians, a newspaper under his arm. He was still holding on to the doorknob of the connecting door as if he might change his mind and flee. It was clear that the source of his outburst was Jack's presence.

"What's the matter?" Jack demanded, wondering if there was some emergency.

Vinnie didn't answer. He glared at Jack for a beat before closing the door behind him. He stood in front of Jack's desk, arms crossed. "Don't freaking tell me you're reverting to your old ways," he said.

Jack could not suppress a smile. He'd suddenly realized the cause of Vinnie's feigned anger. Prior to John Junior's birth, when Jack would come to work early to cherry-pick the autopsy cases, he'd drag Vinnie down with him to the autopsy room to get a jump on the day. In addition to his regular mortuary-tech duties, Vinnie was responsible for coming in early to facilitate the transition from whatever the night techs were doing, although what he mostly did was make the communal coffee and then read the sports section of the *Daily News*.

Although Vinnie always complained about having to start autopsies earlier than the chief medical examiner decreed, he and Jack were a great team despite their merciless teasing of each other. Together they could frequently do one and a half or even two cases while others did just one.

"I'm afraid so, sport," Jack said. "Vacation is over. You and I are going to get back down to work. It's my New Year's resolution."

"But it's not New Year's for another month," Vinnie complained.

"Tough," Jack responded. He reached out and pushed the chart of the twenty-seven-year-old woman in Vinnie's direction. "Let's start with Keara Abelard."

"Not so fast, supersleuth," Vinnie protested, using his old nickname for Jack. He made a production of inspecting his watch as if he were about to refuse Jack's order. "I might be able to accommodate you in, say, ten minutes, after I make the house coffee." He smiled. Feigning the opposite, he'd actually missed his special relationship with Jack based on their early starts.

"It's a deal," Jack said. After a quick high-five with Vinnie, he went back to the stack of charts.

"Since you stopped coming in early when your son was born, I thought it was a permanent schedule change," Vinnie said as he loaded the pot with fresh coffee, whose aroma quickly permeated the room.

"It was just a temporary slowdown," Jack said. Although most everyone at the OCME knew about his child's birth, no one, as far as Jack knew, was aware of the infant's illness. Jack and Laurie were both intensely private people.

"How do you know Dr. Besserman won't want this Keara Abelard for himself?"

"Is that the ME who's on this week and supposed to be here already?"

"None other," Vinnie said.

"I don't think he'll be too upset," Jack said, with his usual sarcasm. He knew full well that Besserman, one of the most senior MEs, would just as soon pass on all autopsies at this stage of his career. Nonetheless, Jack scribbled a quick note to Arnold, telling him he'd taken the Abelard case but would be happy to do another couple of cases if need be. He put the Post-it on top of the pile of records and scraped his chair back.

In less than twenty minutes Jack and Vinnie were down in the autopsy room, which had been renovated to a degree during the previous year. Gone were the old soapstone sinks. In their place were modern composite ones. Gone also were the giant glass-fronted cabinets with the collections of medieval-appearing autopsy tools. In their place were nondescript Formica ensembles with solid doors and significantly more space.

"Let's do it!" Jack said. While he'd filled out the initial paperwork, not only had Vinnie gotten the body on the table and the X-rays on the view box, he'd also gotten all the supplies laid out, including the instruments he thought Jack was likely to want: specimen bottles, preservatives, labels, syringes, and evidence custody tags, in case Jack happened to detect an element of criminality.

"So, what are you looking for?" Vinnie asked, as Jack went through his exhaustive external examination. He ranged over the whole body but devoted particular attention to the head.

"Signs of trauma, for one thing," Jack said. "That would be my number-one guess at this point. Of course, it could have been an aneurysm as well. She apparently became quickly disoriented and spastic, which led to coma and death." Jack glanced into both external ear canals. He then used an ophthalmoscope to look at eye grounds. "Reputedly, she'd been out having cocktails with friends—nonalcoholic, according to history, and no drugs."

"Could she have been poisoned?"

Jack straightened up and looked across the body at Vinnie. "That's a strange suggestion at this point. What made you think of that?"

"There was a poisoning on a TV show last night."

Jack laughed behind his mask. "That's an interesting source for differential diagnosis. I'm guessing that's not too likely, but we'll still need to do a toxicology screen. We'll also make sure she's not pregnant."

"Good point about the pregnancy idea. That was what happened in the show last night. The boyfriend wanted to get rid of the baby and the mom at the same time." Jack didn't respond. Instead, he began carrying out a painstaking examination of Keara's scalp. Her thick, shoulder-length hair made progress slow.

"There's no way this case could be infectious, could it?" Vinnie asked. He had never liked germs. In fact, he hated them. Whether involving bacteria, viruses, or "anything in between," as he called some of the other infectious agents, he'd typically avoided contact as best he could, at least until Jack arrived. Since then, because of the number of infectious cases Jack had done, he'd become inured to his phobia. That morning he and Jack were wearing only Tyvek suits, regular medical masks, surgeon's caps, and curved plastic face guards over their clothes. For a few years the front office had dictated full barrier protection on all cases with what were called "moon suits," but that was no longer the situation, and now each medical examiner could wear whatever he or she wanted provided it was appropriate. Same held for the mortuary techs.

"There's even less chance of it being infectious than it being poisoning," Jack said.

Finishing with the head, Jack carefully examined the neck. When that was completed, he was reasonably certain there was no sign of trauma, as the external exam had been entirely normal. Jack had no more idea of what killed the young woman than he had when they'd started, and feeling less patient than usual, he was briefly and irrationally irritated at the patient for withholding her secrets.

After taking ocular fluid, urine, and blood for toxicology and checking out the X-rays on the chance they might provide a clue about the cause of death, Jack started the internal part of the autopsy. He used the typical Y-shaped incision from the points of the shoulders down to the pubis, then, with Vinnie's help, removed the organs and examined each in turn.

"While you rinse out the intestine, I'm going to make sure there was no venous thrombosis in the deep leg veins," Jack said, wanting to cover all the bases. Increasingly curious about the cause of death, he was now all business and trying to think out of the box. There was none of his signature black humor or teasing of Vinnie.

By the time Vinnie returned with the clean intestine, Jack was able to inform him that in addition to the other negatives there'd been no clotting problems with possible emboli to the brain. The cause of death of Keara Abelard was still a total mystery, whereas with most cases at that point there would have been a good idea.

After the abdominal and chest portions of the postmortem were completed, Jack returned his interest to the patient's head. "This has got to be pay dirt!" he said, as he stepped back to give Vinnie room to use the bone saw to cut off the skullcap.

While Vinnie was busy sawing, several of the other day mortuary techs appeared and prepared to assist their assigned medical examiners. Jack didn't even notice them. As Vinnie continued cutting with the noisy bone saw, Jack began to feel uncomfortable. With no theories as to the cause of death other than a burst aneurysm, which he doubted, he had the sense he was missing something, something important, perhaps even making a mistake.

The moment Vinnie put the calvarium aside and then freed up and lifted out the glistening, furrowed brain, Jack leaned forward and his heart skipped a beat. There was dark blood in the posterior fossa at the very back of the head, and enough such that it was spilling out onto the stainless-steel autopsy table.

"Damn!" Jack snapped with obvious regret while pounding his gloved hand on the corner of the table.

"What's the matter?" Vinnie asked.

"I made a mistake!" Jack said angrily.

Taking a step down alongside the body, Jack peered into the depths of the chest cavity and up toward the head, lifting the anterior wall of the chest. "We've got to do an arteriogram X-ray of the vasculature to the brain," Jack said out loud, more to himself than to Vinnie. He was clearly disappointed with himself.

"You know I can't put the brain back," Vinnie said hesitantly, worried that Jack was blaming him for something.

"Of course I know that," Jack said. "We can't reverse what we've already done. I'm talking about an arteriogram of the vasculature leading to the brain, not of the brain itself. Just get some contrast dye and a big syringe!"

4

Through the shimmering heat, Sana Daughtry could see the Four Seasons Hotel from the taxi as it threaded through traffic. Staying there had been Shawn's idea. Sana was supposed to have stayed at the Semiramis Intercontinental, where her conference was being held. In addition to being one of the principal speakers, she'd also been required to serve on multiple panels, and accordingly needed to be there all four days. It would have been far more convenient for her to have been at the Semiramis, to have had the option of occasionally popping up to her room.

Once Shawn had decided to go along on the trip, he had taken over the travel decision-making. It had been his choice to take the hotel credit from the Semiramis and apply it to a room at the newer and much more posh Four Seasons. When Sana had complained about the unnecessary extra cost, Shawn had informed her that he'd found an archaeology meeting for himself, making the extra cost a tax deduction. At that point Sana hadn't argued. There was no point.

With the driver paid, Sana slipped from the cab. She was glad to get away. The driver had peppered her with questions. Sana was a private person, unlike her husband, who could strike up conversations with just about anyone. From Sana's perspective, he had little sense as to what should be private and what should be available for public consumption. There had even been a few occasions when it seemed that Shawn was making an effort to impress strangers, particularly female strangers, with information about their expensive New York City lifestyle that included their living in one of the few remaining wood frame, clapboard houses in New York City's West Village. Why he would want to brag about such a thing she had no idea, although she assumed, psychologically speaking, that it had to reflect some insecurity.

The doorman greeted Sana welcomingly as she passed into the hotel's lobby. She expected to find Shawn out at the pool, since he was far less concerned than she about actually attending his conference. Over the last few days he'd struck up poolside conversations with one or two women, who would now know more about their life than Sana would have preferred. But she was determined not to allow it to get to her as it had in the past. More than once she'd considered that maybe she was the exception, not Shawn; maybe she was just a private prude and should ease up.

A youngish, elegantly dressed gentleman managed to board the elevator just as the doors were closing. He'd obviously had to run the last few steps and was breathing deeply. He looked at Sana and smiled. Sana looked up at the floor indicator. The man was in a Western suit, complete with a billowing pocket square. Like Shawn, he had a distinctly international air, but he was a much younger, more attractive version.

"Terrific day, isn't it!" the man proclaimed with an obvious American accent. Unlike Shawn, he apparently didn't feel the need to affect an English accent when talking with strangers.

If there'd been anyone else in the car, Sana would have assumed he was talking to them. She met his gaze, guessing he was
close to her age of twenty-eight. Judging by his attire, he was presumably rather successful financially.

"It's a beautiful day," Sana agreed in a tone that didn't encourage conversation. She returned her attention to the floor indicator.
Her fellow passenger had glanced at the buttons but had not
pressed a floor number. Was he staying on her floor, Sana silently
asked herself, and if not, should she be concerned? A second later
she chided herself; maybe she really was a prude.

"Are you from New York?" the man asked.

"I am," Sana said, realizing that if her husband were in the elevator and a woman was asking the questions, he would have launched
into a mini-biography of how he'd grown up in Columbus, Ohio,
gotten full scholarships to Amherst undergrad and Harvard grad,
and then moved up the Met's hierarchy to run the show in Near
Eastern art, all in the time it took to reach the eighth floor.

"Have a nice day," the man said, as Sana exited onto the corridor's plush carpet. He didn't leave the car. As she proceeded
toward her room she questioned her paranoia, wondering if she'd
been living in New York too long. Had Shawn been in the elevator
with a woman, they might have very well ended up on their way
to one of the hotel's many bars for a drink.

Sana came to a halt. Shawn's easy sociability was suddenly irritating. Why? Why now? Her best guess was because it was a new
behavior, and now that her anxiety about her conference was over,
she could think about more personal issues. In the past Shawn had
always been admirably and sincerely thoughtful about her level
of moment-to-moment contentment, especially during their torrid,
six-month courtship. Over the last year or so and certainly on this
present trip, that hadn't been the case. When she'd first met Shawn
at a New York gallery opening almost four years ago, she was defend-

ing her Ph.D. thesis on mitochondrial DNA, and had been bowled over by his affection and attention. She'd also been bowled over by his erudition: He was fluent in more than a half-dozen exotic Near Eastern languages and knew things about art and history that she only wished she knew. The breadth of his knowledge made her seem like the stereotypical narrow-minded scientist by comparison.

Recommencing walking but at a much slower pace, Sana wondered whether her mother had been right. Perhaps the twenty-six-year age difference between them was too great. At the same time, she distinctly remembered the difficulty she'd had dealing with the juvenile nature of men her own age, who wore their baseball caps backward and acted like perfect asses. Unlike most of her girlfriends, she'd never been interested in having children. Early on she recognized herself as an academic and, in that sense, much too selfish. For her, Shawn's two sets of children, from his first and third marriages, were enough to satisfy what meager maternal instincts she possessed.

As Sana retrieved her key card, she considered their departure, scheduled for early the next morning. Before the trip she'd been disappointed that Shawn had been unwilling to take her to Luxor to see the tombs of the nobles and the Valley of the Kings. Without regard for her feelings, he'd said he'd already seen them and couldn't take the additional time off. But now that her DNA conference was over, Sana was relieved they hadn't planned on the detour. She hadn't been working at Columbia University College of Physicians and Surgeons long enough to feel secure, especially with several key experiments under way.

She entered her room in one continuous swift motion, and before the door had time to close, she had undone the top two buttons of her blouse and was halfway to the bathroom. Spotting Shawn, she pulled herself up short as he leaped to his feet. They eyed each other. Sana was the first to speak as she took in a magnifying glass in Shawn's white cotton–gloved hands. "What are you doing here? Why aren't you out at the pool?"

"You could have knocked!"

"I need to knock on my own hotel room's door?" she questioned in a mildly sarcastic tone.

Shawn chuckled, recognizing the unreasonableness of what he'd said. "I suppose that does sound a bit unrealistic. At least you didn't have to come barging in here like there was a fire, scaring me out of my wits. I was concentrating."

"Why aren't you at the pool?" Sana repeated. The door slammed on its own behind her. "It's our last day, if you haven't forgotten."

"I haven't forgotten," Shawn said, a gleam coming into his eye. "I've been busy."

"So I see," Sana said, eyeing the gloves and the magnifying glass. She went back to unbuttoning her blouse and headed into the bathroom. Shawn came to the threshold.

"I just made what I thought was my biggest archaeological find in that antiquities shop I told you about. The one where I got the prehistoric Egyptian pot."

"Excuse me," Sana said, easing Shawn back from the threshold so she could push the door almost closed. She didn't like to change in front of anyone, even Shawn, especially since their level of intimacy had faded of late. "I remember," she called out. "Does it have something to do with your white gloves and the magnifying glass?"

"It certainly does," Shawn said to the door. "The concierge helped me out with the gloves and the magnifying glass. Talk about your full-service hotel!"

"Are you going to tell me about your find, or do I have to guess?" Sana asked, now interested. When it came to his profession, Shawn didn't exaggerate. For sure, he'd made a number of important finds digging in multiple locations throughout the Near

East earlier in his career. That was before becoming a high-ranking curator whose responsibilities had devolved to be more supervisory and fund-raising than fieldwork.

"Come out, and I'll show you."

"Is it not as good as you hoped? I noticed you used the past tense."

"At first I was disappointed, but now I think it is even a hundred times better than my initial impression."

"Really?" Sana questioned. With her bathing-suit bottoms halfway up her thighs, she stopped. Now her curiosity had truly been piqued. What could Shawn possibly have found to warrant such a description?

"Are you coming out? I'm dying to show you this."

Sana wiggled her bottom into the suit and adjusted the crotch, then checked herself in the full-length mirror on the back of the bathroom door. She was reasonably happy with what she saw. A devoted runner, she had a slim, athletic figure and short, dirty-blond but healthy hair. Gathering up her clothes, she opened the door. Depositing the clothes carefully on the bed, she walked to the desk.

"Here. Put these on," he said, handing her a second pair of freshly laundered white gloves. "I got them especially for you."

"What is it, a book?" Sana asked, once she got her hands into the gloves. She could see an ancient-looking leather-bound volume sitting on the corner of the desk.

"It's called a codex," Shawn said. "It's an example of the first books that superseded the scroll, since you can get more in it and access various portions of the text far easier. What makes it different from a real book, like the Gutenberg Bible, is that it was done completely by hand. Handle it carefully! It's more than fifteen hundred years old. It had been preserved for more than a millennium and a half by being sealed in a jar buried in the sand."

"My word," Sana said. She wasn't sure she wanted to hold something quite so old for fear it might disintegrate in her hands.

"Open it!" he urged.

Gingerly, Sana folded back the cover. It was stiff, and the binding audibly complained. "What's the cover made of?"

"It's kind of a leather sandwich stiffened with layers of papyrus."

"What are the pages made out of?"

"The pages are all papyrus."

"And the language?"

"It's called Coptic, which is kind of a written version of ancient Egyptian using a Greek alphabet."

"Truly amazing!" Sana said. She was impressed but wondered why Shawn had said it was such an important find for him. Some of the statuary he'd found in Asia Minor seemed far more substantial.

"Can you see that a large section of the book has been torn out?"

"I can. Is that significant?"

"Very much so! Five of the original, individual texts of this particular codex had been roughly removed in the 1940s to sell them in America. Other pages had been rumored to have been removed to start kitchen fires in a fellahin mud hut."

"That's terrible."

"Indeed. Many an academic has cringed at the thought."

"I also notice that the inside of the front cover has been opened up along its edge."

"I did that myself very carefully with a steak knife about an hour ago."

"Was that wise? I mean, considering the age of this thing. I imagine there are more appropriate tools than a steak knife."

"No, it probably wasn't wise, but I did it because I couldn't help myself. At that point I was horribly disappointed with what's in the codex. I had expected a virtual gold mine, and instead I've rescued the equivalent of the output of one of the world's first copy machines."

"I don't think I'm following you," Sana admitted. She handed the ancient book back to Shawn to absolve herself from responsibility. She pulled off the gloves. His excitement was palpable. She was more than intrigued.

"I'm not surprised." He took the codex and replaced it to its former position on the corner of the desk. In the middle of the desk, under the glare of both a desk lamp and a floor lamp, were three individual pages held flat by various objects, including a pair of Shawn's ancient-coin cuff links. The pages were heavily creased from being folded up for thousands of years. It too was papyrus, like the pages in the codex, but it seemed to be older. The edges had blackened to the point of appearing burnt.

"What's this?" Sana asked, pointing at the papyri sheets. "A letter?" She could see the first page had a possible addressee, the last a signature.

"Ah, the scientific mind immediately homes in on the crux of the matter," Shawn said with glee. Palms down, fingers spread, he reverently passed his hands over the pages as if worshipping them. "It is indeed a letter, a very special letter written in AD 121, by a septuagenarian bishop of the city of Antioch by the name of Saturninus. It was a reply to a previous letter written to him by a bishop of Alexandria named Basilides."

"My gosh!" Sana exclaimed. "That's the beginning of the second century."

"Quite," Shawn remarked, "and within a century of Jesus of Nazareth. It was a fractious time for the early Church."

"Is either man well known?"

"A good question! Basilides is well known among biblical scholars, Saturninus much less so, although I've come across references to him on a couple of occasions. As this letter substantiates, Saturninus was a student or an assistant of Simon the Magician."

"That's a name I've heard in my childhood."

"No doubt. He was and is the quintessential Sunday-school bad guy, as well as the father of all heresies, at least according to a number of the early Christian Church fathers. In point of fact his attempt to buy the ability to heal from Saint Peter is the origin of the word *simony*."

"What about Basilides?"

"He was a very busy man here in Egypt—in Alexandria, to be precise—and a prodigious writer. He's also given credit as one of the first Gnostic thinkers, particularly for putting a distinctive Christian stamp on Gnosticism by centering his Gnostic theology on Jesus of Nazareth."

"Help me," Sana said. "I've heard the term *Gnosticism*, but I wouldn't be able to define it."

"Simply speaking, it was a movement that predated Christianity, ultimately merging aspects of pagan religions, Judaism, and then Christianity into a single sect. The name Gnosticism came from the Greek word *gnosis*, meaning intuitive knowledge. To the Gnostics, knowledge of the divine being was the end-all, and those who had the knowledge believed they had the spark of the divine to the point that people like Simon the Magician actually thought he was, at least partially, divine."

"And you complain that my DNA science is complicated," Sana scoffed.

"This isn't all that complicated, but back to Basilides. He happened to be one of the first Gnostics also to be a Christian, although the name *Christian* didn't yet exist. He believed Jesus of Nazareth was the awaited Messiah. Yet he didn't believe that Christ had come to earth to redeem mankind from sin by suffering on the cross, like most of the rest of his fellow Christians did. Instead, Basilides thought that Jesus' mission had been for the purposes of enlightenment, or gnosis, to show humans how to break free of the physical world and achieve salvation. The Gnostics like Basilides were really high on Greek philosophy and Persian mythology, but they were all very down on the material world, which they thought entrapped humankind and was the source of all sin."

Sana bent over the letter to look at it more closely. From a distance the printing appeared uniform, as if done by a machine, but on closer inspection, slight variations proved that it had been done by hand. "Is this Coptic as well?" she asked.

"No, the letter is in an ancient Greek," Shawn said, "which isn't surprising. Greek, even more than Latin, was the lingua franca of the day, particularly in the eastern Mediterranean. As the name suggests, Alexandria was one of the centers of the Hellenistic world established by Alexander the Great's military feats."

Sana straightened back up. "Was this letter part of the codex or merely stuck into the book as an afterthought?"

"It certainly wasn't an afterthought," Shawn said cryptically. "It was done very deliberately, but not for the reason you might imagine. Remember how I described the codex's cover? Along with other scraps of papyrus, this letter was sandwiched in behind the leather to make it what we would think of as a hardcover book. I'd heard that had been done with other volumes of this particular treasure trove of codices."

"You found more than one?"

"No, I came across only this one codex. But I recognized it instantly. Here, sit down. I've got some explaining to do, especially since we're not going home tomorrow as planned."

"What are you talking about?" Sana demanded. "I've got to get back to rescue several experiments."

"Your experiments are going to have to wait, at least for a day, or maybe two days at most." Shawn placed his hand on Sana's shoulder in an attempt to ease her down onto the couch.

"You can wait if you want, but I'm going back," she said, making a point of pushing his hand off her shoulder. She wasn't going to allow herself to be bullied.

For a moment wife and husband glowered at each other. Then both relented without a harsh word.

"You've changed," Shawn commented at length. He acted surprised rather than angry at her unexpectedly rebellious announcement.

"I think it's safe to say you've changed as well," Sana responded. She made a distinct effort to keep any suggestion of irritation out of her voice. She didn't want to get into a long, drawn-out emotional discussion at the moment. Besides, he was right. She had changed—not markedly, but in a very real way, a response to his changing.

"I don't think you understand," Shawn said. "This letter may very well lead me to the apotheosis of my career. To take advantage of it, I'm going to need your help for a day—two, tops. I have to see if the author, Saturninus, was telling the truth. I cannot imagine why he would have lied, but I have to be sure. To do that, we're going to be flying to Rome early tomorrow morning."

"Do you need my help literally or figuratively?" Sana questioned. To her it made a difference.

"Literally!"

Sana took a breath and eyed her husband. He seemed sincere, which changed things in her mind. He'd never actually asked for her help before. "All right," she said. She sat down. "I'm not yet agreeing, but let's hear your explanation."

With rekindled enthusiasm, Shawn grabbed the desk chair and planted it in front of Sana. Sitting down, he leaned forward, eyes sparkling. "Have you ever heard of the Gnostic Gospels found here in Egypt at Nag Hammadi in 1945?"

Sana shook her head.

"How about the book *The Gnostic Gospels* by Elaine Pagels?"

Sana shook her head again with a touch of irritation. Shawn was always asking her if she read this treatise or that one, and invariably she'd have to say no. As a molecular biologist, she'd not had a lot of time to take many liberal-arts courses, and often felt inferior as a result.

"I'm surprised," Shawn said. "Elaine Pagels was a bestseller, a real commercial hit that put Gnosticism on the map."

"When was it published?"

"I don't know, around 1979, I guess."

"Shawn, I was born in 1980. Give me a break!"

"Right! Sorry! I keep forgetting. Anyhow, her book was about the significance of the Nag Hammadi find, which were thirteen codices, including this one I've come across today. This book was originally part of that find that in one fell swoop doubled the extant books about early Gnostic thought. In many ways the find was in the same league as the Dead Sea Scrolls found in Palestine two years later."

"I've heard of the Dead Sea Scrolls."

"Well there are people who believe the Nag Hammadi texts are equivalently important for understanding religious thought around the time of Christ."

"So, this book you found today is one of those codices found in 1945."

"Correct. It's known, appropriately enough, as the Thirteenth Codex."

"Where are the others?"

"They're here in Cairo at the Coptic Museum. Most had been confiscated by the Egyptian government after a few had been sold.

Those that had been sold eventually made their way back here where they belong."

"How did number thirteen get separated from the others?"

"Before I answer that, let me give you a thumbnail sketch of the story of the discovery of the Nag Hammadi library. It's fascinating. Two young fellahin boys named Khalifah and Muhammed Ali were out at the edge of the desert near modern-day Nag Hammadi, supposedly looking for a kind of fertilizing soil known as *sabakh*. Where they were looking was at the base of a cliff called Jabal al-Tarif, which, by the way, is honeycombed with caves, both natural and ancient man-made. Their method was to blindly poke deep into the sand with their mattocks. I don't know how that helps, but to their surprise on the day of the discovery, instead of coming across the *sabakh* they were looking for, one of them heard a suspicious hollow clunk when he pounded his mattock into the sand. He cleared away the sand and came across a sealed earthenware jar about three to four feet in height. Hoping to find some ancient Egyptian antiquities, they found the codices instead."

"Did they have any idea of the value of what they'd found?"

"Not a clue. They carried the cache home but dumped it next to the family's cooking oven, where the mother used some of the papyri pages to start the family's cooking fires."

"What a tragedy."

"As I said, there are academics who still wince at the thought today. Anyway, friends and neighbors of the boys, including a Muslim imam who was also a history teacher, suspected they were valuable and quickly intervened. The codex that I came across today worked its way down the Nile to reach Cairo via various antiquities dealers. There the five of its missing texts, which also turned out to be the most extraordinary, were removed and smuggled out to the United States. Luckily, by that time Egyptian government agents had been alerted, and they then managed to buy or confiscate the remaining codices, including eight of the pages removed from the thirteenth. The thirteenth itself they didn't find, and somehow it got lost in someone's antiquities inventory to await a safe time to fence it. My guess would be that it somehow got forgotten until recently, when my friend Rahul got access to it. My appearance today was clearly serendipitous. He's in contact with a number of curators around the world. He wouldn't have had a problem disposing of it."

"But isn't it against the law to sell it or even own it?"

"Absolutely!"

"Doesn't that bother you?"

"Not really. I think of myself as its rescuer. I don't intend to keep it. My goal from the beginning was to be the person to publish the contained texts and reap the professional benefits. Unfortunately, that is no longer much of an issue."

"Why not? How many texts are remaining in the codex?"

"Quite a number."

"What exactly are these Nag Hammadi texts?"

"They are Coptic copies of Greek originals with names like the Gospel of Thomas, the Gospel of Philip, the Gospel of Truth, the Gospel to the Egyptians, the Secret Book of James, the Apocalypse of Paul, the Letter of Peter to Philip, the Apocalypse of Peter, so forth and so on."

"What are the names of the texts remaining in the Thirteenth Codex?"

"That's the problem. All of the remaining texts are additional copies of texts previously found in the first twelve codices. Even in the initial fifty-two texts of those twelve volumes, only forty had been new works. It's similar in that respect to the Dead Sea Scrolls, where there was some redundancy as well."

"Which leads us to the letter you found sandwiched in the cover."

"Exactly," Shawn said. He got up, gingerly picked up the three pages, and quickly returned to his chair. "Do you want me to read it, which I'll probably do a shoddy job at, or will you be content for me to paraphrase? One way or the other, it's going to go down as one of the most historically significant letters in the history of the world."

Sana let her mouth drop open in mock astonishment. She even rolled her eyes. "Are you developing a new tendency toward hyperbole? Earlier you said your find today was a hundred times better than your previous most important archaeological find, or something like that. Has it now ascended to being one of the most historically significant letters in the history of the world? Aren't you pushing the envelope here?"

"I'm not exaggerating," Shawn said, his eyes shining.

"Okay," Sana said. "I think you'd better try to read the whole letter to me. I don't want to miss anything. You mentioned Jesus of Nazareth. Does the letter involve him?"

"It does, but indirectly," Shawn said. He cleared his throat.

As her husband started to read, Sana shifted her eyes out the hotel window. The sun reflected in a blaze of light off the Nile's surface in the foreground; on the horizon loomed the famed Pyramids of Giza, with the Great Pyramid towering over the others. If the ancient letter turned out to be half as important as Shawn was implying, she couldn't have wished for a better place to hear a translation.

5

Goddamn it, Vinnie," Jack Stapleton growled. Jack was along the left side of the body of Keara Abelard. He'd been bent over the woman's back for more than twenty minutes, carefully biting off pieces of the cervical transverse processes with his rongeurs, trying to expose the two vertical arteries as they coursed up through the neck. The arteries pierced each vertebra laterally before making an S-curve around the atlas, or first cervical vertebra.

"Sorry," Vinnie said, but without sufficient remorse.

"Can't you see what the hell I'm trying to do?"

"Yeah, I know what you're trying to do. You're trying to expose both vertebral arteries."

Keara's neck was pressed down on a wooden block, her face pointing down at the floor, on the table, her brainless calvarium pointing at the autopsy room's door. The brain sat alone on a cutting board at the foot of the table.

Vinnie stood at the end of the table with his hands on either side of Keara's head, trying to stabilize it as Jack nipped off pieces of bone. It was a slow process. The idea was to expose the arteries without damaging them. Jack recorded his progress with a series of digital photos.

"If you can't hold the head still, I'm going to have to find someone who can. I don't want to make this my life's work."

"All right already," Vinnie complained. "I got the message. For a second there I was thinking about the Giants and the worry they're not even making the Super Bowl much less winning it."

Jack closed his eyes and silently counted to ten. He knew he was being tough on Vinnie. Holding on to a body part while Jack nibbled away was a grunt's job, and he would have hated to do it himself. Still, the case had to get done. The problem was, his emotional instability was causing him to be less patient than usual.

"Just try to focus a little more," Jack said, making a conscious effort to calm his voice. "Let's get this over with."

"Got it, boss," Vinnie said, tightening his grip on the woman's head.

The rest of the autopsy room was a beehive of activity with all eight tables in use, but Jack was oblivious to it all. He now had a preliminary diagnosis as to the cause of Keara's death, and his attention was focused. The arteriogram showed an almost complete blockage of both vertebral arteries, the source of much of the brain's blood supply. The blockage appeared to have occurred over a relatively short period of time. But why? Was it a natural occurrence, as in some sort of emboli, or accidental, like an injury? The fact that it was so symmetrical was the most difficult to explain. It was a unique case for Jack, and he had eased up on himself for not thinking of doing a vertebral arteriogram before removing the brain. It had been a mistake but ultimately not detrimental.

Twenty minutes later, Vinnie leaned down to view Jack's handiwork. "It's looking good to me," he said.

Jack straightened up, pleased. The field looked like an anatomy textbook illustration of the course of the vertebral arteries, particularly at the base of the skull. "Can you see the bluish discoloration and swelling around the S-curves on both sides?" Jack asked. "Come around to get a better look."

Vinnie traded places with Jack. From that vantage point he could see what Jack was referring to. Each vertebral artery had a two- to three-inch section with a swollen bluish cast, the right slightly more pronounced than the left. "What do you think it is?" Vinnie said.

Jack shrugged. "Looks to me like an injury of some kind, but since there was zero bruising on her neck, it's a bit strange. In fact, she had no signs of trauma of any form. And it's peculiar how symmetrical it is."

"Could it be a whiplash injury, something like that?"

"I suppose it could, but there'd be the history of the automobile accident. When I glanced through the medicolegal investigation report, there'd been no mention of any auto accident. I think I might be in for a bit of investigative work myself. There has to be an explanation."

"What now?"

"More photos," Jack said, reaching for the digital camera. "Then we're going to remove both arteries and check the interiors."

Ten minutes later Jack had the vessels on the cutting board with the brain. They looked like two small headless red snakes who'd swallowed something blue. The discoloration was more apparent than when the arteries had been in situ.

"Here goes nothing," Jack said. Steadying each blood vessel between the thumb and forefinger of his left hand, he used his right to make a careful incision through one side of each artery's wall. He then opened both of them lengthwise, spreading them out on the cutting board inside out.

"Would you look at that?" he said, still holding the scalpel.

"What am I looking at?" Vinnie questioned.

"It is called a dissection," Jack said. "A bilateral dissection of the vertebral arteries. I've actually never seen it."

Using the handle of the scalpel, Jack pointed to a spot just before the arteries' S-curve where they looped up and over the first cervical vertebra. "Can you see this tear in the intima, or the inside lining of the blood vessel? In both arteries there is a tear at the point between the atlas, or first vertebra, and the axis, or second cervical vertebra. In such a situation, what happens is that arterial pressure forces blood into the tear and balloons the lining of the arteries away from the vessel's fibrous wall, eventually blocking the vessel's lumen. The brain is then deprived of a major portion of its blood supply and bingo, lights out."

"Meaning curtains for the victim."

"I'm afraid so," Jack agreed.

With the pathology determined, the rest of the autopsy continued apace. Twenty minutes later, Jack exited the autopsy room to learn that Dr. Besserman had assigned him a second autopsy, the private-school meningitis case. While he waited for Vinnie to set it up, Jack ditched his soiled Tyvek suit and took Keara Abelard's chart into the locker room.

Making himself comfortable, Jack carefully reread Janice Jaeger's medicolegal investigation report. As he had noted earlier when he'd skimmed the record, the woman had been brought into the emergency room by her drinking buddies with the sudden onset of confusion and spasticity, leading to unconsciousness. From Janice's choice of syntax, Jack could tell that she had not spoken with the friends directly but rather had gotten her information from a combination of the Saint Luke's ER record, one of the ER nurses, and one of the ER docs. Typical of Janice, the report was complete, with no mention of an auto accident.

Switching to the ID sheet, Jack saw that it had been Keara's

mother who'd made the identification. The woman lived in Engle-
wood, New Jersey, and Jack glanced at her phone number with its
201 area code.

Impulsively, Jack got to his feet. It was clear he needed more
information than what he had. With the OCME record in hand,
he used the back stairs to get up to the first floor, and, passing
though the SIDS investigation area, he walked into the expanded
medicolegal space. He found Bart Arnold, the chief of forensic
investigation, at his desk in cubbyhole number one. He and Jack
had an excellent working relationship, as Jack was one of the few
medical examiners willing to give the investigators the credit they
deserved by letting them know he couldn't do his job without
their help.

"Morning, Dr. Stapleton. Is there a problem?" Bart asked, seeing
the case file under Jack's arm.

"Hey, Bart, I was wondering if during your shift-change report
session this morning Janice happened to mention anything memorable about Keara Abelard?"

Bart looked at his list of the night's cases. "Nope, not that I can
remember. It seemed routine to her, but definitely a case that fell
under OCME jurisdiction."

"I couldn't agree more," Jack said. "But there's so little history."

"She mentioned that the ER docs felt the same, which is why
they left word with Janice to get a callback. They want to know
what's found."

"I didn't see a note to that effect in the record."

"I believe Janice knows the doc in question and was going to
do it herself rather than obligating you."

"Do you know if she spoke to the mother when the mother
came in to make the identification?"

"That I don't know. If I had to guess, I'd say no, because Janice
is so thorough—if she'd spoken with the mother, she would have

written it down. But why don't you call her and ask? What's the problem, not enough info?"

Jack nodded. "It's a curious case. The woman died from occlusion of both her vertebral arteries. Unless she had had some connective-tissue disease like Marfan syndrome, which I seriously doubt, she had to have suffered serious trauma. Her vessels dissected, meaning the lining came off, blocking them up. Vinnie suggested whiplash injury from an auto accident, and he might be right. I think her friends or her mom might have some information. It could be extremely important. If someone ran into the back of her, he or she would now be looking at possible manslaughter, even murder, if the parties knew each other and there was some kind of conflict or controversy between them. I'd give the mother a call myself, but I'd hate to bother her if Janice has already spoken with her."

"As I said, why not give Janice a call?"

With his left hand, Jack twisted up the bezel of his watch tied with the cincture of his scrub pants. "It's a quarter to ten. Isn't that too late?"

"She's a perfectionist. She'll want to help you out," Bart said, handing him Janice's home number. "Call her! Trust me!"

Using the front stairs, Jack hurried up to his office. After propping open his office door, he placed Janice's card in the center of his blotter and pulled over his phone. Before he dialed the woman, he called down to Vinnie.

"I'm bringing in the body of the kid as we speak," Vinnie said. "Five minutes and we'll be ready to go. Calvin, our lovable deputy chief, wants us to do it in the decomposed room." The decomposed room was a separate, small autopsy room with a single table. It was used mostly for putrid bodies.

"Make sure we have plenty of culture tubes," Jack said. "See you in five." He disconnected.

He was about to dial Janice's number when the photo he had

on his desk of Laurie and John Junior caught his eye. It had been taken at a happier time, the day Laurie and the baby were leaving the hospital after the delivery. At the moment there had been no symptoms or signs of the disaster that was to come.

Impulsively, Jack reached out, grabbed the photo, and tossed it into his bottom drawer, pushing it closed with his foot. "God!" he murmured. It was embarrassing how quickly he could be yanked back into a depressing thought, especially since Laurie was the one bearing ninety-nine percent of the burden. He wondered how she'd been able to do it. At least he'd been able to go to work to take his mind off the reality of the disaster.

For a moment Jack rubbed his eyes, causing a squishy sound from both sockets. With his elbows on the desk, he then roughly massaged his scalp. He was back to realizing how much he needed to find something professional to occupy his mind to rein in his fragile emotions.

Opening his eyes, Jack snatched up the telephone receiver and angrily poked the sequence of buttons corresponding to Janice's phone number. When she answered, he snapped back with his name in such a way that he knew he sounded angry. Before Janice could even respond, he excused himself. "That didn't come out right," he said. "I'm sorry."

"Is something the matter?" Janice questioned. As conscientious as she was, her first concern was that she'd done something terribly wrong.

"No! No!" Jack assured her. "My mind was elsewhere for a second. I hope I'm not disturbing you."

"Not at all. I can't sleep for three or four hours after getting off shift."

"I'm looking for more information on Keara Abelard."

"I'm not surprised. There was so little available. Such a sad case, so young, attractive, and seemingly healthy."

"Did you speak to any of the woman's friends who brought her into the ER?"

"I didn't have a chance. They had already left by the time I got there. I was able to get a name and number of one of them, Robert Farrell. I put it down at the bottom of the page."

"Did you get to speak with her mother when she came in to make the ID?"

"I wanted to but got called out on another case before she arrived. And then when I returned, she'd already left. I'm sure Bart would be more than happy to follow up."

"What I think I'll do is call myself. My curiosity has been tweaked."

"If you change your mind, I'm certain one of the day investigators would do it."

"Thanks for your help," Jack said.

"No problem," Janice replied.

Jack disconnected with the forefinger of his left hand while still holding on to the receiver. With his right hand he pawed through the OCME record, looking again for the ID sheet for Mrs. Abelard's phone number. The second he found it, the phone rang under his hand. It was Vinnie, saying all was ready down in the decomposed room.

After a moment's hesitation, Jack replaced the receiver on the cradle. There was no rush to speak with Mrs. Abelard, as it was not a call he relished having to make. He was happy to put it off until he finished the next autopsy, although had he any inkling about what he'd learn from the mother, he wouldn't have put off the call for a second. Mrs. Abelard was going to tell him something he never would have guessed.

6

So there you have it," Shawn said. "Sorry it's taken so bloody long. Greek was obviously not Saturninus's forte. As I mentioned after the first reading, the letter is signed simply Saturninus, with the date of the sixth of April, AD 121."

For a few beats Shawn studied his wife. She didn't move or even blink. She had a dazed expression on her face; she didn't even seem to be breathing.

"Hello," Shawn called, to get Sana's attention. "Say something! Anything! What are you thinking?" Shawn stood up and stepped back to the desk, where he gently deposited the papyri sheets for their protection, using the assorted weights to hold them flat. He slipped off the white gloves, placed them on the desk, and then returned to the straight-backed chair. Sana had followed him with her eyes, but it was clear her thoughts were on what she'd been hearing over the last few hours. When Shawn had laboriously finished reading the letter the first time, she'd seemed equally shell-shocked, managing to say only that she'd needed to hear it again.

"I know I didn't do a good job at translating it," Shawn confessed, "especially that first time. Again, I'm sorry it took so long, but the grammar and the syntax are both so convoluted. It's obvious that Greek was not Saturninus's first language, and because of the sensitive nature of the subject matter, he did not want to entrust the writing of the letter to a secretary. His mother tongue would have been Aramaic, as he was from Samaria."

"What are the chances it is a fake? Perhaps a second-century fake, but a fake nonetheless."

"That's a good question, and if the letter had been addressed to one of the early Orthodox Church fathers, the idea it was a fake might be something I'd question, if only to discredit the Gnostic heretics by making a direct association with them and the arch-villain Simon Magus. But it was sent to an early Gnostic teacher, from someone who had theological inclinations in that direction. This was kind of an 'inside communication' sent to someone with answers to specific questions. There's almost zero chance it's a fake, especially where it ended up. It wasn't as if someone ever expected it to be found."

"When do you believe the codex was put together? I mean, when was this letter presumably sandwiched into the leather cover?"

"Let's say it had to be before approximately AD 367."

Sana smiled. "Approximately AD 367! That's a pretty specific date."

"Well, something specific happened in AD 367."

"So the letter was saved for several hundred years. It was important, but then it became less so?"

"Yes," Shawn agreed. "But it's something I cannot explain."

"What happened in AD 367, and what's the theory of why these codices ended up being sealed in a jar and buried in the sand?"

"In AD 367 the Gnosticism movement had peaked and was on the decline, as ordered by the Orthodox Church. In compliance, the influential bishop of Alexandria, Athanasius, ordered the monasteries under his jurisdiction to dispose of all heretical writing, including the monastery that existed close to modern-day Nag Hammadi. It's supposed that some of the monks rebelled at that monastery and instead of destroying the texts, hid them, with the intention of eventually retrieving them. Unfortunately for them, it didn't happen, and their loss turned out to be our gain."

"And you think this letter is a response to a letter that Basilides wrote to Saturninus."

"There is no question in my mind, considering Saturninus's syntax. He surely didn't pull any punches in his description of his former boss and teacher, Simon the Magician. It is clear to me that Basilides had specifically asked if Saturninus thought Simon was divine, a true Christ in the footsteps of Jesus of Nazareth, and whether or not Simon possessed the Great Power as he claimed. Although Saturninus suggests that Simon himself thought he was either divine or was possessed of a spark of the divine, Saturninus surely didn't. Saturninus clearly states that Simon's magic was trickery, for which Saturninus and Simon's other assistant, Menander, were largely responsible. Saturninus also says Simon was extremely jealous of the supposed curative power of the Apostles, especially Peter. This is a canonical fact. It appears in the Bible's Acts of the Apostles, where it specifically states that Simon tried to buy Peter's power." Shawn paused to catch his breath but then added with a contemptuous chuckle, "Thanks to Saturninus and this letter, we know now that Simon didn't give up after that initial rebuff."

"What I find ironic is that we have this extraordinary historical information because of one person's venality."

"True," Shawn agreed with a more open laugh. "But what I find ironic is that the same venality is quite likely going to vault me into the archaeological stratosphere. Belzoni, Schliemann, and Carter will have nothing on me."

Sana couldn't help but roll her eyes. Although Shawn's seeming self-confidence had impressed her at the beginning of their relationship, she now found it puerile and self-absorbed, again suggesting Shawn harbored insecurity that she had not initially suspected.

Catching her reaction and misinterpreting it, Shawn added, "You don't think this is going to be a big event? You're wrong! This is going to be huge. And you know who I'm going to have the most fun breaking the news to?"

"I can't imagine," Sana said. She was more interested in continuing the discussion of the contents of the shocking letter, rather than its potential effect on Shawn's career.

"His Eminence!" Shawn said with a touch of mock disdain. "James Cardinal O'Rourke, bishop of the Archdiocese of New York." Shawn laughed, savoring the anticipation. "I can't wait to drop in on my old Amherst College drinking buddy, now the most elevated member of the ecclesiastical establishment that I know and the one who's forever lecturing me to mend my ways. I'm going to have a lot of fun rubbing his nose in this letter, proving to him that one of his uppity-up popes, believing he was infallible, was dead wrong. Mark my words!"

"Oh, please!" Sana scoffed. Too often, she'd witnessed her husband and the archbishop arguing uselessly into the wee hours of the morning, particularly about papal infallibility, after a dinner at the cardinal's residence. "You two are never going to agree on anything."

"This time, thanks to Saturninus, I'll have proof."

"Well, I hope I'm not there," Sana remarked. She'd never enjoyed those evenings and lately had stopped participating. She'd asked if they could go out to a restaurant instead, which Sana thought would calm their behavior. But neither Shawn nor James were willing. They enjoyed their endless, seemingly acrimonious debates too much and didn't want to be restrained.

Back at the beginning of their relationship, when Shawn had first told her about his long-standing friendship with the archbishop, she didn't entirely believe him. The archbishop was the most powerful prelate in the country, if not the hemisphere. The man was a true celebrity. There was even talk that he might be destined for the Vatican.

Yet it wasn't just their respective positions that made their friendship seem so unlikely. It was their personalities—Shawn the sophisticated extrovert, constantly seeking opportunities for real or imagined self-aggrandizement, James the ever-modest parish priest who had been waylaid by fate to assume more and more responsibilities for which he was ill prepared. What never ceased to amuse Sana was that these opposite personality styles were denied by the old friends themselves. Shawn would have none of James's expressed modesty, accusing him of unbridled ambition fortified by exceptional pragmatism, shrewdness, and his ability to flatter. James considered Shawn's bravado equally suspect, convinced Shawn was a deeply insecure person, a belief Sana was beginning to share. James never tired of constantly reminding Shawn that God and the Church were there to help him.

From Sana's perspective, even the two men's outward appearances argued against the chances that they would be friends. Shawn was a natural athlete who participated in varsity sports at Amherst. At six-foot-three and two hundred pounds, he was physically imposing and still fit from competitive tennis. James was short and plump, and now, often swathed head to toe in his scarlet robes of office, appeared decidedly elfin. On top of that, Shawn was black Irish, with thick, dark hair and strong angular features. James, on the other hand, had red hair and creamy, freckled, almost translucent skin.

What had drawn the two men together and had cemented their relationship, Sana was later to learn, was first circumstance and later a love of debate. It had started their freshman year when they had been made roommates. Joining them was another student who lived directly across the hallway. His name was Jack Stapleton, and as chance would have it, he too ended up living in New York City. So the Three Musketeers, as they were known in college, miraculously ended up in the same city even if they were worlds apart in their careers.

In contrast to James, Sana had met Jack Stapleton just twice. He seemed such a remarkably private person, she wondered how he'd gotten along with the others. Maybe his seemingly thoughtful, retiring nature and lack of self-reference had made him the glue that had held the group of friends together back in college.

"James is going to come unhinged," Shawn continued, still chuckling to himself at the prospect. "And I'm going to love it. This is going to be my opportunity to put him on the hot seat, and is he going to squirm. I can't wait to revisit the infallibility issue. In light of all the papal shenanigans during the Middle Ages and Renaissance, it's an issue we've argued about hundreds of times."

"What makes you so certain this is going to rank up with Carter's discovery of King Tut's tomb?" Sana questioned to refocus the discussion.

She wasn't certain what the other two archaeologists Shawn had mentioned had discovered, although the name Schliemann was familiar.

"King Tut was an insignificant child ruler whose life was a mere blip in the sands of time," Shawn snapped, "whereas the Virgin Mary was arguably the most important human to have lived, second only to her firstborn son. In fact, maybe they were equally important. She was the Mother of God, for chrissake."

"No need to get yourself riled up," Sana said soothingly. Of late

Shawn often expressed irritation when he thought she was dis-
agreeing with him in his area of expertise. The irony was that in no
way did she question the historical importance of the Virgin Mary,
especially in relation to the puny, teenage Tutankhamen, but Carter
had unearthed a huge cache of treasure. So far, all Shawn had was
three sheets of papyrus of unconfirmed authenticity that talked
about the Virgin Mary's remains. Yet Sana could see Shawn's point
from her own reaction. When Shawn had gotten to the section in
Saturninus's letter that involved the bones of the Virgin Mary, she
had reacted as if Shawn had slapped her across the face.

"I'm not upset! I'm just surprised you don't see the unbeliev-
able importance of this letter."

"I do! I do!" Sana insisted.

"What I think happened was Basilides asked Saturninus not
just his opinion on Simon's divinity but also whether Simon had
written anything of substance and, if he had, where it might be.
Maybe Basilides had his suspicions. That's why I believe Saturninus described the Gospel of Simon along with the fact that he
and Menander put it in the ossuary. I don't believe Basilides had
any idea about the Virgin Mary's remains having been brought
to Rome by Simon, nor did he care. He was interested in Simon's
theology."

"What's the actual definition of the word *gospel?*"

"It's any message concerning Christ, which most people associ-
ate with the first four canonical books of the New Testament covering the teachings of Jesus Christ. More broadly, a gospel is any
message of a religious teacher. That's why it's going to be both thrill-
ing and instructive to learn if the Gospel of Simon is about Jesus
Christ, Jesus Christ and Simon Christ together, or Simon Christ
alone. I say it that way because most people think Christ was Jesus'
last name. It wasn't. Christ was from the Greek *kristos,* meaning
messiah, and it is where the word *Christian* was derived. If Simon

considered himself a messiah, he could have very well referred to himself as Christ. Of course, we already know one thing: There was no resurrection associated with Simon. He stayed dead after he toppled off a tower in the Roman Forum at Nero's behest, trying to prove his divinity, or at least his close association with divinity."

Sana glanced in Shawn's eyes. She could read his mind. Obviously, he thought his chances of finding the Gospel of Simon were good, and she knew exactly why. Five years ago Shawn had prevailed upon James to use his influence with Pope John Paul II to obtain access to the necropolis under Saint Peter's Basilica to carry out the definitive analysis of Saint Peter's tomb. Over a period of six months, Shawn, along with a team of architects and engineers, had studied both the site and two thousand years of available papal records to write the definitive history of the tomb, including the 1968 discovery of a headless first-century male skeleton, heralded by Paul VI as the apostle's remains. The result was that Shawn had become an expert on the gravesite, and if Saturninus and Menander had buried the Virgin Mary's ossuary containing the Gospel of Simon in AD 65 where Saturninus claimed in the letter, Shawn would know where to look.

"I've heard of the Sadducees and the Pharisees, but never the Essenes or the Zealots," Sana said, going back to the letter. "Who were these people Saturninus is talking about?"

"They were all separate Jewish sects, of which the Sadducees and Pharisees were far and away the most important because of their numbers. The Essenes were a small militant, ascetic, communal group who felt the Temple in Jerusalem had been defiled. Although there were Essene cells in most Palestinian cities, their strictest leaders and brethren moved out into the desert along the shores of the Dead Sea at Qumran. They were the transcribers of the Dead Sea Scrolls, as well as the people who hid them to keep them out of the hands of the Romans.

"The Zealots were more politically defined. Their primary goal was to rid Jewish lands of Roman oppressors, and the most fanatical members were called the Sicarii. To understand what was going on in the first century, you have to remember that most everyone wanted the Romans out of Palestine, except, of course, the Romans, and to a large degree that was what a lot of the contemporary messianic prophecy was all about. The Jews expected a messiah to get rid of the Romans, which was one reason why a lot of Jews weren't satisfied with Jesus being the Messiah. Not only did he not get rid of the Romans, he got himself crucified in the bargain."

"Okay," Sana said. "But why would the Zealots and the Essenes plot to steal the body of the Virgin Mary? That doesn't make sense to me."

"Saturninus doesn't say specifically, but here's what I think he is implying. When the Virgin Mary died in AD 62 as he says and was entombed in a cave on the Mount of Olives, perhaps even where her tomb is supposed to be today, some Zealots, probably the Sicarii, saw an opportunity to fan the fires of hatred of the Romans toward the Jews. What they were trying to do was start a revolt, and they didn't care which side was the instigator. Prior to that, the Sicarii had mostly concentrated on intensifying the hatred of the Jews toward the Romans, which is why they spent most of their time and energy assassinating those Jews who they thought were collaborating with or even just soft on the Romans. The rationale was to get the Jews to start the fight.

"Then the death of Mary offered something else. It offered an opportunity to put Roman frustration with the problem of religious strife over the top. You see, at that time in the mid–first century, Jews who had become followers of Jesus of Nazareth were considered Jews and not yet a new religion. Yet they didn't get along with traditional Jews. In fact, they were constantly at each others' throats over what the Romans considered ridiculously petty issues. On top of that, there was infighting among the Jewish Christians. It was pure religious anarchy, and the Romans were fit to be tied."

"I still cannot understand the Virgin Mary's role in all this."

"Think of the Romans' frustration. Saturninus mentions that the Romans thought they had taken care of the Jesus of Nazareth problem by crucifying Jesus. But they were wrong, because Jesus didn't stay dead like all the other crucified supposed messiahs of the time, of which there were a number. Jesus came back in three days, which ended up, in retrospect, magnifying the problem rather than ending it. Saturninus implies that the Zealots counted on Mary's disappearance in three days after her death to suggest that she too had defied death and had joined her son, reconfirming Jesus' mission. The Zealots and the Sicarii stole the body of the Virgin, specifically on the third day, in the hope of terrifying the Romans into believing that there was possibly going to be another serious flare-up of religious fervor as followed Jesus' resurrection, forcing them to crack down to prevent it. The idea was that a crackdown in such a tense environment would cause a cycle of violence, which would cause a harsher crackdown, and so on. As Saturninus mentions, he didn't know if it was the disappearance of Mary's body that did the trick, but soon after its theft, a cycle of violence did occur that grew progressively month by month. Within just a few years the tinderbox that was Palestine exploded into the climactic Great Revolt, with all the Jews uniting together to seize both Jerusalem and Masada from the Romans."

"Do you think it would have been easy to steal the body of the Virgin?"

"Actually, I think it would have been. There seems to have been a surprising lack of interest in the Virgin Mary after the crucifixion, so that her death, according to Saturninus, in AD 62, drew little or no attention. None of the four Evangelists mentions much about her after Jesus' death and resurrection, and Paul gives no indication whatsoever of a special place for her in the early Church. In fact, he mentions her only once in Galatians, and that was fleetingly, without even using her name. It wasn't until toward the end of the first century that Mary began getting more recognition. Today there is no question of her importance, which is why I believe this letter is so significant."

"I didn't get the impression from Saturninus's letter that Simon Magus had any connection with the initial theft of Mary's remains."

"Nor did I. My sense is that his interest was driven by his desire to secure for himself the curative power related to Jesus of Nazareth, and he didn't share the political interests of the Zealots. Saturninus doesn't mention how Simon learned that the Essenes had hidden the body in one of the Qumran caves, nor does he say how he managed to gain control of the bones. Perhaps by then no one cared. Simon was disappointed the remains didn't have the power to heal, which was obviously his reason to gain possession of them, and it was only after the fact that he got the idea to follow Peter, first to Antioch, and then Rome, with the plan to trade them for Peter's curative power."

"But Peter rebuffed him again."

"Apparently so, and according to Saturninus, with equal passion as when he had offered silver."

"Why do you think Saturninus and Menander decided to bury Mary's bones with Peter?"

"I believe for the reason he states in the letter. They were both impressed with Peter's ability to cure by laying on of hands. We know they were impressed, since ultimately both became Christians, and Saturninus became a bishop of a major Roman city."

"I wonder what happened to Simon's remains. It would have been ironic if they ended up with Peter as well."

"Indeed," Shawn said with a smile. "But I doubt it sincerely. Saturninus surely would have said if he and Menander had done it."

"So, what are your plans?" Sana questioned. "Let me guess. You want to go to Rome and see if this ossuary Saturninus described is where he said he and Menander put it?"

"Exactly," Shawn said eagerly. "Apparently, just around the time Simon died during his attempt to rise up to heaven, Peter must have been martyred. With Peter's followers building him an underground tomb, Saturninus and Menander would have had a convenient opportunity to join Mary's ossuary with one of her son's closest apostles. Frankly, I think it was a very respectful gesture on their part, and it certainly suggests that they at least held Mary in high regard."

"I didn't understand the part of the letter describing where they put it," Sana said. "Do you?"

"I do. The tomb was a barrel vault, comprised of two parallel foundation walls holding up a vault. To build such a tomb, a rather large hole has to be excavated so that the walls can be put up. Saturninus says that they placed the ossuary at the base of the north wall outside of the tomb, approximately in the middle, and covered it with dirt. That is consistent with the facts, because the foundation walls of Peter's tomb run east–west."

"Why did they put the ossuary outside the tomb, rather than inside with Peter?"

"Obviously, they had to hide the damn thing outside," Shawn said impatiently, as if he thought Sana's question was inane. "They were doing this sub rosa, so to speak, without anyone else's knowledge."

"Don't be condescending!" Sana snapped. "I'm doing my best trying to understand it all."

"Sorry," Shawn said, realizing that if he wanted her to come, he had to be patient. "Getting back to the ossuary's placement, I have to tell you that it is unbelievably serendipitous for us for two reasons: First, I don't think that area of the tomb has ever been touched; second, the last time the tomb was excavated, which was in the nineteen-fifties, the archaeological team actually tunneled under the area, probably passing beneath Mary's ossuary, to reach the inside of the tomb. What that means is that all we will have to do, at most, is remove maybe a few inches of packed debris and the ossuary will drop down into our waiting hands."

"You make it sound so easy."

"I think it will be. Just before you got here I was on the phone with my assistant, Claire Dupree, back at the Metropolitan. I'm having her overnight my file on Saint Peter's tomb to the Hassler in Rome. I still have the access permit to the necropolis under Saint Peter's Basilica from the Pontifical Commission for Sacred Archaeology, which James arranged directly through Pope John Paul II. The file also contains my Vatican ID card, and most important, the key for the Scavi, or excavation office, which is the same as to the site itself."

"That was five years ago."

"True, but I'd be astounded if anything has changed. It's one of the frustrations as well as joys of Italy that rarely does anything change, at least in the bureaucratic arena."

"What if the keys don't fit or the permit has been revoked?"

"I cannot imagine that happening, but if it does, we'll have to cross that bridge at that time. If worse comes to worst, I'll call James. He can arrange for us to get in there. It just might mean an extra day."

"You think James would do that if he gets to read Saturninus's letter, which I assume he'd demand to do. I don't think so. Also, let's say we do get in there for argument's sake, and we do find the ossuary. What in heaven's name do you plan to do with it?"

"Bring it secretly to New York. I don't want to jump the gun with this windfall project. When I announce it, I want to have studied the bones and fully translated any and all writings, most specifically, the Gospel of Simon."

"It's against the law to take antiquities out of Italy."

Shawn regarded his wife with a touch of irritation. Over the previous year she had developed an independent streak, as well as an aggravating tendency toward negative thinking, and this was a good example. At the same time he reminded himself that in his enthusiasm over the previous hour, he was guilty of glossing over a few pesky details, like how the hell he was going to get his find back to New York. He, more than anyone, knew that Italy had become very protective about its historical treasures being pirated out of the country.

"I'll send the damn thing from the Vatican, not Italy," Shawn decided abruptly.

"What makes you think sending it from the Vatican is going to be any different? It will have to clear customs one way or the other."

"I'll send it to James and label it his personal property. Of course, that will mean I'll have to call him beforehand and tell him it is a surprise, which it certainly will be, and tell him not to open it until I get there."

Sana nodded. She'd not thought of that. She supposed it might work.

"Hell, I'll be giving it back after the fact," Shawn said, in partial justification.

"Wouldn't they let you work on it at the Vatican? Why take it back to New York at all?"

"I can't be sure of it," Shawn said without hesitation. "Besides, a number of people would demand to be involved and share the spotlight. Frankly, I don't want to do that. I'll take some flak for removing it from the Vatican necropolis and sending it to New York, but the positive will overwhelm the negative, I'm certain. To sweeten the deal, I'll even give the Vatican the codex and Saturninus's letter, and they can keep them or send them back to Egypt. It will be their call."

"My sense is that the Catholic Church is not going to like anything about this affair."

"They'll have to adjust," Shawn agreed with a snide smile.

"Adjusting is not easy for an institution like the Catholic Church. The Catholic Church believes the Virgin Mary was assumed bodily into heaven like her son, bones and all, since hers was a virgin birth without original sin." Sana had been raised a Catholic until her father's death when she was eight. From then on she'd been raised an Anglican, her mother's religion.

"Well, as the expression goes, the ball will be in their court to deal with that issue," Shawn added, with his smile lingering on his lips.

"I wouldn't make light of it," Sana said.

"I won't," Shawn said categorically but then added with gathering emotion, "I'm going to enjoy it. You're right about Mary's bones not being here on earth, but that dogma is relatively new for the Catholic Church. For centuries the Catholic Church just avoided the issue, letting people believe what they wanted to believe. It wasn't until 1950 that Pope Pius the Twelfth made the determination ex cathedra and invoking papal infallibility, which for me, as you know, is pure nonsense. I've had this argument with James a thousand times: The Catholic Church wants it both ways. They evoke a divine basis for papal infallibility regarding Church matters and their interpretation of morality based on a direct apostolic lineage to Saint Peter and ultimately to Christ. Then, in the same breath, they dismiss some of the Church's medieval popes as being only human."

"Calm down!" Sana ordered. Shawn's voice had been steadily rising as he spoke. "You and I are having a discussion here, not a debate."

"Sorry. I've been wound up from the moment Rahul placed the codex in my hot little hands."

"Apology accepted," Sana said. "Let me ask you another question about Saturninus's letter. He used the word *sealed* when referring to Mary's ossuary. What do you think they meant by 'sealed'?"

"Offhand, I'd guess wax. Burial practices at that time involved putting a corpse in a cave tomb for a year or so, then collecting the bones and putting them in a limestone box, which they called an ossuary. If the decay wasn't complete, the box could have stunk to high heaven unless sealed. To do that, they would have had to use something like wax."

"Saturninus said that Mary's body was put in a cave in Qumran. How dry is it there?"

"Very."

"And how dry is it in the necropolis beneath Saint Peter's?"

"It varies, but there are times when it's relatively humid. What are you thinking?"

"I'm wondering what kind of condition the bones might be in if the ossuary stayed sealed. If dampness has been excluded, I might be able to harvest a bit of DNA."

Shawn chuckled with delight. "I'd never even considered that. Getting some DNA could add another dimension to this story. Maybe the Vatican could make some money by creating Bible Land, something akin to Jurassic Park, by bringing back some of the original characters, starting with Mary."

"I'm being serious," Sana said, mildly offended, thinking Shawn was making fun of her. "I'm not talking about nuclear DNA, I'm only talking of my area of expertise: mitochondrial DNA."

Shawn held up his hands, again pretending to surrender. "Now, I know you've told me in the past, but I don't totally remember the difference between the two types of DNA."

"Nuclear DNA is in the cell's nucleus, and it contains all the information to make a cell, to allow it to differentiate into, say, a heart cell, and to cause it to function. Every cell has a full complement of nuclear DNA except red blood cells, which have no nucleus. But every cell has only one set. Mitochondria are microscopic energy organelles that in the very distant past when life was just beginning were engulfed by primitive single-cell organisms. Once those single cells had mitochondria, they were able over millions or even billions of years to develop through evolution into multicellular organisms up to and including humans. Since the mitochondria had been freely living organisms, they have their own DNA, which exists in a circular, relatively stable form. And since individual cells have up to a hundred or so mitochondria, the cell has up to a hundred sets of mitochondrial DNA. All that leads to a higher possibility that DNA can be retrievable, even from ancient bones."

"I'm going to pretend I understood all that. Do you really think you might be able to isolate some of this circular DNA? That would be fascinating."

"It all depends on how dry the bones were initially and how dry they have remained. If the ossuary is still sealed, it's a possibility, and if it is possible to retrieve some of Mary's DNA, then it's too bad she had only a divine son and not a divine daughter."

A crooked smile spread across Shawn's face. "What a strange comment! Why a daughter and not a son?"

"Because mitochondrial DNA is passed on from generation to generation matrilineally. Males are genetic dead ends, mitochondrially speaking. Sperm don't have much mitochondria, and what they do have dies off after conception, whereas ova are loaded with them. If Mary had a daughter who had a daughter, et cetera, until current day, there might be someone alive today with the same mitochondrial sequence. By coincidence, the mitochondrial DNA has a two-thousand-year mutational half-life, meaning that after two thousand years, statistically speaking, there'd be a fifty percent chance the DNA sequence would be unchanged."

"Actually, there's a very good chance Mary had a daughter—in fact, not one but three of them."

"Truly?" Sana questioned. "I recall she had only one child, Jesus. That's what I learned in Sunday school."

"One son is Catholic dogma, Eastern Orthodox creed, and even the belief of some Protestant denominations, but there are many people who think otherwise. Even the New Testament in the Bible suggests she at least had other sons, although some people think the term 'brother of Jesus' means another close relative, like a cousin, a debate that arose during translation from Aramaic and Hebrew to Greek and Latin. But I, for one, think a brother is a brother. Besides, it makes sense to me that she had more children. She was a married woman, and having a bunch of kids the normal way certainly wouldn't have taken away from having the first one mystically, if that's what happened. And I'm not making this up. There's an awful lot of early Christian apocrypha, which didn't get chosen to be canonical by being included in the New Testament but which state she had up to eleven children, including Jesus, three of whom were daughters. So there might be someone out there with the same DNA."

"Now, that would put my field of mitochondrial DNA on the map," Sana said, while imagining writing the paper for *Nature* or

Science with such a suggestion. In the next instant, she was mocking herself. She was getting as bad as Shawn by jumping the gun and entertaining far-fetched delusions of grandeur. Maybe she was even worse, since Shawn was already much more famous in his field than she was in hers.

"Getting back to reality," Shawn said, "our Egyptair flight leaves Cairo at ten a.m. tomorrow and arrives in Rome at half past twelve. We're staying at the Hassler. Why not celebrate this coup in style. So, what do you think? Are you coming with me? If all goes well, it's just an extra day, and the payoff will be immense. I'm truly excited about it. As my last hurrah at fieldwork it will seriously aid my fund-raising."

"Do you really need me or am I window dressing to prop you up and keep you company?" Sana asked for reassurance but then inwardly winced the moment the unguarded words spilled from her mouth. It was the first time she'd actually voiced the idea, which she had lately been questioning due to his general behavior plus his lagging interest in intimacy, that Shawn had married her more as a young trophy wife than a true partner. It was an issue that had been progressively bothering her over the previous year and which seemed to be worsening with her own modest professional successes. Although she was planning on bringing the subject up at some point, the last thing she wanted to do was get into a serious row there in Egypt.

"I need you!" Shawn said definitively. If he'd actually heard what she had said, he didn't let on. "I won't be able to do this myself. I imagine the ossuary will weigh ten to fifteen kilograms, depending on its size and thickness, and I'm not going to want it to literally drop out of the ceiling. I suppose I could hire someone, but I'd much prefer not to. I don't want to be beholden to someone for their silence until I publish."

Relieved that her verbal slip had gone over his head, Sana fired off another question: "What are the chances that we could get into serious trouble by sneaking into the crypt under Saint Peter's?"

"We won't be sneaking in! We'll have to get past the Swiss Guards before we even get into the Vatican, and I'll need to show my all-hours-access permit from the Pontifical Commission for Sacred Archaeology. So we'll be perfectly legal."

"So, you can look me in the eye and promise me we're not going to be forced to spend the night in an Italian jail?"

Shawn made a point of leaning over and with his cerulean eyes stared unblinkingly into the depths of Sana's brown ones. "You will not have to spend an evening in an Italian jail, guaranteed! In fact, when we're done, we'll have a late supper with a bottle of the best Prosecco the Hassler can produce."

"All right, I'll come!" Sana said with resolve. She was suddenly enamored with the idea that they were embarking on an adventurous quest together. Maybe it would have a positive effect on their relationship. "But now I want to go down to the pool and get the last bit of sun before we head back to winter."

"I'm with you," Shawn said eagerly. He was pleased. He'd worried she'd turn him down. Although he'd suggested he could hire someone to help get the ossuary from beneath Saint Peter's, he knew he couldn't. The risk of the news getting out would be too great. After all, what he was planning to do was, despite what he'd just said to Sana, totally illegal. At the same time he was convinced it was to be his most brilliant coup.

7

Make sure you disinfect the outside of all the culture tubes and the histology specimen bottles," Jack said to Vinnie at the conclusion of the meningitis case. "I'm serious. I don't want to find out later that it didn't happen and you saying you forgot, understand?"

"I got it," Vinnie complained. "You already told me the same thing two minutes ago. What do you think I am, stupid?"

Vinnie caught Jack's expression through the plastic face mask of his hood and quickly added: "Don't answer that."

Jack hadn't planned on using a hood with a HEPA filter, but he could tell that Vinnie was uncomfortable without one, and his pride wouldn't let him use one unless Jack did. So at the last minute Jack relented for Vinnie's sake. As a rule, Jack didn't like using a hood and the moon suit because they were cumbersome and hard to work in. But as the case proceeded, he was glad he'd changed his mind. The virulence of this particular strain of meningococcus was impressive by dint of the damage it had done to the meninges and the brain itself.

Since they'd done the case in the decomposed room and there were no other mortuary techs around, Jack helped Vinnie get the body into a body bag and onto a gurney. After reminding Vinnie to inform the receiving funeral home that it was an infectious case, Jack removed the moon suit and hood, stripped off and disposed of the Tyvek coverall, and headed up to his office.

His first call was to the deceased teen's private school. Although it was an OCME rule that the public relations office handled all official communication, Jack often took it upon himself to buck protocol. He wanted to be absolutely sure certain things got done, and alerting the school in this instance was one of them. With the evidence of the bacteria's destructive power fresh in his mind, Jack spoke frankly to the headmaster, who assured him that the institution was taking the tragedy to heart. The city epidemiologist had already been there, and extensive decontamination and quarantine had begun. He was appreciative of Jack's concern and effort, and said as much.

Jack's next call was to Robert Farrell, one of Keara's friends. After more than half a dozen rings, the man finally answered, apologizing for the delay. But his tone changed when Jack identified himself as a medical examiner.

"I understand you were one of a group out drinking last night along with Keara Abelard and brought her into Saint Luke's emergency room."

"We could tell she was really sick," Farrell responded.

"Are you aware of the outcome?"

"The outcome of our bringing her to the ER?"

"I'm talking about her outcome."

"I heard she died after we left."

Jack's cynicism antenna went up. "Did that surprise you?"

"Sure. She was young."

"Young people don't usually die."

"That's why I'm surprised."

Jack cleared his throat to give himself a chance to think. His quick assessment was that Farrell was inappropriately defensive. As if to underline this impression, Farrell quickly added, "We didn't give her anything, if that's what you are implying. She wasn't even drinking."

"I wasn't implying anything," Jack said. He congratulated himself for taking a wide sampling of body fluids for toxicology despite the positive finding of bilateral vertebral artery dissection. He now wondered if she'd suffered a peculiar fall that could have sharply twisted, flexed, or extended her neck.

"How many of you brought her to the ER?"

"Three of us."

Jack nodded.

"You guys were drinking but she wasn't?"

"I think I want to talk to my lawyer before I answer any more questions," Farrell said.

Jack pressed on. "How big was your group?"

"There were about a dozen of us, men and women. We went to this dive bar in the West Village. Can you just tell me what she died from?"

"We're working on that. Did you witness the change in her behavior?"

"Yeah, one minute she was lively and talking, drinking a Coke, the next minute she was slurring her words and didn't know where or who she was. Then she stood up, staggered a few steps, and fell. I literally caught her, which is why I ended up bringing her to the ER."

"Why didn't you call an ambulance?"

"We thought she was drunk, to tell you the truth. I didn't learn until later that she was a teetotaler."

In his imagination, Jack could picture the lining of Keara's vertebral arteries balloon up and gradually choke off the blood supply to her brain. "Can you get me the names and phone numbers of the other people who made up this group?"

"I don't know, man." Farrell shied. "I don't know if I want to get any more involved in all this than I already am."

"Look, I'm not accusing anyone of any wrongdoing and I'm not accusing you of anything. I'm just trying to speak for the dead, which is what medical examiners do. I want Keara to tell us what killed her to try to save someone else from the same fate. There is some key piece of missing information involved here. Tell me, did you talk to her directly during the evening?"

"For a few minutes, but not any more than I talked to everyone else. I mean, like, she was a looker, so all the guys talked to her."

"Did she mention anything at all about being in an auto accident in the last week or so?"

"No, nothing like that."

"How about any falls she might have experienced: maybe even earlier last evening, like in the ladies' room." Jack didn't think a fall was a likely culprit with no external evidence of injury, but he didn't want to rule anything out.

"She didn't mention it, no."

Jack finally got the man to agree to make up a list of the other revelers from the previous night, along with their phone numbers. Farrell even promised to have it available by late afternoon.

Jack hung up, then sat at his desk, drumming his fingers on the blotter. Despite his initial suspicions, it now seemed to Jack there wasn't a criminal angle. But he was sure there was some piece of Keara's story that still eluded him. With no other excuse to postpone the call to Keara's mother, Jack dialed the number. He knew too well the woman's plight.

She picked up on the very first ring, her voice strong and expectant. Jack immediately assumed she was in the denial phase and there was still a part of her that hoped it might be a call from someone saying it was all a horrible mistake and that her daughter was just fine.

"This is Dr. Jack Stapleton. I'm calling from the Office of the Chief Medical Examiner."

"Hello, Dr. Stapleton," Mrs. Abelard said in a lilting but questioning tone, as if there was no reason for someone to be calling from the New York City morgue. "Can I help you?"

"You can," Jack said, debating how to begin. "But first I want to express my deepest sympathies."

Mrs. Abelard was quiet. Jack worried she might explode into a tirade with tears, heralding the second stage of grief, the anger stage. But there was only silence, interspersed by the woman's intermittent breathing. Jack was afraid to say anything, lest he make a bad situation worse.

"I hope I'm not bothering you too much," Jack said at length, but only after it had become obvious Mrs. Abelard was not about to respond. "I'm sorry to have to call.

"I know you were here at the morgue last night," Jack continued. "And I'm sure it was difficult. I don't mean to disturb you in this time of grief, but I wanted to let you know that I have carefully examined your daughter, Keara, this morning, and I can assure you she is resting peacefully."

Jack grimaced at what sounded to him like a mawkish attempt at empathy. He wished he could hang up, collect himself, and call back. The idea that an eviscerated corpse was resting peacefully was so absurdly sappy that he was embarrassed it had come out of his mouth. It made him feel guilty that he'd stooped so low in his manipulating. Nonetheless, he forged on as he'd done with the reluctant Robert Farrell. "What I'm trying to do is speak for your daughter, Mrs. Abelard. I'm certain she has something to say to help others, but I need more information. Can you help me?"

"You say she is resting comfortably?" Mrs. Abelard asked, breaking her silence. It was as if she believed her daughter had had some minor mishap.

"She's at peace. But I'm wondering, did she experience any kind of neck injury recently?"

"Neck injury? Like what?"

"Any kind of injury at all," Jack said. He felt like a trial lawyer trying to avoid leading the witness.

"Not a specific neck injury that I can recall, although she did fall from a swing when she was eleven and was bruised all over, including her neck."

"I'm talking about an injury that might have occurred over the last few days," Jack said, "maybe in the last week."

"Heavens, no."

"Is she a yoga enthusiast?" Jack was trying to cover all the bases.

"No, I don't think so."

"What about an automobile accident? Anything like that happen recently?"

"Heavens, no," Mrs. Abelard repeated more forcefully.

"So she'd been completely well up until yesterday. No neck aches or headaches."

"Well, now that you mention it, she did complain of some recent headaches. She's been under stress because of a new job."

"What kind of work?"

"Advertising. She's a copywriter for one of the up-and-coming ad agencies in the city. It's a new position, and a bit of a stressful situation. She'd been laid off recently, so she was feeling pressure to do her best in her new position."

"Did she say where the headaches were centered, like in the front or back of her head?"

"She said they were behind her eyes."

"Did she do anything about them?"

"She took ibuprofen."

"And . . . did it help?"

"Not very much, so she asked one of her friends, and the friend recommended a chiropractor."

Jack sat up in his chair. In the far reaches of his mind, he recalled a case he'd read about in an issue of the *Forensic Pathology Seminars* involving a chiropractor and stroke. "Did Keara go to this chiropractor?" Jack asked, while trying to recall the details of the published case. He remembered it dealt with the vertebral artery dissection, just as he'd found that morning in Keara.

"She did. As I recall, it was this past Thursday or Friday."

"Did the visit help her headaches?"

"It did, at least initially."

"Why did you say 'at least initially'?"

"Because the headache located behind her eyes went away, but then she got a different one in the back of her head."

"You mean like the back of her neck?"

"She said the back of her head. Now that I'm remembering the discussion, she also said she had a bad case of hiccups she couldn't get over, and they were driving her crazy."

"Do you happen to know the name of this chiropractor?" Jack asked, as he supported the phone receiver in the crook of his neck. With his hands free, he went on the Internet and Googled "dissection, vertebral artery."

"I don't. But I do know the name of the friend who recommended the doctor."

"You mean the chiropractor," Jack said reflexively, then regretted it. He didn't want to take any chances of upsetting Keara's mother. While the man may well have been a doctor of chiropractic, Jack knew many people thought they were medical doctors. Jack was leery of chiropractors, although he admitted he didn't know too much about them.

"Her name is Nichelle Barlow," Mrs. Abelard said, indifferent to Jack's comment.

"Thanks for your cooperation," he said, writing down the number. "You've been so generous, especially under such trying circumstances."

Replacing the receiver, Jack stared blankly at the wall. Seventeen years ago when his first wife and children died, he remembered how long he had been in denial as friends and family had called. Shaking his head to free himself from such morbid thoughts, he forced himself to turn his attention to his computer screen, but he couldn't concentrate. Instead he recalled the scene a couple of nights previous, of John Junior sobbing with what he and Laurie worried was bone pain from the tumor in the marrow cavities of his long bones. His tiny, perfectly formed infant hands seemed to gesture toward his legs as if hoping his parents could provide relief, but of course they couldn't.

"Shit!" Jack yelled at the ceiling in hopes of shocking himself out of his downward-spiraling self-pity. At that point, a head poked in through the open doorway. It was Dr. Chet McGovern, Jack's former office mate.

"Is that a reflection of your personal state of mind," Chet joked, "or a general assessment of the current stock-market trend?"

"All of the above," Jack said. "Come on in and take a load off." Despite being preoccupied, Jack welcomed the diversion.

"Can't do," Chet said, with a lilt to his voice. "I met somebody Saturday night, and we're meeting for lunch. She might be the one, my friend! She is hot."

Jack waved him off. He'd become convinced Chet was never going to, find "the one." Chet loved the chase too much to settle down.

"Hey, Chet," Jack called to his retreating friend. "Have you ever had a vertebral artery dissection?"

"Yeah, one," Chet said, returning to lean back into Jack's office. "It was during my forensic pathology fellowship in L.A. Why?"

"I had one this morning. It stumped me until we opened the skull. There wasn't much of a history, and there was no apparent trauma."

"How old?"

"Young. Twenty-seven."

"Check out if she'd seen a chiropractor in the last three days or so."

"I think she did," Jack said, impressed by Chet's suggestion. "I think she might have seen one last Thursday or Friday. She died last night."

"It could be significant," Chet replied. "In my case, the association was easy to make, since the symptoms began moments after the cervical manipulation. But when I looked into the issue in general, I learned the symptoms of VAD can be delayed for days.

"Listen," Chet added. "I'd love to talk more, but I got to go to meet my new honey."

"You're impressing me no end," Jack said, jumping up and following Chet down the hall. "I vaguely remember reading about a case, but I'd never seen one."

"I found it interesting," Chet admitted as he walked, "and I thought I could get some kudos out of it from my chief, so I researched VAD and chiropractic a bit. I found it to be one of those associations which hasn't sparked much interest, nor did it then for me. It turned out my chief went to the same chiropractor and swore by him, so my hand was forced to sign out the case as merely a therapeutic complication."

"What is it that certain chiropractors do that makes VAD possible? Do you know?"

"I assume it is the force of their 'adjustment technique,'" Chet explained. "It's called a high-velocity, low-amplitude cervical thrust. Though it doesn't happen often, there are apparently times when it can cause an internal tear in the vetebral artery, and the blood pressure does the rest. Sometimes the dissection extends all the way up into the basilar artery."

"How often is not often?" Jack asked.

"I don't remember exactly," Chet admitted. "It was a few years ago. In the L.A. medical examiner files I think I found only four or five cases of VAD associated with chiropractic visits." Chet stepped into the elevator, holding the door open with his hand. "Listen, Jack, I gotta go. I'm already late. We can talk more later if you want." The doors closed, and he was gone.

For a moment Jack continued to stare at the blank elevator door. He was now intrigued, thinking he might have stumbled on the diversion he needed. If it turned out that Keara had gone to a chiropractor for her headache and had had cervical manipulation, there was a chance, he had no idea of how much chance, she'd suffered her vertebral artery damage there.

Turning around suddenly, Jack hastened back toward his office, mulling over the fact that he'd read of a case of VAD caused by cervical manipulation, and that Chet had had one himself as well as having found four or five in the L.A. medical examiner data bank. On top of that, Jack thought, he may presently have another. What it was all suggesting to him was that paying a visit to a chiropractor under certain circumstances was not necessarily a benign experience.

Although Jack admitted he didn't know the details of chiropractic therapy, as a form of what was referred to as alternative
or complementary medicine, he knew there was a question about
its efficacy. He had always vaguely lumped together chiropractic,
acupuncture, homeopathy, Ayurvedic tradition, Chinese herbal
medicine, Transcendental Meditation, and a hundred others of
what he considered questionable therapies based more on hope
and the placebo effect than anything else. It surely wasn't science,
as far as he was concerned, but if people believed they got value
for their dollar, it was fine with him. On the other hand if these
therapies could be fatal, it was another story entirely, and he, as
a medical examiner, had a distinct responsibility to blow the proverbial whistle.

Energized by this new crusade, Jack sat back in his desk chair.
He couldn't help but think about his conversation with Laurie and
how she said she'd be willing to try anything for JJ. "I think we'll
pass on chiropractic therapy," Jack said out loud as he pulled his
chair toward his computer monitor.

8

Jack pulled up an eMedicine article dealing with vertebral artery dissection. He began skimming it, learning that VAD was the cause of twenty percent of strokes suffered in patients younger than forty-five years of age, occurring three times more often in females than males. Reading on, he noted that the typical presentation was occipital, or back of the head, headache. He turned to the last page for the causes. The very first risk factor listed was spinal manipulation, just as Chet had suggested.

Intrigued at what the incidence of VAD was from spinal manipulation specifically, Jack went back to his default search engine. A few seconds later, he was scanning through a plethora of articles. He quickly found an article he thought promising and clicked on it. As he read it, he found it far more disturbing than the first as it was a systematic review of thirty-five actual cases of strokes caused by cervical spine manipulation that had been reported in the medical literature from 1995 to 2001. The vast majority involved chiropractors, and most of the lesions were vertebral artery dissections. Outcomes varied from full recovery in six percent of patients to varying levels of permanent neurological deficits or death in the remaining ninety-four percent. One of the listed patients who had died was a three-month-old baby girl.

Jack leaned back and stared up at the ceiling. What malady would lead parents to think an infant's symptoms would be relieved by cervical neck manipulation, suddenly and forcibly twisting the infant's neck beyond a point of normal resistance? And what had gone through the supposed therapist's mind that gave him or her the audacity to do such a thing? Jack wasn't just horrified—he was angry.

Moving on to the discussion section of the article, Jack read that there was evidence that the thirty-five cases discussed were only a small portion of such cases, since underreporting was apparently widespread. To back up this statement a survey of physician specialists at a meeting of the Stroke Council of the American Heart Association reported three hundred sixty unreported cases of stroke after spinal manipulations! *How could this be?* Jack questioned.

Placing his hands on either side of his head, Jack shook it in disbelief, questioning why this issue was not more commonly known. After puzzling over the situation for a few minutes and coming to no conclusion, Jack returned his attention to Keara Abelard's case.

He angrily riffled through the mass of papers on his desk until he located the telephone number of Keara's friend who'd allegedly recommended chiropractic. He dialed, then tried to calm himself as the call went through. He knew it could be counterproductive to intimidate Keara's friend. When she answered, Jack identified himself and mentioned his official title in as poised a manner as he was capable. His introduction was greeted with silence.

"Are you still there?" Jack inquired. "You are Nichelle Barlow, aren't you?"

"Are you calling from the morgue?" the woman asked, with obvious concern.

"I am. Are you Nichelle Barlow?"

"Yes," she replied reluctantly, apparently trying to prepare herself for what couldn't be good news.

"I got your number from Mrs. Abelard. I hope I'm not disturbing you."

"It's okay," she said hesitantly. "Are you calling me about Keara?"

"I am. I suppose you weren't out with her and her friends last night."

"No, I wasn't, but don't tell me she . . ." Nichelle said but was unable to complete the sentence.

"Unfortunately, Keara passed away last night," Jack said. "I'm sorry to be the bearer of bad news."

"What happened?"

"She had a stroke."

"A stroke?" Nichelle said with disbelief. "Keara was my age, only twenty-seven."

"Strokes are more common the older one gets, but even children can have them."

"I can't believe this. Is this some kind of sick prank?"

"I'm afraid not, Ms. Barlow," Jack said calmly. "The reason I'm calling is because I'm investigating your friend's death. Any sudden passing of an individual in apparent good health and with no known cause falls under the jurisdiction of the medical examiner's office. What I need is some information. You were aware that Keara was suffering from headaches?"

"That's what she said. But I didn't get the impression they were particularly bad. More nuisance than debilitating."

"Did she describe them to you?"

"Sort of. She said they were behind her eyes, more on the right than the left. She said she gets them when she is under stress, and with her new job she said she was under a lot of stress."

"Her mother told me you had suggested she see a chiropractor." Jack kept his voice neutral to avoid casting blame.

"She said ibuprofen wasn't helping, so I suggested my chiropractor."

"Did she take your advice?"

"It sounded like she was going to, but I don't know for sure. The last time I spoke with her was last Wednesday."

"What is this chiropractor's name?"

"Dr. Ronald Newhouse. He's a wonderful doctor."

"When you say 'doctor,' you are aware he's not a medical doctor?"

"He's a doctor, he just can't do surgery or prescribe drugs."

Jack felt his anger seeping back, but he fought against it. He wasn't going to be able to change Nichelle's ideas about this, but he couldn't let her misconception go completely unchallenged. "Your chiropractor calls himself a doctor, but he is a doctor of chiropractic, not a doctor of medicine. Can you tell me where Dr. Newhouse has his office?"

"Fifth Avenue between Sixty-fourth and Sixty-fifth. Hold on and I'll get you the telephone number."

In a moment Nichelle came back on the line. After she gave Jack the number, he asked, "How long have you been a patient of his?"

"About eight years. He's been my savior. I see him for almost everything."

"What do you see him for specifically?"

"Whatever ails me: sinusitis, mostly. That and gastric reflux. I'd be a wreck if it weren't for Dr. Newhouse."

"Ms. Barlow," Jack began, then paused. For a moment he mulled over what he wanted to say. "I'm curious to know how your chiropractor treats your sinusitis."

"He adjusts me. Usually he works on my cervical vertebrae, but sometimes my lumbar. I've got one hip higher than the other, and my back is a mess, but it's definitely getting better. You should see the changes in my X-rays. It's remarkable."

"Does he take spine X-rays often?" Jack asked, horrified at the thought. The radiation required for spinal radiology was significant.

"Most every visit," Nichelle said proudly, as if she thought the more X-rays, the better. "He's a very, very thorough doctor. The best that I've ever been to, truly."

Jack cringed at this inappropriate glowing assessment of someone who was treating sinusitis undoubtedly caused by an overgrowth of bacteria with potentially dangerous cervical manipulation and unneccessary radiation to boot! Even if the machine was digital, over time the dose would add up.

"Thank you for your help, Ms. Barlow," Jack said, making an effort to avoid the temptation to contradict the woman. The fact that a seemingly intelligent and educated person could hold such off-the-wall opinions in this day and age was a mystery to him. But he didn't dwell on it.

Jack disconnected rather abruptly. He knew that had he not done so, he surely would have ended up lecturing Nichelle about her need to apply a modicum of her intelligence to her health-care choices. She was admittedly using her chiropractor as a GP. Without even replacing the handset, he began dialing Ronald Newhouse's office. At about the halfway point he stopped, paused, then put the receiver it its cradle. He still felt enraged, and in that state of mind he was prescient enough to know he couldn't have a coherent conversation. The idea that the man truly believed he could treat a sinus infection with spinal adjustment was execrable. The man had to be a charlatan.

To calm himself, Jack turned to composing an e-mail asking the thirty-plus other New York City medical examiners if they'd had any cases of VAD, particularly chiropractor-induced VAD. He was about to send the message when he decided to expand the request to deaths involving all types of alternative medical therapy, including but not limited to homeopathy, acupuncture, and Chinese herbal medicine.

Jack then searched the Barnes & Noble website for alternative-medicine titles and was amazed at the number available. Reading through the descriptions, he noted that there seemed to be many more pro than con, despite what he felt was the shaky underpinning of the various therapies. This only added to his curiosity, especially in an era when conventional medicine was moving toward more evidence-based therapy.

One title struck him: *Trick or Treatment*. He called one of the Barnes & Nobles on the West Side and asked that a copy be put aside. He was motivated to rectify his shameful ignorance of the subject.

Feeling more like himself, Jack went back to telephoning Ronald Newhouse. Again, halfway through the dialing process, he stopped and hung up the phone. He suddenly decided a site visit was in order, even though he knew very well that the powers-that-be frowned on site visits by the MEs. The OCME protocol called for site visits to be made by the well-trained medicolegal team, not medical examiners, unless extraordinary circumstances demanded the presence of a trained forensic pathologist. Although Jack guessed that neither the deputy chief nor the chief would see the current situation as one of those "extraordinary circumstances," he decided to do it anyway. He had an irresistible urge to look the chiropractor in the eyes while he explained how spinal manipula-

tion could cure sinusitis. He also wanted to see his expression
when he told the guy he'd killed Keara Abelard, treating her for a
garden-variety tension headache.

It had been a while since he last made a site visit. Back when
he was newly hired, especially when he was involved in a complicated infectious-disease case, he made a lot of them, and almost
got himself fired several times. The chief, Dr. Harold Bingham, had
come within inches of dismissing Jack for willful insubordination.

As he waited for the elevator, Jack realized that if Ronald
Newhouse had treated Keara with the suspected cervical manipulation, Jack wasn't required to put "therapeutic complication"
as the manner of death on the death certificate, which would be
what everyone from Bingham on down would expect. He didn't
even have to put "accidental," which was the designation for such
a case before "therapeutic complication" had been devised in the
mid-nineties. Jack realized he could put "homicide" as the cause of
death, then turn the case report over to the DA as was done in
more typical cases of criminality. "What a stir that would cause,"
Jack said to himself with a mischievous smile as he boarded the
elevator. And thinking in that vein, he thought that perhaps such
a "political bomb" was what was needed to draw attention to the
dangers of cervical manipulation.

9

By the time Jack braked to a stop in front of Ronald Newhouse's Fifth Avenue office, he felt better than he had in months. He was motivated, thanks to Keara Abelard, by having stumbled on the perfect diversion: a crusade of exposing the dangers of alternative medicine. He couldn't wait to come face-to-face with the man.

Jack hopped off his bike and went about applying the collection of locks he used to secure his Trek. As he was applying the last one, someone tapped him on the shoulder.

Jack looked up into the face of a uniformed doorman, looking like he stepped off a movie set in his old-fashioned greatcoat with two rows of shiny brass buttons. "Sorry," he said in a tone that suggested he wasn't sorry at all. "You can't leave your bike here. It's against the rules."

Redirecting his attention to the final lock, Jack finished the task of securing the bike.

"Hey, buddy!" the doorman said. "Did you hear me? You can't leave the freaking bike here. It's private property."

Standing up without saying a word, Jack fished in his pants pocket, pulled out his wallet, and flashed his official New York City medical examiner's badge. It looked to all the world like a policeman's badge, unless you looked closely.

"Sorry, sir!" the doorman said hastily.

"It's quite all right," Jack said. "The bike won't be here long."

"No problem, sir. I'll keep my eye on it. Can I help you in any way?"

"I'm here to see Ronald Newhouse," Jack said. He couldn't bring himself to use the title "doctor." Nor did he say whether he was there in an official capacity or as a patient.

"This way, sir," the doorman said obsequiously, gesturing toward the front door and leading Jack into the foyer. He opened the inner door with a key and pointed. "Dr. Newhouse's office is down the hall, first door on the left."

"Thank you," Jack said, wondering if the man would have been equally gracious if he knew Jack was a medical examiner.

DR. RONALD NEWHOUSE AND ASSOCIATES was stenciled in gold leaf on the door. When he walked in, it was immediately apparent that Newhouse ran a successful practice. Not only could he afford the Fifth Avenue rent, which Jack assumed was significant, he'd had the waiting room decked out in style. There were original oil paintings on the walls, plush furniture, and a large Oriental rug. What made it appear different from any successful medical doctor's office he'd seen were three stools with contour seats connected to their bases by a movable ball joint. A woman in her twenties occupied one of the stools. With her hands on her knees and her legs spread apart such that her dress drooped between her knees, she was in constant motion in a manner that reminded Jack of his daughters using their hula hoops. While he watched her, the woman caught his eye and smiled. She appeared completely unself-conscious, leading Jack to believe the unique activity was normal in the environment.

"Can I help you?" a pleasant female voice asked from Jack's right. He turned to face an immaculately dressed woman with every strand of dark hair in place. Jack was impressed. Even her manicure was perfect.

"I think so," Jack said. He stepped over to the woman, who smiled up at him. "To be perfectly honest, I've never been in a chiropractor's office."

"Welcome," the receptionist said. Her nametag read LYDIA.

"That's an interesting piece of furniture," he remarked, tilting his head toward the woman rotating and counter-rotating on the stool.

"She's using one of our swivel chairs. It's great for the lumbar vertebrae of the lower back," Lydia explained. "It causes the intervertebral discs to lubricate themselves and actually swell to a degree. We encourage people to do it before their adjustment session."

"Interesting," Jack said. "Is Dr. Ronald Newhouse available?" He gritted his teeth after forcing himself to use the appellation "doctor."

"He is here," she said. She gestured toward the woman on the swivel chair. "He has his next patient at one-twenty-five. Do you have an appointment?"

"Not yet," Jack said.

"Would you like to make one?"

"I'd like to see the doctor," Jack said ambiguously. "I don't know nearly as much about chiropractic therapy as I would like."

"Dr. Newhouse is always interested in new patients. Perhaps he could see you for a few minutes before he sees Ms. Chalmers. If you don't mind waiting for a moment, I'll go ask him. Who may I say wishes to see him?"

"Jack Stapleton."

"Okay, Mr. Stapleton. I'll be back presently."

"I appreciate your help," Jack said. While the receptionist was out of the room, he glanced back at Ms. Chalmers as she dutifully continued her hip rotations. She had her head back, her eyes closed, and her lips slightly parted. For a moment Jack was mesmerized. She seemed to be in a trance.

"The doctor will see you now," Lydia said, breaking Jack's concentration. He followed her through an interior door and down a short corridor passing a series of closed doors. At an open doorway she stepped back and gestured for Jack to enter.

The office looked out on Fifth Avenue and beyond into Central Park. Inside there were two men, one sitting behind a desk, the other in a visitor's chair. The man behind the desk, who Jack assumed was Ronald Newhouse, immediately stood up and leaned over the desk, stretching a beefy hand in Jack's direction.

"Welcome, Mr. Stapleton," Ronald Newhouse said with a salesman's enthusiasm.

Jack allowed his hand to be vigorously pumped. Newhouse was about an inch or so taller than Jack's six feet, and one and a half times his hundred-and-eighty-pound weight. Jack estimated he was in his mid-forties. His coloring was dark with carefully groomed eyebrows on prominent brow ridges. His eyes were dark and piercing. But the most striking aspect of the man's appearance was his hairstyle, or, more accurately, the lack of it. His hair was medium-length, dark, and shiny, as if slathered with styling gel, but totally uncombed. Spiky clumps sprang from his scalp at odd angles.

"Meet one of my associates, Carl Fallon," Newhouse said, gesturing toward the gentleman in the visitor's chair.

On cue, Fallon sprang to his feet, and with alacrity that matched Newhouse's, gave Jack's hand a second spirited shake. "Very nice to meet you," he said to Jack. He gathered the remains of a pastrami sandwich and a half-eaten dill pickle along with a small brown bag. "I'll catch you later," he said to Newhouse.

"A great guy," Newhouse commented. He pointed to the chair Fallon had vacated. "Please, sit! I understand you are interested in chiropractic therapy. I'm happy to give you a quick intro before I see my next patient. But before I do, how did you find me? Was it through my new website? We've been putting a lot of effort into it, and I'm curious to know if it's working."

"I was referred," Jack said. He was aware he wasn't quite telling the truth, but he wanted to see how things would play out.

"Wonderful!" Newhouse responded smugly. "Would you mind if I asked the patient's name? I can't tell you how rewarding it is to get positive feedback from a satisfied patient."

"Nichelle Barlow."

"Ah, yes! Nichelle Barlow. A lovely young lady."

"I'm interested to know what you as a chiropractor feel competent to treat?"

Newhouse's smile deepened, and for a moment he seemed to be deciding where to begin. Jack focused on a series of books on the windowsill directly behind him, held upright by bright brass caduceus-shaped bookends. The titles were telling: *How to Build a Million-Plus-Dollar-a-Year Chiropractor Practice* and *How an E-meter and Applied Kinesiology Can Double Your Practice Income.* Jack had vaguely heard of e-meters, which had been described as bogus technology when a number had been confiscated by the FDA. He'd also heard of applied kinesiology, which had been discredited as having no medical value by controlled trials.

"I'd have to say chiropractic therapy in my hands can treat just about any medical ailment known to man. Now, to be fair, I'd have to qualify that by admitting up front that chiropractic cannot cure every ailment, but it most definitely relieves the symptoms of those problems it cannot cure."

"Wow!" Jack said, as if impressed. Actually, he was impressed by the sheer boldness of the claim. "Do all chiropractors feel the same about the field's capabilities?"

"Heavens, no," Newhouse said with a sigh. "There's been an unfortunate falling-out, so to speak, since the field's great founder, Daniel David Palmer, discovered the techniques in the nineteenth century and founded the Palmer School of Chiropractic in Davenport, Iowa."

"Davenport, Iowa," Jack repeated. "Isn't Iowa where the Transcendental Meditation movement is based?"

"Indeed, it is, although different towns. Fairfield, Iowa, is the location of the Maharishi University. I suppose you could say Iowa's the nation's most fertile center for the development of alternative medicine. Of course, the most important discovery of all remains the chiropractic movement."

"Can you give me a thumbnail sketch of the scientific basis for chiropractic's therapeutic power?"

"It's based on the flow of *innate intelligence*, which is a kind of life force or vital energy."

"'Innate intelligence,'" Jack repeated, to be certain he'd heard correctly.

"Exactly," Newhouse said, raising his hands palms out with fingers spread like a preacher about to make an important point. "Innate intelligence has to move freely about the body. It's the basic governing force making sure all the organs and muscles work together for the common good."

"And when this flow is impeded, then there's disease."

"Exactly!" Newhouse seemed pleased.

"What about bacteria, and viruses, and parasites," Jack said. "How do they fit in when it comes to disease—let's say with sinusitis."

"Very simple," Newhouse said. "With sinusitis there is a sharp decrease in the flow of innate intelligence to the sinuses. There is a resultant decrease in the normal physiological function of the sinus cavities, opening up the opportunity for any resident bacteria or fungus or whatever to grow."

"So let me see if I understand this," Jack said. "The pathological process starts with the blockage of the flow of innate intelligence, or life force, and the overgrowth of the bacteria is a result, not a cause. Am I getting this right?"

Newhouse nodded. "You're getting it perfectly."

"So, the chiropractor's job is to restore the flow, and as soon as he or she does that, the bacteria, or whatever is secondarily involved, goes away."

"You are exactly right."

"I said 'he or she,' but it seems to me there are more men chiropractors than women."

"I think that is safe to say."

"Is there some reason?"

Newhouse shrugged. "Probably the same reason there are more surgeons who are men than women. Chiropractic therapy takes a certain amount of strength. Maybe men find it easier."

Jack nodded while in his mind's eye he could see the internal tears in Keara's vertebral arteries. He had to agree. It took strength to cause the kind of damage she'd suffered. After clearing his throat, Jack asked, "How is it that the innate intelligence gets blocked?"

"One of Daniel David Palmer's very first patients had a severe hearing problem brought on seventeen years previously while straining to pick up a heavy load. When Dr. Palmer examined him, he determined a cervical vertebra had been racked out of position. When he replaced it, the patient's hearing returned. What had happened, simply put, was the displaced vertebra had been pressing on the nerves, enervating the ears. When the pressure had been released the flow was reinstated and function returned."

"So, the innate intelligence flows through the nerves."

"Of course," Newhouse said, as if this particular fact was self-evident.

"So, it's the backbone that's the culprit," Jack said, "when it comes to blocking innate intelligence."

"Yes," Newhouse agreed. "You have to realize that the spine is not just a stack of bones but rather a complex organ, with each vertebra able to influence the other as well as the group as a whole. It's what supports us, holds us all together, and integrates us. Unfortunately, it has a strong tendency to get out of line. That, in a nutshell, is the responsibility of we chiropractors. It's our job to diagnose the irregularity—or *subluxation*, as we call it—and restore the involved vertebra to its normal position, and then make sure that it stays there."

"All this is accomplished by spinal manipulation, correct?"

"You got it. We, of course, have a special name for it. We call it *adjustment*."

"Are you saying you can function as someone's GP?"

"Absolutely," Newhouse said, pronouncing each syllable as if it were a separate word. "I believe I serve as your friend Nichelle Barlow's GP. And I'm sure she'll tell you she is in terrific health. I adjust her regularly, because her spine needs constant attention."

"I suppose you don't have a strong feeling about antibiotics."

"Generally, they are not needed. Once I get the innate intelligence flowing normally, any infection clears up rapidly. Besides, antibiotics are dangerous. You see we dispense remedy, not drugs."

"How about vaccinations?"

"Not needed and dangerous," Newhouse said without a second of hesitation.

"All vaccinations for all kids?"

"All vaccinations for all kids," Newhouse echoed. "Vaccines are more dangerous than antibiotics. Look at this autism tragedy. I tell you, it is a terrible shame, if not a national disgrace. If one of those kids had come to me before getting vaccinated, they'd be normal today."

Jack literally had to bite his tongue to resist arguing with this off-the-wall charlatan. Though it seemed Newhouse believed what he was saying, Jack couldn't tell whether he was a well-intentioned but misguided therapist or a modern-day snake-oil salesman.

"What about infant colic?" Jack asked hesitantly, since the issue struck too close to home. "Can you treat that?"

"Not a problem," Newhouse said confidently.

"You'd treat an infant with spinal manipulation?" Jack asked nervously. He couldn't help but envision JJ being tortured by the man sitting in front of him.

"Well, first there'd be the diagnostic stage."

"Which would involve what, exactly?"

"Visual examination, careful palpation, observation of movement, and, of course, X-ray."

"You'd do a full spinal X-ray on an infant?" Jack asked, just to be certain. He was incensed. He wondered just how many infants Newhouse had exposed to the amount of radiation necessary for spinal films, even if his equipment was digital.

"Of course. It's a major part of our thorough diagnostic and therapeutic process. We use X-rays to diagnose, to document the course of treatment, and to make sure troublesome vertebrae stay in place. Since X-ray is so central to our mission, we have the latest digital system. Would you like to see it?"

Jack didn't answer. He was still trying to digest the information about infants being bombarded by ionizing radiation to make a bogus diagnosis of their youthful normal spines being somehow out of line.

Taking Jack's silence as acquiescence, Newhouse leaped from his chair and motioned for Jack to follow him. Dutifully, Jack got to his feet and shadowed him out into the hall and through one of the previously closed doors. The calm he'd achieved during the bike ride had been replaced by anger directed at Newhouse and his like-minded colleagues. Jack felt personally embarrassed, as if their existence was his fault.

The X-ray unit was impressively state-of-the-art. Knowing approximately how much such a unit cost, Jack could guess why they used it as much as they apparently did: It had to be paid for. Jack didn't listen as Newhouse, like a proud father, went through a litany of the machine's attributes.

In the middle of Newhouse's spiel, Lydia poked her head through the doorway to tell him that Ms. Chalmers was waiting in treatment room one.

"Have Dr. Fallon see her!" Newhouse said, hardly breaking stride with his presentation.

"I don't think she's going to be happy about that," Lydia said.

In an instant, Newhouse's demeanor changed from jovial to malevolent. "I said have Dr. Fallon see her!" He repeated each word with equal force.

"As you wish," Lydia said, beating a hasty retreat.

Newhouse took a deep breath. In a blink of the eye, the storm had cleared and sunlight had burst forth. Jack was astounded at the transition.

"Now, where was I?" Newhouse questioned, glancing over the keyboard and up at the monitor as if the X-ray machine would tell him.

"So, you follow people with X-rays," Jack said, ignoring Newhouse's question.

"All the time. We are interested in documenting the patient's progressive improvement, and the patients find it particularly reassuring."

"Could you show me such a progression?" Jack asked.

"Absolutely," Newhouse said. "We have a series available as a presentation for prospective patients like yourself, since we'd love to fulfill your health-care needs. Please, come back into my office. I'll show it to you on the computer."

Jack marveled at the effort Newhouse was willing to expend to gain another client. Until his last comment, Jack had wondered why Newhouse was being so generous with his time.

Jack moved behind Newhouse's desk so the two of them could view the monitor. Newhouse brought up a lateral cervical X-ray, allegedly that of one of his patients. Superimposed on the film were a number of straight red lines intersecting carefully measured angles. It all looked legitimate, as if it was some complicated system to analyze the film. Yet the more Jack looked at the X-ray and the profusion of red lines, the less sense it made to him. The one thing he did notice was that the patient's head was bent forward, with the chin practically resting on the anterior chest.

"In this preliminary film," Newhouse said, "the curve of the cervical spine in this symptomatic patient is just the opposite of normal. As you can see, it exits the skull not curving forward as it should, but rather backward. Now, this was the initial film before therapy commenced. As I show you subsequent films of this patient, watch how the cervical spine changes as therapy progresses."

Jack watched subsequent lateral films and could clearly appreciate the cervical spine change from curving backward to curving forward. At the same time he could see that the change was not from any therapy but due to the fact that the patient was slowly raising his head on each successive X-ray.

"Pretty dramatic, isn't it," Newhouse cooed.

Jack glanced from the monitor to the man who was admiring the final film of his presentation as if it were a piece of art. What it was, in reality, was a bit of trickery involving X-rays, used to fool an unsuspecting public. What Newhouse and his ilk were doing was lending a false sense of legitimacy to chiropractic therapy by using something that was a legitimate tool in the hands of conventional medicine. Not only was that fraudulent, it was dangerous, exposing people to harmful radiation.

Newhouse acted surprised when he turned to find Jack staring at him with silent intensity. Newhouse quickly misconstrued Jack's expression as awed appreciation. "Lydia will be happy to make you an appointment. I'm sure we'll have an opening within the month, if your symptoms can wait. We are booked solid with follow-ups, and initial visits take considerably more time to go through the diagnostic procedure and X-rays. Don't take the relaxed situation today as typical. Monday afternoons are booked lightly for continuing educational purposes. Usually, it's pandemonium around here."

Jack couldn't believe what went on in that office. If it wasn't so pathetic, it would have been funny. Understanding Newhouse was one thing. But what about the patients? Nichelle Barlow seemed intelligent and educated. So how could she be so foolish as to trust this man peddling phony therapy based on screwball ideas of innate intelligence?

"Mr. Stapleton?" Newhouse questioned. "Hello! I didn't mean to overwhelm you quite so much. Are you *okay?*"

Jack shook himself out of his mini-trance. "Earlier, in the beginning of our conversation," he began, "you said there'd been a falling-out among chiropractors? Somehow we became distracted and you never finished what you were going to say."

"You're right! We got off the track of talking about Daniel David Palmer, the founder of chiropractic, to talking about Davenport, Iowa, where he set up the first chiropractic medical school."

"What kind of falling-out were you referring to?"

"Simple! During the nineties a whole bunch of turncoat chiropractors allowed themselves to be browbeaten by conventional doctors into limiting themselves to treating back problems alone."

"You mean, giving up on treating such things as acute sinusitis."

"Exactly! The AMA had been against chiropractic forever, insti-
gating lawsuits and the like. They were afraid we'd steal their business,
which of course we were doing, because patients aren't stupid."

Jack wasn't so sure of that, but he didn't interrupt.

"Anyway," Newhouse continued, "sometime around 1990 the
Supreme Court finally silenced the AMA, ruling in favor of chiropractors by stating categorically that conventional medicine
through the AMA had tried to discredit chiropractic therapy to
maintain a monopoly over health care in this country."

Jack made a mental note to look into that ruling. Considering
what he'd learned that afternoon about chiropractic, it seemed
inconceivable the Supreme Court would have ruled in chiropractic's favor, although he assumed that the ruling involved the monopoly issue only and had nothing to do with efficacy.

"You'd think that such a ruling would have helped chiropractic,"
Newhouse continued. "But strangely enough it split us. A number
of conventional doctors, obviously from seeing our benefits, started
working with us, at least with those chiropractors willing to limit
themselves. Over the years these traitors have been dubbed 'mixers'
because they've been duped into limiting themselves to back problems exclusively and by doing so betraying the chiropractic movement." Newhouse paused momentarily, then added derisively:
"Meaning, of course, they are not real chiropractors."

"And what are you stalwart patriotic chiropractors called?" Jack
demanded, allowing a full dose of his infamous sarcasm to mani-
fest itself.

For a beat Newhouse gazed at Jack almost as if Jack had slapped
him. It was apparent the sarcasm hadn't been lost on him, but he
appeared more confused than affronted. Ultimately he ignored it
and said: "We're appropriately call 'straights' because we are true
to our beginnings."

For the hundredth time during his relatively short conversation with Newhouse, Jack had to restrain his reflex urge to speak his mind. Modulating his voice carefully, he said, "I'd like to ask you about another patient. Her name is Keara Abelard."

"Ms. Abelard," Newhouse repeated, allowing his sunshine face to reappear. "Another classy young lady. Did she also refer you to me?"

"Ultimately, I'd have to give that a qualified yes."

Newhouse's smile faltered. He was mildly confused again. Jack's response seemed unreasonably convoluted. "She was a new patient," Newhouse said. "Did she say something to you about her experience here?"

"Indirectly," Jack said, purposefully trying to be somewhat mysterious to fan Newhouse's curiosity. "Ms. Barlow told me she had suggested Keara come to see you but didn't know if Keara had followed through."

"She did. She came in as a new patient this past Friday. We squeezed her in because she said she was in considerable pain."

"So you remember her distinctly?"

"Oh, yes. Quite distinctly."

"How is that possible, given how busy you are? You must see a lot of patients to cover your overhead and pay the installments on your digital X-ray machine."

"I remember names," Newhouse said, looking askance at Jack. Jack's comment seemed inappropriate at best. "I have a facility for it."

"Do you remember her complaint?"

"Certainly. She had a severe frontal headache that was unresponsive to drugs. She'd had it for weeks."

"So, you thought you could help her."

"Most definitely, and I did. She said her headache melted away like magic."

"Did you take an X-ray?"

Newhouse nodded. He was sensing there was something wrong

with the conversation, but he didn't know what it was or when it had started. Jack's attitude had suddenly changed from being impressed to being strangely challenging.

"Where exactly were her subluxations?" Jack questioned.

"All up and down her spine," Newhouse said, with a new edge to his voice. He didn't like being challenged, especially on his own territory. "Her spine was a mess from ignoring it for so long. She'd never been to a chiropractor."

"How about her cervical spine? Was that a mess?"

"The whole spine, including the cervical area."

"So, you thought she was in need of an adjustment."

"Many adjustments," Newhouse corrected Jack. "We discussed a treatment schedule. I'll be seeing her again twice this week and for four subsequent weeks. Then once a week for four weeks."

"And if I remember correctly, an adjustment is another word for spinal manipulation. Is that correct?"

Newhouse made a show of looking at his watch. "I'm afraid it is getting late. I do have a few patients I must see. I'm going to have to ask you to leave."

"I'd like you to give me the courtesy of answering my question," Jack said, standing his ground.

A wry smile crept across Newhouse's face. He suddenly decided this uninvited visitor was a possible troublemaker and ought to be thrown out on his ass. Yet an inkling of concern that Jack might be some sort of city inspector instead of an oddball made him hesitate. Jack had, Newhouse thought, an authoritative air, an unexpected inquisitiveness, and a bold confidence that gave weight to his possibly being an official. And even though Newhouse's office had never previously been inspected, he thought there always could be the first time, which could be a disaster. He knew for a fact that his X-ray room was not properly shielded in the ceiling. With all that in mind, he asked, "What was your question again?"

"I want to know if Keara Abelard had a manipulation of her cervical spine."

"Generally, we don't divulge confidential information about our patients," Newhouse said defensively.

"Do you keep records of what you do to patients?"

"Of course we keep records! We need to document the course of improvement. What kind of question is that?"

"I can subpoena your records, so you might as well just tell me."

"You can't subpoena my records," Newhouse declared, although without much confidence. He was now more worried Jack was not quite what he'd assumed: a prospective new patient with the thought of making an appointment.

"You said Keara Abelard's headache went away after your treatment. Did you know it came back?"

"No, I didn't know. She didn't call me. If she had, I would have seen her immediately."

"The headache came back with a vengeance," Jack snapped. "And I need to know if you adjusted her cervical spine."

"And why do you need to know, Mr. Stapleton? Who are you, anyway?"

"I'm Dr. Jack Stapleton," Jack spat. "New York City medical examiner." He flashed his badge in Newhouse's face. "Keara Abelard died suddenly last night, without apparent cause, which makes her a medical-examiner case. I am the investigating medical examiner. I need to know if you manipulated her neck when you saw her on Friday. If you don't tell me, I'm going to get the police over here to take you in."

Jack knew he was exaggerating his power and a bit out of control. There was no way he could have Newhouse arrested. But Jack was furious enough to make such a claim, because the man had snuffed out the life of a beautiful, promising young woman.

What was really at the bottom of Jack's over-the-top behavior—
which he would have realized if he'd stopped to think about
it—was his anger at his son's illness and his inability to do anything
about it.

"All right," Newhouse shouted, after recovering from the shock
of learning of Keara's death. "I manipulated her cervical spine like
I've done for thousands of others. And you know something? It
worked. It worked because I fixed her subluxated fourth cervical
vertebra. And she walked out of here a grateful, well woman, without pain for the first time in weeks. If she died, she died of something else, something that happened to her over the weekend, not
because of my treatment, if that's what you are implying."

"Of course I'm implying your treatment killed her," Jack yelled.
"And do you know how you did it? Your thrust, as you call it, tore
the delicate lining of her vertebral arteries, which in turn caused
bilateral vertebral artery dissections and ultimately blockage. I
trust you know what the vertebral arteries are?"

"Of course I know what they are," Newhouse shouted back.
"Now get out of my office. You can't prove I did anything wrong,
because I didn't. And I cannot imagine it's okay for you to be accusing me like this. You have some nerve coming in here under
false pretenses. You are going to hear from my lawyer. I can promise you that."

"And you'll be hearing from the DA," Jack yelled. "I'm going to
sign the death certificate as homicide. 'Innate intelligence,' my ass!
That's the screwiest nonsense I've heard in my life. You mentioned
you 'straight' chiropractors call your colleagues mixers or traitors
who restrict their work to back problems exclusively. What do the
mixers call you guys, quacks?"

"Get out!" Newhouse roared, his face threateningly close to
Jack's.

It was as if a lightbulb went off in Jack's head. He suddenly realized he was within inches of an enraged man, nearly to the point of fisticuffs. What was he doing? What was he thinking?

Jack backed up a step. He wasn't necessarily afraid—Newhouse didn't look especially fit—but Jack didn't want to make a bad situation worse. What he wanted to do was get the hell out of there.

"Now that we see eye to eye, I think I'll be going," Jack said, reverting to sarcasm. "Don't bother to see me to the door," he added, holding up his hand as if waving Newhouse off. "I'll see myself out."

Jack made a beeline out of the inner office. Lydia and several patients had heard at least part of Jack and Newhouse's shouting match. All were sitting tensely, ready to bolt for safety's sake. Their mouths were slightly open, eyes unblinking, as they watched Jack transit reception. Jack's last gesture was to wave 'bye at Lydia before ducking through the office's outer door.

Outside Jack went straight to his bike, fumbling with the multiple locks while glancing nervously over his shoulder. He was astonished at his behavior, marveling at how out of control he'd become with Newhouse. Of course, now that he was thinking rationally, he recognized it all went back to JJ, emphasizing how important it was for him to get a grip on that situation. It also emphasized the importance of his crusade to help in that regard, but he needed to be thinking of the forest, not the trees. He had to focus on alternative medicine in general, not just chiropractic nor Newhouse because of an emotional response to Keara Abelard's tragedy.

Once his bike was free, Jack jumped on and sped away, heading south. Reaching speed he began to worry about the potential repercussions of his ill-considered site visit. If Bingham or Calvin got word of his latest shenanigans, it could very well cause a premature end to his nascent crusade. It might even be serious enough to get him put on administrative leave. From Jack's perspective either outcome would be a serious problem.

10

Shawn looked out the window as the Egyptair Boeing 737-500 made its final approach into Rome's Fiumicino airport. He could see nothing but the plane's wing. It was as if they were in a San Francisco fog bank. They had been circling the airport for almost a half-hour.

Other than the current tension, the day's travel had been enjoyable. They easily passed through Egyptian passport control and security. Shawn was a bit concerned because the codex was in his carry-on, wrapped in a towel in a Four Seasons pillowcase. If it had been found, Shawn would have been disappointed, although he didn't worry about legal consequences. He was prepared to tell the truth—that he'd bought it as a souvenir—and then lie that he'd been sure it was a fake like most everything else sold in Khan el-Khalili antiquities shops.

Saturninus's letter was a different story. Shawn had carefully covered each sheet of papyrus with clear plastic wrap he'd gotten from the Four Seasons kitchen, and then glued each between separate pages of a large, coffee table–style photography book of ancient Egyptian monuments hastily purchased in the hotel's gift shop. Through security Shawn had carried it in full sight in his hands. If the letter had been discovered there would have been a definite problem, but Shawn felt there was little risk. To Sana he'd downplayed it completely, falsely saying he'd done it in the past without the slightest difficulty. "As long as the book goes through the scanner, they're happy," he'd said to reassure her.

There was a sudden hard bump that made Shawn start. The plane had dropped below the low cloud cover. Through the now-rain-streaked window, Shawn could see soggy green fields and traffic-clogged roads. Despite it being the middle of the day, most of the vehicles had their headlights on. Looking ahead, he could dimly see the airport and, more important, the oncoming runway. A moment later, the plane touched down and the engines reversed.

Shawn let out a minor sigh of relief and glanced at Sana. She smiled. "Doesn't look like the best weather," she commented, leaning forward so she could see out.

"It can be rainy in winter."

"I don't think it's going to matter to us," Sana said, adding a wink to her smile.

"I think you're right," Shawn agreed. He reached over and gave his wife's hand a squeeze, and she squeezed back. Both were tense with anticipation.

"I'll tell you what," Sana said. "Why don't I go to baggage claim, and you go get the rental car? It's got to save us time."

"That's a super idea," Shawn said. He glanced back at his wife. He was genuinely surprised and appreciative. Usually, she left all the planning to him. Now she was being proactive and offering to help. To his delight, it seemed that she was equally as excited as he was. She had peppered him with questions about early

Christianity, Judaism, and even Near Eastern pagan religion throughout the flight.

"So, what do you think our schedule should be once we leave the airport?" Sana asked eagerly.

"We'll check in to the hotel, have a bite to eat, then find a place to get some basic tools. Then I think we should check out the necropolis or Scavi, so there will be no surprises when we sneak back tonight to get the ossuary. As I recall, the Scavi is open until five-thirty or thereabouts."

"Like what kind of tools?"

"A hammer and a chisel and a couple of flashlights. Maybe a battery-powered cutting device, just to be sure."

"For cutting what?"

"Soft rock and maybe brick. I'm hoping we don't need it. Power tools were actually banned by the pope when he authorized the modern excavation, to avoid any collateral damage, but we're not going to worry about that detail. Where we'll be working, the only thing we might damage is the ossuary itself."

"Aren't you expecting we'll be digging in just plain dirt?" Sana asked. In her mind, the idea of cutting into rock made the scope of the project significantly more daunting.

"No, it's going to be more like hardpan, a claylike layer mixed with gravel but highly compacted to seem like very soft stone. As I mentioned, the tomb that Peter's followers made for him on the Vaticanus hill adjacent to Nero's circus was an underground chamber with a barrel vault. They dug a large hole and then built two parallel brick foundation walls oriented in an east–west direction. Saturninus's letter says that the ossuary was placed midway at the base of the north wall and concealed before the excavation hole outside the walls was filled back in."

"And the base of the north wall is where we're going to find the ossuary?"

"That's right. During the last major excavation, more than fifty years ago, the archaeologists tunneled under that north wall to get inside the original tomb's chamber, to avoid destroying the mishmash of graves, altars, and trophies clustered above Peter's underground tomb. Starting from soon after his death until not that long ago, people clamored to be buried as close as possible to him. Anyway, it's in the roof of that tunnel where we are going to find the ossuary."

"I'm having trouble picturing all this."

"For good reason. Soon after Peter's death, the whole hill became not just the place for future popes to be buried but a popular Roman necropolis filled with graves and mausoleums. Today, because of its location beneath Saint Peter's, only a small portion of it has been excavated. And within a twenty-foot or so cubic area right around Peter's tomb, there is such a hodgepodge of ancient construction, you can't believe it. To make things more complicated, sometime in the first century a monument called the Tropaion of Peter was built just above his grave. Then in the fourth century, Constantine built his basilica around this monument, using it as an altar. During the Renaissance, Saint Peter's was built on top of Constantine's basilica, locating the high altar directly atop what had been Constantine's altar, now some forty feet above the floor of Peter's original tomb."

"It sounds like a layer cake," Sana said.

"That's a good analogy," Shawn agreed.

Once inside the terminal and through passport control, Shawn and Sana split up, with Sana heading for the baggage area and Shawn for the rental-car stands. Within half an hour they were on their way.

The drive into Rome was fine until they got into the city limits. Rain, traffic, and the lack of a decent map left them praying they'd eventually come across a recognizable monument.

After fifteen white-knuckled minutes, they spotted the Colosseum. Shawn quickly pulled over, and from there they plotted their way to the top of the Spanish Steps and the Hotel Hassler.

The route they'd chosen took them along the Foro Romano to the wedding cake monument to Vittorio Emanuele II. From there they headed north on the busy Via del Corso.

"My, this looks different than it does in the sunshine," Sana said, eyeing the pedestrians as they scurried about, huddled under their black umbrellas. "The dark clouds, the rain, and all the ruins make it seem sinister. Certainly not the Hollywood image as the city of love."

After several more key turns they found themselves on Via Sistina and then in front of the hotel. The doorman immediately came to Shawn's side.

"Are you checking in?" he asked graciously.

When Shawn indicated yes, the doorman waved to a colleague, who emerged with a second umbrella to shelter Sana while a porter gathered the luggage.

Once inside, they were whisked through check-in. Shawn was particularly pleased that the overnight package sent by his assistant from the Metropolitan Museum was waiting for him.

Shawn immediately began chatting up the attractive desk clerk.

"You're not Italian, I don't believe," he said. "You have a most charming accent."

"I'm Dutch."

"Really," Shawn said. "Amsterdam is one of my favorite cities."

"I see you are from New York," the receptionist said, cleverly diverting the conversation away from herself and to Shawn.

Oh, please! Sana thought. Impatiently, she shifted her weight from one hip to the other. She was afraid Shawn would launch into his life history. Thankfully, the well-trained receptionist expertly handled the situation by coming out from behind the counter to show them to their room, while maintaining a continuous flow of conversation describing the hotel's amenities, including the restaurant and its spectacular view.

The room was on the third floor. Shawn went to the window, which looked out over the Spanish Steps. "Come out here and see this," Shawn called to Sana, who'd gone into the bathroom to see if it was as posh as everything else.

"Pretty amazing, wouldn't you say?" Shawn said as Sana joined him and both gazed out at the Spanish Steps. Despite the rain, tourists were taking pictures of themselves. "Even though we can't quite see it, we're facing the dome of Saint Peter's. If it doesn't clear by morning, we'll have to come back someday when it's not raining so you can appreciate it."

Turning back inside, Sana unpacked and Shawn opened his package, dumping the contents on the desk. "Thank you, Claire!" he said, surveying the objects.

Sana came up behind him and peered over his shoulder. "Did you get everything we need?"

"I did. Here's my Vatican picture ID," Shawn said, handing her the laminated card.

"This picture looks like a mug shot," Sana joked.

"Okay, enough teasing," Shawn joked back, snatching the photo from her hands. In its place he handed her the access permit to the Vatican's necropolis, the Scavi, meaning "excavation" in Italian. It was a very formal document, complete with the official seal of the Pontifical Commission for Sacred Archaeology. "This is what is going to get us past the Swiss Guards tonight."

"I'm impressed," Sana said, handing the paper back. "Things seem to be falling into place. What about the keys?"

Shawn held them up and jangled them before pocketing them along with the ID card and the access permit.

"Looks like we are in business."

A few minutes later, Shawn and Sana headed down to the concierge's desk and asked where they could get a quick bite.

"Caffè Greco," one of the two concierges said without hesitation, the other concierge nodding in full agreement. "It's just down the steps and straight on Via Condotti. It's on the right."

"Can you also tell me where I can find a hardware store?" Shawn asked.

The concierges eyed each other quizzically. This was a first.

After some charades and a quick dictionary consult, Shawn and Sana were directed to a nearby *ferramenta* called Gino's on the Via del Babuino.

With map in hand and two hotel umbrellas, the couple first went to Caffè Greco, where they made short work of lunch. Next they used the hotel's map to seek out Gino's *ferramenta* shop, which was, as the concierges promised, a short walk up Via del Babuino. As they approached the shop, the dusty window display of tools and housewares appeared as if it hadn't been changed in years. When the door closed behind them, they were instantly enveloped in a palpable silence. The interior was as dusty as the window display. At the register were a half-dozen customers patiently and noiselessly waiting for service. A lone employee scanned a thick catalog.

Shawn and Sana were taken aback by the silence. It was heavy, like a church. What minimal sound there was seemed to be dampened by the plethora of merchandise, much of which was stacked in variously sized cardboard boxes. A black-and-white cat slept curled up on a humidifier carton. The atmosphere was a far cry from the hardware stores Shawn remembered from his youth growing up in the American Midwest. There, hardware stores were usually busy and loud, as much a hangout as a place to buy hardware.

Shawn motioned for Sana to follow him into the depths of the store. "Let's do our shopping ourselves," he whispered.

"Why are you whispering?"

"I don't know," he whispered back, but then in a normal voice said, "It's ridiculous to be whispering. I suppose I was just following the old adage: When in Rome, do as the Romans do."

Shawn first went to the area where the cleaning products and utensils were located, Sana following. He handed two stackable buckets to her, then moved on to flashlights and batteries. He selected two large torches with several sets of replacement batteries for each. As he was putting them into the nestled buckets, his eye caught something he'd not thought of: yellow plastic construction helmets with battery-powered headlamps. "I hadn't thought of headlamps," he admitted. "But they could come in quite handy." He tried one on, Sana doing the same.

They laughed at each other conspiratorially.

"Let's get them," Shawn said. Sana nodded, and both of them left them on as they moved on to the tool section. There Shawn got a masonry hammer and several masonry chisels. Then he saw three other things he'd not thought of but which would be undeniably helpful: plastic eye-protection goggles, work gloves, and knee protectors. The last item he selected was a Black & Decker drill with a battery pack and a number of interchangeable cutting and drill bits. With that, they paid for their selections and headed back to the hotel, where they stashed them. Shawn also plugged in the battery pack to charge.

"Look at the time," Sana said. "We've only got an hour."

"It will be close," Shawn said, checking his watch.

"Maybe we should plan to stay in Rome an extra day. The Scavi might be closed before we get there."

Shawn glanced at his wife with surprise. Just the day before, she'd been eager to go home immediately. Now she was the one suggesting they stay yet another day. "What about the experiment you were so worried about?"

"You've convinced me how important this could turn out to be."

"I'm pleased," he said. "But let's give it a try to get to the Scavi today. To tell you the truth, I'm so excited I can't put it off. I might even insist we try to get the ossuary tonight whether or not we're able to reconnoiter this afternoon."

"Okay, fine," Sana said. "Let's give it a go."

Despite it being rush hour, the Hassler doorman hailed them a taxi in minutes. As they were driven across the city Shawn and Sana were too tense to make conversation.

The cabbie, perhaps noting his passengers constantly checking their watches, drove like he was a Formula One racer. Weaving in and out of the traffic, he was able to deposit them just shy of twenty minutes at the Arch of the Bells, or Arco delle Campane, in the shadow of Saint Peter's. The rain was now coming down in sheets. Shawn and Sana huddled together under a single umbrella and made a run for the relative protection of the arch. The moment they stepped out of the rain, their further progress was blocked by two Swiss Guards dressed in their colorful black-and-orange vertical-striped uniforms accented by white ruffs and floppy black berets. One of the guards accepted Shawn's Vatican ID, checked the photo against Shawn's rain-soaked face, handed it back, saluted, and waved them in. There had been no words.

Emerging into the open, back into the wind-whipped rain, they ran across the cobblestoned piazza abutting the south side of Saint Peter's basilica. Now they were fighting not only the rain but also the torrents of water issuing forth from the church's gargoyles as well as splashes of water from fast-moving traffic heading out of Vatican City.

Gesturing with his head, Shawn said, "Can you see that flat black stone with a white border set into the ground we are passing?"

"Yes," Sana said without much enthusiasm. She was intent on getting out of the weather.

"Remind me to tell you about it when we get indoors."

Luckily, they didn't have far to go, and a few moments later they ducked in under a portico. They whisked the water off themselves as best they could and stomped their feet.

"That black stone out there in the piazza is supposed to mark the center of Nero's circus, where many early Christians, including Saint Peter, were martyred. For many years the Egyptian obelisk that's now in the center of Piazza San Pietro stood there."

"Let's get inside," Sana said. She wasn't interested in touristic details. She was wet and chilled, and night had fallen.

A few steps away, they entered the office of the Necropoli Vaticana. Despite it looking ramshackle to Sana to the point of resembling an inner-city principal's office, she was glad to be out of the weather. A large old-fashioned steam radiator hissed and thumped in the corner. Facing them was a counter fronting a battered government-issue desk. A man's head bobbed up. His expression suggested he was not happy about being disturbed.

"The Scavi is closed for the day," he said with a heavy accent. "The last tour left half an hour ago."

Without speaking, Shawn handed over his Vatican ID and the access permit. The man examined the permit closely. When he read Shawn's name his eyes lit up. He raised his head and smiled. "Professor Daughtry! *Buona sera*." As it turned out, the man recognized Shawn's name from his work at the site five years previously. He introduced himself as Luigi Romani.

Shawn vaguely recognized the name.

"Are you going down into the Scavi?" Luigi asked.

"Yes, just for a short visit. We just came into Rome this afternoon, and we're leaving tomorrow. I wanted to show my wife some of the more interesting details. We won't be long."

"Will you be exiting back this way or through the basilica? I'll be leaving shortly."

"In that case, we'll leave through the basilica with the tour group that's down there."

"Do you need me to let you in?"

"No, I have my keys, unless the locks have been changed."

"Changed?" Luigi laughed. "Things like that never change."

Leaving the Scavi office, Shawn led the way down a gently sloping, completely deserted marble corridor. "We're actually about ten feet or so below the floor level of the basilica above us."

"The fact that Mr. Romani recognized you—does that matter?"

"I can't imagine," Shawn replied in a hushed voice. "Since no one but us knows about the ossuary, if we find it and take it, no one's going to be the wiser."

They reached a flight of marble steps that descended more than a full story. Shawn started down.

Sana hesitated, pointing ahead. "Where does this corridor lead?"

"It winds up in the newer crypt beneath Saint Peter's."

At the base of the stairs was a narrow stone passageway blocked by a locked metal grate. "Here's the test!" Shawn said, pulling out one of the sets of keys. He remembered the correct key, and it slid into the lock with ease. "So far so good," he said. After a moment's hesitation to bolster his courage, he tried to twist the key, and to his joy it did so with ease.

After passing through a humidity-control door and descending more stairs, they reached what had been ground level in ancient Roman times.

"It is quite humid," Sana commented. She wasn't pleased.

"Does that bother you?"

"Only if the seal on the ossuary is broken."

"Right!" Shawn said, realizing that Sana's interest was primarily to find ancient DNA.

"Why don't they have more light down here?" Sana complained. "It feels claustrophobic." The illumination was very dim, mostly from recessed lighting at floor level. The ceiling was completely lost in shadow.

"For atmosphere, I suppose. To tell the truth, I don't really know. It gets even more claustrophobic around Peter's tomb. Are you going to be able to handle it?"

"I think so. Where are we now?"

"We're in the middle of the Roman necropolis that Constantine had completely filled in the fourth century to form the foundation for his basilica. What's been excavated is this single east–west path between two rows of tombs. Most were first- through fourth-century pagan mausoleums, although a few Christian mosaic images and inscriptions have been found."

"This place gives me the creeps. Where's Peter's tomb, so we can check it out and get on our way?"

Shawn gestured to his left, up the ancient Vaticanus hill. After they'd walked for fifty feet he pointed to a Roman sarcophagus in a dark corner. "If we have to store any debris, I thought we'd hide it in there. Okay?"

"Sure," Sana said, curious why he was even asking her.

"Are you interested in getting a closer look at any of these ancient Roman tombs?" Shawn asked. "Some of them have interesting decorations."

"I want to see Peter's grave and where we will be working," Sana replied. Her pant legs felt sodden, and her whole body was cold.

"This is the 'red wall,' " Shawn explained as they rounded the crumbling end of a brick wall. "We're getting close. The wall is part of what's considered Peter's tomb complex." To Sana, it didn't look particularly special. Ahead they now could hear a tour guide lecturing.

"Stop a minute," Shawn said, where there was a breach in the red wall. "Take a look in this hole. Can you see a white marble column?"

Sana did as she was told. She could easily see the column Shawn referred to beyond the red wall, as it was illuminated. It appeared to be about six inches in diameter.

"That's part of the Tropaion of Peter that was built over Saint Peter's tomb. So, where we are standing now is the floor level of Constantine's basilica."

"So Peter's tomb is below us."

"That's right. Below us and to our left."

"Where will we be looking for the ossuary?"

"We're now on the south side of the structure. We have to go around to the north side."

"Let's do it," Sana said.

As they skirted the complex and arrived at the north side, they ran into the tour group, which included about a dozen adults of widely varying ages. The only unifying aspect was that everyone spoke English. Some were listening to the guide, others were staring off into space, while still others rudely carried on their own hushed conversations. It was hardly the kind of group Sana expected.

Shawn waited for a break in the guide's description before urging Sana forward to follow the tour group. After ten feet, on their right they came to what the guide had been describing. It was a bluish-white plaster wall with a profusion of incised epigraphs one on top of the other, such that it was difficult to discern any one epigraph in particular. "It's called the graffiti wall," Shawn explained in a hushed voice. "As I told you, during the last excavation, in order to get into Peter's tomb without disturbing anything, in particular this graffiti wall, one had to tunnel under the wall, and then under the wall that supports the original vault over Saint Peter's tomb. The ossuary is going to be between the two walls, back close to the red wall, which cuts across both at right angles."

"My goodness," Sana exclaimed. She shook her head in exasperation. It was too confusing.

"I know," Shawn said sympathetically. "It's extremely complex. The site has been added to and altered continuously over almost two thousand years. I might not be explaining it well, but I know what I'm talking about. My only concern is that when the red wall was in the process of being built by the Romans around the turn of the first century, they might have inadvertently stumbled across the ossuary and either moved it or destroyed it. There's no doubt in my mind that its original location had to have been close to the red wall, which is just behind us."

"Where does the tunnel start?" Sana questioned as she gazed around the chamber they were in.

"The tunnel is directly below where we are currently standing. At the moment, we are at the level of the floor of Constantine's basilica. We have to descend to the level of the floor of Peter's tomb. To get there we have to go into the next chamber. Are you ready to move on?"

"More than ready," Sana said. Thanks to her discomfort, she wanted to see where they would be working later that night, then leave. Under the circumstances, the three-dimensional details of what Shawn was patiently describing were not registering.

Shawn led the way down a number of metal steps into a relatively large room, where the tour group had reassembled. The guide was explaining that the Plexiglas boxes seen through a small wall opening into Peter's tomb contained the bones of the saint.

"Is that true?" Sana whispered to Shawn.

"Pope Pius the Twelfth said they were," Shawn answered softly. "They were found scattered in the tomb within a V-shaped niche in the red wall. I think what swayed the pope was the lack of a skull. Saint Peter's head historically was supposed to have been in the basilica of San Giovanni in Laterano."

"Okay, so where is the tunnel?" Sana asked impatiently. She'd had enough history for the moment.

"Follow me!" Shawn said. They passed behind the tour group and approached a large decklike structure reached by several descending steps. It had a gridlike metal frame and handrails. The surface was comprised of large squares of clear three-quarter-inch glass. Standing on the deck, one could look down to the lowest point of the excavation about five feet below.

"That's the level of the floor of Peter's tomb," Shawn explained. "To get to the tunnel, we have to go down there and then back under where we are standing in front of the graffiti wall."

"How are we going to get down there?" Sana questioned, as her eyes ran around the transparent deck. There didn't seem to be any opening.

"The glass panel in the far corner lifts up. It's heavy as hell, but we'll be able to do it together. What do you think? Will you be able to manage all this?"

The thought of crawling through a tunnel pricked at Sana's mild claustrophobia. Knowing she was already some forty to fifty feet underground didn't help.

"Having second thoughts?" Shawn asked when Sana didn't answer.

"Are these lights going to be on?" Sana asked in a scratchy whisper. She ran her tongue around the inside of her mouth to try to drum up a bit of saliva. Her throat had suddenly gone dry.

"We can't have the lights on," Shawn said. "They are on an automatic timer, and if someone were to open either of the doors to the necropolis and see the lights, they'd know something was wrong. Besides, we need the lights off to act as a warning system. If anyone goes through the basilica while we are using the chisels, they might hear it, despite it being forty or fifty feet away. Remember, marble is a great sound transmitter. If they come to investigate, they'll turn on the lights, which will warn us someone is coming. Does that make sense?"

Sana reluctantly nodded. It made a lot of sense, but she didn't like it.

"Talk to me," Shawn said. "Are you going to be able to handle this?"

Sana nodded again.

"Tell me!" Shawn demanded, raising his voice and giving it an edge. "I have to know for sure!"

"Okay! Okay!" Sana said. "I'm with you all the way." She glanced around self-consciously at the nearest members of the tour group, several of whom were eyeing them curiously. Sana looked back at Shawn. "I'll be okay. Don't worry!" she assured him in a whisper, but had she known what was to transpire several hours hence, she might not have been quite so confident.

11

How was lunch yesterday?" Jack asked. He'd stuck his head into Chet's office, where his colleague was at his microscope studying a set of slides. Chet looked up and then pushed back from his desk.

"It wasn't quite what I expected," he confessed.

"How so?"

"I don't know what I was thinking Saturday night," he said with a shake of his head. "I must have been bombed outta my freaking mind. That woman was the size of a horse."

"Sorry to hear that," Jack said. "So, I guess she's not going to be 'the one' after all."

Chet made a gesture as if waving away a noisome insect while chuckling derisively. "Mock me!" he challenged. "I deserve it."

"I want to ask you about that VAD case of yours you mentioned yesterday," Jack said, trying to rein in his enthusiasm for his crusade concerning what he thought was the irrational popularity of alternative medicine. He was now even more convinced it was generally ineffective beyond the placebo effect as well as being expensive: a bad combination. And as if that wasn't enough, he now knew it was, at times, dangerous. In fact, he felt personally embarrassed that forensic pathology had not taken a more responsible stand on the issue.

Jack's opinion had hardened after the site visit he'd made to Ronald Newhouse's office the previous afternoon, even though, in retrospect, he admitted it had been a mistake, as he had allowed his fragile emotions to get the better of him. Later in the day he'd done an Internet search and had found an enormous amount of information, which would have precluded the need to confront Newhouse. He'd been unaware of the thousands of "studies" that had been done to prove or disprove the efficacy of alternative or complementary medicine. His search also highlighted what he saw as the Internet's biggest drawback: too much information, with no real way to evaluate the bias of the sources.

By chance he'd come across a number of references to the book, *Trick or Treatment*, he'd earlier put on hold at Barnes & Noble. A check of the authors' credentials left him unquestionably impressed. One was an author of a book that he had enjoyed several years earlier, called *Big Bang*. The man's grasp of science, particularly physics, was awe-inspiring, and Jack was duly encouraged he'd trust the man's opinions concerning alternative medicine. The second author, educated as a conventional medical doctor, had taken the time and effort to train in some types of alternative medicine, and had had the experience of practicing both. Such a background could not have been better to evaluate and compare without prejudice the two approaches. Duly encouraged, Jack had decided to give up on the Internet and had left work early to pick up the book.

When Jack had arrived home the previous evening, he'd been disappointed to find both Laurie and JJ fast asleep and a note on the console table by the front door: "Bad day, lots of tears, no sleep but asleep now. I have to get mine when I can. Soup on the stove. Love, L."

The note had made Jack feel guilty and lonely. He'd not called all day for fear he'd wake them, which had happened in the past. Although he always encouraged Laurie to call him when she could, she never did. He hoped the reason wasn't out of resentment that he got to go to work while she remained at home, but even if it was, he knew she wouldn't have it any other way.

But his guilt wasn't just about not calling—it was because he actually didn't want to know what was going on at home. Sometimes, he didn't even want to go home. Being in the apartment made the tragedy of his son's illness and Jack's inability to affect it unavoidable. Although he'd never admitted it to Laurie, just holding the suffering infant was a strain on his emotions, and he hated himself for it. At the same time he understood what was behind his feelings: He was vainly trying not to get too attached to the child. The unspeakable reality lurking in the recesses of his mind was that JJ was not going to survive.

Jack took advantage of the house's peacefulness by diving into *Trick or Treatment*. When Laurie awoke four hours later, she found him so completely absorbed that he'd forgotten to eat.

Jack listened while Laurie recounted her day. Just like every other day, the more he heard, the more he felt she was a saint and he the opposite, but he let her get it all out. When she'd finished, they'd gone into the kitchen, where she insisted on heating up some soup for the two of them.

"It's ironic that you brought up trying alternative medicine this morning," he'd said as they'd eaten. "I can tell you one thing, we might be desperate, but we are never going to use alternative medicine." He told her about Keara Abelard and his decision to look seriously into the alternative-medicine issue. As physically and mentally exhausted as she was, she listened to his impassioned lecture with only half an ear until he got to the fatal case of the three-month-old dying from chiropractic cervical manipulation. From that point on, Jack had had her full attention. He described how *Trick or Treatment* was opening his eyes to all the mainstream alternative-medicine fields, including homeopathy, acupuncture, and herbal medicine, in addition to chiropractic.

When Jack had finished his mini-lecture, Laurie's response was to congratulate him on finding a worthy subject to occupy his mind while the family was treading water regarding JJ's treatment. She even confessed to some jealousy, but that was as far as it went. When Jack again brought up the subject of getting her back to work with the aid of round-the-clock nurses, she'd again refused, saying she was doing what she needed to do. She then went on to mention three cases of alternative-medicine fatalities that she'd had herself. One was a case of an acupuncture victim who'd died when the acupuncturist inadvertently impaled the victim's heart with an acupuncture needle right in the area of the sinoventricular node. Two others died from heavy-metal poisoning from contaminated Chinese herbs.

Jack was pleased to get Laurie's cases and had admitted he'd sent out an e-mail to all their M.D. colleagues, asking for similar cases, to try to estimate the incidence of alternative medicine–induced deaths in New York City.

"Hey!" Chet called out while giving Jack's arm a forceful nudge. "What are you having, a psychomotor seizure?"

"Sorry," Jack said, shaking his head as if waking from a trance. "My mind was someplace else."

"What did you want to ask me about my VAD case?" Chet asked. He had been waiting for Jack to finish his question.

"Could you possibly get the name or accession number of that case so I can get the details?" Jack said, but he didn't listen for Chet's response. His mind was back, remembering that morning when he'd awakened at five-thirty, still in his clothes, still sitting on the living-room couch. On his lap was *Trick or Treatment*, open midway through the appendix.

The book had solidified his negative feelings about alternative medicine and boosted his interest in the issue. Although there were certain sections of the book that he'd skimmed, for the most part he'd read the entire volume, even underlining certain key passages. Its message surely meshed with his own stance on the subject, and he felt the arguments the authors used to justify their conclusions were clear and unbiased. In fact, Jack felt they had bent over backward to try to make a case for alternative medicine, but in their summary all they could say was that homeopathy provided only a placebo effect; acupuncture, besides placebo, might have an effect on some types of pain and nausea, but it was minor and short-lived; chiropractic, besides placebo, showed some evidence of efficacy in relation to back pain, but conventional treatments were usually equally beneficial and far less expensive; and herbal medicine was mostly placebo, with products of little or no quality control, and for those products with a pharmacological effect, drugs that contained just the active ingredient were decidedly more safe and more efficacious.

Having slept just a couple of hours, Jack thought he'd be exhausted. But, at least initially, that hadn't been the case. After an exhilarating cold shower and a bite to eat, Jack had cycled to the OCME in near-record time.

As keyed up as he was with newfound knowledge about alternative medicine, Jack immersed himself in his work, signing out several pending cases before grabbing an unwilling Vinnie to start work in the autopsy room. By the time Jack had come by Chet's office he'd finished three autopsies, which included a shooting at a bar in the East Village and two suicides, one of which Jack found definitely suspicious and about which he'd already put in a call to his buddy, Lieutenant Detective Lou Soldano.

"Hey," Chet called out again. "Anybody home? This is ridiculous. It's like having a conversation with a zombie. I just told you the name of that VAD case of mine, and you look like you're back having another petit mal seizure. Didn't you sleep last night?"

"I'm sorry," Jack said, squeezing his eyes together and then blinking rapidly. "You're right about me not getting much sleep last night, and I'm running on nervous energy. Tell me again the name!"

"Why so interested?" Chet questioned, writing the name on a piece of notepaper and handing it to Jack.

"I'm looking into alternative medicine in general, and chiropractic VAD in particular. What did you find when you looked into VAD back then?"

"You mean above and beyond the fact that no one wanted to hear about it?"

"You mean besides your chief?"

"When I presented the case on grand rounds, it ignited a kind of debate, with half the audience for and half against chiropractic, and those who were for it were really for it. It was an emotional issue that took me by surprise, especially that my boss was such a fan."

"You said you'd gathered four or five cases. Do you think you could find their names as well? It would be interesting to unofficially compare the incidence of VAD between New York City and L.A."

"Finding the name of my own case was relatively easy; finding the others is asking for a miracle. But I'll check. How are you going to look into it around here?"

"Have you checked your e-mail lately?"

"Can't say I have."

"When you do, there's one from me. I sent an e-mail to all the city MEs, looking for cases. Later this afternoon I'm going to go over to records and see if I can find any there as well."

Suddenly, Jack's BlackBerry buzzed. Always concerned it might be Laurie and a crisis at home, he snatched it out of its holster and glanced at the LCD screen. "Uh-oh!" he said. It wasn't Laurie. It was the chief, Harold Bingham, calling from the front office downstairs.

"What's up?" Chet asked, noticing Jack's reaction.

"It's the chief," Jack said.

"Is that a problem?"

"I made a site visit yesterday," Jack confessed. "It was to the chiropractor involved in my case. I wasn't my usual diplomatic self. In fact, we almost came to blows."

Chet, who knew Jack better than anyone else in the office, grimaced. "Good luck!"

Jack nodded thanks and clicked to accept the call. Bingham's no-nonsense secretary, Mrs. Sanford, was on the line. "The chief wants you in his office, *now*!"

"I heard that," Chet said, making the sign of the cross. The meaning was simple: Chet was convinced Jack's situation needed prayer.

Jack pushed away from Chet's desk. "Thanks for the vote of confidence," he said sarcastically.

As he walked to the elevator, Jack thought the summons had to be about good old Newhouse, the chiropractor. Jack had fully expected to have to answer for the episode but didn't think it would happen so quickly. This probably wasn't due to just a phone call from the irate chiropractor but rather a call from a lawyer. Consequences could be a slap on the wrist—or a drawn-out civil suit.

Stepping out of the elevator, Jack thought that instead of defending himself in front of Bingham, which he knew would be difficult if not impossible, perhaps he should go on the offense.

"You are to go right in," Mrs. Sanford said, without looking up from her computer. Since she'd done the same thing the last time he'd been called on the carpet ten years previously, he was once again mystified how she'd known it was him.

"Close the door!" Bingham demanded from behind his mammoth wooden desk. The desk was set back below high windows covered with ancient venetian blinds. Calvin Washington, the deputy chief, was sitting at the large library table, with the glass-fronted bookcases behind him. Both men stared at Jack unblinkingly.

"Thanks for calling me down here," Jack said earnestly, walking directly up to Bingham's desk and giving it a thump with the bottom of his fist for added emphasis. "The OCME must take a responsible stand on alternative medicine, particularly chiropractic. Yesterday we had a death by bilateral vertebral artery dissection caused by unnecessary cervical manipulation."

Bingham looked confused by the way Jack took the wind out of his sails. "I've taken the lead," Jack continued, "by forcing myself yesterday to take the time and effort to conduct a site visit to the offending chiropractor to confirm that he performed the cervical manipulation. As you might gather, this was not the easiest task, and I needed to be forceful to get the information."

Bingham's blotchy face paled slightly, and his rheumy eyes narrowed while he stared at Jack. Then he removed his glasses to clean them—and to buy himself time. Snappy repartee had never been one of his strengths.

"Sit down!" Calvin boomed from the back of the room.

Jack sat in one of the chairs in front of Bingham's desk. He didn't look back. As he expected and feared, Calvin was not taken in by his tactics the way Bingham was.

Calvin's imposing bulk appeared out of the corner of Jack's line of vision. Slowly Jack raised his eyes to look at him. Calvin had his hands on his hips, his face drawn, his eyes blazing. He towered over Jack. "Cut the bullshit, Stapleton!" he thundered. "You know damn well you're not supposed to be out there running around the city, flashing your badge around like a renegade TV cop."

"Looking back, I realize I didn't handle it well," Jack admitted.

"Was this some kind of personal vendetta against chiropractic?" Bingham demanded.

"Yes, it was personal."

"Do you care to explain?" Bingham demanded.

"You mean other than chiropractic has no business treating illnesses that have nothing to do with the spine? Or that chiropractic bases its rationale for such treatment on an idiotic outdated mystical concept of innate intelligence that has never been found or measured or explained? Or that such treatment often involves cervical manipulations that can cause death, like in my twenty-seven-year-old patient?"

Bingham and Washington exchanged a dismayed glance at Jack's emotional outburst.

"That all may or may not be true," Bingham said, "but what makes it personal?"

"I'd rather not get into that," Jack said, forcing himself to calm down. He knew he was letting his emotions get the better of him, just as he had at the chiropractor's office. "It's a long story and the association is what you would call rather indirect."

"You'd rather not get into that," Bingham repeated scornfully, "but we might feel it is necessary, and that if you don't do it, it might be at your peril. Since you might not have been served with a subpoena yet, it's my unpleasant responsibility to inform you that you and the OCME are being sued by a Dr. Ronald Newhouse. . . ."

"He's not a doctor, for chrissake," Jack blurted. "He's a goddamn chiropractor."

Bingham and Washington exchanged another quick glance. Bingham was clearly frustrated, like a parent with a recalcitrant teenager. Calvin was less generous. He was just plain furious and finding it difficult to hold his tongue.

"For the moment, your opinion of chiropractic doesn't matter," Bingham said. "It was your actions that are in question here, and the gentleman in question is most likely a doctor of chiropractic. You and the OCME are being sued for slander, defamation of character, assault—"

"I never touched the guy," Jack interrupted. He was finding it difficult to follow his own advice in regard to his emotions.

"You do not have to touch someone to be sued for assault. The plaintiff only has to believe you are about to injure him in some way. Were you in his office yelling at him?"

"I suppose," Jack admitted.

"Did you threaten to have him arrested for killing his patient?"

"I suppose," Jack said sheepishly.

"You suppose!" Bingham echoed with heightened scorn, momentarily throwing up his arms toward the ceiling in exasperation. Then, raising his voice, he yelled, "I'll tell you what I think it is: It's an egregious misuse of official authority. I have the mind to kick your ass outta here and put you on unpaid administrative leave until this mess is sorted out."

A chill went down Jack's spine. If he was put on leave, his lifeline to emotional sanity would be cut. He'd have to stay home, and Laurie would have to come to work instead. He'd have to assume responsibility for taking care of JJ. *Oh my God!* Jack voiced inwardly. He suddenly felt desperate, even more than he'd been feeling up until then. The last time he'd been in a similar circumstance facing Bingham's wrath, he didn't care about himself. But now he couldn't afford to be self-destructive. His family needed him. He couldn't get depressed. Bingham was right; it was a mess.

Bingham noisily took in a deep breath and blew it out through pursed lips. He looked up at Calvin, who still glared down at Jack. "What do you think, Calvin?" Bingham asked. His voice had calmed to near normal.

"What do I think about what?" Calvin demanded. "Whether we put this asshole on administrative leave or beat him to a bloody pulp?"

"You met with the general counsel, not I," Bingham said. "What was her opinion about the indemnity issue? Is she confident our insurance will cover this episode whether the suit settles or goes to trial?"

"She thought it should. After all, it's not a criminal suit."

"What about the possibility of Stapleton's actions being considered purposefully malicious?"

"She was less sure about that possibility."

Jack looked from Bingham to Calvin and back. For the moment they were ignoring him, as if he wasn't even there. After several more exchanges between the two men, Bingham switched his attention to Jack. "What we're talking about here is whether you're going to be covered by insurance. According to your contract, the OCME indemnifies you for malpractice, except if the malpractice involves criminality or is considered malicious, meaning you were doing it on purpose instead of by accident."

"I didn't go to the chiropractor's office to injure anybody, if that's what you mean," Jack said contritely. He had the sense that the situation was spiraling out of control.

"That's reassuring," Bingham said. "We have to decide if we are going to defend you or not. Of course, it has some bearing whether or not our insurance will cover a judgment against you. If it won't, then you'll probably have to defend yourself, which could be expensive, I'm afraid."

"My motives were definitely not malicious," Jack said, as his heart skipped a beat at the prospect of having to defend himself. With Laurie on leave and the extra expenses of JJ's illness, he didn't have money for a lawyer. "I didn't go to the chiropractor's office with any other intent except to find out if he had seen my patient professionally, and whether or not he had manipulated her cervical spine."

"What was the cause of death again?" Bingham asked.

"Bilateral vertebral artery dissection," Jack said.

"Really!" Bingham commented, as if he'd heard it for the first time. Immediately, his eyes glazed over. It was a physiological reflex for him whenever his brain sifted through the thousands of forensic cases in which he'd been involved over his extensive career.

Although Bingham could struggle at times with remembering recent events, like the cause of death of Keara Abelard, which Jack had mentioned only moments earlier, his distant recall was encyclopedic. A moment later he blinked and roused himself, as if waking from a trance. "I've had three cases of VAC," he reported.

"Were they caused by chiropractic manipulation?" Jack asked hopefully. Still, it was becoming clear to him that he wasn't going to be able to keep his private life separate from his professional life if he wanted to avoid being put on administrative leave or worse. He was going to have to admit to JJ's illness and his difficulty dealing with it. Only then might Bingham and Calvin excuse his unthinking behavior the day before.

"Two of them were associated with chiropractic care," Bingham said. "The other was idiopathic, meaning we never did find out. Now, let me tell you . . ." For the next few minutes, Jack and Calvin had to listen to Bingham retell the stories of his three VAD cases. Although it was always impressive to hear the level of detail Bingham could remember, at the moment Jack found it tedious at best, yet common sense told him not to interrupt. Having decided to reveal John Junior's cancer, he was eager to do it and get it over with.

At the moment Bingham finished his detailed remembrance, Jack began his mea culpa of sorts. "A few moments ago I said I didn't want to explain how my behavior at the chiropractor's office was personal. I'd like to amend that."

"I'm not sure I want to know if you were acquainted with your VAD patient personally," Calvin growled.

"No, no!" Jack assured them. It had never occurred to him that Calvin might think such a thing. "I had no association whatsoever with the patient. I had never seen her, met her, or knew anything about her. The origin of this mess is my new baby boy."

Jack hesitated a moment to let his statement sink in. Immediately, he could see a softening in the expressions of both men, particularly with Calvin, whose concern instantly replaced his anger.

"I'd like to ask one thing before I reveal what I'm about to," Jack said. "I would ask that it doesn't leave this room. It is a highly personal matter."

"At this point I believe you will have to let us decide," Bingham said. "If this suit goes forward, we could easily be deposed. If that were to happen, you can understand that we might not be able to honor a promise we make to you."

"That I understand," Jack said. "Short of being deposed, I would trust that you could keep Laurie's and my secret."

Bingham looked at Calvin. Calvin nodded in agreement.

"Is the baby okay?" Calvin demanded hastily.

"Unfortunately, no," Jack admitted, and the moment he did, there was a catch in his voice. "I know you are aware Laurie has not returned from maternity leave as originally planned."

"Of course we're aware," Calvin said impatiently, as if Jack was deliberately extending his story.

"Our child is gravely ill," Jack managed. He'd not told anyone about JJ, for fear that the mere telling would somehow make the situation more real. Jack had been using a kind of denial as a way of dealing with the shock since JJ's diagnosis.

Jack hesitated while he took a few deep breaths. Bingham and Calvin waited. They could see Jack's jaw quiver and knew he was fighting back tears. They wanted to hear more details but were willing to give him time to collect himself.

"I know I haven't been myself work-wise over the last three months or so," Jack managed.

"We had no idea," Bingham interrupted, suddenly feeling guilty about coming down so hard on Jack.

"Of course you didn't," Jack said. "We've told no one other than Laurie's parents."

"Do you mind telling us the diagnosis?" Calvin asked. "I suppose it's none of our business, but I'd like to know. You know my feelings about Laurie. She's like family."

"Neuroblastoma," Jack said. He had to take another deep breath to continue. "High-risk neuroblastoma."

A hush fell while Bingham and Calvin digested this revelation.

"Where is he being treated?" Calvin asked gently, breaking the silence.

"At Memorial. He's in a treatment program, but as luck would have it, they had to put it on hold once he developed an anti-mouse antibody. After he finished his chemo, his treatment has been based on a mouse monoclonal antibody. Unfortunately, he is not being treated at the moment. As you might expect, Laurie and I are having trouble dealing with the delay."

"Well," Bingham said after another short, uncomfortable silence. "This does put a different spin on the current situation. Perhaps you need a leave of absence, but a paid leave of absence. Perhaps you need to be home with your wife and child."

"No!" Jack said forcefully. "I need to work! Seriously, the last thing I need is a leave of absence. You cannot believe how frustrating it is to watch your child suffer and not be able to do anything about it. Threatening me with a leave of absence is what pushed me to tell you about this in the first place."

"Okay," Bingham said. "No leave, but in return you must promise me you will refrain from making site visits, particularly to chiropractors."

"I'll promise that," Jack said. From his perspective, that was hardly a concession.

"I still don't quite understand your behavior at the chiropractor's office," Bingham said. "Was it something specific or just your general dislike for the field? It's pretty obvious from what you said when you first came in here that you do not have a high regard for chiropractic therapy. Have you had a bad experience with a chiropractor yourself?"

"Absolutely not," Jack said. "I've never been to one, nor did I really know much about them, but because of my VAD patient yesterday, I decided to look into chiropractic and alternative medicine in general to occupy my mind. Obviously, I've been obsessed about JJ, particularly with him off treatment. Before this VAD case, I hadn't really thought about people dying from alternative medicine. When I began to look into it, one of the first articles I read described a case of a three-month-old infant having died from chiropractic cervical neck manipulation. I was appalled, especially since JJ is nearly the same age.

"I didn't dwell on it, at least not until I started talking with Ronald Newhouse. As he was describing the insane rationale for chiropractic treatment for things like childhood allergies, sinusitis, or even something as benign as fussiness, and killing the kid in the process, I saw red. It's one thing for an adult to be stupid enough to put themselves in jeopardy with a snake-oil salesman, but not a child. With a child it is criminal."

Jack's voice trailed off. Once again a heavy silence settled over the room.

Bingham broke the silence by announcing, "I believe I can speak both for myself and Calvin by saying how very sorry we are about JJ's illness. Although I certainly cannot condone your behavior vis-à-vis the chiropractor, I can say I understand it better now. I can also say that I strongly encourage your investigating alternative medicine; from the forensic pathology point of view, it will be good for you for the reasons you gave, and good for forensic pathology. I can envision a valuable paper for one of the major forensic pathology journals, which will add to the alternative-medicine debate. However, during your investigation, I must insist you do not make any site visits to any alternative-medicine provider. Also, I want you to avoid any statements to the press on your own. Any releases have to go through public relations after being screened by me. The alternative-medicine issue is more political than scientific. In my opinion, there is very little science involved at all. To emphasize this point, in addition to getting the lawsuit this morning, I got a call from the mayor's office. It seems you were picking on His Honor's favorite health provider."

"You are joking," Jack said. It seemed impossible. Jack had met the mayor and had been impressed by the man's intelligence, at least until that moment.

"I'm not joking in the slightest," Bingham continued. "Apparently, Mr. Newhouse is the only person who can relieve the mayor's lumbar back pain."

"I'm shocked," Jack admitted.

"Don't be," Bingham shot back. "As for this current lawsuit, we will make every effort to defend you."

"Thank you, sir," Jack said, relieved.

"We will also honor your wish for privacy, depositions notwithstanding. We will not divulge your secret, particularly here at the OCME."

"I appreciate that," Jack said.

"If you change your mind and want a leave of absence, consider the request already granted."

"I appreciate that as well. You're very kind."

"Now, I assume you have work to do. Calvin tells me you have more cases pending than usual. So get to work and get them signed out."

Jack took the cue and rapidly disappeared.

For a few moments, neither Bingham nor Calvin moved. They stared at each other, still shocked.

"Has his work really been suffering?" Bingham asked, breaking the silence.

"Not from my vantage point," Calvin said. "It's true he's more behind than usual, but the quality is up to par, and, although he's behind, he's still been by far our top producer, with about one and a half times the output of everyone else."

"You didn't have any idea about this terrible news concerning his child, did you?"

"Not the slightest," Calvin said. "Even Laurie's decision to extend her maternity leave didn't raise any red flags for me. I just thought she was loving being a mother. I knew how much she'd wanted children."

"He's always been such a private person. I've never understood him, to tell you the honest truth, especially back when he first started here. He was self-righteous and self-destructive, and I'm not sure which is worse. When the suit came in this morning and I fielded the call from the mayor's office, I thought he was reverting to bad habits."

"The thought went through my mind as well," Calvin confessed, "which, I suppose, is why I didn't give him the benefit of the doubt with this current affair."

"Talk to the general counsel," Bingham said. "Tell her we're going to defend the case unless she thinks we should settle. And with that said, get out of here so I can get some real work done."

12

The flash of the one hundred million volts of electricity came first, followed by a sputtering crackle as it knifed through the humid air to ground itself on the ancient Egyptian obelisk in the center of Piazza San Pietro. A blink of the eye later came the sharp crack of thunder that literally shook the Fiat.

"What the hell was that?" Sana demanded, before her mind told her exactly what it was.

"Thunder and lightning," Shawn said disdainfully, although he had jumped nearly as much as his wife had. He'd never seen a bolt of lightning so close. "For God's sake, calm down! You're out of control."

Sana nodded as she looked out the rent-a-car's windows. In the darkness there were lots of pedestrians on their way home, bent into the wind using their umbrellas like shields against the near-horizontal rain. "I can't help it. Are you sure we should be doing this?" Sana questioned. "I mean, we're sneaking into an ancient Roman cemetery on a rainy night to steal an ossuary. It seems more like the script for a horror movie than something appropriate. What if we get caught?"

Shawn drummed his fingers irritably on the rent-a-car's steering wheel. He too was tense, and Sana's second thoughts were only magnifying his anxiety.

"We're not going to get caught," Shawn snapped. He didn't want to hear any negativity. He was on the verge of making his most spectacular find, provided Sana cooperated.

"How can you be so sure?"

"I worked in there at night for months, and unless I brought people in with me, I never saw a soul."

"You were using pencil and paper and photography. We're going to be using a drill and hammer and chisel. As you suggested, what if someone up in the basilica hears us?"

"The basilica is closed up tight as a drum," Shawn spat. "Look, don't do this to me. You already agreed to do it. The time is right. We've got the tools. We know where to look. And by using the drill to probe for the stone ossuary, we should be in and out in a couple of hours. If you're dying for something to worry about, worry about lugging the ossuary out of the necropolis and into the trunk of the car."

"You make it sound so easy," Sana commented. She stared out the windshield into Piazza San Pietro with Bernini's curved, elliptical colonnades sweeping off on either side.

"I'm telling you it will be easy," Shawn said with apparent conviction, though Sana's misgivings were heightening his own. In reality he knew there were plenty of opportunities for things to go wrong. Despite what he'd just said, he was aware they could get caught. A more probable problem was they wouldn't find the ossuary. If they didn't, he'd have to tell the authorities about Saturninus's letter and share the prestige if the ossuary was eventually found. Of course, that would happen only if the pope allowed the search to take place—unlikely, since the ossuary's discovery would put Church dogma and papal infallibility in question.

"All right," Sana said suddenly. "If we're going to do this, let's do it and get it over with. Why are we still sitting here?"

"I told you. We got here faster than I thought. The last security sweep of the basilica is at eight p.m. I want to give them plenty of time to finish and get the place locked up tight."

Sana looked at her watch. It was almost eight-thirty. "What if they find something amiss, like the *Pietà* is gone?"

Shawn turned to study his wife's profile in the dark. He was hoping she was teasing him, but that didn't seem to be the case. She was looking out the car windows like some kind of hyperalert prey about to be eaten. "Are you being serious?"

"I don't know," Sana admitted. "I'm nervous and exhausted. I mean, we traveled all the way from Egypt today. That might be easy for you, but it's not for me."

"You can be nervous, that's okay. Hell, I'm nervous, too. It's natural to be a little nervous."

"What if I get claustrophobic?"

"We'll make sure you don't. I won't make you come into the tunnel. There probably won't be room for you anyway."

Sana regarded her husband in the half-light of the car's interior. Headlights from the multitude of passing cars played intermittently across his face. "Are you sure you won't need me in the tunnel?"

"If we're down there and you don't want to go into the tunnel, we'll deal with it. Let's think positively. Can I count on you?"

"I suppose," Sana said, without a lot of confidence.

At quarter to nine Shawn started the car and eased away from the curb. With the windshield wipers struggling to keep up with the rain, he had to strain to see. The traffic entering the piazza careened past them at breakneck speed. Entering Saint Peter's

Square, he drove along Bernini's Colonnade toward Arco delle Campane. "If the Swiss Guards question why you don't have a Vatican ID card, let me do the talking," Shawn said. The two dark-brown guard shacks loomed out of the mist ahead. The guards stepped out, wearing dark rain capes over their black-and-orange uniforms. They didn't look pleased to have pulled guard duty on such a night. Shawn lowered his window as he came abreast of the guard shacks and stopped. A few wayward raindrops immediately blew in through the open window and danced in the swirling air.

"Good evening, gentlemen," Shawn said pleasantly, making an effort to suppress any nervousness in his voice. As he had expected, the shift had changed. They were different guards.

As was the case that afternoon, the guard took Shawn's Vatican ID card without a word. He examined it with a flashlight, comparing the photo to Shawn's visage. As he handed it back, he asked, "Where are you going?"

"To the necropolis," Shawn said, while handing over his access permit. "We're going to do a little maintenance work."

The Swiss Guard studied the permit for a minute before handing it back. "Pop the boot," he said, disappearing toward the rear of the car.

Sana sat uncomfortably as the second Swiss Guard shined his flashlight in her face. Prior to that, he'd used the flashlight and a mirror on a long stick to inspect the underside of the car for bombs.

Shawn heard the trunk slam, and a moment later the guard returned to Shawn's open window.

"What are the tools for?" the guard asked.

"For our maintenance work," Jack said.

"Will you be entering through the Scavi office?"

"We will indeed."

"Should I call security to open it?"

"No need. We have keys."

"Okay," the guard said. "Just a moment." He returned to the tiny guardhouse for a parking permit. A moment later he was behind the car to copy down the license plate number, before returning to the open window. There he tossed the permit onto the dash. "Park straight ahead in the Piazza Protomartiri and leave the parking permit visible on the dash." He then saluted.

"Phew," Sana voiced as they pulled away. "I was afraid we were already dead meat when they looked in our trunk and saw the tools."

"Me, too. During the months I worked here I never got that kind of attention. They've certainly beefed up security."

Shawn parked where he'd been told but as close as possible to the Scavi office. "I'll get the tools. You get yourself over to the shelter of the portico. I don't want you getting wet, like this afternoon."

"Will you be able to manage?" Sana asked while getting an umbrella from the backseat.

Shawn grabbed her arm. "The question is: Will you?"

"I'm better now that we're here."

Sana was about to climb from the car when Shawn tightened his grip. "Wait for these cars," he said. Sana turned to see a line of cars bearing down on them in the darkness. They went by with a *whoosh* on the slick, puddle-filled cobblestones, sending a heavy spray of water to splash against the Fiat. Shawn and Sana turned to watch the red taillights speed away, passing through the Arco delle Campane without even slowing.

"That must have been one of the bosses, maybe even the big boss himself," Shawn commented.

"Thank you for keeping me from opening my door," Sana said. "I would have been drenched."

A few minutes later they were inside the darkened Scavi office.

Shawn had carried the tools and other paraphernalia in the two buckets. Now that he was this close, his excitement and anxiety ratcheted up several degrees.

"What should I do with the umbrella?" Sana asked guilelessly.

"Jesus H. Christ!" Shawn exploded. "Do I have to tell you what to do with everything?" He'd been pushed beyond his patience. First, she threatened not to go through with their plan, and now she was asking stupid questions.

"You don't need to speak to me like that. It's a reasonable question. If I leave it here, someone may come along and then suspect someone is down in the excavation."

"Why on earth would someone jump to the conclusion that a trespasser was down in the Scavi when an umbrella is left in the Scavi office? That's ridiculous."

"Fine!" Sana snapped back. She extended her arm and let the Hassler Hotel umbrella fall to the floor. She felt that Shawn's concern for her feelings had descended to a new low.

Shawn was equally unhappy. Over the last year, as her career blossomed one moment she was an independent firebrand, cutting her hair short against his wishes; in another she was as petulant as a child dropping the umbrella as she'd just done.

For several beats they stared daggers at each other. Sana was the first to relent. "We're both being foolish," she said. She picked up the umbrella and leaned it up against a wooden bench.

"You're right. I'm sorry," he said, but without much sincerity. "I'm uptight because I was afraid you were not going to go through with this, which is of vital importance to me."

In Sana's mind any benefit of Shawn's halfhearted apology melted away like a snowball in the tropics. Instead of taking responsibility for his behavior, he blamed it on her. In other words, the reason he'd hurt her feelings was her fault, not his.

"Let's get this over with," Sana said. At this point, the last thing she wanted to do was get into an argument. What she really wanted to do was get back to the hotel and go to bed.

"Now you're talking."

Each picked up a bucket and passed through the glazed Scavi inner office door. The corridor beyond was illuminated only by a series of low-intensity night-lights along the marble baseboards.

When they arrived at the flight of steps that descended to the necropolis entry, Shawn paused to look down the corridor toward the basilica's crypt. He saw no one.

"All right," he said. "Let's do it."

They descended the stairs. At the bottom, Shawn opened the grate with the appropriate key, let Sana pass, then stepped in himself before locking the metal barrier behind him.

With only scant illumination descending from the night-lights in the corridor above, the couple immediately took out their respective construction helmets and switched on the headlamps.

"Not bad," Sana commented, using the headlamp to look down the narrow stone passageway to the solid, humidity-proof door to the necropolis. Just a moment earlier, she'd experienced a touch of claustrophobia. The headlamp changed everything.

"Here, take this in one hand and the bucket in the other," Shawn said, after switching on one of the flashlights.

"I don't think I need it with the headlamp."

"Take it," Shawn insisted.

Shawn squeezed past Sana and quickly descended to the solid door. With every step he felt his excitement grow. He couldn't help feeling optimistic. He was convinced that the ossuary would be where Saturninus said he'd put it almost two millennia ago.

After unlocking the solid door, he once again moved aside so Sana could precede him. Then, after relocking it, he pushed past his wife to descend quickly to the level of the Roman-era cemetery. He was ready to turn west but sensed Sana wasn't behind him.

"What the hell are you doing?" he asked as he looked behind to see her descending slowly, her headlamp and flashlight moving erratically in rapid arcs.

"I don't like this," Sana said.

"What don't you like?" Shawn demanded, and under his breath he murmured, "What the hell now?" They were just beginning, and he was already finding his wife a progressively frustrating handicap. For a moment he thought about having her wait in the car, but then he remembered he needed her. What he was planning was defnitely a two-person job.

"My lights don't seem to reach the ceiling. It gives me a strange feeling."

"The ceiling has been purposefully darkened so visitors don't see the steel supports. It's for atmosphere."

"Is that what it is?" Sana said. She reached the ancient cemetery level and allowed her lights to play across the dark entrances of the mausoleums.

Shawn rolled his eyes.

"This place is even eerier at night than during the day," Sana remarked.

"Because the freaking lights are turned off, for shit's sake," Shawn growled.

"What was that noise?" Sana demanded with desperation.

"What noise?" Shawn questioned with near equal concern.

For a few moments of frozen panic they strained to hear sound—any sound. The silence was deafening.

"I don't hear anything," Shawn said finally. "What did you hear?"

"It sounded like a high-pitched voice."

"Good grief! Now you're imagining things."

"Are you sure?"

"I'm sure, but what I'm not sure is whether you can do this. We're so close."

"If you're sure I didn't hear anything, let's finish this and get out of here."

"Can you calm down?"

"I'll try."

"All right, let's go, but stay close."

Shawn led the way west in the direction of Peter's tomb. Sana followed a step behind, avoiding glancing into the mausoleums as they passed their dark, foreboding entrances.

Suddenly, Shawn stopped, and Sana jolted into him.

"Sorry," Sana said. "You have to let me know if you stop."

"I'll try to remember," Shawn said as he pointed off to the left with his flashlight. "There's the Roman sarcophagus I pointed out this afternoon. That's where we'll put our excavated debris. Do you think you will be able to bring it back here while I dig?"

"You mean by myself?"

Shawn silently counted to ten. "If I'm digging, of course it would be by yourself," he said impatiently.

"We'll see," Sana said. The idea of wandering around in the necropolis alone was daunting, and hardly alluring. All she could hope was that somehow she'd adjust.

Shawn held his tongue. Instead, he continued on, rounding the southern tip of the red wall. Despite the climb, Sana stayed close. A few moments later, they were standing in the large chamber on the east side of Peter's tomb complex near the original monument called the Tropaion of Peter. Shawn shined his flashlight down through one of the many glass panels of the deck, which had been built to allow modern-day tourists to see into the tomb's interior.

"We're almost there," Shawn commented, his voice brimming with excitement. "We'll soon be at the level of the floor of Peter's tomb."

"I'll take your word for it," Sana said. "Let's get on with this."

"Right!" Shawn agreed with alacrity. It was what he wanted to hear.

Lifting the three-quarter-inch glass panel in the far corner that served as access to the lower level took considerably more effort than Sana expected. After much straining, they got the panel on end and leaning against the wall.

"Let me go first," Shawn said. Sana nodded. Descending below the glass deck was the part that she was looking forward to the least, and if she was going to have a problem with claustrophobia, this was where it would begin.

Shawn took the time to strap on his knee pads and pull on his work gloves, and advised Sana to do the same. From then on they would need to be crawling about, as the height of the excavated floor to the glass deck didn't allow either of them to walk upright. Sitting on the edge of the deck with his feet dangling though the open space, Shawn inched himself forward and then swung down to stand on the earthen floor. After Shawn had ducked down and moved away from the opening, Sana mimicked his motions, and soon they were crawling ahead, pushing their respective buckets in front of them.

The floor was what Shawn had originally described, a kind of compacted clayish dirt mixed with gravel. Although Sana was becoming progressively anxious as they moved away from the opening in the deck, she was encouraged by one thing. The dirt, unlike the other areas in the necropolis, was bone-dry, suggesting the ossuary, if they found it, would be as well.

After advancing diagonally under the glass deck, they reached the section of the excavated space that extended under the level above. The ceiling now matched the hardpan of the floor. Sana noticed that there were no supports, and she stopped crawling, eyeing the ceiling with distrust.

Shawn continued forward for another ten feet and stopped to shine his flashlight down a tunnel to his left. "Here we are," he said. He turned to see that Sana had halted about eight feet back. He waved to her to follow him. He wanted to show her where he believed they were going to find the ossuary.

"Is it safe?" Sana questioned while eyeing the ceiling.

"Perfectly safe," Shawn said, following her line of sight. "The dirt at this level is like concrete. Trust me! You've come this far. I want to show you where I'll be digging."

Reluctantly, Sana crawled forward and found herself looking down a narrow tunnel about four feet wide, three feet high, and five feet deep. At the mouth of the tunnel and at its end were supports of rough lumber, each consisting of two stout vertical members and a thick crossbeam forming a truss.

"Why are there supports in there and not here?" Sana asked. She couldn't help but worry that nothing was holding up the ceiling above where she and Shawn were currently crouching.

"The first support here at the lip is holding up the graffiti wall, while the inner one is supporting the foundation wall for the vault of Peter's tomb. The space beyond the inner truss is the interior of the tomb. If you want to crawl in there, you'll be able to see a notched niche in the base of the red wall if you look to the right. That's where the bones the pope claimed were Saint Peter's were found, the ones they have a level up in the Plexiglas boxes."

"I think I'll pass," Sana said. The thought of crawling on her stomach through the low tunnel into Peter's tomb made her queasy and awakened the claustrophobic fears she'd been trying to suppress. It took all of her self-control to keep from fleeing back out to the area under the glass deck and then back up through the opening to the gallery above.

"Let me show you something else," Shawn said as he crawled into the tunnel and then rolled over on his back. He pointed up at the ceiling using his flashlight and tapped the ceiling between the two trusses. "The ossuary will be up here, if it wasn't discovered by accident when either the red wall or the graffiti wall was erected. Now, hand me the drill and the goggles. I'm going to probe a bit and see if I can make contact with stone."

Sana concentrated on Shawn's commands to avoid thinking about the entire mass of Saint Peter's Basilica pressing down on top of her. When Shawn was ready to begin, she said: "If you don't mind, I'm going to move out to the more open area under the glass deck. I'm having a bit of trouble breathing here."

"Suit yourself," Shawn said, distractedly. He was thrilled to be back to field archaeology. After he put the pail next to his body, he tried the drill. Its whine seemed particularly loud in the confined space. Satisfied with the drill's performance, he put the tip of the bit up against the ceiling. The bit cut through the hardpan like a knife through butter. Within seconds it buried its four-inch-long shaft up to the hilt. Dry dirt rained down mostly on his chest, although some went into the bucket. Mildly disappointed not to hit stone on the first attempt, he pulled the drill bit out and moved six inches to the left and tried again.

After thirty minutes he still hadn't hit stone, despite covering the ceiling with dozens of probing holes. He was ready to switch to the masonry hammer and chisel when he noticed something: The excavators had not burrowed under the vault's supporting wall as he'd thought, but rather had poked directly through its base. When he looked carefully, Shawn could actually see butt ends of the wall's brick just outside the vertical supports of the inner truss.

"My God!" Shawn called out for Sana's benefit. He couldn't see her, but he knew she was out in the area under the glass deck. He knew where she was because of her impatient questions every five minutes on how he was doing. By the sound of her voice, he could tell she was getting progressively anxious, but there was nothing he could do about it other than keeping her in the loop about his progress.

"Did you find it?" Sana responded hopefully.

"No, not yet, but I discovered something else. The vault foundation goes down deeper. The ossuary had to have been deeper as well. If it is still here, it's got to be on the right of the tunnel in the direction of the red wall."

After picking the drill back up and turning onto his left side, Shawn began making holes in the tunnel's right wall. The first one was midway from the floor to the ceiling and midway into the tunnel, with the result the same as all the holes in the ceiling. Pulling the bit free, Shawn started a second hole at the same level but deeper into the tunnel. Just three inches in, he hit something hard enough to make the drill practically leap out of his hand. Encouraged, he started another hole three inches above the last. He held his breath as the drill bit knifed through the hardpan. Again, the drill bit hit a hard surface.

Shawn could feel his pulse in his temples. Again, he drilled a new hole a few inches away from the last and felt resistance at the same depth. His excitement grew by leaps and bounds, but he wasn't ready to celebrate. Instead, he quickly sank more than a dozen new holes, effectively outlining a perfectly flat stone approximately fifteen inches square embedded three inches into the tunnel's wall. At that point, he called out to Sana. "I found it! I found it!" he repeated with great excitement.

"Are you sure?" Sana yelled back.

"I'd say ninety percent sure," Shawn called out.

With such encouraging news, Sana overcame her reluctance and returned to peer into the tunnel. "Where is it?"

"Right here," Shawn said. He knocked with a knuckle against the tunnel's wall at the very center of the covey of holes he'd drilled.

"I don't see it," Sana said, with gathering disappointment.

"Of course you can't see it," Shawn barked. "I haven't dug it out yet. I've just located it."

"How can you be so sure?"

"Listen, just hand me the hammer and the chisel. I'll show you, you nonbeliever."

Sana didn't necessarily disbelieve Shawn, but like him, she didn't want to get her hopes up. Sana got the tools and handed them in to Shawn.

Shawn attacked the tunnel's wall. The process was more difficult than he'd expected, and it took many blows to drive the chisel several inches into cement-like dirt after which he'd wiggle the chisel free. The noise of the steel hammer against the steel chisel was sharp and penetrating, almost painful in the narrow confines. In an attempt to speed up the process, Shawn almost buried the chisel, before pounding it laterally to loosen the surrounding dirt. This took a lot of blows, and each reverberated with a sound like a gunshot, leaving both Shawn's and Sana's ears ringing. Sana found she had to cup her ears with her palms to protect herself from the near-painful noise.

After half an hour of pounding the hammer while on his side, Shawn had worked up a mild sweat, and his shoulder was aching. Needing a rest from the continuous effort, he put down the tools and rubbed his complaining muscles briskly. A moment later the beam from Sana's headlamp merged with his. To his surprise, Sana had actually poked her head into the tunnel.

"How's the progress?" she asked.

"Slow going!" Shawn admitted. With his gloved hand he wiped off the limestone surface he'd been laboriously exposing. Despite trying to avoid striking the stone with the chisel, he'd nicked it half a dozen times. The nicks stood out sharply as light cream-colored defects against a field of brownish tan. As an archaeologist, he regretted having to employ such a heavy-handed technique, but he had little choice. He knew security made their rounds at the eleven p.m. shift change and he wanted to be long gone. It was already close to ten.

"Do you still think that's it?" Sana questioned.

"Well, let's put it this way: It's a dressed piece of limestone that is surely not indigenous, and it is exactly where Saturninus said he'd placed it. What's your take?"

Sana couldn't help but take offense at Shawn's condescending tone. She was asking a legitimate question because all that was visible was a flat piece of stone, and considering all the construction and modifications that had occurred around Peter's tomb over thousands of years, there'd probably been multiple opportunities for a stone slab to have been accidently buried where this stone was. With an edge to her voice, Sana made her thoughts known.

"So, now you're the expert," Shawn replied sarcastically. "Let me show you something." Shawn directed the beam of his headlamp to the lower edge of the limestone, where he'd begun the even harder job of undermining the object. At that moment, the entire lower edge was exposed. "Notice something curious," he said, in the same condescending tone he'd used a moment earlier. "The 'slab,' as you call it, is perfectly horizontal and vertical. If it were debris from some other project, chances are it wouldn't have ended up so perfectly level and perpendicular. This piece of limestone was carefully placed. It wasn't haphazard."

"How much longer?" Sana asked in a tired voice. There was no doubt in her mind that her sacrifice of struggling with her claustrophobia was not appreciated. If she'd felt capable of leaving on her own, she would have done it at that moment.

Ignoring Sana's question and with the circulation restored to his shoulder muscles, Shawn went back to work. Rapidly he completed the filling of the first bucket with dirt. He then called out for the second to be handed in. Twenty minutes later he had a slit-like opening about four inches deep and four inches wide exposing the end of what he now knew to be a limestone box. The cover was about an inch thick, and was sealed with caramel-colored wax. Giving up on the masonry hammer because of the confined space, Shawn switched to using the chisel as a scraper before pulling out the debris by hand.

Suddenly, Shawn froze. He sucked in a lungful of air as his heart skipped a beat. The lights in the necropolis had flashed on, accompanied by the low rumbling sound of electrical transformers being activated.

13

Jack was thoroughly disgusted with himself. For the second time in two days, he'd completely lost control. Yesterday it had been with Ronald Newhouse, illustrating just how poorly he was handling his son's illness. Thinking back on his actions in the chiropractor's office embarrassed him, especially since it was Laurie who bore the brunt of the tragedy, while he fled the house on a daily basis to avoid even thinking about it. Today he'd essentially blamed his four-month-old son for his lapse of sanity, which was even more embarrassing than railing against a quack chiropractor. Guiltily, he thought about how Laurie would respond when she learned he'd told Bingham and Calvin about JJ. Although they hadn't discussed it openly, both saw the situation as an utterly private affair.

Jack was still sitting at his desk, where he'd retreated after the dressing-down in Bingham's office. He looked at his in basket, which was overflowing with laboratory results and information he'd requested from the medicolegal investigators. He knew he should get to work, but he couldn't get himself to start.

He glanced over at his microscope and the stacks of beckoning microscope slide trays, each representing a separate case. He couldn't do that, either. As preoccupied as he was, he worried he'd miss something important.

Seemingly paralyzed, Jack put his head in his hands. With his elbows on the desk and his eyes closed, he tried to decide if he was actually getting depressed. He couldn't let that happen again. "Pitiful!" he snarled out loud through clenched teeth, his head still bowed.

Vocalizing such a harsh opinion of himself was like being slapped. Jack sat back upright. Having in a sense hit bottom, he rallied. With the same rationale that the best defense was a good offense, the way he approached the meeting with Bingham and Calvin, a state of mind that he wished he'd maintained rather than becoming the wimp he had for fearing to be put on leave, Jack steered his mind back to his alternative-medicine crusade. "The hell with you, Bingham!" Jack snapped. Suddenly, instead of being cowed by Bingham, he was defiant. Though he was initially motivated by a desire to distract himself from JJ's illness, he now thought of the crusade as a legitimate goal in and of itself and certainly not simply a writing exercise for a forensic pathology journal. Instead it was a bona fide way to inform the public about an issue they should care deeply about.

His motivation restored, Jack raised his head and scooted his chair over from the work area of his desk to his computer monitor. With a few clicks of his mouse, he was looking at his e-mail, checking to see if any of his colleagues had responded to his request for cases involving alternative medicine. There were just two: Dick Katzenberg from the Queens office and Margaret Hauptman from

Staten Island. Jack cursed under his breath at the lack of response from the others.

Taking out a couple of three-by-five cards, Jack wrote down the names and accession numbers. He then sent another group e-mail to all the MEs, thanking Dick and Margaret by name for responding, and exhorting the others to follow their lead.

Jack grabbed the index cards and his jacket and headed out. He wanted to pull the files on the two cases, which meant dashing over to the records department in the new OCME DNA building on 26th Street.

Jack hurried past the old but newly renovated Bellevue hospital complex and into the new OCME DNA building, which was set back from First Avenue by a small park. The building itself was a modern skyscraper sheathed in a mixture of blue-tinted glass and light tan polished limestone and towered over the old hospital. Jack was proud of the structure, and proud of New York for having built it.

Jack flashed his OCME ID card and was buzzed through the security turnstile. The records department was on the fourth floor in a spotless office lined with floor-to-ceiling faux-hardwood vertical drawers. Each massive drawer held eight four-foot-wide horizontal shelves. At the end of the day, each aisle had a fold-out wall of the same faux wood that was closed and locked.

The front desk of the department was staffed by a smiling woman named Alida Sanchez. "What can we do for you?" she asked in a lilting voice. "You look particularly motivated."

"I guess I am," Jack admitted, returning the smile. He handed over the two index cards, asking to see the records.

Alida glanced at them before standing up. "I'll be right back."

"I'll be waiting," Jack said. He watched her walk away in the direction of the East River, visible through the windows. A few moments later, she reappeared with a folder. She returned to the desk and handed it to Jack. "Here's the first, to get you started."

Jack opened the record and pawed through the medicolegal report, autopsy notes, autopsy report, telephone-notice-of-death forms, and case worksheet until he came to the certificate of death. Pulling this form out from the others, he noticed that the immediate cause was the same as Keara Abelard's, vertebral artery dissection. On the next line of the form, after the phrase "due to or as a consequence of," was written "chiropractic cervical manipulation."

"Perfect," Jack murmured to himself.

"Here's your second file," Alida said, returning from a more distant aisle. Curious, Jack opened the second folder and pulled out the death certificate. Glancing at the "immediate cause of death" line, he was surprised to see that it included "melanoma." Lowering his eyes to the next line, he saw that the death was a consequence of cancer that had spread to the liver and brain. Confused as to why Margaret would have sent the case, he moved on to part two of the cause of death. There was a line designated as "other significant conditions contributing to death," where Margaret had written that the patient had been advised to use only homeopathy for six months.

"My goodness," Jack said.

"Is something wrong, doctor?" Alida asked.

Jack looked up from the death certificate, and then held it up in the air. "This case has opened my eyes to another negative side of alternative medicine I'd not given any thought to."

"Oh?" Alida questioned. In her job, she wasn't accustomed to having conversations with the MEs, especially after the records department had moved away from the morgue to the new building.

"I used to think that alternative medicine like homeopathy was at least safe, but it isn't so."

"What is homeopathy exactly?" Aida asked.

As Jack had read an entire chapter on it the previous evening in *Trick or Treatment*, he had a rapid answer he wouldn't have had otherwise. "It's a type of alternative medicine based on the very unscientific idea that "like treats like." In other words, if a plant causes nausea when it's been eaten, then the same plant will cure nausea when it's taken in a very diluted amount, and I'm talking about a severe dilution such that there might be only a molecule or two of the active ingredient."

"That sounds rather strange," Alida commented.

"Tell me about it," Jack said with a laugh. "But as I said, at least I thought it was safe until you gave me this case." He again waved the death certificate in his hand. "This case underlines the fact that people can buy into alternative-medicine therapies like homeopathy to the extent that they might forgo conventional medicine, which, in certain circumstances, can offer a cure only if the conventional therapy is started early enough, like with certain cancers. This case that you gave me is such a case."

"That's terrible," Alida voiced.

"I agree," Jack said. "So thank you for your help."

"You're most welcome. Is there anything else I can do for you?"

"There's been talk of digitalizing OCME records. Has that started?"

"Most definitely," Alida said.

"How far along is it?"

"Not very far. It's time consuming, and there are only three of us."

"How many years do you go back?"

"We haven't even done a year yet."

Jack rolled his eyes in disappointment. "Not even a year yet."

"It's a very laborious process."

"How could I search through all the OCME records for deaths

associated with alternative medicine, like the two you pulled for me?"

"I'm afraid it would have to be record by record, which could literally take years, depending on how many people were tasked to do it."

"That's the only way?" Jack asked. It was not what he wanted to hear.

"That's the only way until all the records are digitalized. And even with the digital records, you'd only find those charts where the medical examiners added the words *alternative medicine* in the cause-of-death box."

"Or *chiropractic* or *homeopathic*, et cetera, et cetera," Jack added. "Whatever type of alternative medicine was involved."

"Correct, but I wouldn't imagine too many medical examiners would add such a thing. After all, on the death certificates of people dying of therapeutic complications, you don't see conventional or orthodox medicine stipulated as a contributing factor, or orthopedic surgery, or any other specialty, for that matter. The only possible place it might turn up, if the medical examiner didn't include it on the death certificate, would be in the investigator's report under 'other observations.' Even then it would be unlikely, since in my experience, investigators rarely write anything there at all."

"Shit!" Jack exclaimed. Then, realizing what he'd said, he excused himself. "I'm just so desperate for this information," he said. "I wanted to know how many deaths the OCME has seen over the last thirty years or so that involved alternative medicine. It's that type of statistic that gets people's attention."

"Sorry," Alida said with a forced smile.

14

J ust keep your eyes closed!" Shawn whispered. "Don't open them, no matter what! Just imagine you're on a beach and the sun is streaming down, and white, puffy clouds are passing overhead against a faraway blue sky."

"It's too cold to imagine I'm on a beach," Sana said, with desperation in her voice.

"Then for chrissake, imagine you're lying in the snow at Aspen, looking up at a crystalline winter sky that makes you feel you're seeing beyond the Milky Way."

"It's not that cold."

For a moment, Shawn didn't respond. He was running out of patience and things to say to Sana, whom he'd been comforting the entire time they'd been hiding, pressed together in the tunnel. He'd known her for nearly five years, and never suspected the severity of her claustrophobia or the panic it was capable of creating. She began vociferously complaining from the moment they turned off their headlamps and dove into the tunnel headfirst, ending up on their sides facing each other in an uncomfortable embrace. Initially he had just shushed her, as he was nearly as ter-

rified as she was, though his fear was driven by the real danger of
discovery by Vatican security, not claustrophobia.

Unfortunately, her panic was such that he had had to try to calm
her or she would have been the reason they were discovered. Looking
at her with the meager light creeping in from both ends of the tunnel,
he had seen she was trembling, her forehead was dotted with perspiration, and her eyes were thrown open to their absolute limit.

"You have to calm down!" Shawn had snapped in a hard
whisper.

"I can't," she had cried in the softest voice her panic would
allow. "I can't stay here. I've got to get out. I'm going crazy!"

Forced to be creative, he ordered her to close her eyes and keep
them shut. To his unexpected gratification, it had had the desired
effect. She'd immediately calmed enough to stay put.

"How are you doing?" Shawn finally asked. Although she didn't
answer, he was encouraged. She'd not opened her eyes or complained about her panic for several minutes, giving Shawn a moment to calm himself. When the lights had suddenly popped on
twenty minutes earlier, he'd panicked, too, rushing from inside the
tunnel out to the area beneath the glass deck. He knew he had to
replace the heavy glass panel they'd left leaning against the wall.
There'd been no doubt that if the glass had been seen standing
open, they would have been found.

Just minutes after they'd gotten the glass panel back in place
and had scrambled back to the tunnel, they had heard the voices
of people arriving on the scene, mounting the glass deck and carrying on a conversation.

While Sana had struggled with her panic attack, Shawn had to
fight his own fears that he and Sana might have left some of their
equipment in view through the glass deck. For the ten minutes the
security people were in the area, Shawn was driven to distraction
worrying that they'd be discovered.

He wondered what had attracted the security people. He'd never know for sure, but he admitted that Sana had been surprisingly clairvoyant. It had to have been the piercing, metallic clang of the masonry hammer against the chisel being conducted by the hardpan and marble up into the basilica.

"Can I open my eyes now?" Sana asked suddenly, breaking the heavy silence in the confined tunnel.

"No, keep them closed!" Shawn snapped. Dealing again with Sana's claustrophobia was not something he needed at the moment.

"How long are we going to stay like this?" Sana asked tremulously. It was apparent she was still struggling, but before Shawn could answer, the lights in the necropolis went off, throwing them into absolute blackness.

"Did the lights go off?" Sana asked nervously but also with a touch of relief.

"They did," Shawn said, "but keep your eyes closed until you get your headlamp on." He began wriggling backward in an attempt to extricate himself from the tunnel. When he was free, he turned on his headlamp. Sana joined him a moment later, switching hers on as well.

At first they sat staring at each other. Although Shawn had worried that Sana's panic might reappear when she opened her eyes, it didn't happen. Getting out of the cramped tunnel had been enough of a relief to keep her claustrophobia under control.

"Remind me never to take you on another dig," Shawn said irritably, as if blaming Sana for the scare.

"Remind me never to go!" Sana shot back.

They continued staring at each other for another few seconds, both of them panting as if they'd just run a hundred yards instead of being immobilized for half an hour.

"Let's get the hell out of here," Sana said. "So far, this ranks up there as one of my least favorite experiences. Get in there and get that damn ossuary!"

The last thing Shawn wanted was to be bossed around by Sana after he'd had to hold her hand, at least figuratively, through the entire ordeal. Dealing with her fears had been worse than the fear of discovery.

"I'm going to get the ossuary because I want to get it," Shawn retorted, "not because you're ordering me to do so." He grabbed the chisel and the bucket, and crawled back into the tunnel.

Sana could hear him scraping the dirt from around the ossuary, but unfortunately she had nothing to do and her mind reverted back to obsessing about the situation. Now that the glass access panel had been lowered in the deck, she was completely at Shawn's mercy by being truly imprisoned. As a consequence, her panic and anxiety threatened to return.

"Shawn!" Sana called out over the scraping and grunting noises he was making in the tunnel. "I need us to go back and raise the glass panel."

"Go do it yourself," Shawn yelled back, along with something Sana couldn't hear but could guess.

Knowing she couldn't handle the glass panel herself, and knowing that Shawn knew it too, made her furious, but there was a good side.

She quickly realized that anger mollified her claustrophobia. The more angry she was at Shawn, the less anxious she was about being in a confined space. Recalling that closing her eyes had worked so well in the tunnel to lessen her panic, she did it again.

"Voilà!" Shawn shouted from inside the tunnel. "It's free! It's coming out!"

As if waking from a hypnotic state, Sana's eyes popped open. As far as she was concerned, Shawn could have been talking about her. The ossuary's freedom was her freedom as it meant they would soon be leaving. Completely forgetting her phobia, she crawled forward to the mouth of the tunnel and watched Shawn slide out the stone ossuary from the niche in the wall.

"Is it heavy?"

"Heavy enough," Shawn said with a grunt, settling the limestone box onto the tunnel's floor. Repositioning himself, he pushed it out of the tunnel and emerged himself.

Squatting on their knees and gawking at the ossuary between them, the couple instantly forgot their irritation. Shawn reached out reverently with his gloved hand and gently brushed off the residual dirt from its top. He was momentarily overwhelmed by the possibility it could contain the relics of one of the most revered people in history. The surface was covered with what appeared to be indecipherable scratches. Once he was able to make sense of them, it all clicked into place.

"I was hoping to see a name," Sana said, disappointed.

"There is a name!" Shawn said. "And a date." He rotated the ossuary so that the script that had been facing him was now turned toward Sana. She studied it, recognizing only the Roman numerals of a date: DCCCXV, which she figured out was 815. She slowly raised her eyes to Shawn's. It seemed all their effort had been for naught.

"Oh, no!" she cried. "The damn thing is from the Dark Ages!"

Shawn smiled slyly. "Are you sure?" he asked teasingly.

Confused, she looked back at the Roman numerals and again translated them into numbers. It still came out to 815. She was going to have to convince Shawn that they had failed. As she'd said the artifact was obviously from the Dark Ages.

Then Shawn pointed at the Roman numerals and asked, "Can you see the Latin letters that follow the Roman numerals?"

Sana looked back at the date. After peering at the maze of scratches, three letters emerged. "Yes, I see them. It looks like AUC."

"It is exactly AUC," Shawn said triumphantly. "It stands for ab urbe condita, referring to the supposed founding of Rome in 753 BC, according to the Gregorian calendar, which wasn't introduced until AD 1582."

"I'm confused," Sana said.

"Don't be. Romans didn't use BC or AD. They used AUC. To convert from the ancient Roman calendar to our Gregorian, you have to subtract seven hundred fifty-three years."

Sana did the subtraction in her head. "Then the date is AD 62."

"Correct. What I'm guessing is Simon Magus believed the Virgin Mary died in AD 62."

"I suppose that's a reasonable possibility," Sana said, nodding her head while thinking back to her catechism.

"I would say so," Shawn said. "Assuming Mary had her first child, Jesus, in 4 BC, and that she was about fifteen years old, then she would have been eighty-four at her death. That's certainly long-lived for the first century, but it is possible. Look, there's also a name."

"I don't see one," Sana said, returning her gaze to the tangle of scratches around the date.

"Here. It's in Aramaic, just above the Roman numerals."

"I truly cannot see any letters."

"I'll draw them for you when we get back to the hotel."

"Great! But what is the name?"

"It's Maryam."

"Good Lord!" Sana whispered. Something she never thought might come to pass was seemingly happening.

"Good choice of words," Shawn said happily. "Let's get this thing back to the hotel so we can celebrate." He gradually worked the box out to the area beneath the glass deck. It was difficult because he couldn't stand upright.

"What about the tools and the buckets?" Sana asked. "If I carry them, I'm not going to be able to help you carry the ossuary."

Shawn scratched his head and nodded. The ossuary had to weigh forty to fifty pounds, which he could certainly manage, but he'd need to rest, especially going up the multiple flights of stairs. "I know," he said. "Let's give some future archaeologist something to find in its place. Let's entomb everything except our helmets in the ossuary's former resting spot. After all, we have to get rid of the dirt."

"Good idea," Sana said, but as Shawn started crawling back toward the tunnel, she stopped him by grabbing his arm. "Before you do that, can I ask you a big favor?"

"What?" Shawn demanded. Despite their apparent success, he wasn't in the mood for largesse.

"Can we lift the glass panel? It will make me feel a lot less panicky. Then, while you're burying the tools, I'll get the ossuary over in the corner under the access panel."

Shawn looked back and forth from the tunnel to the ossuary. He even briefly glanced at his watch, knowing he wanted to be exiting the Scavi office by eleven. "Oh, all right!" he said, as if making a big concession. A few minutes later, he was back in the tunnel, busily sealing their equipment in the hole vacated by the ossuary by shoveling the dirt in with his hands and packing it in. He wasn't able to return the wall of the tunnel completely to its original state, but he did his best, and when he was through it looked better than he'd expected.

After smoothing out the dirt floor and making sure he wasn't leaving anything lying around, he beat a fast retreat to where Sana was waiting for him at the exit in the far corner of the glass deck. With the two of them working together, they got the ossuary up to Shawn's chest height and then laterally over onto the deck's surface.

With much effort, they made the long walk though the necropolis toward the exit, stopping repeatedly to catch their breath, Shawn urging them onward. At one of their rest stops near the necropolis entrance door, Sana said, "You know what I'm most excited about?"

"Tell me!" Shawn said, massaging the aching muscles of his upper arms.

"The fact that the top of the ossuary is still sealed all the way around."

Shawn bent down and looked. "I think you're right."

"If that box had been sealed in Qumran, and Qumran is as dry as you said, I think I've got a good chance of finding some first-century mitochondrial DNA."

"And a rather special DNA sample at that. Come on, let's get this thing in the trunk of the car."

The last portion of the trip was the most nerve-wracking. As close to eleven as it had become, there was the small but definite risk of running into security between the Scavi office and the Piazza del Protomartiri Romani, where the car was waiting. Luckily it didn't happen. Once outside, Shawn carried the ossuary himself so Sana could hold the umbrella. She didn't want to risk even getting the outside of the ossuary wet.

With the relic safely ensconced in the trunk of the car, there was some mild concern as they bore down on the Swiss Guards' shacks under the Arco delle Campane. But the concern was unnecessary. Perhaps because of the rain the guards didn't even come out of their guardhouses as Shawn and Sana zipped by, heading out into the dark, wet city.

"Well, that was easy," Shawn said as he settled back into his seat. Sana had her construction helmet on her head with the headlamp illuminated. On her lap was a hotel map with which she hoped to guide them back to the hotel.

"I don't think I'd describe it as easy," she said, not realizing Shawn was joking. She shuddered at the memory of her panic attack. She had never before experienced such anxiety.

"My only regret is allowing myself to be talked into leaving the masonry hammer and chisel behind," Shawn added, continuing his attempt to be humorous. He knew full well it had been his idea to leave all the tools behind.

Sana looked over at the silhouette of her husband and fumed, as she completely missed the fact that he was trying to be funny. How could he be so insensitive? she marveled. Why would he take the risk of hurting her feelings like that? It didn't make sense, especially since they'd found what they were looking for and managed to snatch it from beneath everyone's nose.

"It would come in handy to open the ossuary."

Sana's irritation at Shawn instantly shifted to concern about Shawn's intentions. "When are you planning on opening it?" she asked, afraid to hear his response.

"I don't know exactly," Shawn said. He glanced at his wife, surprised at her tone and the fact that she was staring at him so intently. "I might allow myself to have a drink first, but I want to know if there are any documents inside, and I want to know sooner rather than later."

Sana didn't laugh or even smile at what she now sensed was a feeble attempt at humor. There was nothing funny about opening the ossuary prematurely. In fact, she was afraid his impatience might put her interest in the ossuary in jeopardy.

"Why the long face?" he asked, while shielding his eyes from Sana's headlamp.

"You can't open the ossuary until I can stabilize the relics biologically," Sana blurted, as she turned off her headlamp and tossed the helmet in the backseat. "Otherwise, we'll be taking a risk of lessening the chances of isolating any mitochondrial DNA."

"Oh, really?" Shawn questioned mockingly. He was shocked that his wife could think it was her position to preempt what was sure to be his premier archaeological find. "I'm opening the damn ossuary tonight! We'll worry about your DNA stuff when the time comes."

"You could be cutting off your nose to spite your face," Sana replied with emotion. "Your impatience could be costly. Remember, this thing's been sealed for nearly two thousand years. If there are documents in it, you'd better be prepared to conserve them immediately or you might lose them, along with any biological material."

"Okay, maybe you are right," Shawn reluctantly admitted, "at least about the documents. But really, except for vague scientific interest, what would knowing the Virgin Mary's mitochondrial DNA sequence mean, anyhow?"

"I'm not sure how to answer that. We might be able to trace her genealogy quite a ways back because we'd already be two thousand years back before we start. But more important, because mitochondrial DNA is inherited solely from the mother, with no recombination involved, you will be ultimately responsible for learning the mitochondrial DNA sequence of Jesus Christ."

"Really!" Shawn repeated, suddenly awed.

"Really!" Sana echoed. "You would be included in that rarified group of scientists who have made extraordinary contributions to knowledge, probably more than any documents could provide."

"My word," Shawn said, visualizing the accolades.

"So, can I have your word we won't open the ossuary until we get to New York? You'll only have to wait a few days."

"You have my word."

Sana took in a deep breath and let it out in a huff. She was relieved. She was also a little embarrassed at her stooping so low as to manipulate Shawn with his own vanity. Yet she wasn't embarrassed enough to admit to it. She was intent on maximizing the chances of isolating Mary's DNA, because she, as the molecular biologist, rather than Shawn, as the archaeologist, would ultimately be credited with having deciphered Jesus Christ's mitochondrial DNA sequence.

15

Well, there's no question what killed him," Jack said. He had just sliced open the heart of a sixty-two-year-old African-American male named Leonard Harris. A large, sausage-shaped blood clot completely filled the right atrium.

"Did that clot come from the legs?" Vinnie asked.

"We'll just have to check that out," Jack answered.

The autopsy room was in full swing, with all eight tables in use. Jack and Vinnie were already deep into their third case, while most of the other MEs were still doing their first.

Jack's first case had been a teenager shot in Central Park. There was a question of whether it was a suicide or a homicide. Unfortunately, there had been a mistake made by the OCME medicolegal investigator, George Sullivan, who had been bullied by the detective in charge to rush his investigation. The result was that he'd forgotten to bag the victim's hands, possibly causing a loss of critical evidence. Since the victim was the son of a politically connected lawyer, Calvin had been called in, ordering Jack on the case.

Jack's other two cases were a bit more straightforward, but just.

The second case was a drug overdose of a college freshman. But the third case, the one he was on, presented a surprise challenge. Jack was confident the cause of death was a pulmonary embolism, but the manner of death was not necessarily natural.

"Vinnie, my friend, do you know—" Jack began as he sliced open the rest of the heart, looking for more blood clots, particularly at the tricuspid and pulmonary valves.

"No!" Vinnie interrupted, without even letting Jack finish his sentence. "When you start a question by being nice to me, I know you have something on your mind that I want no part of."

"Am I that bad?" Jack asked, as he moved up to the bifurcation of the pulmonary artery looking for more clots.

"You're wicked bad!" Vinnie declared.

"Sorry you feel that way," Jack said. "But let me finish my sentence. Do you know what is particularly special about this case?"

Vinnie looked down at the large, dark clot and then over at the flayed-open corpse, trying to come up with something humorous. When he couldn't, he fell back on the truth: "No!" he said.

"This case is a perfect example of just how important the medicolegal investigators are in forensic pathology. Because Janice asked all the right questions, this case will be viewed in a different light. I would have been certain it was a natural death, but because she asked the wife if he'd been taking any medication, she learned something the ER docs didn't know: that he'd been taking an herbal remedy on his own, PC-SPES, made of Chinese herbs, which was supposed to be taken off the market but which is still available. Janice Googled the drug and learned that it was an FDA-unapproved medication that had often been contaminated with female hormones and was therefore associated with clotting problems and fatal pulmonary emboli."

"So, the herbal remedy killed the man."

"Possibly," Jack said.

"Will you be able to prove it?"

"Perhaps. Let toxicology have a go at the samples we've taken and see if we can get some of the medication he's been taking from the wife."

"Hey, keep working!" Vinnie complained. Jack had stopped while he was talking.

"Do you take any herbal medicine, Vinnie?" Jack asked, going back to work.

"Sometimes. There's a Chinese aphrodisiac called Tiger Stamina I use once in a while. And occasionally my acupuncturist gives me something for some minor complaints I have."

Jack stopped working and stared at his favorite mortuary tech.

"What's wrong? Why are you looking at me like that?"

"As the saying goes, I knew you were dumb, but I didn't think you were stupid."

"Why? What are you talking about?"

"I had no idea you were a user of alternative medicine. Why?"

Vinnie shrugged. "I guess because it's natural."

"Natural, my ass," Jack said scornfully. "The worst poison known to man comes from a tree frog in South America. You cannot imagine how small an amount would be necessary to kill you, and it's natural. Calling something natural is a meaningless marketing ploy."

"All right, calm down! Maybe I like alternative medicine because it's been in use for more than six thousand years. After all that time, they have to know what they're doing."

"You mean the wacky idea that somehow in the distant past people had more scientific wisdom than they do today? That's both crazy and counterintuitive. Six thousand years ago people thought thunder was a bunch of gods moving around furniture."

"All right," Vinnie repeated, with a touch of irritation. "I like alternative medicine because it treats my whole body, not just my arm or spleen or whatever."

"Ah!" Jack said, his voice rising and tinged with more scorn than when he spoke about the "natural" fable. "The holistic myth or the more-holistic-than-thou nonsense is just as crazy as everything else you've said. Regular medicine is a thousand times more holistic than alternative medicine. With conventional medicine, they're even taking into account individual genetic profiles. How much more holistic can you be than that?"

"How about we get this autopsy over with," Vinnie suggested. "And maybe you should stop yelling."

Just as he had a few days ago in Ronald Newhouse's office, Jack suddenly came to his senses. Again, he'd allowed his emotions to get the best of him. The room had gone silent, and everyone was staring at him. When he glanced down at his hands, he realized one hand was still grasping the heart and lungs he'd been examining while the other hand still held the butcher knife. As suddenly as the buzz of conversation stopped it now resumed.

"Wow!" Vinnie murmured. "You're getting awfully touchy in your old age."

"I've been looking into alternative medicine since our case of vertebral artery dissection on Monday, and I've become a touch emotional about what I've been learning."

"A touch?" Vinnie questioned mockingly. "I'd say it's over the top, but I tell you what I'll do: I'll give up on the acupuncture if it will make you feel better."

"It would," Jack said, "especially if you ditch the herbs as well."

Vinnie leaned toward Jack and squinted. "Are you pulling my leg now or what?" He wasn't certain.

"Half and half," Jack said. "Meanwhile, let's knock out this autopsy."

They completed the pulmonary embolism case in near record time, too uncomfortable to talk. When they did finish, Jack said, "Sorry, my friend. I was definitely out of line."

"You're forgiven. To pay me back, you can promise me we won't start autopsies until everyone else does."

"Dreamer," Jack said, snapping off his gloves and heading for the washroom.

Jack cleaned up and returned upstairs to his desk. Still feeling uncomfortable about his mini-blowup in the autopsy room, he closed his office door. For a while, at least, he didn't want to see or talk to anyone. Forcing himself to work, he dictated all three autopsies he'd just completed so he was sure not to forget any of the details, using his scribbled notes to remind him of specific important points.

With the dictation out of the way, Jack looked at his crowded inbox, but, like many days of late, he couldn't find the motivation to start. Instead, he opened up his center drawer and pulled out a large envelope where he'd been storing all his alternative-medicine data. As of that moment, he had a total of twelve cases from his colleagues. Keara Abelard made thirteen, and his herbal case that morning made a grand total of fourteen.

Jack should have been pleased with his progress, but he wasn't. He'd come to the conclusion that the number of cases he was going to find, no matter what he did, was going to be seriously lower than the true number, for a complex of reasons. One problem was the lack of digitalization of the OCME records, meaning a search was not possible. Even if the records were digitalized, there would be no coding for alternative medicine in general, nor for specific types of alternative medicine in particular. On top of that, even if he was able to find VAD cases, there was no guarantee that the records would say anything about chiropractic, even if chiropractic therapy was involved in the cause of death.

In situations involving herbal medicine, the cases would be signed out as accidental poisoning, with the cause of death attributed to the specific poison involved. It would be the exception, not the rule, if herbal medicine was mentioned at all.

Although Jack thought his crusade of exposing the risks of chiropractic and other forms of alternative medicine was still a great idea and more than worth pursuing, his enthusiasm was being dampened by these tactical obstacles. Fourteen cases over some indeterminate period of time was not enough to attract the public's attention. When he had started, he'd envisioned a grand exposé involving hundreds of cases capable of dominating the media for days. Jack could already assume that was not going to happen.

As Jack's zeal for his crusade sagged, his problems at home only loomed larger. His out-of-control emotions, as the recent minor episode with Vinnie exemplified, were a clear sign he still lacked focus. For a few moments Jack debated whether he should stick with the alternative-medicine idea in hopes of solving the problems of researching it or whether he should switch and try to find something more engrossing.

The ring of the telephone startled him out of his reverie. He glared at the phone with a sudden flash of anger, suppressing an urge to rip the blasted cord out of the wall. He didn't want to talk to anyone.

But what if it was Laurie? Perhaps there'd been a sudden change for the worse with JJ's condition. Perhaps she was calling from Memorial's emergency room. Jack snatched up the handset and barked, "Yes?"

"Hey, big guy," Lou Soldano rumbled. "Am I catching you at a bad time? You sound harried."

It took Jack a moment to reboot his brain. He'd been so certain it would be Laurie calling about some kind of disaster. "It's okay," he said, struggling to calm himself. "What's up?"

Next to Laurie, Lieutenant Detective Lou Soldano was one of his favorite people. In many ways, Lou and Jack's friendship had a curious twist. Before Jack had come on the scene, Lou and Laurie had dated for a time. Luckily for Jack, their relationship had changed from rocky romantic to pleasant platonic, and when Jack and Laurie began dating, Lou championed Jack on multiple occasions. At one particularly difficult juncture, it was Lou's belief that Jack and Laurie were made for each other that probably saved the day.

"I wanted to give you some follow-up," Lou said, "on that suicide gunshot case you called me about Tuesday. You know which case I'm talking about?"

"Of course. The woman's name was Rebecca Parkman. That was the case that the husband was dead set—excuse my pun—against his wife having an autopsy, supposedly for religious reasons."

"It appears he had other reasons, too," Lou said.

"I'm not surprised. Although the entrance wound was somewhat stellate, it wasn't stellate enough, which suggested it was not a contact wound. How far away did I guess the gun was when it was fired?"

"Two inches!"

"In my entire forensic career, I've never seen a suicide with a gunshot wound to the head that wasn't a contact wound."

"Well, with your suspicions we got a warrant and burst in on the guy. And guess what, he was entertaining this young chick. Can you imagine? Two days after his wife is supposed to have killed herself, he's boffing this cheerleader type."

"Did you find anything incriminating?"

"Oh, yeah!" Lou said with a confident chuckle. "In the dryer we found a recently washed shirt of his. Of course it looked clean, but the lab guys found some blood, which turned out to be the wife's. I think that's pretty damn incriminating. I have to give it to you guys at the OCME. Chalk up another victory for justice." One of the things that had propelled Jack and Lou's friendship was Lou's high regard for forensic pathology and what it could do for law enforcement. Lou was a frequent visitor to the OCME, and a frequent observer of autopsies on criminal cases.

"Hey, how's that new kid of yours?" Lou asked.

"It's a struggle," Jack said, without supplying any details. He hadn't told Lou about JJ's illness, nor did he want to. At the same time, he didn't want to lie. Wasn't life with an infant a struggle for everyone?

"Isn't it, though?" Lou laughed. "Talk about changing one's lifestyle. I remember with my two I didn't sleep for months."

"How are your children?" Jack asked.

"They aren't kids anymore," Lou said. "My baby girl's twenty-eight, and my baby boy is twenty-six. I tell you, it goes by fast. But they're fine. How's Laur?" Laur was Lou's nickname for Laurie.

"She's fine," Jack said, and before Lou could follow up, Jack added, "Lou, do you mind if I ask you a personal question?"

"Hell, no! What's on your mind?"

"Do you use alternative medicine?"

"You mean like chiropractors and acupuncture and all that kind of shit?"

"Exactly! Or homeopathy or herbal medicine or even some of the more esoteric therapies involving buzzwords like energy fields, waves, magnetism, and resonance."

"I have a chiropractor I go to once in a while to get adjusted, especially when I don't get a lot of sleep. And I tried acupuncture to stop smoking. Somebody here at headquarters recommended it."

"Did the acupuncture work?"

"Yeah, for a couple of weeks."

"What if I told you alternative medicine isn't risk-free? In fact, what if I told you cervical manipulation by chiropractors kills people every year? Would that influence you?"

"Really?" Lou questioned. "People die?"

"I just did a case Monday," Jack said. "A twenty-seven-year-old female who died from having arteries torn in her neck. It was the first such case I'd seen, but I've looked into it over the last few days. I'm surprised at the number of cases I've found. It's influenced my opinion of alternative medicine."

"I never knew people died from chiropractic treatment," Lou admitted. "How about acupuncture? Anyone die from that?"

"Yes. Laurie had such a case."

"Jeez!" Lou remarked.

"What if I told you alternative medicine really doesn't deliver the kind of health benefits it claims? That beyond providing a placebo effect, it doesn't do much at all. You know what the placebo effect is, don't you?"

"Yeah, that's when you take some kind of medicine, like a sugar pill, that actually has no medicine in it, but you feel better."

"Exactly. So, to reword what I'm saying, what if I told you alternative medicine doesn't do anything other than provide a placebo effect, but in the process puts you at risk?"

Lou laughed. "Maybe I'll just go out and buy me a bottle of sugar pills."

"Lou, I'm being serious about this. I want to understand why you won't question the rationale of going to a supposed health provider, paying good money, possibly putting yourself at risk of death, when I'm telling you all you're getting is a placebo effect. Help me understand."

"Maybe it's because I can go and see this chiropractor guy."

"I still don't understand. What do you mean you go because you can go?"

"It's harder than hell to get in to see my general practitioner. His office is like a fort with a couple of witches who act like they need to protect him from me, the grunt. And when I do get in to see him, he tells me to lose weight and stop smoking, as if that's easy, and I'm in and out so fast that half the time I forget why I went in to see him in the first place. Then I call up the chiropractor, they take your call right away and are pleasant. If you want to speak to the chiropractor, you can. If it's an emergency and you want to come in right away, you can. And when you do get into the office, there's not the hour-long wait, and when you see the therapist, you don't have the feeling he's rushing you through an assembly line like a hunk of meat at a slaughterhouse."

For a few moments there was a silence. As a benefit of controlling his own emotion to a reasonable degree, Jack could hear Lou's breathing. The man was mildly vexed. Jack cleared his throat. "Thank you!" he said. "You've taught me something I needed to know."

"You're welcome," Lou said with little sincerity.

"I said I have been looking into alternative medicine, and I've been mystified by the general public's willingness to embrace it despite the fact it appears to me to be nearly worthless efficacy-wise, yet it costs the public billions upon billions of dollars a year. Herbal medicine alone, I found out, rakes in some thirty billion, which reminds me, do you take any herbal medicine?"

"Occasionally. When my weight spikes over two hundred pounds, I go on a weight-loss kick, which includes an herbal product called Lose It."

"That's not good," Jack said. "As your friend, I'd advise you not to use it. Many herbal weight-loss products, especially those from China, are accidentally contaminated with lead salts or mercury salts, or both. On top of that, often the natural plant content has been known to be purposefully contaminated with dangerous pharmaceuticals to be assured that there will be some sort of a mild positive effect, meaning weight loss. My advice is to stay away from such remedies as much as possible."

"You are such a wonderful bearer of good news today. I'm so glad I called."

"I'm sorry," Jack said. "But I'm pleased you've called. You have actually taught me something I needed to know, although probably something I didn't want to know—namely, why the public is so willing to embrace alternative medicine and resistant to hear why they shouldn't."

"Now you have me curious," Lou said. "What did I teach you?"

"You taught me that conventional medicine has a lot to learn from alternative medicine. The way you described your experiences with the two is truly telling. Alternative medicine has good customer relations with their patients, treating them like people, making the visit a positive social experience, even if there is no real curing going on. Conventional medicine, on the other hand, too often is the opposite, acting more as if they are doing you a favor. And worse still, if conventional medicine thinks they cannot help you, they ignore you; you're out in the proverbial cold." Jack couldn't help but think that's where he and Laurie were right now, treading water while they waited until JJ's allergy to mouse protein went down, if it was going to go down. That was not a given.

"Why do you say you didn't want to know that?" Lou asked.

Jack had to think for a moment, because the question had to do with his crusade, which had to do with JJ's illness. Jack did not want to talk about JJ. "I didn't want to know because learning that there is a legitimate reason for people to want to use alternative medicine means that my efforts to expose its limitations and even its risks will probably fall on deaf ears."

"Sometimes I think you are the most irritatingly arcane person I know. But let me add another reason why people will fight you tooth and nail about alternative medicine: Alternative medicine doesn't seem scary. If you say a handful of people die every year from going to an alternative-medicine therapist, they won't blink an eye. Thousands upon thousands more people die who go only to conventional medical doctors than the people who go to a chiropractor. In fact, people who go to chiropractors want to believe in chiropractic specifically because they don't want to go to conventional doctors, where they might get a diagnosis that will involve discomfort and pain and possibly death. At the chiropractor, that never happens. Everything is optimistic, every complaint can be treated, and it doesn't hurt, and even if it is placebo, who cares?"

There was another period of silence until Jack said, "You're right!"

"Thank you. Now let's get back to our respective work, because we're on city time. And one last thing, keep the forensic tips coming, because this last one on Sam Parkman was right on target."

"But isn't there going to be a problem with the Parkman case about the blood being circumstantial evidence? I mean, there's no way to prove when the wife's blood got on the shirt. The defense can argue it was a month ago or a year ago."

"That's not going to be a problem. The cheerleader girlfriend is singing at the top of her lungs, trying to avoid being considered an accomplice. The DA is very happy and considers the case a slam dunk."

After Jack hung up the phone, he sat unmoving for a time. What little wind he'd had remaining in the sails of his alternative-medicine crusade was gone. Again, he felt discouraged. He took all his notes and dumped them back into the large envelope. Then, instead of returning it to his center drawer, he opened his bottom drawer containing the framed photo of Laurie and JJ, and tossed it in. He then kicked the drawer shut.

Prepared to get down to real work, Jack reached for his inbox with the intention of lifting out the material onto his blotter to begin to sort it. But his hand never made it. His phone's jangle again pierced the room's stillness. Sure it would be Lou with another thought about the alternative-medicine issue, Jack answered the phone as informally as he did earlier. But the caller wasn't Lou. It was perhaps one of the last people in the world Jack expected to hear from.

16

D r. Jack Stapleton, I presume!" The clear, mellifluous tenor voice came over the receiver like a breath of fresh air. It was somehow familiar to Jack, and his brain desperately scanned though its auditory memory bank.

Jack was silent a moment. Listening more closely he could hear a slight wheeze. Someone was still on the line but deliberately not speaking. Almost half a minute went by before Jack said, "We're going to be here awhile unless I get a bit more information."

"It's one of your oldest and dearest friends."

The voice was again familiar, but Jack could not quite pin it down. "Since I've never had a surplus of friends, this should be an easy task, but it's not. You have to give me another hint."

"I was the handsomest, tallest, smartest, most athletic, and most popular of the Three Musketeers!"

"Will wonders never cease," Jack said, now at ease. "James O'Rourke. Although I can grant you the other less significant qualities, I'm going to contest the tallest."

James burst out with his familiar high-pitched laugh, which

grated on Jack's nerves like sandpaper on the tips of his fingers, just as it had when they met at Amherst College in the fall of 1973.

"The moment I hear your voice, do you know what I visualize?" James said with another giggle.

"I can't imagine," Jack said.

"I see you walking out of Laura Scales House at Smith College, lugging the bust of Laura Scales, with your face as red as mine would have been. It was hilarious."

"That was because Molly stood me up," Jack said, quickly defending himself.

"I remember," James said. "And you did it in broad daylight."

"I brought it back the next month with great fanfare," Jack added. "So no harm done."

"I remember. I was there."

"And you're hardly the one to be throwing stones," Jack said. "I can remember the night you carried out the club chair from Dickinson House at Mount Holyoke College because you were pissed off at . . . what was her name?"

"Virginia Sorenson. Beautiful, sweet Virginia Sorenson! What a doll!" James said with a hint of nostalgia.

"Have you heard from her since—"

"Since I went into the seminary?"

"Yeah."

"No, I haven't. She was sweet but hardly understanding."

"I can see her point, considering how tight you guys were. Do you regret your choice?"

James cleared his throat. "The difficulty of having to make the choice has been a source of both joy and sadness, which I would prefer to discuss over a glass of wine and a roaring fire. I have a place on a lake in northern New Jersey where I'd love to have you and your wife come some weekend."

"That might work," Jack said vaguely. It seemed a surprising invitation after not having heard a whimper from James since they graduated from college in 1977. Of course, it was also Jack's fault, since he hadn't tried to contact James, either. Although they'd been good friends in college, their postgraduate interests had been totally divergent. With the last member of the Three Musketeers, it had been different. Jack had been enthralled by Shawn Daughtry's field of Near Eastern archeology, and they had stayed reasonably in touch until the death of Jack's first wife and children. After that, Jack didn't keep in touch with anyone, not even family.

As if sensing Jack's thoughts, James said, "I have to apologize for not getting in touch with you when you moved here to the city. I heard you were here, working at OCME. I've always meant to give you a call to get together and laugh at old times. No one seems to realize when you go to college what a wonderful experience it is. At the time it always seems so hectic, with some giant paper or exam weighing you down. And when someone tries to tell you how special college is while you're there, all you can say to yourself is, *Oh, sure! If this is the best that it gets, I'm in serious trouble!*"

It was Jack's turn to chuckle. "You're so right. It's the same with medical school. I can remember my old family doc telling me medical school was going to be the emotional highlight of my professional career. At the time I thought he was crazy, but it turns out he was right."

There was a short pause in the conversation as the two old college friends silently reminisced. But then James's attitude and tone abruptly changed as he broke the silence. "I suppose you'd like to know why I have suddenly called you out of the blue."

"It's crossed my mind," Jack admitted, trying to sound casual. James's voice had become decidedly somber, almost grave.

"It's simply that I am in desperate need of your help, and I pray that you will be willing to indulge me."

"You have my attention," Jack said warily. There had been times when listening to other people's problems had awakened his own. Much as he wanted to avoid that, he couldn't help but be curious. Still, Jack could not believe that he, a die-hard agnostic, could possibly help the archbishop of New York City, arguably one of the most powerful leaders in the world.

"It involves our mutual friend, Shawn Daughtry," James added.

"Have you been playing cards again?" Jack asked, in an attempt at humor. Back in college, James and Shawn would play poker at least once a week and get into heated arguments about how much one owed the other. Several times, Jack had to intervene to get them back to talking to each other.

"This issue is of extraordinary importance," James said. "I would prefer you not make light of it."

"Excuse me, Father," Jack said, realizing James was dead serious. Still trying to lighten the sudden downturn in the tone of the conversation, Jack added, "Am I supposed to call you Father, Father?"

"My title is Your Eminence," James said, easing up a trifle. "But you can call me James, which from you I vastly prefer."

"I'm glad," Jack responded. "Knowing you from college as I do, it might be difficult to call you Your Eminence. It sounds too much like a rude anatomical statement."

"You haven't changed, have you?" James said, even more light-heartedly.

"Unfortunately, yes, I have changed. I feel like I'm living a second life totally separate from the first. But I'd rather not get into it, at least not now. Maybe when you call me in another thirty years, I'll be ready to talk about it."

"Has it been that long?" James said, with a touch of regret.

"Actually, it's been thirty-one; I rounded it off to the nearest decade. But I'm not blaming you. I'm just as guilty."

"Well, it's something that should be rectified. After all, we live and work in the same city."

"It seems that way," Jack said. Jack was one of those people who refrained from spur-of-the-moment social commitments. Considering how long it had been and how divergent their careers had become, he didn't know if he wanted to reopen a relationship from what seemed like a previous life.

"What I'd like to propose," James said, "is we get together just as soon as possible. I know it is short notice, but would you consider coming here to the residence for a quick lunch?"

"Today?" Jack asked with utter surprise.

"Yes, today," James reiterated. "This problem has just been dumped in my lap, and I don't have a lot of time to deal with it. That's why I need to ask your help."

"Well," Jack said, "it's short notice, and I was invited to lunch with the Queen, but I can give her a call and tell her we'll have to reschedule, as the Catholic Church needs my intervention."

"I beg to differ concerning your assessment of yourself. You haven't changed one iota. But thank you for being willing to come. And thank you for your irreverent humor. It would probably be best for me to lighten up a bit, but I am very concerned."

"Does it have something to do with Shawn's health?" Jack questioned. That was the main thing he was worried about: some health issue like cancer, as it would be too close to his own problems.

"No, not his health but his soul. You know how headstrong he can be."

Jack scratched his head. Recalling Shawn's loose sexual mores from college, Jack would have thought his soul was in jeopardy from the age of puberty on, which begged the question of why there was such a rush today. "Can you be a bit more specific?" he asked.

"I'd rather not," James said. "I'd rather discuss the issue tête-à-tête. When can I expect you?"

Jack glanced at his watch. It was ten minutes until noon. "If I leave now, which I can do, I'll be there in fifteen or twenty minutes."

"Wonderful. I do have an official reception I must attend with the mayor at two p.m. I look forward to seeing you, Jack."

"Likewise," Jack said as he hung up the phone. There was a strange unreality to James's request. It was like the president calling and saying get down here to Washington immediately: The country needs you. Jack laughed out loud, grabbed his leather jacket, and headed down to the basement.

As Jack was unlocking his bike, he became aware that someone had come up behind him. Turning around, he found himself confronted by bulldog-faced Chief Bingham. As usual, his expression was grim, perspiration dotting his forehead.

"Jack," Bingham began. "I wanted to say again how sorry Calvin and I are about your son. Having had children ourselves, we can, to some degree, imagine how very difficult it must be. Remember, if there's anything we can do, just let us know."

"Thank you, Chief."

"Are you heading out?"

"No, I just drop down here every so often to unlock and lock my bike."

"Always joking!" Bingham commented. Knowing Jack as well as he did, he wasn't about to take offense the way he used to when Jack first came on board at the OCME. "I assume you're not heading out to lunch with a chiropractor friend."

"Your assumption is entirely correct," Jack said. "Nor am I heading out to see an acupuncturist, a homeopathist, or an herbalist. But I am going to lunch with a faith healer. The archbishop of New York just called and asked to have lunch with me."

Bingham burst out laughing despite himself. "I have to hand it to you. You're creatively quick on the retort. Anyway, ride carefully, and if truth be known, I wish you wouldn't ride that bike. I'm always terrified you're going to come in here feet first." Still chuckling, Bingham turned and walked back into the depths of OCME.

Jack rode uptown on Madison, the fresh air reviving him. In fifteen minutes he arrived at the corner of 51st Street.

The archbishop's residence stood out dramatically from the neighboring modern skyscrapers, a modest, rather severe three-story slate-roofed house of gray stone. The windows on the lower floors were covered by heavy iron bars. The only sign of life was a glimpse of Belgian lace seeming out of place behind a few of the barred windows.

With the bike secured along with his helmet, Jack mounted the granite steps and gave the shiny brass bell a pull. He didn't wait long. As the locks clicked open, the heavy door swung inward, revealing a tall, thin, red-haired priest whose most prominent feature was a hatchet-like nose. He was dressed in a priest's black suit and a heavily starched, old-fashioned white clerical collar.

"Dr. Stapleton?" the priest questioned.

"Yes, indeed," Jack said casually.

"My name is Father Maloney," the priest said, stepping to the side.

Jack entered, feeling somewhat intimidated by his surroundings. As Father Maloney closed the door behind him, he said, "I will show you to His Eminence's private study." He strode off, forcing Jack to run a few paces to catch up.

The sounds of busy Madison Avenue had disappeared behind the heavy front door. All Jack could hear besides the tick of the grandfather clock were their footsteps on the highly polished oak floor.

Father Maloney stopped before a closed interior door. As Jack came up to join him, the priest opened the door and stepped aside to allow Jack to enter.

"His Eminence will join you momentarily," he said, backing out of the room and quietly closing the door.

Jack glanced around the spartan room, which smelled of cleaning fluid and floor wax. The only decoration besides a small crucifix hanging on the wall above an antique prie-dieu were several framed formal photos of the pope. Besides the prie-dieu the furniture was limited to a small leather couch, a matching leather chair, a side table with a lamp, and finally a small lady's writing desk with a straight-backed wooden chair.

Jack walked across the glossy wooden floor, his leather soles tapping loudly. He sat on the sofa without leaning back, feeling as if he were someplace he didn't belong. Jack had never been religious, as his schoolteacher parents had not followed any faith themselves. As he grew up and was forced to think about the issue, he'd decided he was an agnostic, at least until the tragedy that had stripped him of his family. From then on, Jack had given up on the comforting idea that there was a God. He didn't think a loving God would let his beloved wife and his darling daughters perish as they did.

Suddenly, the door burst open. Already on edge, Jack leaped to his feet. In walked His Eminence James Cardinal O'Rourke in full regalia. For a beat the men regarded one another, each resurrecting a flash of pleasant memories. Although Jack could definitely see a glimpse of his old friend in the cardinal's face, the rest of his appearance surprised him. Jack didn't remember him being as small as he now appeared to be. His hair was shorter and not so vibrantly red. But it was the clothing, of course, that had changed the most: James reminded Jack of a Renaissance prince. Over black pants and white collar, James wore a black cassock enhanced with cardinal-red piping and buttons. Over the cassock was an open scarlet cape. On his head was a cardinal-red zucchetto skullcap. Cinched around his waist was a broad scarlet sash, while around his neck hung a jeweled silver cross.

The two men threw their arms around each other. They hugged for a moment before stepping back.

"You look terrific," James said. "You look like you could run a marathon this minute. I don't think I could run the length of the cathedral if I had to."

"You're too kind," Jack said, as he gazed down at James's gentle face with soft, freckled, shiny red cheeks and pleasantly rounded features. His sharp, sparkling ice-blue eyes told a different story, and one more consistent with what Jack knew of his old friend, who was now a powerful, ambitious prelate. The eyes reflected James's formidable and canny intelligence, which Jack had always envied.

"Truly," James continued. "You look like a man half your age."

"Oh, stop it," Jack said with a smile. Suddenly he remembered how facile James was at flattery, a trait he'd always used to great advantage. Back at Amherst, there wasn't a person who did not like James, thanks to his ability to beguile others.

"And look at you," Jack said, trying to return the compliment. "You look like a Renaissance prince."

"A chubby Renaissance prince whose only exercise is at the refectory table."

"Think about it," Jack continued, ignoring James's comment. "You are a cardinal, one of the most powerful people in the Church."

"Fiddlesticks," James remarked, waving him away as if Jack was teasing him. "I'm just a simple parish priest caring for my flock. The Good Lord has put me in a position that's way over my head. Of course, I can't question the Lord's ways; I do the best I can. But enough of this small talk. We can indulge ourselves more at lunch. First, I want to show you something."

James led the way out of the study, down a long hall, and past a formal dining room, where there were two place settings at a table for twelve, and into a large kitchen with modern appliances but old-fashioned soapstone countertops and sinks. A woman was at the sink washing a head of lettuce. She was a big woman, about four inches taller than James, with her dark hair pulled back in a severe bun. James introduced her as Mrs. Steinbrenner, the house-keeper, and the absolute ruler of the residence. Her response was to shoo James out of what she called *her* kitchen and to feign anger when he stole a carrot stick from a carefully arranged veg-etable platter.

"That is your lunch," she scolded with a heavy German accent, slapping James's hand. Pretending to be intimidated, James mo-tioned for Jack to follow him down the cellar steps.

"She pretends to be Brunhild," James explained, "but she is a lamb. I could not do without her. She does all the cooking, except for large parties, keeps the place spotless, and keeps everyone, my-self included, in line. Now, where is the light switch?"

They had reached the concrete basement, which was divided into rooms by rough, white-stained lumber. James flicked a switch, reveal-ing a central corridor lined with padlocked doors on either side.

"I really, really appreciate your coming over on such short no-tice," James said as he stopped in front of one of the doors. He took out a key, opened the lock, and pulled open the hasp. The door's hinges squeaked as the door opened outward. He fumbled again to get the lights before proceeding into the room and motioning for Jack to follow.

It was a rectangular room about twenty feet long and ten feet wide with a nearly twelve-foot ceiling. The end wall was made of exposed, roughly dressed granite blocks that also served as the building's foundation. Shelving ran down the walls, supporting carefully labeled cardboard moving boxes. Down at the end of the room stood a yellowed wooden packing crate whose metal straps had been cut but were still in place. Again motioning for Jack to follow him, James walked to the crate and bent the cut metal straps back to expose the top, which clearly had been opened and then put back.

"This is what has started the dilemma," James said. Then he sighed. "Notice it is addressed to me. Also notice I am supposedly the sender, and also notice it says that it contains personal items."

"Did Shawn send this to you?"

"He did indeed, the clever guy. He also phoned me to tell me it was coming. He said it was a surprise, and he knows I like surprises. Actually, foolish me thought it was something for my upcoming birthday, which I now know it isn't, but it is a surprise that has turned out to be a much bigger one than I could have imagined."

"Oh, yeah," Jack said, his face brightening. "Your birthday is coming up. In fact it's tomorrow, the sixth of December, right?"

"He hasn't given me a present since I don't know when," James said, ignoring Jack's question. "Why I let myself believe he was going to give me one this year, I truly don't know. But since Shawn is both a biblical scholar and archaeologist, I thought it might be some wonderful early Christian relic. Little did I know."

"Is it?" Jack asked.

"Let me finish," James said. "I want you to understand why I am in such a difficult situation."

Jack nodded, his curiosity building. The crate probably did contain an antiquity. Something unusual, judging from James's reaction.

"Sending this crate to me from the Vatican saying it contained my personal effects meant it wasn't stopped by customs, either in

Italy or here in New York. It came overnight by air freight, deliv-
ered here directly from JFK. Since I thought it was a birthday
present, I had it placed in here with the rest of my personal items.
As he promised, Shawn showed up yesterday right from JFK,
shortly after the crate arrived. He was in a very strange mood, kind
of tense with excitement. He was very impatient to open the box,
as was I, to see if the contents had arrived safely. So we came down
here and cut the metal strips and unscrewed the top of the
wooden crate. Initially, all we saw was foam board, as the object
had been extremely well packed. When the top piece of foam
board was removed as I will do now, this is what I saw." James
insinuated his fingers between the rough wood and the packing
material and lifted the latter.

Jack leaned forward. The light in the basement was not the
best, but he could plainly see a tarnished, rectangular stone with
a flat, scratch-covered surface. He wasn't impressed. He'd expected
something eye-catching like a gilded cup, or a statue, or maybe a
heavy gold box. "What is it?" Jack asked.

"It's an ossuary. Around the time of Christ, give or take a
hundred years, Jewish burial practices in Palestine involved putting corpses in cavelike tombs for a year or longer to permit the
body to decay. After that the family would return, collect the
bones, and place them in a limestone box of varying size and
decoration, depending how wealthy the family was. The box is
called an ossuary."

"Wasn't there a controversy recently about an ossuary that
supposedly had an inscription saying James, son of Joseph, brother
of Jesus."

"Absolutely. In fact, there were some recently discovered ossuaries with inscriptions claiming they contained the remains of
Jesus Christ and his immediate family. Of course, the whole troublesome incident was proved to be pure chicanery by some un-

scrupulous forgers. Thousands of first-century ossuaries have been found over the last twenty years as a result of the building boom in Jerusalem. It's hard not to find ossuaries when you dig in that city. I am confident this ossuary here will turn out to be a similar fake, as to whose relics, if any, are supposed to be inside."

"Whose remains are supposedly involved?" Jack asked curiously.

"Holy Mary, Mother of Christ, Mother of God, Mother of the Church, second only to Jesus himself, the most holy person to have walked this earth," James said, finding it difficult to get it all out.

For almost a full minute Jack and James stared at each other. Jack's disappointment concerning the contents of the box edged upward. He wasn't interested in a box of bones; treasure held more allure for him than historical objects. James, on the other hand, was overwhelmed. Simply talking about the supposed contents only made him more desperate to find a solution.

"Okay," Jack said at length. He broke off staring at James and his brimming eyes and looked back down at the lid of the ossuary. He'd expected James to continue, but the man was too distraught to speak.

"I must be missing something here. If there are lots of ossuaries and lots of forgers, which it seems there are, what's the problem?"

James had his lips pressed together, and a single tear fell in a rivulet down his right cheek. Without speaking, his eyes momentarily closed, he raised his palms toward Jack and gently waved them in a narrow arc. He shook his head, as if apologizing for not being able to explain his feelings. A moment later, he gestured for Jack to follow him.

Upstairs, as they passed back though the kitchen, Mrs. Steinbrenner took one look at His Eminence and instantly recognized his emotional state. Although she didn't say anything, she glared at Jack, whom she suspected was the source of her boss's tears.

James took the seat at the head of the dining table and gestured for Jack to take the one to his right. Between them was the vegetable platter. The moment they pulled themselves to the table Mrs. Steinbrenner appeared with a large tureen in her hands. While the intimidating woman ladled out the soup, an excellent eggplant bisque, Jack kept his eyes focused on his bowl.

When the housekeeper finished serving and had closed the swinging door to the kitchen behind her, James used his cloth napkin to blot his eyes, which had become significantly red. "I sincerely apologize for my maudlin behavior," he said.

"That's okay," Jack responded quickly.

"No, it isn't," James answered, "not in front of a guest, and especially not in front of a good friend I am about to ask for a serious favor."

"I disagree," Jack said. "This shows me how important this is to you, whatever it is you're going to ask me."

"You are too kind," James said. "Now permit me to say grace."

After James had voiced his final amen, he glanced up at Jack and said, "Please start. I'm sorry we don't have much time, as I mentioned earlier, but I have to be at Gracie Mansion at two p.m."

Jack picked up the heaviest silver soup spoon he'd ever had the opportunity to use and took a taste of his soup. It was sublime.

"She's a good cook. Not the most pleasant personality, but definitely a good cook."

Jack nodded, glad that James had recovered from his emotional outburst.

"As I said, I believe the ossuary downstairs will eventually be proved to be just another unfortunate forgery. I say 'unfortunate' because before it is proved to be a forgery, it can cause a good deal of harm to the Church, its followers, and to me personally. The problem is that proving it a fake is not going to be easy and may ultimately rely mostly on faith."

Jack silently acknowledged that in science, proof that relied on faith was hardly proof at all. In fact, it was an oxymoron.

"The biggest problem we face is that the ossuary was discovered by one of the most renowned archaeologists in the world."

"You mean Shawn?"

"Yes, I mean Shawn. After we opened the crate and looked at the top of the ossuary, Shawn pointed out two things. Among all those scratches are a date and a name. The date is in Roman numerals and is 815 AUC, which in a Gregorian calendar is AD 62."

"What the hell is AUC?" Jack asked, then blushed. "Excuse my French."

"I remember your French, as you call it, was significantly more colorful in college. No need to apologize, I'm as immune to it now as I was then. But AUC stands for ab urbe condita, referring to the supposed date of the founding of Rome. In other words, it's a date appropriate to such a find. And when the date is combined with the name, it becomes truly disturbing—the name Maryam, written in Aramaic characters, which when translated into Hebrew is Miriam or the English Mary."

"So Shawn is convinced the ossuary contains the bones of the Virgin Mary, Jesus' mother?"

"Precisely. Shawn is an extremely credible witness and can prove that this ossuary has not seen the light of day since the time it was interred almost two thousand years ago. He found it nestled next to the tomb of Saint Peter. Furthermore, the ossuary is sealed. All other ossuarys as far as I know have not been sealed."

"Wasn't Mary a common name back then? Why does he believe it's the Mary who was Jesus' mother?"

"Because Shawn has discovered an authentic second-century letter that claims the ossuary contains the bones of Jesus' mother. And it was the letter that led Shawn to the bones."

Jack raised his eyebrows. "I see your point. But what about the letter? Couldn't that be fake?"

"Although it is somewhat tautological, finding the ossuary where the letter says it will be proves the authenticity of the letter, and vice versa. Both are such extraordinary finds that that fact alone will convince people that the bones in the ossuary are the Holy Mother's."

Jack thought about the issue while using a pair of silver tongs to help himself to some of the raw vegetables that had been waiting on the table. He could see James's point. But then he had another idea. "Did you see the letter?"

"I did. I saw it yesterday."

"Who wrote it?"

"A bishop of Antioch called Saturninus."

"I never heard of him."

"He's a known figure, not very well known, but he was a real person."

"Who did he write to?"

"Another bishop, a bishop of Alexandria, named Basilides."

"I never heard of him, either."

"Do you know anything about Gnosticism?"

"Can't say I do. It's a subject that doesn't come up often at the morgue."

"I'm sure not," James said with a laugh. "It was a serious heresy in the early Christian church, and Basilides was an early leader."

"Would Saturninus have had any reason to lie to Basilides?"

"Clever idea," James said, "but unfortunately no."

"Does Saturninus take responsibility for actually burying the ossuary?"

"Most definitely."

"Does he say how he came to have the relics or who gave them to him?"

"He does, and you are cleverly enough coming to what I think is the weakest point in the chain of custody, so to speak. Do you know who Simon Magus was?"

"You have me there, too. Never heard of him."

"He is the archvillain of the Bible's New Testament, a true scoundrel who tried to buy Saint Peter's healing powers. From him we get the word *simony.*"

Jack smiled inwardly when he realized that Jesus Christ was the most famous provider of alternative medicine, and Saint Peter was the second.

"Simon Magus is also considered by some to be one of the earliest Gnostics," James continued. "And Saturninus, who was much younger, worked for him, helping him with his magic. So to prove whether the bones in the ossuary are the Holy Mother's, which they certainly are not, it all depends on Simon Magus, perhaps the most notoriously poor witness of all."

"There's another way," Jack said. "A particularly straightforward way."

"Which is?" James asked eagerly.

"Have an anthropologist check the bones, if there are bones, and first make sure they are human. If they are human, then make sure they are female, and if they are female, check whether or not the woman had given birth. We know Mary had at least one child."

"An anthropologist can tell those things?"

"A definite yes on the first two points: whether or not the bones are human and whether or not they are female. It is a little less certain on whether one can tell if the woman was parous or not. If the changes one looks for are present, the woman definitely had children, and generally, the more prominent, the more children. However, if they are not there, you cannot say with certainty the woman didn't have, perhaps, one child."

"Fascinating," James said. "Especially with the idea the bones could be male. If they are, the nightmare would be over."

"Have you seen the bones?" Jack asked.

"No. Shawn and his wife were only interested in making sure the ossuary had not been broken during transit. They did not want to open the ossuary itself, since it is sealed with wax. Both are concerned, as you might imagine, with the state of the contents after two thousand years, and didn't want to expose them to air and moisture without having laboratory facilities available. Have you met Shawn's wife?"

"Maybe," Jack said. "The last time I saw him was two years ago, and considering the speed with which he goes through wives, I don't know if I'm current. I've seen Shawn only twice in the fourteen years I've been here in the city. In that time I know he's been married and divorced at least twice."

"Totally shameless," James remarked. "But not totally out of character. Remember how many girlfriends he had in college?"

"Do I ever," Jack said. "I remember one weekend when two showed up. One was supposed to be for Friday night and the other for Saturday, but the Saturday one mistakenly thought it was for the whole weekend. Fortunately, I was able to help out. I ended up entertaining the Friday-night choice, and we hit it off."

"Shawn's current wife is named Sana."

"Oh, yes," Jack said, remembering. "I have met her. She was very shy and retiring. All she did was cling to his arm and dreamily stare into his face. It was a little embarrassing."

"She's changed. She's a molecular biologist who has gained a lot of notice in her field. She's now a scientist at the medical school up at Columbia University. I think she's really blossomed since they first met. I have a sense that the marriage won't last too long, given Shawn's preference for adoring, docile women. Socially, he's never going to be content. I'm no expert, but I don't think he's capable of being faithful."

"Maybe so," Jack said. He'd never admired Shawn's behavior in regard to women, but he'd never commented on it. But it had always been a bone of contention between James and Shawn.

"How is your relationship with Shawn?" James asked.

Jack shrugged. "As I mentioned, I've seen him only twice since I moved here to New York City. He was nice enough to invite me to his home for dinner on those two occasions. I suppose I should have returned the gesture, but I've become a bit of a hermit these days."

"You alluded to that on the phone," James said. "Would you care to explain?"

"No. Maybe some other time," Jack said, trying to avoid thinking about his first family or his second. "Why don't you tell me how I can help you? I assume it involves the box downstairs."

James took a deep breath to steel himself. "You are right, of course," James began. "It does involve the box downstairs. What do you think would happen if a significant percentage of people came to believe, even briefly, that the ossuary downstairs actually contained the bones of Mary, the Mother of God?"

"I suppose it would disappoint a lot of people," Jack said.

"That's a lot more diplomatic than I would have expected."

"And less sarcastic than I've been of late."

"Does that have anything to do with me being a cardinal?"

"Obviously," Jack said.

"I'm sorry you feel that way. Old friends should feel able to be themselves."

"Maybe if such meetings became a habit. For now, why don't you tell me what you think would happen?"

"It would be a disaster for the Church, at a time it can least afford it. We are still suffering from the damage caused by the priest molestation scandal. It has been a true tragedy for the people involved, and for the Church itself. So too would the belief that the Blessed Virgin Mary had not been assumed body and soul into heaven as promulgated ex cathedra by Pope Pius the Twelfth with his *Munificentissimus Deus* in 1950. This promulgation has been the only use of the solemn declaration of papal infallibility declared by Vatican One on July eighteenth, 1870. Shawn's claim that he has found the bones of the Most Holy Mother of God would seriously threaten and undermine the authority of the Church. It would be a disaster bar none."

"I'll take your word for it," Jack said, watching James's face turn increasingly red.

"I'm being very serious," James declared, afraid Jack wasn't really getting the message. "As a direct religious descendant from Saint Peter himself, when the pope speaks ex cathedra on faith or morals he is making divine revelation as the Holy Spirit works in the body of the Church as *sensus fidelium.*"

"Okay, okay," Jack conceded. "I understand how Shawn claiming Mary did not rise up to heaven when the Church has declared she had would be a serious blow to the Catholic faith."

"It would be an equally disastrous blow to those who venerate Mary almost as they do Jesus Christ. You have no idea of her position among the Catholic faithful, who would be cast adrift if Shawn has his way."

"I can see that, too," Jack said, sensing that James was working himself into a minor frenzy.

"I can't let that happen!" James snapped, slapping his palm on the table hard enough to cause the dishes to rattle. "I can't let that happen, both for the Church's sake and my own!"

Jack raised his eyebrows. Suddenly, he saw his friend as he was back in college, sensing James's beneficence and concern about the bones in the basement was based on more than the Church's well-being. James was also a skilled politician. Though Jack had doubted his chances, James ran for class president in college. Jack had underestimated James: With an innate sense of people's inner needs, fears, and sensitivities, plus his ability to flatter, James was a natural. He was also driven, pragmatic, and shrewd. Everyone liked him, and to Jack and Shawn's amazement, he won the election. Jack had every reason to believe it was these same qualities that helped James rise to the exalted level of cardinal.

"An added problem," James continued, "is that that clever Shawn has me by the balls."

Jack's head snapped back as if he'd been slapped. Such language coming from a Roman Catholic cardinal was completely unexpected. Of course, he'd heard this all the time in their college days.

Catching Jack's reaction, James guffawed. "Oh! Sorry!" he said. He then purposefully echoed Jack by following up with "Pardon my French."

Jack laughed, realizing he had been guilty of stereotyping his old friend, who, despite outward appearances, was still the same person he'd been. "Touché," he said, still smiling.

"Let me put it this way," James continued. "By sending the ossuary from the Vatican to me with my name as the sender, he avoided customs *and* took advantage of my covetousness, since I was so quick to imagine it was a birthday present. By accepting the crate and signing for it, I have become, if you will, an accessory. I should have refused the carton so that it would have ended up back at the Vatican. As it is, whatever havoc it will evoke, I will be personally implicated, since it was my involvement that got him access to Peter's tomb in the first place. I am in this hook, line, and sinker."

"Why don't you just call the media and confess right off the bat that you had no idea what you were signing for?"

"Because the damage is done. I am, as I said, an accessory. Besides, Shawn would go to the media himself and accuse me and the Church of trying to prevent the object from reaching the light of day, saying we've denied him the chance to examine the contents. That would sound like a conspiracy, which to many people would be akin to proving the object's authenticity. No, I cannot do that! I have to let Shawn do whatever he is going to do, which he believes will take a month if there are no documents to deal with, or up to three months if there are documents in with the bones, if there are bones. I hope there aren't. That would make everything easier."

"Are there usually documents in ossuaries?" Jack asked. He found his interest in the contents growing.

"Usually not, but according to the letter from Saturninus to Basilides, this ossuary contains the only known copy of a Gospel of Simon Magus, along with the bones."

"Now, that would be an interesting manuscript, from what you've mentioned of the guy," Jack said. "Bad guys are always more interesting than the good guys."

"I will have to contest that."

"Okay, so, what are you going to do and what is my role?"

"Shawn and Sana want to keep the ossuary secret until they complete their work. And I forgot to mention this, but Sana intends to try to salvage some DNA."

"I suppose that's possible. Biologists were able to extract DNA from the much more ancient ice man found in the Alps in 1991. It's been estimated that mummy was more than five thousand years old."

"Well, to keep their respective labs ignorant of what they are doing, they need someplace to work where they can keep their work a secret. It's an idea I'm in full agreement with. I suggested the OCME's new forensic DNA facility. I thought of it because I'd gone to its grand opening along with the mayor and a few other city officials. Do you think that is possible, and could you arrange it?"

Jack gave the idea some thought. The building had been built with more space than was currently needed, a rare incidence of foresight on the side of city planners. Jack knew that the chief had supported other research projects from NYU and Bellevue Hospital, so why not this one? It would also be good public relations, which would please Bingham to no end. "I think it is definitely possible," he said, "and I'll talk with the chief as soon as I get back to the OCME. But is that all you want me to do?"

"No, I'd like you to help me try to change Shawn and Sana's opinion on publishing their work. I want to make them realize how much harm will come from it by appealing to their better judgment. I know Shawn is a good man, even if he's somewhat vain and self-indulgent."

Jack shook his head. "If what I remember about Shawn's desire for fame and fortune is still true, it's going to be a tough sell. Changing his mind is going to be nearly impossible. This is the kind of story that will take him out of the dry archaeological journals and catapult him into *Newsweek, Time,* and *People.*"

"I know it will be difficult, but we must do it. We must try."

Although Jack wasn't optimistic about changing Shawn's mind, which he imagined was set in stone, he had no idea about Sana.

"There's one other thing," James added. "Whether or not you're willing to help, I must ask you to keep this in the strictest confidence. You cannot tell a soul, not even your wife. At the moment, the only people who know of the ossuary's supposed contents are the Daughtrys, me, and you. It must stay that way. Can I have your word on that?"

"Of course," said Jack, though he knew he would have a difficult time not telling Laurie. It was a truly fascinating story.

"Oh, dear God," James voiced after glancing at his watch. "I must leave at once for Gracie Mansion."

They stood, and James enveloped Jack in a rapid hug. As Jack returned the gesture, he could feel how plump his friend had become. Jack vowed to take him to task at a more opportune moment. Jack could also hear a slight wheeze when James breathed.

"So, you are willing to help in this most unfortunate episode?" James asked, as he snapped up his skullcap that he'd put on the chair to his left and returned it to his head.

"Of course," Jack said, "but can I have permission to tell my wife? She's the soul of discretion."

James stopped abruptly. "Absolutely not," he said, staring into Jack's eyes. "I don't know your wife, although I do hope to meet her. But I'm sure she has a friend whom she trusts as much as you trust your wife. I must insist you not breathe a word of this to her or anyone. Can you promise me that?"

"You have my word," Jack responded quickly. He felt impaled by James's glare.

"Good," James responded simply. He turned and continued out of the room.

As if by magic, Father Maloney appeared near the foyer and handed His Eminence his coat and a stack of phone messages. While James struggled into his coat, Jack mentioned that his bomber jacket was in the study. Without a word, the priest quickly disappeared.

"I'll hear from you soon?" James asked Jack.

"I'll talk to the chief as soon as I get back to the OCME," Jack assured him.

"Excellent! Here are the numbers for my cell and my private line here at the residence," James said, handing Jack his personal business card. "Either call or e-mail as soon as you have Dr. Bingham's response. I'll be happy to talk with him directly, as need be."

He gripped Jack's forearm and gave what Jack felt was a pathetic squeeze.

Father Maloney returned with Jack's coat, bowing as Jack thanked him.

The next moment they were out the door. A shiny black limousine idled on the street, the liveried driver holding open the rear door. The archbishop climbed in, and the door was shut behind him. The car pulled away into the uptown traffic.

The next thing Jack heard over the sound of traffic was the slamming of the formidable residence's door and the metallic and final click of its brass hardware. Jack looked back. Father Maloney was gone. Jack returned the glance at the quickly disappearing limo and wondered what life would be like being the archbishop and having a bevy of assistants to fulfill his every need. At first it sounded tempting, as it would certainly make life more efficient, but then he quickly realized he wouldn't want to feel responsible for the emotional and spiritual well-being of millions of people, as he had a difficult enough time with one.

17

Jack unlocked his bike and tried to beat the rain as he headed downtown. He almost did, but just before he was about to pull into one of the OCME loading bays, the heavens opened and drenched him.

Jack hung his damp jacket in his office and descended to the first floor to stand like a penitent in front of Mrs. Sanford's desk. When employees showed up uninvited, she usually ignored them, as if she was so busy she couldn't even look up. Jack imagined it was her way of demanding respect, which she thought she deserved, since she'd been there guarding Bingham since before the flood. There was no sense trying to fight her. She wouldn't even let Bingham know that you were there until she felt like it.

After several minutes, she finally glanced up at Jack and did a fake mild double take.

"I need to see the chief," Jack said, not fooled in the slightest.

"What about?"

"It's personal," Jack said, with a slight smile of satisfaction. He wouldn't be intimidated by her nosiness. "Is the chief in?"

"He is, but he's on the phone and has a call waiting," she said with satisfaction. She tilted her head toward her phone, where a light blinked insistently. "I'll let him know you are waiting."

"That's all I can ask," Jack said, continuing the game.

Jack took a seat on a bench directly across from Mrs. Sanford's desk. It reminded him of all the times he had to wait to see the principal in middle school. He'd been labeled an incessant talker.

While he waited, Jack mulled over the unexpected conversation with James and found himself intensely curious about what was in the ossuary, and if there were bones and some sort of manuscript, how the episode would play out. Even though he initially was sure James wouldn't be able to convince Shawn not to publish his findings, Jack remembered he'd misjudged James in the past. And Shawn had been raised a Catholic by two very devout parents, both of whom served in lay societies and who had even tried to talk Shawn into the priesthood. Though no longer a practicing Catholic; Shawn was very knowledgeable about the Catholic Church, and might be more respectful of the potential problems he might cause by denigrating the concept of papal infallibility and, to a degree, the reputation of the Virgin Mary herself. He certainly knew more than Jack. So Jack was no longer sure what the final outcome was going to be.

"Dr. Bingham is ready to see you now," Mrs. Sanford said, interrupting Jack's thoughts.

"Have you changed your mind about wanting to take a leave of absence?" Bingham asked when Jack entered his office and before Jack had a chance to speak. He peered at Jack over the tops of his wire-rimmed glasses. "If so, the answer is yes. Please take care of that child of yours! I've been worried sick since you told us about him."

"Thank you for your concern. But he is in excellent hands with Laurie in charge, I can assure you. In comparison to her, I'm a basket case."

"Somehow I find that hard to believe, but I'll take your word for it."

How wrong you are, Jack thought to himself. Out loud he said, "I know you are busy, but the archbishop requests a favor."

Bingham sat back in his chair, gazing at Jack in shock. "You really went to the archbishop's for lunch?"

"Yeah, why not?" Jack asked. Having known the man for so long, visiting him didn't seem so special.

"'Why not?'" Bingham questioned. "He's one of the most powerful and important people in the city. Why the hell did he invite you to lunch? Was it something to do with your boy?"

"Heavens, no!"

"Then what? If you don't mind me asking. I suppose it's none of my business."

"Not at all," Jack said. "We are old friends of sorts. We went to college together, and were quite close. We graduated together along with another fellow who also lives here in the city."

"That's extraordinary," Bingham said. He was suddenly self-conscious at his overreaction to celebrity, but as a politically oriented person, he was already thinking about whether there was a way to take advantage of Jack's friendship with the archbishop. "Do you and His Eminence get together often?"

Jack smiled. "If you call every thirty-one years often, then yes, we get together often."

"Oh, it's like that," Bingham said, mildly disappointed. "It's still surprising to think of the two of you having a shared past. Are you serious about his asking for a favor? Excuse the pun, but what in heaven's name is it?"

"He humbly requests the use of lab space in the OCME DNA building."

"Now, that is an unexpected request from the most powerful prelate in the country."

"Actually, it's not for him but rather for our mutual college friend, although he will consider it a favor to him if you grant the request."

"Well, we do have quite an excess of lab space, and I certainly cannot see it as detrimental extending a hand to the archbishop, but who is this friend, and is he a competent lab scientist? We can't have just anybody working over there, whether he knows the archbishop or not."

"I'm not sure if he is a lab scientist or not," Jack admitted, "but his wife is a DNA expert from Columbia University's College of Physicians and Surgeons."

"That constitutes expertise," Bingham said. "I'd also like to have some idea of what they'll be doing and how long they'll need."

"The archbishop's guess is around two months."

"And what is it exactly that they plan to do?"

"The husband, whose name, by the way, is Shawn Daughtry, is a Ph.D. in Near Eastern archaeology and biblical studies. He has found what is called an *ossuary*. Do you know what that is?"

"Of course I know what an ossuary is," Bingham snapped in his signature impatient style.

"I didn't," Jack admitted. "It's rather unique in that it is sealed, and they are hoping to isolate some ancient DNA. The reason they would like to use our lab is to keep the project secret until they finish analyzing all the ossuary's contents, which will supposedly include a document or two in addition to the bones."

"I've never heard of an ossuary with a document of any kind."

"Well," Jack said, "that's the story I've been told."

"All right," Bingham said. "Considering we're doing it as a favor for the archbishop, I'll allow it, provided Naomi Grossman, the DNA department head, doesn't have an objection."

"Fair enough," Jack responded. "I'll thank you for my friends." Jack turned toward the door, but before he could exit, Bingham called out to him, "By the way, how's that case where the tour doctor forgot to bag the hands?"

"Fine," Jack said. "There's no way that bullet was fired by the victim. It was definitely a homicide. The hands could not have had any gunpowder residue on them."

"Good," Bingham said. "Have it on my desk ASAP! The family is going to be pleased."

Jack was about to leave for the second time when he stopped himself and again turned back to Bingham. "Chief," he called out, "can I ask you a personal question?"

Without looking up, Bingham said, "Make it quick."

"Do you use a chiropractor?"

"Yeah, and I don't want to hear any grief about it. I already know your feelings."

"Understood," Jack said. He turned and walked out of the office.

Despite Bingham's final body blow to his alternative-medicine crusade, meaning Jack could not expect support from the front office, Jack felt content as he headed up to his office to retrieve his jacket. He now had another project to keep his mind busy. With Bingham on board for the Daughtrys, he couldn't imagine Naomi Grossman turning down the request, especially since she was already permitting three other research groups to use the facilities.

He grabbed his jacket and an umbrella, anxious to connect with Naomi and get the lab space set up. Lost in thought, he literally bumped into Chet coming out of the elevator.

"Hey, what's the hurry?" Chet asked, nearly dropping the tray of microscope slides he was carrying.

"I could ask you the same thing," Jack answered.

"I was about to stop by," Chet said. "I've got some more names and accession numbers for those old VAD cases."

"Hold up on looking for more VAD cases," Jack said. "My interest has cooled."

"How come?"

"Let's just say I've run into pretty much the same response as you did back when you looked into the issue. My sense is that the public's reaction to alternative medicine is almost a religious thing. People have faith in alternative medicine because they want to believe. They can dismiss as irrelevant any proof that it doesn't work or might be dangerous."

"Okay," Chet said. "Suit yourself. If you change your mind, let me know."

"Thanks, buddy," Jack said, getting on the elevator.

Jack emerged outside back into the downpour he'd almost missed coming back from his meeting with James. With only a travel umbrella, by the time he reached the DNA building he was soaked from mid-thigh down.

Naomi Grossman's office was on a high floor. As Jack approached Naomi's secretary, he worried he should have called first. Naomi was the director of the largest single department at the OCME. DNA science had come into its own, thanks to the enormous contributions it made to law enforcement and identification.

"Is Dr. Grossman available?" Jack asked.

"She is," the secretary said. "And you are?"

"Dr. Jack Stapleton," Jack said, relieved at Naomi's availability.

"Nice to meet you," the secretary said, extending her hand. "I'm Melanie Stack." She was young and friendly, especially compared to those ancient secretaries in Bingham's office. Instead of being confrontational, she was open and eager to help. She was dressed in an attractive, youthful style, with her radiant long hair pulled back from her healthy, smiling face with a barrette.

To Jack, Melanie was a typical representative of the OCME

DNA building. Most of the people working there were young and energetic, and seemed to be generally happy and appreciative of their jobs. DNA was a new science with immense potential, and it was appropriate that it was centered in a bright, brand-new building. In many ways, Jack regretted that he didn't work there, too.

"Let me check with Dr. Grossman," Melanie said, pushing back from her desk.

As Melanie disappeared for a moment, Jack made eye contact with the other secretaries. Each one returned his smile with one of her own. For Jack the office was a breath of fresh air and optimism despite the rain pattering against the glass.

"Dr. Grossman can see you," Melanie said, reappearing in the blink of an eye.

Jack stepped into the inner corner office with a stunning view over the East River. Naomi was seated behind a large mahogany desk with an in basket that reminded Jack of his own. Like most everyone else in the building, Naomi was relatively young, perhaps mid-thirties. She had an oval face framed by a nimbus of remarkably curly hair. Her dark eyes were bright, and her expression was cheerful but questioning, as if her obviously sharp mind was always a bit dubious about what she was hearing.

"What a nice surprise!" Naomi said as Jack approached her desk. "To what do we owe this honor?"

" 'Honor'?" Jack questioned with a chuckle. "I wish I had your facility to make people feel good."

"But it is an honor. We're here to help you medical examiners. We're just an adjunct to the process."

Jack chuckled anew. "Let's not carry it too far. With the rapid advances in DNA science, I think we'll soon be working for you. This time, though, I'm here to ask you a favor."

"Ask away."

Jack quickly went through the same spiel he'd given Bingham, mentioning the archbishop, the ossuary, and its expected contents but nothing about the Virgin Mary.

"That's utterly fascinating," Naomi said when Jack finished. "Tell me the wife's name?"

"Sana Daughtry."

"I've heard of her," Naomi said. "She's really making a name for herself in the mitochondrial DNA field. I certainly wouldn't mind having her work here for a time, and the project itself sounds intriguing, especially if it turns out that there are documents which might prove the body's identity. But why don't they do their work up at Columbia? Their facility might not be as new as ours, but I'm confident it is just as good."

"For privacy purposes. They want time, I presume, to complete their studies before anyone knows about the find. And you know how it is in the academic world: Everybody knows everyone else's business."

"Truer words have never ever been spoken. They won't have to worry about any leaks here. Have you spoken with Dr. Bingham?"

"I just came from his office, and he's on board, provided you have no objections. And though he didn't say so directly, I'm sure he likes the idea of having the archdiocese beholden to the OCME."

Naomi laughed in a way that was infectious enough to bring a smile to Jack's face. "I wouldn't put it past him, given he's such a political animal. But I shouldn't cast aspersions. If not for him, I wouldn't be sitting in this grand building."

"So, you're okay with this?" Jack asked.

"Absolutely."

"When can they start?" Jack asked. "I have to confess from the moment I first heard about this, I've been dying of curiosity about the contents of the ossuary myself."

"It's tantalizing," Naomi agreed. "Whenever the Daughtrys

want to start is fine with me. We still have plenty of lab space lying fallow."

"How about tomorrow? Is the lab open on weekends?"

"Absolutely, although at a skeleton-staff level. But we have numerous projects that need to be looked after on a daily basis, so we're open twenty-four-seven."

"I'll let them know. I don't even know if they want to start so quickly, and perhaps I'm guilty of projecting my impatience onto them. But if they do want to start tomorrow, how would we get the ossuary into the building?"

"They could bring it through the front door if they so desire. How big is it, do you know?"

"I'm not sure, but I'd estimate roughly two feet long and one foot wide and deep."

"It could fit through the front door without a problem, but there's also a loading dock on the Twenty-sixth Street side, where most normal deliveries are made. Since tomorrow's a Saturday, we'd have to make arrangements in advance."

"The front door will be fine," Jack said. "It all depends on them. In the meantime, would you mind showing me the lab area they will be using? I can help them get set up."

A few moments later they were on the eighth floor, which was one of the floors devoted to laboratory space.

"How does the building function?" Jack asked. Though he'd toured the building before, he was curious about how the department handled the number of specimens they processed.

"Specimens are received on the fifth floor," Naomi explained. "Then they work their way upstairs maintaining a chain of custody. First the samples are cleaned as a preparation for DNA extraction. The isolated DNA then heads up to the sixth floor for preamplification. When that's completed, it's on to the seventh floor for postamplification and sequencing."

"It's a type of assembly-line approach."

"Very definitely," Naomi said. "Otherwise, we'd never be able to process the number of specimens we get."

"We're now on the eighth floor," Jack said, peering into the lab space through closed but glazed doors as they walked east from the bank of elevators. Through floor-to-ceiling windows on his left he could see Bellevue Hospital. "What happens here?"

"The eighth floor is out of the assembly line," Naomi explained. "These labs are mostly for training. But in this direction toward the river are labs specifically for research projects. The pace of change in DNA science is rapid, and we have to keep up. Here's the lab the Daughtrys may use."

Naomi used a key to open the door, then handed it to Jack.

The room was constructed of white laminate plastic with bright recessed fluorescent lighting, giving it a futuristic look. There was a large center table the size of a library table. Along the east wall was desk space with cabinets above and below. On the west wall were floor-to-ceiling lockers with keys in each lock.

"What do you think?" Naomi asked.

"It's perfect!" Jack said. He peered through a glazed door on the south wall into a bio-vestibule for gowning and degowning to prevent DNA contamination. Through yet another door was the lab itself, with all the instruments necessary for extraction, amplification, and sequencing DNA. He was impressed. It was a totally self-contained laboratory.

"There are even lockers here if they're particularly paranoid," Naomi joked, pointing to the full-length cabinets. "But let them know our security in this building is very good. Which reminds me, they are going to need photo ID cards. Security downstairs can set them up tomorrow, as long as I give them the heads-up today. And they'll also have to sign a comprehensive waiver from all liability. If they do want to start tomorrow, I'll leave a copy here on the table, and I'll ask you to be sure it gets signed."

"I'll be happy to do that," Jack agreed.

"Okay, then. We're set," Naomi said. "Unless you have additional questions."

"I don't think so," Jack said. "This is a perfect setup. Shawn can work in this room with the bones and perhaps documents, and Sana has the laboratory. It couldn't be better. Thank you. If you have a couple of friends that would like to come over and do a few autopsies, let me know. I feel like I'd like to repay you in kind."

Naomi laughed. "I've heard about your sense of humor."

He thanked her again and left the building, suddenly aware that the rain had stopped. Looking up, he even saw a small but definite patch of clear sky, reminding him how quickly weather could change in New York.

Jack jogged back to the OCME. With both Bingham's and Naomi's consent, the Daughtrys' work would go ahead. With the elevators in use he used the stairs, eager to let James know that he'd been successful. Sitting down at his desk, Jack checked the time while he got out the card James had given him. It was after four o'clock. Thinking James had probably long since left the reception at Gracie Mansion, he called his direct line rather than his mobile.

"I have some good news," Jack said when he heard James's voice.

"That's a welcome relief," James replied. "Is Dr. Bingham going to allow Shawn and Sana to use his crowning-glory facility?"

"He is indeed!" Jack reported proudly. "It's a perfect situation. It's one of several completely self-contained laboratories, with space for both Shawn and Sana and all the equipment they should need. It's very private and secure. They can start tomorrow if they like."

"Praise the Lord," James said. "I spoke with Shawn not an hour ago. I told him you had agreed to intervene on his behalf as far as the lab space was concerned, and that you'd call later today to give him the news."

"You want me to call him rather than yourself?"

"I do. I think it is more appropriate. I know he wants to thank you directly for your help. That's what he said, but between you and me, I think he wants to make sure that I adequately emphasized the secrecy involved. He's as paranoid as I am about leaks."

"I don't mind telling him, especially since it's good news."

James gave Jack Shawn's office number at the museum and his home number, then said, "Let me know as soon as you and Shawn talk! I'm nervous about all this, and the more information I have, the better I'll feel because the more I think about it all, the more damage I'm afraid this could wreak on the Church, and my career."

"I'll call you right after I speak with him."

"I'd appreciate it," James said before hanging up.

Jack tried Shawn's office number but got a busy signal. Foiled for the moment, he turned to locating all the material on the teenage shooting death in Central Park, where the hands had not been bagged by the tour doctor. Jack wanted to stay on Bingham's good side, and one way was to sign out that case as soon as possible, as he had asked. Once Jack had the necessary information, he was able to complete the paperwork in less than twenty minutes and e-mail Bingham saying that he'd done so.

Trying Shawn again, he got through but instead of getting his old friend, he got Shawn's secretary. It seemed that Shawn was out of the office but was due back shortly.

Jack decided not to wait. "Can you tell me when the museum closes?" he asked the secretary. "I think I'll stop in and wait for him."

"Nine p.m., but I'll be leaving at four-thirty."

"Would you take a message for him? Please tell him Dr. Jack Stapleton is coming in for a visit. I can't make it before you leave, but I should be there before, say, four-forty-five."

After hanging up, Jack took a few minutes to straighten up his very messy office. While he did so he located the paperwork and slides on the suicide case Lou had called about. He knew the DA would be looking for it. When he was finished, he grabbed his damp bomber jacket from behind the door and his bike helmet from atop the file cabinet and was out the door.

18

The sky was clear and the sun near the western horizon when Jack emerged from the OCME and turned northward on First Avenue. The temperature had dropped to a bracing level, and his cheeks burned as he raced the traffic uptown.

At 81st Street he turned west, and soon had the Metropolitan Museum of Art directly before him.

With its tan, neoclassical façade brightly illuminated against the coal black of Central Park, the huge building momentarily took Jack's breath away. As night had now fallen, the building looked like a jewel on a square of black velvet.

Jack checked his watch. It was exactly quarter to five. Hurrying forward and up the front steps, he entered the renowned museum, asking himself why he didn't take advantage of its treasures. Somewhat guiltily, he couldn't even remember the last time he'd been there.

The huge multistory lobby was filled with people. Jack had to wait at the large oval information booth in the center of the room to talk to one of the museum's employees. When he asked for the location of Shawn Daughtry's office, he was given a map with the route drawn with a marker.

As Jack approached the office, he was pleased to see the door ajar. He walked in and found himself in an outer office with a secretary's desk. Beyond the desk was a second door, also ajar. Jack continued in and, reaching the threshold, he rapped forcefully on the jamb.

"Aha!" Shawn voiced, leaping to his feet. "Here's a sight for sore eyes. How the hell are you?"

Shawn moved toward Jack with his hand extended.

"I got your note," he added, with a smile splashed across his face. "I'm so pleased you stopped by. And look at you, you look as fit as you did the last time we were together. How do you do it?"

"Mostly street basketball," Jack said, a bit taken aback by Shawn's exuberance.

"I should follow your example, buddy," Shawn said. He leaned back and stuck out his already protruding gut, patting himself as if proud of it.

"So, how long's it been?"

"I don't remember exactly," Jack admitted. He glanced around the spacious office whose windows looked out on Fifth Avenue. A number of early Christian artifacts sat on a large rectangular center table. An entire wall of bookshelves was filled with an impressive collection of art books. The far wall was dominated by an enormous dark green leather couch.

"Beautiful office," Jack remarked, thinking of his own tiny cubicle.

"Before I say anything else," Shawn began, "I want to thank you for being willing to help in this affair. It truly means a lot to me, for many reasons, but mostly because I think this extraordinary find is going to define my career."

"I'm happy to do it," Jack said, wondering what Shawn would

think if he knew that Jack was doing it as much for himself as for Shawn. Being involved in Shawn's project was a hundred times more absorbing than investigating alternative medicine, the results of which people didn't want to hear.

"What's the bottom line? Have you had a chance to ask your chief about lab space?"

"I did. There's no problem. You and your wife will have to sign a comprehensive liability waiver, but that's it. No one has even spoken of any charges."

Shawn clapped his hands loud enough to make Jack jump. "All right!" he cried, before placing his palms together, closing his eyes, and tilting his head up at the ceiling in a crude mime of praying. A moment later he leaned forward and assumed a serious expression. "Jack," he said. "I'm thrilled you got us permission to use OCME lab space, but there is one thing I do want to talk to you about. It's an important issue, and one that His over-the-top Holiness said he'd already mentioned. I'd just like to emphasize the fact that we want this whole project to stay completely secret, especially as it pertains to the Virgin Mary. Are you okay with that? If what we expect is in the ossuary, we want to be able to break the news only after we've totally finished our respective studies. I want to be entirely sure of the facts when we make the announcement."

"James was very clear about the secrecy issues. In fact, he's probably more interested in secrecy than you. I don't know if you are aware of this, to the extent that you should be, but he means to launch a serious campaign to convince you never to publish anything at all about the Virgin Mary's connection to the bones. I believe he's already mentioned to you that he's totally convinced this is an elaborate fake: a first-century fake but a fake nevertheless, which he is certain you will learn eventually, as a consequence of your investigations."

Shawn slapped the surface of the desk with open palms, put his head back, and let out a guffaw. When he'd regained control of himself, he shook his head in disbelief. "Isn't that typical of James? I spent four years arguing with him about the abuses of organized religion, including papal infallibility, and now that I'm closing in on evidence to refute it, he wants to deny my use of it. What a joke."

"He's worried it might have a tremendously negative effect on the Church, undermining clerical authority and the reputation of the Virgin," Jack said. "He's also worried that he'll be considered an accomplice because of how you tricked him into signing for the ossuary as well as his being responsible for your access to Saint Peter's tomb. I think he believes his career could be over."

"As far as his being responsible for access, he's correct. But no one is going to blame him for that. This is five years after the fact, and I did produce the definitive work on Saint Peter's tomb, which was the reason the access was granted originally. It's the Vatican's fault that the access has remained on the books. As far as signing for the crate, he did that entirely on his own accord. I didn't trick him. Personally, I suspect he believed he was getting a gift, a decision made entirely on his own. I never said anything about the crate containing a gift."

"Well, I'm not going to get between you two guys," Jack said, not wishing to take sides. "You're going to have to work it out yourselves. I just wanted you to know his mind-set."

"Thanks for warning me," Shawn said with a grumble.

"I have a question for you," Jack said, wishing to go on to another issue.

"Ask away."

"When do you want to start?"

"As soon as possible."

"How about tomorrow around eight? I have to meet you to usher you through some details."

"Fine with me, but let me give Sana a quick call, if you don't mind waiting."

"Not at all," Jack said, and meant it. As usual, he was reluctant to go home for fear of what he'd find. Of course, he didn't like the feeling and didn't like himself for feeling it.

Shawn reached Sana at the medical school. She'd gone in that day to try to salvage some of the ongoing studies her graduate-school assistants were trying to keep afloat. It sounded as if things had not gone well in her absence. Even Jack could hear the stridency of her voice as Shawn held the receiver away from his ear. Shawn finally got a word in and told Sana the plan.

He listened intently and soon held up his thumb for Jack's benefit.

"All right!" Shawn said, hanging up. "Eight it is. Where will we meet you?"

"In the lobby of the DNA building," Jack said. "What about the ossuary?"

"Sana and I will stop at the residence and pick it up on the way."

"I have to admit," Jack said, "I'm wildly curious to see what is in the ossuary. You really think there are bones and documents in there?"

"Very confident," Shawn said. "And if you think you are curious, you cannot imagine how curious I feel. My wife had to literally talk me out of opening it the moment we got it back to the hotel in Rome."

"What about the letter? Do you have it here?"

"Absolutely. Would you like to see it?"

"I would," Jack said.

Shawn retrieved a large volume from the bookcase and placed it on the central library table.

"I used this photography book of Egyptian monuments to get the letter out of Egypt. I'll have the letter's pages conserved, but for now it's keeping them flat."

Shawn exposed the first page of the letter.

"It looks like Greek," Jack said, bending over the text.

"It looks like Greek because it is Greek," Shawn said with a condescending chuckle.

"I thought it was going to be in Aramaic or Latin," Jack said.

"This is not what we call Attic, or classical, Greek but Koine Greek, which was the language of the western Mediterranean during imperial Roman times."

"Can you read it?"

"Of course I can read it," Shawn said, taking mild offense. "But it's rather poorly written, which makes translating it difficult. It's easy to tell that Greek was not Saturninus's first language."

Jack straightened up. "Amazing! It's like a treasure hunt."

"I thought the same thing," Shawn said, "which is one of the reasons I went into archaeology in the first place. It seemed to me the field was one big treasure hunt. Unfortunately, that's more romantic than realistic, but finding this letter and then the ossuary has returned me to that romantic notion. Ironically enough, I feel truly blessed."

"I thought you were agnostic?"

"I still am, for the most part," Shawn said. "And you?"

"I suppose," Jack said, thinking of all his personal trials and the damage done to any religiosity he did have. To change the subject, he pointed to the letter and asked Shawn how he'd found it.

"Do you have time for the story?" Shawn asked.

"Absolutely," Jack said.

Shawn described the whole thing, beginning with an explanation of a codex and continuing on to his visit to Antica Abdul.

"It was pure luck that I stopped in the shop when I did," Shawn admitted. "Rahul was about to sell it. He has the e-mail addresses of the curators of the world's famous museums. He's in regular contact with the who's who of the field of ancient Near Eastern antiquities."

"And it's just a modest hole-in-the-wall antiquities shop in the middle of the Cairo souk?"

"That's right," Shawn agreed, "with ninety-nine percent of its inventory being modern fakes. It's more of a souvenir shop than a true antiquities shop, but it obviously does have some real relics, as I've proved on two occasions."

"So, you'd been there before?"

"I had," Shawn admitted. He told Jack about his first visit ten years earlier, when he stumbled on the piece of pottery in the window. "You can imagine my shock," Shawn continued, "when one of my Egyptian department colleagues convinced me it was not a fake. In fact, it is on display downstairs in a prominent location in the Egyptian collection."

"Did you see the codex in the window like the pot and recognize what it was, or did he just bring it out?"

"It wasn't in the window," Shawn said with a smile, "and he didn't just bring it out. We'd talked awhile, and I guess he decided I was an okay risk. It is seriously illegal to sell such a relic in Egypt."

"Did you know it was authentic right away?"

"Absolutely."

"Was it expensive?"

"I certainly overpaid, but I was dying to get the codex back to the hotel room to see what texts it contained."

"Was the letter part of a text or just inserted into the codex?"

"Neither. It was sandwiched in between the leather covers to stiffen it, along with other scraps of paper. At first I was disappointed, because all I found in the codex were copies of texts that had been in previous codices. Then I remembered to check inside the cover. Bingo, I found the Saturninus letter."

"So the letter not only explains that the ossuary contains Mary's bones but also exactly where to locate it."

"It does indeed. I don't know if you're aware of this, but my last professional publication was called *Saint Peter's Burial Complex and Environs.* Did you happen to read it?"

"I didn't get a chance to read it," Jack commented. "I thought I'd wait for the movie."

"Okay, wise guy!" Shawn laughed. "It wasn't meant to be a bestseller, but it was meant to be the definitive work on a very complicated structure that had been under almost continual renovation for two millennia. Currently I'm probably the most knowledgeable person on the complexities of Saint Peter's tomb. From Saturninus's letter, I had a good idea of where the ossuary would be in relation to one of the tunnels dug during the tomb's last excavations.

"So, the tunnel was reasonably accessible?"

"Very much so. I knew the tunnel had not been filled in from my work at the site. My only mistake was that the ossuary was in the wall and not in the ceiling."

"It's an amazing story," Jack said. "Is it your intention to open the ossuary tomorrow?"

"You bet your life! Thanks to your arranging access to a modern lab facility."

"Would you mind if I stuck around to watch after I get you and your wife settled in the lab?"

"Not at all. We'd love to have you. In fact, if we find what we hope to find, we'll have to have a celebration tomorrow night at our house in the West Village, and you'll be invited. We'll even pressure His Holiness into joining us. It will be the Three Muske-teers all over again."

"If you find what you want to find, I'm not sure James will be in the mood to celebrate," Jack said, shaking Shawn's hand in prep-aration of leaving.

"I think we'll be able to twist his arm," Shawn said, walking Jack to the office door. "See you tomorrow for what should turn out to be a remarkable unveiling."

"Looking forward to it," Jack said. Remembering a question he'd been meaning to ask, he added, "If there are bones in the os-suary, would you want the OCME anthropologist to look at them? He's an expert on old bones, and can probably tell you some in-teresting things about them."

"Why not, provided there's no mention of whose bones they are. 'The more information we can get, the better' has always been my motto."

19

Jack took the elevator down to the museum's first floor in anticipatory excitement. Although the lobby was still as crowded as it had been earlier, Jack hardly noticed the people. Instead, he thought about how good it had been to see two of his best friends from a time in his life he'd so enjoyed, especially catching up with them as this mesmerizing narrative unfolded. Jack could not remember another occasion when he'd been more eager for time to pass and questions to be answered. The only dubious element was the history of his two friends' propensity to clash. Jack had the disturbing feeling that he'd again be called to referee a serious conflict between the two men, as he'd done in college, each steadfastly convinced of the validity of his position. Little did Jack know how prophetic and deadly his intuition would prove to be.

Jack didn't waste time riding home, thanks to the cold air. Pushing himself to generate as much body heat as possible, he rode uptown at breakneck speed. Within fifteen minutes he'd traversed the park and reached 106th Street, heading for his house, a fourth-floor walk-up that he and Laurie had recently renovated.

Directly across the street was the playground Jack had refurbished at his own expense. As he glided to a stop, he eyed the basketball court he'd had illuminated. It was covered with shiny black pools of rainwater, meaning there would be no games that night.

Hoisting his bike onto his shoulder, he climbed the eight front steps of the stoop and stepped inside. He glanced at the console table and the mirror directly above it. There was no note waiting for him to let him know if Laurie and the baby were asleep.

Jack couldn't decide if he preferred a note or not. When there was a note, he'd instantly feel lonely. When there wasn't, he'd have to gird himself from getting too emotional hearing about the invariable bad day.

"We're up here," Laurie shouted from the kitchen.

Jack felt a bit of relief, as Laurie's voice sounded less strained than usual. Perhaps it had been a good day. When it had been a bad day, Jack could always hear it in her tone.

After stashing his bike in a custom-sized front-hall closet and hanging up his leather jacket, he slipped off his shoes, put on his slippers, and climbed upstairs. As he had expected, Laurie and JJ were in the kitchen. On the surface, it looked like a normal domestic scene. JJ was on his back in the playpen, reaching for the mobile suspended above him. Except for his slightly bulging eyes and the dark circles below them, he looked like any baby. Laurie was at the sink, preparing artichokes for their evening meal. Except for her pale skin and the dark circles under her eyes that rivaled JJ's, she looked terrific. Her lustrous brown hair glinted with auburn highlights.

Noticing Jack's gaze, she said, "JJ let me take a shower! He's had a better day today than any other day this week. I feel like I've been on vacation."

"That's fabulous," Jack said.

Laurie rinsed her hands and dried them on her apron as she walked over to Jack and enveloped him in her arms. For a full minute, the husband and wife embraced, speaking volumes without words. Laurie was the first to pull back to give Jack a peck on the lips. Then she went back to the sink and the artichokes.

"How was your day?" she asked. "How's your crusade going?"

Jack thought for a moment about what to say. The day had been irritating and exhilarating. He'd gone from squabbling with Lou and Vinnie to lunching with the archbishop and meeting Shawn at the Metropolitan Museum of Art.

"Cat got your tongue?"

"It's been a full day," Jack said, but he didn't know where to go from there. His promise to James not to tell Laurie about the ossuary put him in a fix, because it was the only thing he wanted to tell her. He didn't want to revisit his embarrassing behavior with Lou and Vinnie, and if he mentioned Shawn and the museum, he'd have to bring up the ossuary.

"Well, was it good full or bad full?"

"A little of both."

Laurie leaned her hands on the edge of the sink. "So I guess you don't want to talk about your day."

"Sort of," Jack said evasively. He felt penned in. "I've kinda given up on the crusade idea."

"Why?"

"No one wants to hear criticism about alternative medicine, at least none of the people who use it, and there are a lot of people who use it. The only way I might influence their opinion is by having lots and lots of cases, which I'm not going to be able to find. I'm sure there are hundreds of cases locked up inside the OCME records, but there's no way to get at them. I'm kind of spinning my wheels. The biggest problem is that the crusade is not keeping me from obsessing about you-know-who."

"I guess I can understand, but it sounded like such a good idea when you told me about it Monday night. I'm sorry."

"Hey, it's not your fault."

"I know, but I'm still sorry. I know you need a diversion. I could use one myself."

Jack winced at Laurie's comment, exacerbating his omnipresent guilt of not sharing the burden of JJ's illness. "I can well imagine you could use one," he said. "Do you want to rethink the nurse idea so you could come back to work, maybe on a half-time basis?"

"Absolutely not!" Laurie said with an edge to her voice. "I didn't mention the issue to bring it up for discussion."

"Okay, okay," Jack repeated, getting the message loud and clear.

"Anyone say anything about JJ since you spoke to Bingham and Calvin yesterday?"

"No one except Bingham himself."

"That's good. Maybe they'll honor their word and respect our privacy."

Jack walked over to the playpen and looked down at his son. He longed to bend down and pick him up and hold him against his chest to feel his heart beat, to feel his warmth and smell his sweet smell, but he didn't dare.

There was also a more practical reason he was reluctant to pick him up—because he'd probably start to cry. Jack thought JJ's extensive bone tumors caused him tremendous pain, which seemed to be aggravated when he was picked up.

"He's been a real soldier today," Laurie said, watching Jack observe the baby. "I hope this is the start of a new trend, because this has been a tough week."

"Should I try to pick him up?" Jack asked, melting as he saw JJ smile up at him.

"Well . . ." Laurie debated. "It might be best to just let him be while he's so quiet."

"That's what I was afraid of," Jack said, relieved.

Guiltily, Jack turned away from JJ. He stepped behind Laurie and massaged her shoulders. She closed her eyes and leaned back against Jack's hands.

"I'll give you a half-hour to stop that," she purred.

"You deserve it. I'm continually amazed at your patience with JJ. And thankful, too. I don't want to beat a dead horse, but I don't think I could do it."

"You are in a different place than I am. You already lost two children."

Jack nodded. Laurie was right, but he didn't want to think about it.

"I'm sorry it rained so hard today," Laurie said. "I guess it rained out your basketball for tonight."

"It happens," Jack said, starting to feel depressed. He always looked forward to the diversion his Friday-night basketball games afforded him. To avoid obsessing on the loss, he turned his thoughts to his new diversion: the ossuary and the idea that that coming morning he and the others would learn what was inside. He suddenly then remembered he had promised James that he would call him right after seeing Shawn.

Jack gave Laurie a final squeeze. "I think I'll take a shower. What time are you planning for dinner, provided you're not interrupted?"

"As if I can plan anything." Laurie laughed good-naturedly. "Enjoy your shower and then come down. As usual, it will depend on the squirt and how long this amnesty lasts."

Climbing the stairs, Jack again marveled at Laurie's attitude. Despite everything she'd been through following JJ's diagnosis, and everything she was destined to endure, she was still capable of putting it aside and pretending everything was normal. "If only I could be so giving," Jack murmured to himself.

Inside the bathroom and still feeling a bit guilty, as if involved in some kind of conspiracy, Jack used his mobile phone to call James. He didn't want to do it in front of Laurie, concerned that doing so would elicit a blizzard of questions, all of which he wouldn't be able to answer without violating his promise.

"My savior!" James offered humorously, having seen Jack's name pop up on his LCD screen.

"Is this a good time to talk?" Jack asked softly. "Sorry I failed to call right away. In fact, I biked all the way home, which is where I am now."

"I have been saying my prayers, but He will understand if I take a break since you are one of my prayers. Tell me what happened. When is he going to open the ossuary?"

"I actually stopped in to see him at the Met. I was interested in seeing Saturninus's letter."

"What did it look like? Did it look authentic?"

"Very much so," Jack said, and then paused. He suddenly heard JJ's cry, which quickly grew louder. In a minor panic, he realized that Laurie was rapidly approaching. "Just a minute, James!" Jack pushed away from the sink, where he'd been leaning. Feeling even more guilty holding the phone, he opened the door just as Laurie was approaching with the unhappy infant. JJ was screaming, and his face was bright red.

Laurie's expression reflected her exasperation. "Change of plans," she said while gently bobbing the baby. "I'm thinking we'll have to eat takeout again. You'll have to run down to Columbus Avenue after your shower."

Jack nodded and could tell she was quizzically eyeing the cell phone in his hand. He held it up. "I'm just on a quick call to someone about tomorrow's plans."

"I can see," Laurie said. "In the bathroom?"

"Just before I was about to shower, I remembered I was supposed to call this person earlier."

"Whatever," Laurie said. "JJ and I will be lying down in the bedroom." She moved on down the hall.

"I'll be in there as soon as I finish the shower," Jack called after her.

Jack closed the door, wondering if he was going to have to explain himself more. Returning to the phone, he apologized to James.

"No apology needed," James insisted. "I'm just crushed I've been reduced to a mere someone."

"Sorry to sound so impersonal. I'll explain next time I see you."

"That sounds like a newborn."

"Four months."

"You didn't tell me. Congratulations!"

"Thank you. Now, back to Shawn and the letter. As I said, it looked authentic because it appeared very old, with edges so dark they almost looked burnt. Of course, I couldn't read any of it since it's written in Greek."

"I surely wouldn't have expected you to be able to read it," James said. "Was he happy about you obtaining permission for them to use the lab at the OCME DNA building?"

"He was thrilled."

"When are they starting?"

"Tomorrow. Actually, I'm surprised he hasn't gotten in touch with you. He told me he was going to stop by the residence and pick up the ossuary, and then meet me in front of the DNA building before eight."

"Typical Shawn," James said. "Thinking of others has never been his strong suit. I'll give him a call as soon as we hang up."

"He's extremely excited about this discovery. He sees it as his path to glory and comeuppance for the Church. My guess is that he feels strongly that if the Church is wrong in relation to the Virgin Mary, it can be wrong in other arenas."

"I agree, but I am also confident of his strong sense of ethics, despite his questionable sense of morality. Among other issues, he and I have argued endlessly about sex, which he believes is a gift to humanity in exchange for the burden of having to anticipate our death. He believes sex should be enjoyed, and he's angry at the Church for its propensity to label as sin any aspect of sex beyond a narrow interpretation of its procreative role. But he knows right from wrong in every other arena, which is why I'm confident he will realize that he cannot prove any bones inside the ossuary are those of the Virgin Mary. Saturninus's letter is certainly suggestive, but as we've discussed, it all rests on Simon Magus. Did Simon tell Saturninus the truth? No one knows, and no one will be able to know."

"What about the Gospel of Simon that Shawn expects to find in the ossuary?"

"What about it?" James asked hesitantly.

"What if it talks about this specific issue?"

"I hadn't really thought of that," James confessed. "I suppose it is a possibility. That would complicate things." There was a moment of silence. "You are supposed to be helping me, not vice versa," he added with a nervous laugh.

"Sorry," Jack said. "But consider this. Saturninus said something about Simon being disappointed that the bones didn't convey to him the healing power by themselves. That means that Simon was convinced the relics were real."

"Okay, that's enough!" James pleaded. "At this point, you're just making me feel less secure in my thinking. Even if what you say is true, there's still the issue of hearsay."

"You are reaching for a technicality when you say something like that. The ossuary will be opened tomorrow. Let's wait and see what's in it. It could be cow bones and a scroll that's pure fictional grandiosity."

"You're right," James said. "My anxiety has me envisioning the worst."

"I've asked Shawn if he would mind if I observed, and he said I was welcome. I also asked if he would like to take advantage of the OCME's new anthropology department, and he said he would, provided that no one was told the identity of the individual."

"Does that mean the bones will be able to be identified as human, and the gender determined right away?"

"If an anthropologist sees them, absolutely."

"If you are there, will you call me as soon as you can?"

"Of course! And I hope I'll be able to put your mind at rest."

"Oh, glory days! I will pray that such will be the case."

After appropriate good-byes, Jack hung up. He opened the bathroom door. JJ was still crying, more insistently than before. Once again it was going to be fast food, and a painful evening.

20

As the sun rose above the buildings to the east, it looked as if a million diamonds were scattered across Sheep Meadow in Central Park. Even with his cycling sunglasses, Jack had to squint into the dazzling glare.

He had awakened an hour earlier despite the fact that he and Laurie had been up most of the night with a very unhappy baby. For a few minutes he had watched the play of light on the bedroom ceiling, obsessing about how they were going to manage to get through the next few months until they could possibly restart JJ's treatment. With no real answers, he'd slipped from the warmth of his bed, dressed, and breakfasted on cold cereal. Leaving a note for Laurie that said simply, "Off to OCME—call me on my cell when you have the time," he'd hit the street just as dawn was breaking.

The air was arctic. Despite his exhaustion, Jack felt wonderfully alive as he pedaled south. The mystery of the ossuary would either blow up in a puff of smoke or rise to another more fascinating level. And unlike his friend the archbishop, Jack hoped it would be the latter.

Jack regretted that Laurie was to have no relief. Her day was going to be the same emotional disaster as yesterday and the day before. A good day was defined as one that was less bad.

Twenty minutes later, Jack pulled into one of the OCME loading bays to leave his bike where he knew it would be safe. It wasn't much of an inconvenience. All it meant was walking the final four blocks south to the DNA building, which turned out to be pleasant in the crisp, clear morning.

He glanced at his watch. His timing was near perfect. It was five of eight. He checked with security to make sure Shawn and Sana hadn't arrived early. As he'd assumed, the couple had yet to be seen. When Jack knew Shawn back in college, Shawn was always late.

Jack sat on one of the lobby's upholstered, backless benches and looked out at the scant traffic on First Avenue, thinking about the ossuary and growing increasingly excited.

At twenty after eight, Shawn climbed from a taxi that had pulled onto 26th Street. Behind him emerged Sana. The couple went to the rear of the car, joined by the driver.

As Jack stepped back into the wintry air, Shawn and the driver lifted the ossuary from the trunk. Jack dashed over and took the driver's end.

"How nice to see you again, Dr. Stapleton," Sana said.

Jack drew up one knee to rest the corner of the ossuary and extended a hand toward Sana. "Wonderful to see you as well," he said. "But the name is Jack."

"Jack it is," Sana said happily. "And before I say anything else, I'd like to thank you for arranging this lab space for us to use."

"My pleasure," Jack said, as he and Shawn began walking sideways, the ossuary between them. Having seen just the top nestled in the foam board, Jack could now appreciate the whole object. It looked bigger out of the crate. It was also heavier than he had expected.

"Did you have difficulty picking it up from the residence?" Jack asked.

"No, it was a breeze," Shawn said, "but I don't think His Most Reverend Holy Eminence muckety-muck wanted to part with it. He tried to suggest we could examine it there in his dusty old basement. Can you imagine? I mean, the man has no idea about science."

"Careful!" Sana warned, as they walked through the building's glass door. Once inside, they carefully lowered the ossuary onto the same bench Jack had been sitting on earlier.

Jack turned to Sana, and they greeted each other for the second time. "I'm not sure I would have recognized you," Jack said. "You look different. Must be the haircut."

"Funny you should mention it," Shawn complained. "Her coiffure was one of her best features, if you ask me. You must have liked it, too, if you remembered it."

"I did like it," Jack said. "But I like it now, too."

"That's being diplomatic," Shawn commented sourly.

"So, this is the famous ossuary," Jack said, to change the subject. The air had become charged, and the last thing he wanted to do was get caught in the middle of a marital disagreement. Jack could sense there was some definite mutual hostility about Sana's hairstyle.

"This is it," Shawn said, recovering and giving the limestone box a tap on its top like a proud parent. "I'm psyched. I think it's going to change a lot of people's view of the world and their religiosity."

"Provided it's not empty," Jack added. Uncertain of the power of prayer, he had a sense that James was giving it all he had.

"Of course provided it's not empty," Shawn rejoined sharply. "But it's not going to be empty. Anyone want to bet?"

Neither Jack nor Sana responded. Both were a bit intimidated by the edge in Shawn's voice.

"Hey, come on! Lighten up!" Shawn said. "I think we're all a bit tense."

"I think you're right," Sana agreed.

"Okay, one last step," Jack said. "We need to get your IDs."

While Shawn and Sana were taken to the security department to fill out paperwork and have their photos taken, Jack turned back to the ossuary. Now that it was out of the carton, he could examine it with ease, especially with the natural light streaming through the building's front windows.

The Roman numerals scratched on the top were far more visible than they'd been in James's basement. Mary's name, supposedly rendered in Aramaic, was still indecipherable to Jack. The sides of the limestone box were similar in appearance to the top but with fewer scratches. On one end, there was a shallow drill hole whose interior color was far lighter than the rest of the box's surface. There were also four small chipped areas on the same end, which were the identical light color.

"All right, we're ready to rumble," Shawn called out to Jack, as he and Sana appeared with their new ID cards suspended around their necks.

"Can I ask you something?" Jack asked Shawn as they prepared to pick up the ossuary.

"By all means."

"I noticed this light tan drill hole," Jack said, pointing. "And these chip marks. They look new. What are they?"

"They are new," Shawn admitted. "I used a power drill to find the ossuary. I know it is far from standard archaeological technique, but we were crunched for time. As for the chipped areas, they were from the chisel I had to use. Once we'd found the box, I had to get the damn thing out of the hardpan as soon as I could because of Sana. You should have heard her complaining about how long it was taking."

"I think under the circumstances, I was doing damn well," Sana snapped.

"I'm glad you think so," Shawn snapped back.

"Okay, okay!" Jack said. "Sorry I asked." He'd been with the couple for only ten minutes and already he could sense why James felt as he did about their marriage.

"You couldn't have done what you did without my help," Sana continued, "and this is the thanks I get."

"Come on, you guys!" Jack cried. "Cool it! We're here so you people can realize the benefits of all your efforts. Let's see what's in the ossuary." Jack inwardly groaned. He was worrying about refereeing between Shawn and James, and had no interest in doing the same between Shawn and Sana.

Sana continued to glare at Shawn while he stared out the window for a beat.

"You're right!" Shawn suddenly said. He gave Jack a playful slap on the shoulder. "Let's get this thing up to the lab and proceed!" He emphasized the word *proceed* by raising his voice and pro- nouncing it as if it were two words, not one. Then he bent over and picked up one end of the ossuary while Jack quickly did the same on the other. Together they carried it toward the turnstile and the elevator beyond.

On the eighth floor, they walked nearly the length of the build- ing to reach the lab. Sana and Shawn were full of compliments about the building and the impressive view. "I hope I don't get too spoiled," Sana said. "This building is like laboratory paradise."

Pausing at the door, Jack asked Sana to hold his end of the ossuary as he put the key in the lock.

"I like the fact that we can lock up," Shawn said.

"There are lockable lockers inside as well," Jack said as they entered the room.

He and Shawn set the ossuary down on the large center table.

"My goodness," Sana exclaimed. She looked through the glazed door into the gowning room and then through the door beyond, to the laboratory itself. "I can see a brand new Applied Biosystems three thousand one hundred XL from here. This is terrific."

They all took off their coats and other outerwear and stowed it all in the lockers, except for Shawn's backpack. He put that on the table next to the ossuary.

"The time has finally arrived," Shawn exclaimed, eagerly rubbing his hands together and eyeing the ossuary. "I can't believe I've been able to keep my hands off this thing for four days. It's all your fault, Sana, dear."

"You'll be thanking me to no end if we can salvage some mitochondrial DNA," Sana said. "It will add a whole new dimension to this discovery."

Shawn zipped open his backpack and pulled out an extension cord and a hair dryer, then a small hammer and chisel.

"How about we all gown up and put on hats and latex gloves," Sana suggested. "I don't want to leave even the slightest chance of DNA contamination."

"Fine with me," Shawn said, glancing at Jack.

"Absolutely," Jack said. "But first you guys have to sign the indemnity waiver."

After the husband and wife signed all the legal papers absolving the OCME from any damages on every front known to man, the three went into the gowning room with ever-increasing anticipation.

"When I first thought about going into archaeology, this is the kind of experience, of significantly adding to history, I thought would be a routine event," Shawn said, pulling on his gown. "Unfortunately, it is not, so now I'm enjoying every second of it."

"In molecular biology, we have experiences like this all the time," Sana said, snapping on her gloves.

"Really?" Shawn questioned.

"I'm joking," Sana said. "Come on, you guys! Both of you know that science is a slow, plodding affair with only very rare eureka moments. I have to confess, I've never before felt this excited in my career, not even close."

When all three were gowned, gloved, hooded, and masked, Shawn pushed back into the outer room. Plugging in the hair dryer, he turned it on high. Using it like a blowtorch, he directed the hot air at the caramel-colored wax-filled groove between the ossuary's side and its top. The wax eventually softened enough for him to insert the chisel. After a few taps with the hammer, the chisel hit rock.

"This is going to take a wee bit longer than I expected. The ossuary's top is rabbeted. Sorry, guys!"

"Take your time!" Sana said.

"Don't hurry on my account," Jack said.

Slowly, Shawn inched around the entire periphery of the ossuary, first softening the wax with the hair dryer, then poking in with the chisel and tapping it with the hammer until it hit up against the rabbet. When he'd gotten all the way around, he pushed in the chisel and now tried to rotate it. There was no give. Moving the chisel along in the groove, he tried again. Nothing. A new location, and nothing again. Another new location, and there was a slight cracking sound.

"I think I could feel some movement," Shawn said. He was encouraged but concerned that if he applied too much torque, he could snap off a piece of the ossuary's top. The ossuary had been intact for two millennia, and he wanted it to stay that way.

"Can't you speed this up," Sana said, beside herself with excitement. From her perspective it seemed that Shawn was dragging this part out unnecessarily.

Shawn paused and glanced up at his wife. "You're hardly being helpful," he snapped. Repositioning himself, he went back to work with the chisel. There was no telling how long it would take, or if it would work at all.

Just when he paused to stop and rethink the situation, there was another cracking noise, and Shawn's heart skipped a beat. Quickly, he pulled out the chisel, expecting to see a crack in the limestone, but there was none. He ran his hand along the edge to see if he could feel a crack that for some reason he could not see, but there was no discontinuity.

Gingerly, he reinserted the chisel and tentatively began to rotate it. To his relief, the top, in its entirety, lifted off the base. It was free! He looked at the others and nodded. "This is it," he said, grasping both ends of the top with his hands. He gently lifted it high enough for the rabbet to clear the sides and placed the top on the table. Then they leaned over and peered into the ossuary that had been hermetically sealed for two thousand years.

21

D ear Lord, I beseech You," James prayed. "Show me the way to deal with the ossuary." He was in the exquisite private chapel dedicated to Saint John the Apostle on the third floor of the archbishop's residence, kneeling on an antique French prie-dieu beneath an ebony wall plaque.

On the plaque was a superbly rendered image of the Assumption of the Blessed Virgin. The Mother of God was standing on clouds with two cherubs at her side. Attached to the plaque's base was a finely wrought sterling-silver holy-water font. James had always loved the piece, and that morning its image had particular significance.

"I never question Your will, but I fear that my capabilities involving the task You have placed in my unworthy hands may not be sufficient. I firmly believe that whatever remains might be found in the ossuary are not those of Your Virgin Mother. It is my humble wish that there will be no possibility anyone will believe whatever relics are found are those of a woman. Only then may I feel capable of dealing with this problem. I also pray that my friend Shawn

Daughtry will disavow any and all association he might have originally felt between the ossuary and Your Blessed Mother." Crossing
himself, he rose, saying a fervent "May Your will be done. Amen."

James's torment had made sleep difficult, and his eyes had
popped open that morning before five. Rousing himself from the
warmth of his narrow metal bed, he'd prayed a similar prayer to
the prayer he'd just voiced in the chapel, using another more
simple prie-dieu in his ascetic, cold bedroom.

From then on, the morning had been similar to other Saturday
mornings. He'd read his breviary, celebrated Mass with his staff,
and breakfasted with his two secretaries. There had been a short
ten-minute interruption when Shawn and Sana arrived to pick up
the ossuary. James had watched with mild distress as Shawn and
Father Maloney carried the box up from the basement and placed
it in the trunk of a dirty yellow cab. When the trunk had been
slammed shut, James had winced. Even though he trusted the relic
did not contain the bones of the Virgin, the rough treatment
seemed sacrilegious.

After the Daughtrys had left, James had returned to his private
quarters to change into his full regalia as the day was to include an
official visit at the Church of Our Lady of the Holy Rosary. At that
point, fully dressed, he had gone into the tiny chapel.

With some effort, James got to his feet. Then, dipping his
fingers into the holy water, he made the sign of the cross before
descending to his office on the floor below. Checking his e-mail
was part of his morning routine. Just as his computer monitor
awoke, his phone rang, drawing his eyes to the caller ID screen.
When he saw it was Jack Stapleton, he snatched up the receiver.
Unfortunately, he wasn't quite fast enough. He got a dial tone
instead of Jack's voice, meaning Father Maloney or Father Karlin
had beaten him to the punch. Impatiently, he drummed his finger-
tips on his blotter. The intercom buzzed a moment later.

"It's a Dr. Jack Stapleton," Father Karlin said. "Are you avail-able?"

"Yes, thank you," James said. But he didn't answer immediately, knowing that Jack's call meant the ossuary was now open. Reciting another quick prayer, James eyed the small blinking light. He sud-denly felt less confident, as if he somehow knew the Good Lord meant for his torment to continue.

Taking a deep breath, James answered softly.

"Is that you, James?" Jack asked.

"It is I," James said in a depressed tone. He could hear laughter in the background and excited conversation, erasing any last hope in his mind about what he was about to learn.

"I'm not sure you want to hear this," Jack said. "But—"

James could tell that Jack had been cut off by the ecstatic Shawn, who was apparently fighting with Jack for the phone. James could clearly hear Shawn say, "Is that His Eminent Excel-lency, hoping soon to be wearer of the Fisherman's Ring? Let me talk to that pudgy bum!"

James cringed and considered hanging up, but his curiosity pre-vented him.

"Hey, brother!" Shawn said blithely, coming on the line. "We hit gold!"

"Oh?" James questioned with feigned disinterest. "What did you find?"

"Not one scroll but three, and the biggest says in Greek on the outside: GOSPEL ACCORDING TO SIMON. We have the gospel of Simon Magus. Isn't that a gas?"

"Was that all that was in the ossuary?" James asked, with a glimmer of hope appearing on the distant horizon.

"No, that was not all, but I'll give you back to Jack for that. Talk to you soon."

A moment later Jack came back on the line. "He is one happy

archaeologist," Jack explained. "I'm certain he doesn't mean to be disrespectful if you heard what he'd said before he got the phone away from me."

"Just tell me, were there bones in the ossuary?" James asked. At the moment, he was uninterested in manners.

"There were," Jack admitted. "To me, it looks like a complete skeleton, including a skull that's in reasonably good shape. It could be more than one skeleton, but there's only one skull."

"Holy Mary, Mother of God," James murmured, more to himself than to Jack. "Can you tell if the remains are human?"

"That would be my guess."

"How about the sex?"

"That's harder to say. The pelvis is in pieces, which is the way I'd try to tell. But as soon as I saw the bones when we got the top off the ossuary, I called Alex Jaszek, the head of the OCME department of anthropology, told him what we were doing in a very general way, and asked him if he'd like to come over. He's on his way."

"You didn't mention anything about the Virgin Mary, did you?"

"Of course not. I just said we opened a first-century ossuary."

"Good," James said, trying to think of what he should do. He was tempted to go over to the city DNA building himself to view the relics, but to do so would require changing again, lest his visit appear on the cover of tomorrow's *Times*. Since he had to be at the luncheon at noon in his ecclesiastical finery, he decided he didn't have enough time to change and then change back.

"James, Shawn wants to talk with you again. Is it okay if I hand him the phone?"

"Yes, it's okay," James said warily. He assumed Shawn wanted to hit him a few more times while he was down for the count.

"Hey!" Shawn said, coming on the line. "I just remembered it's your birthday! Happy birthday, Your Eminent Excellency."

"Thank you," James said. It took him by surprise. As upset as he was over the ossuary and its potential ramifications, he'd totally forgotten his own birthday. He also wondered why his staff had not said anything, even though he'd never been a stickler for such things. "My title is Your Eminence or Your Excellency," James said in partial rebuke. "But from you I would prefer James."

"Right you are," Shawn said with indifference. "I have a suggestion. How about we throw a party tonight, provided you don't have to dine with some country leader or other muckety-muck. We'll celebrate your birthday and our breakthrough find together. What do you say? The simultaneity is a bit ironic, of course, but life is like that."

James's first reaction was to say absolutely, categorically, no. He didn't want to listen to Shawn bragging about how he was going to shock the world with his revelations. But as James quickly thought about the invitation, the more he began to believe it might be a good idea to bear the burden. He needed to be part of the investigation from the beginning so that he could keep a healthy amount of skepticism alive in the minds of all concerned, if he was to have any hope of ultimately talking Shawn out of publishing anything about the Virgin Mary. Perhaps it was a long shot, but for the moment it was the only strategy James could imagine beyond prayer.

"I'm thinking about picking up some steaks, salad makings, and some terrific red wine on the way home," Shawn went on when James didn't respond. "We can grill the steaks on the back porch. What do you say?"

What made James continue to hesitate was the worry of Shawn being insufferable and riding him the whole evening. James doubted he could endure such an evening on so little sleep.

"Instead of staying in we could always go out," Shawn persisted in the face of James's silence. "I just thought you don't like to go out."

"Only with you," James said. "We always get into an argument over dinner. I'm not blaming you, I'm just as guilty, and even if I go as a civilian, someone always recognizes me. I don't need that type of publicity. Let me talk again with Jack!"

"He wants to talk with you," Shawn said, with frustration.

"What is it?" Jack asked with a tired voice. He had a premonition of what was coming, meaning the refereeing was already beginning.

"Jack, Shawn's planning a celebration dinner tonight at their home. You've got to be there."

"I haven't actually been officially asked, and besides, I have to get home to help Laurie with JJ, our son."

"Jack, I need your help, as I made clear yesterday. If you'll come to this impromptu dinner party, I'll do the same, but I'm going to need a buffer with Shawn, especially with the current high he is on. I need to know more about what he's found and what he's thinking, but you know it'll be torture."

"So I'll play referee once again," Jack said grudgingly. He'd never liked the role.

"Jack, please!"

"All right, if it's not going to be late."

"It won't be late. I have to say Mass in the cathedral early in the morning. On top of that I slept poorly last night. Believe me, it is not going to be a late night. Listen, I'll bring my car, and I'll drive you home."

"Okay, I'll come," Jack said, "but I have to check with Laurie."

"Fair enough," James said. "Put Shawn back on."

James told Shawn what had been decided and asked what time.

Shawn shrugged. "Let's say seven. I think I'd be speaking for Sana if I say we'll want to get an early start in the lab tomorrow. We'll want to break up on the early side."

"I couldn't agree more."

22

Only a little more than ten minutes after the conversation with James, Alex Jaszek, the anthropologist, arrived. During the brief interim Shawn and Sana continued to whisper epithets back and forth. Despite their earlier joy over their discovery, they had begun arguing about the evening's plans until Sana, in disgust, had disappeared into the laboratory to check out the equipment.

Alex looked young for a seasoned Ph.D., with a skimpy beard on his youthful face. He was built like the quintessential high-school football player, with broad shoulders and a narrow waist. He wore khaki pants and an old-fashioned flannel shirt.

"Is this the way the bones looked when you got the top off?" Alex asked, peering into the ossuary.

"Pretty much," Jack said. He was looking in as well. "The three scrolls were inside as well. Shawn carefully lifted them out. The thigh bone might have moved a tiny bit when he did so, but we took plenty of photos."

"It looks like quite a complete skeleton."

"That was our guess as well," Shawn said.

"You could have lifted the bones out," Alex said. "The position is not going to tell us anything, since this was, as I'm sure you know, a reburial. When ossuaries were in use, the body was first left to decompose, then the bones were gathered up and put into the ossuary in no particular order. So let's go ahead and lift them out one by one and arrange them on the table in their general anatomical position."

Sana emerged and joined them around the table, and Jack made introductions. Sana made a big show of shaking Alex's hand while expressing unctuous gratitude that he'd sacrificed part of his Saturday to lend them his extraordinary expertise.

Jack could sense that Sana's over-the-top performance was to irritate Shawn, which seemed to be working. So, while Sana was helping Alex in the gowning room, Jack leaned over and quietly asked, "Are we still on for tonight, or should we reschedule?"

"You bet your sweet ass we're still on," Shawn snapped. "I don't know what's come over her sometimes. Whatever it is better stop."

Sensibly, Jack refrained from further commenting but rather plucked a bone from the ossuary and tried to figure out what it was.

After returning from the gowning room Sana carried on for another five minutes with Alex, who was obviously charmed by her attention. But seeing that Jack and Shawn were having some trouble with determining where the bones belonged anatomically, she and Alex pitched in to help. Then, after several minutes, Alex took over completely since he had begun to comment on each bone as he took it from the ossuary and added it to the expanding skeleton. After a half-hour it was done.

For Sana the most interesting were the skull and lower jaw, because there were some teeth in their original sockets. On the other hand, Shawn was most interested in the bones of the pelvis. While handling each fragment, Alex had commented casually that the woman had had children, most likely multiple children.

"This is a remarkably intact skeleton," Alex said, examining it in its totality and adjusting the position of a few of the individual bones. "Notice that even the tiny finger bones from both hands are all here. That is remarkable indeed. In all the ossuary cases I've had the pleasure of investigating, this has never happened. I've never seen all the finger bones together. Whoever did this was remarkably respectful of the deceased."

"You said it's a woman," Shawn pointed out excitedly. "Are you certain this skeleton is that of a woman?"

"Absolutely! Look at the delicate brow ridges," he said, pointing toward the skull, "and notice the delicate arm bones and long bones of the legs. And if I put the pubic bones together"—Alex lifted the bones and held them together as they would have been in life—"look how wide the pubic arch is! It's definitely female. No question!"

"Especially since you said she'd had multiple children," Shawn said, with a self-satisfied giggle.

"That's an issue I can't be dogmatic about," Alex said.

Shawn's smile faded a degree. "Why not?"

"These are really prominent preauricular sulci," Jack said, picking up an ilium and showing it to Alex. "I've never seen bigger."

"What are sulci?" Shawn asked.

Jack pointed to grooved areas on the edge of the bone. "The sulci appear after childbirth. These are some of the deepest I've ever seen. I'd say she had had close to ten children."

Alex raised a finger and shook it in disagreement. "The depth of the sulci on the ilia and the dots on the pubic bones at the pubic symphyses are not completely proportional to the number of children a woman has given birth to."

"But they usually are," Jack pointed out.

"All right," Alex said. "They usually are, I'll admit that."

"So, this woman's sulci and dots strongly suggest she had had multiple children. It doesn't prove it, just strongly suggests it. Would you agree to that?"

"Yes, Jack, I would. But I'd also say it might be wrong. Do you people have any idea of the identity of this person and how many children she actually had? Is there a name or a date on the ossuary? What about the scrolls? Do they mention children?"

For a second, no one moved. It was silent except for a refrigerator compressor in the background. Sensing a suddenly strained atmosphere, Alex added, "Did I say something wrong?"

"Not at all," Shawn said hastily. "We're not sure of this skeleton's identity, but there is a date on the ossuary's cover. It's AD 62, but we don't know if that's the date of her death or the date of her reburial. We're hoping the scrolls may shed some light on her identity, but we have not yet unrolled them and obviously have not read them."

"What about the woman's age?" Sana asked. "Can you tell that?"

"Not with much precision," Alex said. "Unfortunately, bones are not like tree branches, where you can count the rings. In fact, throughout the individual's life the bone is being constantly replaced, which is why we can accurately carbon-date. You might want to think of going that route with these bones to check on the date on the ossuary. The necessary sample size is extremely small with the newer techniques."

"We'll keep that in mind," Shawn said.

"If you had to guess her age, what would you say?" Sana asked.

"I'd say over fifty to be safe. If I wanted to go out on a limb, I'd say eighty. My sense is this is an old individual, based on the amount of arthritis in the finger bones and feet. What would you say, Jack?"

"I think you are right on the money. The only other thing I note is some mild evidence of tuberculosis on a couple of vertebrae, but otherwise she was in very good shape."

"Remarkably so," Alex agreed.

"I'm psyched," Sana said. "The water seal must have functioned perfectly. I wasn't completely optimistic about finding DNA, but I am now. With those teeth still in their sockets, and as dry as these bones are, there has to be some intact mitochondrial DNA."

"Don't jinx yourself," Shawn warned.

"Why do you want to find DNA?" Alex asked. "Do you have anything in particular in mind?"

Sana just shrugged. "I think it will be interesting and a challenge. It might be fun to see where she was from, genealogically speaking. The ossuary was found in Rome, but that doesn't mean she was from Rome, or even Italy. In the first century AD, there was a lot of migration because of the Pax Romana. And it will be an interesting addition to the international mitochondrial database, having a first-century woman."

"How are you going to do it?" Alex asked. "What procedure are you going to follow?"

"First I'll try a tooth as a source," Sana said. "If that doesn't work, I'll use bone marrow. Either way, it's not a complicated process. It will involve a thorough cleaning of the outside of the tooth to remove any DNA contamination. Then I'll cut into the crown of the tooth, pull out the dried pulp material from the pulp cavity, suspend it with detergent to break open the cells, treat it with proteases to eliminate the proteins, then extract the DNA. Once I have the DNA in solution, I'll amplify it with a PCR, then quantify it, then sequence it. It's as simple as that."

"What's your time frame?" Alex asked. "I'd be interested in a follow-up, if you wouldn't mind."

Sana glanced at Shawn, who gave an almost imperceptible nod of approval. "It depends to a degree on that first rate-limiting step. Whether there is intact mitochondrial DNA available. If there is, I should have it in a few days or up to a week. Some of the steps function best when they are allowed to percolate overnight."

"Well," Alex said, getting up from his chair and giving Sana's back a pat, "I want to thank you all for including me. It's been a terrific morning." His eyes happened to catch the three ancient scrolls as he started toward the gowning room to take off the protective gear. He stopped and looked back at Shawn. "I've been so engrossed with this skeleton, I forgot to ask about the scrolls. What's the plan with them?"

"To read them," Shawn said, with a touch of jealousy at the man's apparent informality with his wife. "But first I have to unroll them, which is going to be a task. They are, excuse the pun, drier than a bone, and quite fragile."

"Are they made of papyrus?" Alex asked. He bent over and looked at each closely. He didn't dare touch them.

"They are papyrus, yes," Shawn said.

"Will they be easy to unroll?"

"I wish," Shawn said. "It is going to be a painstaking process that has to be done millimeter by millimeter. They could disintegrate into thousands of tiny pieces, and on top of that, we have to be careful."

Everyone laughed, even Shawn.

"What a pleasant fellow," Sana said after Alex left, then to herself she added, "in comparison to my husband."

"Oh, you noticed," Shawn said mockingly out loud, then to himself added, "I know exactly what you are doing, and I am going to ignore it—I'm not going to get jealous. It's not worth getting riled up, and I won't give you the satisfaction."

"All right, people!" Jack said suddenly, clapping his hands loudly to get everyone's attention. "Let's get to work! Let's crank out what has to be done so you two can get under way. I'm going nuts about whether you're going to make a positive identification of these bones. But let me warn you, if you continue to quarrel with each other, I'm out of here, and I'm off your dinner list, and if I'm off, then I believe James is off, meaning party over!"

For a moment Shawn and Sana glared at each other. After several minutes, Sana put her head back and laughed. "God, what a couple of children we are."

"Speak for yourself!" Shawn snapped. He didn't like the new Sana.

"I am. I think we are beginning to become too similar, like a dog and its master."

Now it was Shawn's turn to laugh. "So, which one is the dog?"

"That's easy to tell, the way you've been barking lately," Sana teased, still smiling. She turned to Jack. "He knows better than to invite people to dinner without discussing it with me first. If we've talked about it once, we've talked about it a dozen times."

"You always have to have the last word," Shawn snapped.

Jack stepped between the husband and wife and motioned as if he was calling for a time-out in a basketball game. "Stop!" he said. "Stop taunting each other. You guys are pathetic! Loosen up and let's get to work."

"I'm going to Home Depot," Shawn said abruptly. "Jack, can you lend me a hand?"

"I might need a pair of pliers," Sana said. "Let me see if one of the eye teeth comes out with ease." She picked up the skull and pulled on the right eye tooth, which was in remarkably good shape. The tooth came out easily with a slight popping sound. "That was easy. Nope! I don't need any pliers."

"What do you need from Home Depot?" Jack asked.

"A bunch of plate-glass sheets," Shawn said. "And a small sonic humidifier that I can jury-rig to direct a tiny puff of water vapor where I want it to go. I already have several pair of tongs like those used by philatelists in my backpack. Unrolling these scrolls is not going to be easy. The papyrus will flake, so I'll need to protect it immediately under glass. For all I know, as I said to Alex, the papyri may all come apart in pieces and have to be put together like a jigsaw puzzle. I don't know what to expect, to be completely truthful."

"While you boys go to the Home Depot, I'm going to go into the laboratory and get going with my end of the project," Sana said, brandishing the eye tooth. "The quicker I get it into a sonicator with the detergent, the quicker I can saw off the crown to get at the pulp."

"What about tonight?" Jack asked. "Are you two going to behave? Is the dinner party still on or what?"

"Of course it is still on," Sana said. "I hope our testiness with each other doesn't make you feel too uncomfortable or unwelcome. We'll promise to be good. I just don't like it when Shawn doesn't discuss the idea with me before he invites people over. It's not that I don't enjoy having people over, I do. I actually like to cook and rarely get the chance, so I'm going to enjoy tonight. In fact, as soon as I get my pulp extraction into the incubator to dry overnight, I'm out of here to shop and have some fun preparing what I hope you two and James will enjoy. It will be fun, provided Shawn and James behave."

"Okay. You've put my mind at ease," Jack said. "But, as far as my coming is concerned, I do need to check in with my wife to see if she minds. We have a new baby, and she's doing the lion's share of caregiving."

"A new baby, how nice," Sana said, without the excitement most young women would have expressed. Nor did she invite mother and baby. "Surely she won't begrudge you an evening with your old college buddies."

"It's more complicated than you might think," Jack explained, not wanting to be more specific.

"Well, we'll understand if you can't come," Shawn said. "But we do hope you can. What we've found in the ossuary is incredible, and I'm going to enjoy riding His Excellency James."

"Please don't overdo it," Jack said. "He's really upset about this whole thing and its potential repercussions."

"He should be," Shawn said.

"I wouldn't be so blithe," Jack warned. "James is married to the Church. If nothing else, he is fearsomely loyal."

Their mission to Home Depot accomplished, with what seemed like a ton of glass panes in a taxi's trunk, Jack again tried to encourage Shawn to go easy on James that evening, reminding him that he had a long way to go before he could prove he'd discovered the bones of the Virgin Mary.

"I haven't proven it," Shawn agreed, "but it is coming whisker-close, wouldn't you say, old boy?"

"No, I wouldn't say that," Jack replied.

"Let's put it this way. If I were to take this story as we know it today, combining Saturninus's letter with the fact that the ossuary was right where he said he'd put it, and it hadn't been touched for almost two thousand years—what if I were to take the story, the letter, and the ossuary to Vegas and ask the bookmakers if I had the Virgin Mary in the box. What kind of odds do you think they'd give me?"

"Stop it!" Jack snapped. "This is all ridiculous supposition."

"So that's how it is!" Shawn said suddenly. "You're on James's side, just like you always were in college. Some things never change."

"I'm not on anybody's side. I'm on my side, right in the middle, always trying to keep the peace between you two hard-asses."

"James was the hard-ass, not me."

"Excuse me. You're right. You were the airhead."

"And you were the asshole. I remember it well," Shawn said. "And as the asshole, you were almost always on hard-ass's side, just as I'm beginning to think you'll be tonight. I'm warning you that tonight I'm looking for a bit of payback. During all our debates over the years, we'd always get to a point where James would throw down his trump card: faith! How can you debate that? Well, tonight we'll revisit a couple of those debates, only this time I have facts on my side. It's going to be entertaining. I can promise you that."

Suddenly the two old friends sitting in the back of the taxi stared at each other and smiled. Then they laughed.

"Can you believe us?" Shawn questioned.

Jack shook his head. "We're acting like teenagers."

"Kids is more like it," Shawn corrected. "But I'm just blowing off steam. Don't worry, I'll go easy on Jamie boy tonight."

Their taxi pulled up to the OCME DNA building, and Jack ran in to ask the guards for a cart to meet them at the receiving dock. Arriving about the same time, Jack and Shawn unloaded the glass and stacked it on the cart. Jack patted the top of the last stack, somewhat out of breath. "Glass might not look like much when you are looking through it, but I can tell you it's damn heavy stuff." Shawn nodded as he ran the back of a hand across a sweaty brow.

"Can I trust that you'll be able to get this unloaded upstairs?" Jack asked, with his hand still resting on the glass.

"No problem," Shawn said confidently. "I'll have Ms. Flirtatious Independence upstairs lend a hand."

"I wouldn't take offense at Alex," Jack said. "He's just one of those very friendly, outgoing people. He likes everyone, and everyone likes Alex."

"I don't have any beef with Alex. My problem is that Sana has been slip-sliding to I don't know exactly where. You know what I'm saying? Take her hair as we discussed. It was gorgeous long, and I told her not to cut it, so she cuts it. I ask her to do small things around the house, like iron my shirts; she tells me she works as hard as I do. I tell her I shovel the snow and take out the trash. You know what she said then?"

"I have no idea," Jack said, hoping his tone conveyed that he didn't know or care.

"She says she wants to trade. I do the ironing; she does the trash and the shoveling. Can you imagine?"

"I'm sorry to hear that," Jack said vaguely, refusing to be drawn into a discussion of marital difficulties. "What is your address again?" he asked, to change the subject.

"Forty Morton Street. Do you remember how to get there?"

"Vaguely," Jack admitted. He took out a small pad and wrote down the address. "Okay. Unless my wife has other plans, I'll be there at seven. And what about tomorrow? Are you guys planning to work? If you are and you don't mind, I'd like to stop in and see how things are going."

"I'll let you know what's up. Sana might like to sleep in. As for me, I'm too psyched, so I'll be here. Just as soon as I can I've got to know what Simon Magus has to say and see if he can redeem himself. I've always wondered if he'd just been a whipping boy. The first-century Church had been in such a disarray it needed someone to blame and there was poor Simon Magus and his wish to be a more effective healer, and of course his pals the Gnostics."

"You sure you can handle all this glass?" Jack asked again, as he backed away. He was eager to get home to see if he could clear the deck for the evening event, hoping just maybe to convince Laurie to take some time to get out of the house. He knew it was a long shot, but he was going to try just the same.

"Sana and I will handle it fine," Shawn said with a wave. "See you tonight."

"I hope," Jack said, giving a thumbs-up sign. Feeling progressively nervous and rather guilty since it was now a little after noon, Jack jogged back to the main OCME building at 30th Street and First Avenue. Resisting heading up to his office, he merely grabbed his Trek, waved to security, and headed uptown.

Once on his bike, he felt better knowing he'd be home in thirty minutes, where there would at least be a slight chance to assuage at bit of his guilt, provided he could get Laurie out of the house. Of course, if JJ was having a bad day, that probably wouldn't happen, as Laurie would be reluctant to leave the poor child in Jack's relatively incapable hands. Above and beyond the personal emotional issues, Jack admitted he was not a natural with sick children, as his rotation in pediatrics in third-year medical school had amply displayed.

Jack's mental state progressively improved as the weather was near perfect with a crystal-clear sapphirine sky and a temperature that had risen to be mild for New York in December. There was also a festive feeling in the air, as the city was alive with early Christmas shoppers hoping to beat the crowds.

Jack's route home took him past the Central Park Zoo, which was clogged with children and parents. Jack felt a sudden catch in his throat as he wondered if there would be a chance for him to enjoy such an outing with JJ. A little farther on, and coming abreast of a beautiful playground with a slide built of polished granite, Jack stopped for a minute to watch the children squealing, shrieking, and laughing. Their glee was infectious, and it almost brought a smile to Jack's face, remembering his own exuberant childhood. But a moment later his thoughts were dominated by JJ's neuroblastoma and the heavy question of which was going to triumph, the mystical power of JJ's body to heal itself with the help of modern medicine if and when the medicine could be restarted, or the equally mysterious power of the DNA-driven neuroblastoma cells: a classic collision of right and wrong.

Experiencing another, more powerful catch in his throat, Jack jumped back on his bike and pedaled furiously to clear his mind. Luckily, because of the springlike weather, he quickly found himself enveloped in a mob of other bikers, runners, in-line skaters, roller skaters, and mere walkers such that thinking was difficult to avoid running into someone.

Jack exited the park at 106th Street. As he pedaled he could clearly see his house, which stood out sharply as the only one on the block that had been totally renovated. Then he caught a glimpse of something he wished he hadn't: the sight of his neighbors warming up on the outdoor playground's basketball court. Unable to resist, Jack jumped the curb and glided to a stop at the chain-link fence.

As soon as Jack had come to a halt, one of the players sauntered over to him. His name was Warren Wilson, and he was by far the best player. Over the course of Jack's years in the city living in the neighborhood, he and Jack had become the best of friends.

"Hey, man, you coming out? I still got room for one."

"I'd love to," Jack said, "but Laurie's been cooped up in the house with JJ, and I've got to go and relieve her. You know what I'm saying?"

"Yeah, I know. Catch you later, then."

Struggling with his conscience, Jack watched Warren rejoin the group. Reluctantly, he turned his bike and headed across the street, hoisting it onto his shoulder to carry it up the front stone steps.

After unlocking the door, Jack poked his head in and listened. No crying. Carrying the bike inside, he placed it in its designated closet and started up the stairs.

As Jack climbed the stairs he began to hear some telltale sounds from the kitchen. By the time he arrived there he assumed he would find the baby in the playpen and Laurie at the sink, as he had the previous evening. "Hello, dearest!" he called out, seeing Laurie out of the corner of his eye as he stepped over to take a peek at JJ in the playpen. At that point he did a double take, because JJ was nowhere to be seen.

"Where's the boy?" Jack questioned with mild concern, since the situation was so unique.

"The little guy is sleeping," Laurie announced with pleasure. "And since I had a reasonable night's sleep last night, I thought I'd get a jump on dinner. It's quite a luxury."

Some luxury, Jack thought but didn't express. He walked directly up to her, got his two hands around her waist from behind, and directed her forcibly out of the kitchen, down the short hall, and into the family room. He made her sit on one of the love seats, which was upholstered in a bright-yellow-and-light-green-checked fabric. Jack took the seat opposite.

"I need to talk," Jack said in an authoritarian voice.

"Okay," Laurie said, looking at Jack askance. The situation seemed mildly out of character, and she didn't know whether or not to be concerned. She couldn't read Jack's emotions, although she could sense he was not entirely himself. "Is everything all right at the office?"

Jack hesitated a moment, not knowing where to start. He hadn't given any thought to what he specifically wanted to say. Unfortunately for Laurie, every minute of silence on Jack's part fanned her concerns about what he was struggling to bring up.

"I need to ask you something," Jack said. "Something that makes me feel quite guilty."

Laurie took in a sudden breath and felt her extremities go cold. "Wait!" she said with a touch of desperation, her mind reflexively drudging up the curious cell-phone-in-the-bathroom episode the night before. "If you are about to tell me you are having an affair, I don't want to hear it. That's something I cannot deal with! I've got about as much on my plate right now as I can handle, and sometimes I'm not even sure I've got what it takes to handle this much." The words tumbled out in a rush of emotion as Laurie fought to avoid tears. Quickly, Jack leaped up to sit next to her. He put his arm around her shoulder.

"I am absolutely not having an affair," Jack said, shocked at the suggestion. "What I wanted to ask you is whether you would mind if I went out to dinner tonight with two college friends. One you've met, Shawn Daughtry."

"The archaeologist?" Laurie questioned with relief, as tears brimmed in her eyes. "The archaeologist with the fawning wife."

"Exactly," Jack said. Stunned by Laurie's idea that he might be having an affair, his mind went to his promise to James. He'd sworn not to mention the possibility of finding the bones of the Virgin Mary, not about the existence of the ossuary itself. There'd been no concern about letting Alex Jaszek in on the existence of the relic. Jack wanted something significant to share with Laurie to totally eliminate her concern about his having an affair.

"Last night I told you that I was giving up on my crusade about alternative medicine, even though I'm in sorry need of a diversion. Well, as luck would have it, a diversion has literally dropped into my lap."

"Wonderful," Laurie said, still struggling to recover her composure. "I'm glad to hear it. What is it?"

Jack told the story about the ossuary from the beginning, and as he knew it would, it totally captivated and fascinated Laurie, even without the possible association with the Virgin Mary.

"I had no idea you even knew the archbishop of New York," Laurie said, truly shocked.

"It was part of my old life which I've tried to forget," Jack explained. "Actually I was surprised Shawn didn't mention it when we had dinner with him and his wife."

"I wonder," Laurie said. "But no matter. I just find it astonishing, as is the whole story of the ossuary and the scrolls. I can't wait to hear more."

"I feel the same. As a diversion, I couldn't have asked for anything more engaging. If I believed in a merciful God, I'd think it heaven-sent." Jack smiled inwardly, realizing how true this really was.

"I apologize for even thinking about you having an affair," Laurie murmured. "I'm not myself these days."

"No need to apologize," Jack said. "Neither of us are ourselves, me in particular."

"Of course you can go to dinner tonight," Laurie said, "with my blessing."

"Thank you," Jack said. "But it makes me feel more guilty than I already feel. Can you understand that?"

"I do."

"And can you understand that I would prefer you were coming along," Jack said, while suppressing the thought about wishing they'd not had the child, especially since it had required in vitro fertilization assistance.

"Of course I can understand, and under different circumstances I would love to come, if not just to meet the archbishop."

"You'll meet the archbishop," Jack said. "Especially since he said he specifically is looking forward to meeting you."

"Now, with the dinner issue out of the way, there's one more point I want to make. It's a beautiful day, and since JJ is asleep, why don't you head outside for a while for some air?"

A broad smile spread across Laurie's face. "I appreciate your concern, but I'm okay."

"Oh, come on. You haven't been out for days. The sun is out and it has warmed up considerably."

"Where would I go?" Laurie questioned with a shrug.

"That doesn't matter," Jack encouraged. "Take a walk in the park, go Christmas shopping, visit your mother. Just enjoy some freedom."

"JJ will know I'm gone the second I walk out the door. I'll be worried sick."

"You don't have much confidence in me."

"As a pediatrician? No, I don't. Look, I feel lucky to be able to be home with JJ full-time. It would be a lot tougher if I had to go back to work and entrust his care to someone else. Think of it more like that. You are making it possible for me to do what I want to do, rather than me being stuck."

"Do you mean that?"

"I do. It's not easy right now, but we'll be able to start treatment again soon. And the more effort I make, the more confident I am about the ultimate outcome."

"Okay," Jack said. He wished he shared her optimism. Giving her a squeeze, he got to his feet and walked to the window. Warren and the others were in the midst of their first game, running up and down the basketball court.

"I think I'll head out for a little b-ball," Jack said.

"Good idea, provided you don't get hurt," Laurie said. "I'd rather not have another patient in the house."

"I'll try to keep that in mind," Jack said before heading upstairs to change.

23

James had Father Maloney bring James's beloved Range Rover around from the garage and park it momentarily on the 51st Street side of the residence. A 1995 model, it was hardly a new car, but to James it represented freedom. In the fall and winter months, he used the car to drive to Morris County, New Jersey, to a small lake called Green Pond to spend random solitary weekends at his cottage. It was a heavenly sanctuary from the weekly blur of his endless official responsibilities.

James climbed up into the driver's seat, heading west, then south along the Hudson River on the West Side Highway.

The drive was scenic, and he allowed himself to relax and think about the upcoming evening, which he hoped would not be quite as ghastly as he'd originally feared, especially with Jack present. His mind also drifted back to his major problem: how to talk Shawn out of publishing anything about the possibility the bones in the ossuary belonged to the Blessed Virgin. He shuddered anew at the thought of the consequences if he were unsuccessful. With the Church still reeling from loss of clerical authority due to the molestation crisis, the news would be devastating to the Church. It would be crushing to him personally as he believed the Holy See would be forced to sacrifice him as a scapegoat, thanks to Shawn's machinations. With a profound sense of sadness, James found himself reminiscing over his journey of achieving his current position and his hopes for higher office.

James sighed as he wistfully recalled all the twists and turns of his career and now its possible end at the hands of a friend. It seemed the ultimate betrayal, a thought that suddenly gave him an idea. He realized it was the personal angle that would most likely affect Shawn's decision to publish. James was well aware of Shawn's negative attitude toward organized religion, such that any appeal in that arena would fall on deaf ears. James was also aware that Shawn was not particularly moral, but he was definitely a commited friend. With a modicum of new optimism, James decided that his approach with Shawn was going to emphasize that his actions would injure him, James, and more or less downplay what they might do for the Church in general and its laity.

James exited the highway into the West Village and made his way to Morton Street, taking the first parking place he found. As an admittedly poor parallel parker, it took him ten minutes to get the Range Rover into the spot, and even though it ended up two feet away from the curb, he considered it parked well enough.

Five minutes later James turned into the walkway that led to the Daughtrys' wood-frame house and stopped. He'd visited before but had forgotten how charming it was. Nothing about it was square or plumb for its entire four floors. All the window frames and even the front-door casing were leaning slightly to the right, suggesting that if the door was inadvertently slammed shut, the entire building might fall to the right against its more solid-appearing brick neighbor. The clapboard siding was stained a light gray, while the trim was painted a pale yellow. The roof, although hard to see except for just the corners of the fourth-floor dormers, was a medium-gray slate. The front door with several bottle-bottom windows was dark green, almost the same color as James's Range Rover. In the middle of the door was a brass door knocker in the shape of a human hand holding a ball. Just to the left of the door was a sign that said CAPTAIN HORATIO FROBER HOUSE, 1784.

James found himself inwardly smiling. He recognized it was just the kind of off-the-wall residence Shawn would choose. There was no doubt Shawn liked to stand out from the rest of the crowd, a thought that gave James another idea. Perhaps he could arrange to have Shawn given some kind of high award if he promised not to publish anything about the Blessed Virgin's relics, something like being inducted as a modern Knight of Malta.

With the comforting sense of having come up with something of a plan, even if of dubious efficacy, James reached up and used the brass knocker to announce himself with a few healthy clangs against its brass base. After doing so he cringed, remembering the entire house's precarious lean to the right.

Within seconds the door was yanked open by a euphoric Shawn with a scotch on the rocks in one hand and a smile to beat the band on his face. "The guest of honor has arrived!" he shouted over his shoulder back into the house from whence a most delightful aroma of grilled meat wafted. A Beethoven piano concerto was playing as background music. Both Sana and Jack materialized out of the smoky, candlelit background on either side of Shawn. There was a buzz of voices, hugs, and slaps on the back as James was welcomed into the living room. A small fire was comfortably crackling in the fieldstone fireplace behind an appropriate-size screen.

"My word," James said, pressing a palm against his chest in a gesture of being overwhelmed. "I'd forgotten how very cozy you have it. My highest compliment is that it out-cozies, if that's a word, my lakeside retreat in Jersey."

"Well, sit down and enjoy, birthday boy!" Shawn said, guiding James gently by the elbow to a club chair and hassock situated just to the side of the fireplace. The light from both the fireplace and the candles made his chronically red cheeks look almost like bruises. "What is your preference? We have a terrific vintage Pétrus that's been breathing for several hours or your usual favorite, single-malt scotch."

"My word," James repeated, taken aback. Such extravagance immediately caused him concern about a possible breakthrough with the ossuary. "Pétrus! This is a celebration!"

"You bet your life it is!" Shawn confirmed. "What will it be?"

"Pétrus is a rare pleasure, and provided I'm not taking it away from dinner, I would love a glass."

"No problem, old friend," Shawn said, scuttling off after Sana to the kitchen.

Suddenly becalmed after the tsunami of the welcome, James and Jack exchanged glances. "Thank you for coming," James said pianissimo. "Although I really need to be here to start my campaign, I'm not sure I would have been able to force myself without your presence."

"I'm actually pleased to be here," Jack responded equally softly, even though with the music playing there would be little chance of being heard from the kitchen. "But I feel obligated to warn you that Shawn seems hell-bent on publishing this Virgin Mary story. I've tried to help as you asked me, but I'm feeling less and less optimistic that he'll even consider not publishing, and for a kind of scary reason. Well, two scary reasons, one more so than the other."

"What are they?" James demanded, with a sinking feeling in his stomach.

"I think he's beginning to believe that there is a religious component involved. Several times he's alluded to the possibility that he has been singled out by the powers that be to bring what he considers this enlightenment to the world at large."

James's eyes opened wide. "Are you saying that he's beginning to believe he is acting as a kind of messenger of the Lord?" James exhaled through partially open lips. To him, such thinking smacked of blasphemy, if not mental illness. He'd seen it before with certain zealots, but he hardly considered Shawn a zealot. Either way, James did not consider it a positive sign, or even healthy. "What's the other reason?"

"Just the one we've already mentioned, that he sees this whole affair as his crowning contribution to archaeology and firmly believes it is going to make him famous. That's always been his number-one goal, and until now, he'd resigned himself to the fact that as an archaeologist he'd been born a hundred years too late to achieve such a status."

"Nectar of the gods," Shawn announced loudly, as he came in from the kitchen with a crystal goblet nearly filled with ruby-red claret. "Your Eminence," he said with a bow, handing James the stemware.

"How gallant," James remarked, taking the wine. After holding up the glass in the form of a toast to his two friends, he swirled the goblet, took a whiff of the wine's full aroma, and then tasted it. "Truly the nectar of the gods," he agreed.

At that point the three men took seats at the points of an equilateral triangle, with James and Shawn on opposite sides of the fireplace and Jack on the sofa directly in front.

"Is Sana going to join us?" James asked.

"I believe she will after finishing the final preparations for dinner. Or maybe she'll just give a yell when all is ready."

"James," Jack said. "It's great to see you in mufti. In my mind you look better in jeans, shirt, and sweater than those Renaissance prince costumes. They are too intimidating."

"Here, here!" Shawn said in agreement, motioning with his scotch as if making a toast.

"If it were up to me, this is how I'd dress most every day!" James said, settling back into his club chair and putting his feet up on the hassock, pretending to be relaxed instead of as tense as he was. "So bring me up to date about the contents of the ossuary!"

"It is turning out to be better and better," Shawn said, looking back and forth between the others. "I haven't even told you yet, Jack, but I was able to unroll with great difficulty two pages of the first scroll of the Gospel of Simon, and it is terrific. Unfortunately, at that pace it might take more than a month to do all three."

"In what possible way is it terrific?" James asked, studying his cuticles as if not particularly interested.

Shawn sat forward, and the firelight sparkled off the surface of his eyes. "It was like being transported mystically back to the first century as a witness to the struggles of the early Church."

"You could more effectively do that with Henry Chadwick, *The Early Church*, and with a good bit more confidence in the accuracy of the material," James said, taking a sip of his wine.

"Not the same by any stretch of the imagination," Shawn said. "I was hearing directly from a man who was there and believed himself to be intimately involved."

"How so? By trying to buy Peter's powers from the Holy Ghost?" James laughed.

"James, I already know your opinion about the ossuary and its contents," Shawn gently chided. "But I think you should hear more. You're not going to change my mind by mocking what we have learned so far before you have even heard it."

"I think my role is to keep your feet on the ground," James

retorted. "My sense is that you are the one who is apt to jump to conclusions."

"Perhaps I might need a reality check at some point, but surely not before you understand what we have already learned and what we will learn from the scrolls and the bones."

"You're right," James agreed. "Let's hear what you have supposedly learned so far."

"The gospel starts out with what I'd call a bang," Shawn said. "Simon describes himself as Simon of Samaria, to be sure the reader differentiates him from another relatively contemporary figure, Jesus of Nazareth."

Despite having just moments earlier resigned himself to be polite while Shawn talked, James burst out laughing. "You mean to tell me that Simon, in a sense, in his own gospel, is putting himself on equal or better footing than Jesus of Nazareth?"

"I am indeed," Shawn said. "Simon, with obvious reverence, gives Jesus of Nazareth full credit for being the logos, or word, and for having been the redeemer in relation to sin, particularly original sin, but he also says of himself that he is gnosis, or knowledge, the great power, who has come to bring knowledge of truth and in that way supersedes Jesus just as he believed Jesus superseded the Temple and the Laws of Moses."

"So Simon writes that he is divine?" James questioned, a wry, mocking smile of disbelief still on his face.

"Not in the same sense as Jesus of Nazareth," Shawn continued. "I have to let you take a long look at the text and see for yourself when it is totally unrolled and fully protected under glass. Simon believed, like other Gnostics, that he had a divine spark because he'd been blessed with gnosis, or special knowledge."

"This is early Christian Gnosticism," James said for Jack's benefit.

"Absolutely," Shawn stated, now smiling himself. "It seems that Simon was perhaps the first Christian Gnostic, which is why Basilides was so eager to ask Saturninus about his master. Simon goes on to say that the violent Jewish god who created the world was not the same god as the Father of Jesus of Nazareth, who is the true God, the perfect God who has had nothing to do with the vastly imperfect and dangerous physical world."

"So, Simon was then an early Platonist eschewing his Jewish roots."

"Exactly," Shawn said, still smiling. "Simon was more Paul than Peter; some thought he had more in common with Peter in his early life as far as we know, since he grew up in less-than-prosperous surroundings in Samaria, while Peter did the same in neighboring Galilee. Anyway, I find all this fascinating, and I've unrolled only two pages. What I find so fascinating is Simon's idea of adding to Jesus of Nazareth's mission, giving Jesus the credit for doing the redeeming about sin, while he, Simon, would take on the issue of knowledge. What I'm wondering is whether Simon in his gospel, when I get it completely unrolled and translated, might actually redeem himself from being the convenient whipping boy down through the ages."

"I sincerely doubt that," James said. The last thing James wanted at this point was for Simon Magus to redeem himself. "His perfidy is canonical and unchangeable, and certainly not by something he might have written himself."

"Dinner, everybody," Sana said, coming in from the kitchen and sipping a glass of wine.

The men struggled to their feet, and while Shawn tossed a couple of logs on the fire to keep it going, James and Jack followed Sana to the very back of the house, where there was a dining table in an attached greenhouse-like structure. "This ossuary mess keeps getting worse," James mumbled to Jack, when he and Jack were sitting and when he knew neither Shawn nor Sana could hear.

Jack nodded, but from his perspective it was the opposite, although he did not let on to James, whom he could tell was clearly more anxious now than when he'd arrived.

A few minutes later they were all seated, and Shawn asked James for a blessing, which he was happy to provide. It was a pleasant setting, and both James and Jack commented that one would never know they were in the middle of the West Village in New York City, as quiet as it was. There was not a single siren in the distance. Shawn had switched on a group of lights that illuminated their carefully planned and enchantingly serene Japanese garden bordered by a rough-hewn cedar fence. Nothing of the enormity of New York was even vaguely visible.

"A toast to our hostess!" Jack said, lifting his wine goblet and nodding toward Sana at the right end of the table. Shawn was at the left end and James directly across. In front of each person was a plate of grilled meat with a curiously orange-colored, pungent-smelling sauce, couscous with slivered almonds, and an artichoke with a vinaigrette dip.

"We're eating lamb loin with Indian spices," Sana announced. "Unfortunately, the lamb got to marinate for only slightly less than two hours, whereas the minimum is supposed to be a full two hours, but I did the best I could with the time I had after getting my samples into the incubator to dry overnight."

"I assume you are trying to obtain DNA from the ossuary bones?" James asked. With the idea the bones might be those of the Blessed Virgin, albeit a very slim chance, James felt unease about trying to isolate DNA, without knowing why he felt that way. He imagined it was a privacy issue about someone he held inordinately dear.

"That's correct," Sana responded. "But our current attempt is from a tooth, not from bone."

"Is that a lengthy process?" James inquired.

"Not if we're lucky," Sana answered. "It should take only a few days, although maybe as much as a week. I'd rather be careful than quick. There's lots of opportunity for DNA contamination, which I'm intent to avoid."

"What about the bones?" James asked. "What did you learn from the anthropologist? Are they human? Are they female? Is it more than one person?"

"Yes, yes, and no," Shawn responded. "They are definitely human, without doubt female, and it is only one person."

"And there is a suggestion the individual was multiparous," Jack added. "In fact, significantly multiparous, like more than five, maybe even up to a dozen children."

James felt his pulse hammer at his temples and for a moment he was overheated, thinking of removing his sweater. After taking a sip of wine to relieve his suddenly parched throat, he asked, "What about the age of the individual?"

"That's difficult to ascertain, but the anthropologist was willing to guess over fifty, probably more like eighty-plus."

"I see," James said simply. Doing a quick calculation in his head, he realized with yet another start that such an age would have been entirely appropriate for the Blessed Mother, considering Jesus' birth around 4 BC and her death in AD 62. She would have been in her eighties.

James felt his general anxiety rising. Although he knew everything he was hearing was only circumstantial, he feared that such evidence could not help but harden Shawn's opinion, making James's job that much more difficult. It also suggested to him that he could not wait any longer. He had to state his case; otherwise, he would have to resort to plan B. Of course, the big problem with plan B was that there was no plan B.

With a shaking hand that he tried to hide, James took a fairly large mouthful of wine, savoring the taste, which was absolutely heavenly. Slowly he swallowed, bit by bit. Then, sitting up straighter in his chair, he began, first by thanking his hostess.

"This has been the best dinner I've had since I can remember," James said, looking to his left at Sana. "It has the most exquisite flavors and aromas, and strikingly tasty meat prepared perfectly. I salute you, young lady." James raised his glass, and Shawn and Jack followed suit. Then, turning to Shawn, he again held up his glass. "Adding to this fine dinner has been this superb wine, which I pray did not require mortgaging the house."

Shawn rocked forward and chortled appreciatively. "It's been worth every penny to celebrate your birthday, which when we were in college always seemed to come at the most opportune time as an excuse to party rather than study, and to celebrate our favorite ossuary and the promise it has brought. Cheers!"

Everyone took a drink of their extraordinary wine.

"But now I must turn the conversation over to a more serious matter," James said, looking to his right and engaging Shawn directly. "I can appreciate your excitement about the contents of the ossuary, but I must, I'm afraid, tamp your enthusiasm down a significant degree, as eventually you will come to realize as I mentioned back at the residence that this whole affair is all an elaborate fake, promulgated apparently by this mysterious Saturninus. After giving the affair considerable thought and prayer, I am even more certain this is the case. Why this individual did what he did I have no idea, nor do I care to know, for it is the work of Satan himself. Perhaps he had some personal grudge against the developing Church, most likely from the Church's appropriate condemnation of the Gnostic heresy, which I understand his letter supports. At the same time, perhaps he was prescient about the future role of Mary as the single most important symbol of Catholic spirituality and faith, and the fact that a huge number of current-day Catholics consider praying to her as an extraordinary aid in the search

for personal holiness. Popes have always highlighted the close connection between Mary and the total acquiescence of Jesus of Nazareth as the Son of God. The Church is the people of God, and
she is the Body of Christ. And for women, in general, she is the
redemptrist for the sins of Eve. As much as Eve turned away from
God, Mary accepted His wishes without question and bore His
Son in perpetual virginity."

"How can you possibly declare this affair a fake at this early
stage of investigation?" Shawn shouted, after pounding the table
hard enough for the dishes and flatware to jump noisily.

"Faith, my son," James said authoritatively, holding up one hand
like a policeman stopping traffic. "By the Holy Spirit working both
through the body of the Church as *sensus fidelium* and through the
hierarchy, particularly the pope, through sacred magisterium."

Shawn threw his hands above his head and glanced at Jack
while mockingly rolling his eyes. "Can you believe this guy? Now
he's trying to add Latin to confuse and impress me as a way of
having a debate. It's college all over again. And do you know where
he is going with this? He's going to the infallibility argument, the
same one we had in college. Certain things never change!"

Shawn redirected his attention back to James, who was still
holding up his hand like a traffic cop. "Am I right, lardo? Isn't this
about to dissolve into our old argument about papal infallibility
such that when he speaks ex cathedra, meaning from the his official position as Bishop of Rome and head of the Church, on
matters of faith or morals he is infallible? Isn't that what this discussion is coming down to?"

"Let me finish my major point before we get sidetracked,"
James said, forcing himself to stay calm in the face of Shawn's
impertinence. "The fact of the matter is this: Any publication about
the contents of the ossuary and the Blessed Virgin, the Mother of
the Church, the Mother of God, according to the patriarch Cyril

of Alexandria and the founder of the study of Mariology, and the Mediatrix Extraordinaire, according to Bernard of Clairvaux, will do irreparable harm to the Church in this regrettable era of low clerical authority stemming from the child-molestation crisis. Hundreds of thousands of people will have their faith challenged unreasonably. The celibacy issue, already being challenged, will be further challenged; priestly numbers will drop beyond their critical numbers today. I have over ten parishes under my authority of the Archdiocese of New York without a pastor. I don't have enough priests as it is!"

"That's not my problem," Shawn snapped. "It's the Church's fault. They have to come out of the Dark Ages and stop painting themselves into the corner by relying on this infallibility issue rather than dealing with fact. It's like the Galileo affair all over again."

"That affair was not about papal infallibility."

"Well, you could have fooled me. Galileo was tried for heresy because with his telescope he proved Copernicus's heliocentric theory to be correct, whereas Church dogma said the Earth was the center."

"It was an issue of sacred magisterium and *sensus fidelium* but not papal infallibility," James snapped back.

"Whatever," Shawn flaunted. "It was an inexcusable disregard of fact and truth."

"That's your opinion."

"Of course it's my opinion!"

"Episodes like the Galileo affair have to be viewed in the context of the time at which they occurred."

"I don't think fact and truth are contingent on time," Shawn stated, interrupting James. His words were becoming progressively slurred from the scotch and wine, as he had started drinking before Jack and then James had arrived. "Does anyone else here besides James believe such a thing?"

Shawn glanced at both Sana and Jack and swayed slightly in the process, but neither responded. Neither wanted to take sides in an argument that clearly was not yet over, and by participating, someone's feelings would get hurt.

"Would you please let me finish?" James demanded of Shawn.

Shawn made a spectacle of spreading his hands widely, giving James free rein to say what he wanted.

"Publishing an article about the ossuary bones being those of the Virgin Mary, therefore directly contradicting *Munificentissimus Deus*, Pope Pius the Twelfth's 1950 infallible declaration regarding the Assumption of Mary, not only would have a devastating effect on the Church by undermining both the reputation of the Virgin Mary and clerical authority, but I fully believe it will have an equivalent effect on my career. As the issue is investigated, as it undoubtedly will be, it will soon come to light that it was my intervention with the Pontifical Commission for Sacred Archaeology that provided you, Shawn, access to the necropolis, which made it possible for you to steal the ossuary, which is what you have done."

"I prefer to think of it as *borrow*," Shawn said with a snide smile.

"For someone who purportedly likes to deal with truth and fact, *steal* is a much better term than *borrow*. Quite quickly, the truth and the facts of the matter will be that the archbishop of New York made it possible for the thief to take the ossuary without the knowledge of the Pontifical Commission for Sacred Archaeology, nor any of its archaeologists, and then compound the theft by illegally removing the important artifact from the Vatican and Italy and having it transported to New York, where it was violated without its rightful owner's knowledge. With such an involvement coming to light, I would give the Holy Father about one week to recall me to Rome and then post me to some monastery, perhaps in the jungles of Peru or the deserts of Outer Mongolia."

Once James had finished, a silence settled over the cozy dinner party such that the only sound came from the Daughtrys' cat scratching in its litterbox down the hall. No one spoke. No one even looked at one another. The uncomfortable sense of betrayal hung in the air like a miasma.

Suddenly, Sana pushed back her chair and stood. "Why don't all of you head back into the living room, where I'll bring dessert. Shawn, you see to the brandy." Sana took her plate and James's back into the kitchen proper as the others got to their feet. Still, none of the men spoke. Instead, everyone carried either their plates or other objects from the table back to where Sana had retreated.

"It's actually easier if you all head into the living room as I suggested," Sana said, as the men divested themselves of their loads, trying vainly to put them directly into the dishwasher but bumping into one another in the process.

"Who's for brandy, and who's to stick with their wine?" Shawn gaily questioned. He grabbed the nearly full second bottle of Pétrus and started for the living room, weaving precariously. "If you want wine, bring your goblet," he added, as he snatched his own from the countertop.

In the living room, each took his original spot. Prior to sitting down, Shawn put the wine bottle and his glass on the coffee table, then got several more logs to lay on the glowing coals, which the original fire had been reduced to. He then got James the brandy he'd requested and then filled Jack's wineglass and finally his own.

"Such contentment," Shawn voiced, after finally sitting down. He stared into the now softly crackling fire. He was content, except he knew the ball was in his court to respond to James's comments. Thanks to Jack's warning him the night before in his office, Shawn had thought about the issue and had decided the ossuary affair too important to be put off, even if there was the slight possibility the Church might be foolish enough to shoot itself in the foot by punishing one of its best and brightest for something that was clearly not his fault. Shawn had decided not to allow himself to be goaded by any of James's entreaties.

"James," Shawn said, taking a small gulp of wine. "Do you really, truly believe the pope would punish you for something clearly not your fault? I mean, I take full responsibility for what I've done and will do."

"I think there is a distinct chance I will be punished."

"Ah," sighed Shawn, content to hear that James's supposed banishment had gone from a closed deal to a chance in five minutes, which is quite a rapid change of probability. "I believe the Church makes some strange decisions, like not allowing condom use in sub-Saharan Africa to prevent massive death and suffering from AIDS, but I don't think they'd be stupid enough to terminate your career because of my transgressions."

"I believe I know the inner workings of the Church better than you."

"That might be, but it's my opinion. Most significantly, you are not going to goad me into abandoning a project that I see as inordinately important. From my perspective, presenting a challenge to papal infallibility is a positive, not negative, thing, particularly since his infallibility supposedly extends to the arena of morals. The mystical workings of the Holy Spirit aside, it strikes me as nuts to let a supposedly avowed celibate dictate morals in relation to sex and marriage, and declare him to be infallible. It's contrary to human intuition and cognition, and besides, when you consider *sensus fidelium*, which you brought up, the Church via the pope and the Catholic laity have been at odds about sex for years, even probably several generations."

"And I suppose you would be a better arbiter of sexual mores?" James questioned superciliously. He knew his old friend was in his cups.

"I'd be more popular than the current arbiters," Shawn said.

"Why is it that the Catholic Church, particularly the American Catholic Church, has had such a hang-up about sex?"

"The Christian Church from its early days has always felt that marriage and sex have been an impediment to a true union with Jesus Christ, which is certainly the origin of celibacy being required of priests. It is certainly the reason I have been celibate all these years. The sacrifice has made me feel decidedly closer to God, without an ounce of doubt."

"I'm glad you feel that way, but it doesn't surprise me because you're crazy. After all, you had Virginia Sorenson in the palm of your hand and then let her go. Was she a piece of ass, Jack, or what?"

"She was definitely a looker," said Jack, who was equally aware of Shawn's mental state. "And a smart, lovely person as well."

"You've never come clean about Virginia," Shawn continued, his slurring increasing. "Did you nail her homecoming weekend, James? Here's your chance finally to let your buddies know. After all, we were rooting for you and purposefully cleared out to give you space and privacy."

"I refuse to be drawn into a conversation that might be disrespectful of Virginia," James said with definite resolve. "Let's get back to our discussion. How did we start out talking about papal infallibility and get bogged down about sex?"

"Because it is related," Shawn said, glancing at Jack, whose silence he felt was out of character.

"How can it be related?" James questioned. "In modern times, the power of papal infallibility has been used only twice, and neither time did it in any way involve morals or sex. In fact, ironically enough, both times it has been used, first in 1854 and second in 1950, it has involved dogmas associated with the Blessed Virgin. In 1854 Pope Pius the Ninth proclaimed the Immaculate Conception an ex cathedra dogma, which, contrary to many people's belief, is not about the conception of Jesus Christ, Mary's son, but rather

about Mary herself, so like her son, she too would be free of original sin. Of course, the second time was the *Munificentissimus Deus*
of Pius the Twelfth, as I've already mentioned, concerning Mary's
Assumption to heaven body and soul. How on earth do you get
sex out of that?"

"It's not those two episodes of infallibility that has caused the
current problem. From most of the popes down through the ages,
there has been this evolving papal dialogue that sex is evil. I suppose
Pope Gregory the Great was the worst offender, as he's the one who
said all sexual desire was sinful in and of itself. Now, because of the
modern declaration of papal infallibility, these old beliefs have been
given a new legitimacy, at least from the pope's perspective. A modern pope cannot overrule an older pope without undermining his
own legitimacy. And in the arena of attitudes toward sex, this is a
particular problem, because a good portion of the laity has a new,
much more modern view of sex not as sin but as evidence of divinity
itself. The sacrament of marriage, providing a loving sexual union, is
now more sacred in many people's eyes. And far from being evil, it
is both an affirmation of and gift from God. I believe the Church
must abjure its old knee-jerk reaction against sex as sin and rather
affirm that pleasure is divine and that sensual mutuality is something
to strive for. It only makes sense. Why would an all-powerful God
create the pleasure of sex and then insist his children don't use it?"

"It seems to me you are justifying a very self-serving theology,"
James said.

"Maybe so," Shawn agreed. "But I'll tell you, it makes more
sense to me as an individual than the Church's position, and the
Church better recognize that most of its laity agrees with me."

"That is a leap I'm afraid I cannot accept."

"At your and the Church's peril. As a good example is the
celibacy issue. By making celibacy an individual's decision rather
than the Church's, you'd solve the molestation problem and the

priestly recruiting problem both. Just make it a personal decision so there can be crazy priests like you and normal priests who will be in a much better position to advise their flocks on marriage and parenting, the center issues of most people's lives."

"Shawn!" James said. "You are drunk or close to it, so I refuse to take offense, no matter what you call me or what you say. But let me be clear. If you publish anything about the Blessed Virgin's bones being in the ossuary that you have stolen from the Vatican, you will not only hurt me, your friend, but hundreds of thousands of other people, particularly poor, poverty-stricken people, like those of the interior of South America, whose most cherished possession is their faith, which often is centered on the Virgin Mary, whom they look to as the absolute model of faith and spirituality. Shawn, don't do this, especially when it is mostly based on personal vainglorious goals."

" 'Vainglorious goals'!" Shawn shouted. "So you believe you are the only one on a mission here! Well, screw you. This ossuary fell out of the blue into my hands. How do I know it isn't the Lord himself involved, knowing I was someone who would instantly see the power of its truth and be able to use it constructively?"

"You don't know it is the truth," James countered. "That's the point!"

"And that's why I'm investigating," Shawn said. "When I finish with the scrolls—"

"What language are they written in?"

"Aramaic," Shawn blurted.

James's heart fell. He'd had a sudden hope that Simon's scrolls would be in an inappropriate language, to help him discredit them, but Aramaic would have been Simon's native tongue.

"When I finish with the scrolls and Sana finishes with her work—"

"How is Sana's work going to help or deny the authenticity of the bones?" James interjected irritably.

"I have no idea," Shawn said. "I don't totally understand what she does, but it's indicative of our wish to properly investigate the contents of the ossuary to the limits of our abilities."

"In spite of whom you may injure in the process?"

"I see it more in terms of whom we might help, and I include in that the Church itself."

"Do you honestly believe that you may have been selected by Jesus Christ to help guide his Church? Is that what I'm hearing?"

Shawn spread his hands as if exposing himself. "It's possible," he said, but it came out as "ossible," as he was unable to pronounce the *p*.

James let his head fall forward until his chin hit his chest. "This is worse than I imagined."

"How so?" Shawn asked. He wasn't so drunk not to notice a true change in his friend's demeanor.

"I'm beginning to fear for your eternal soul," James said. "Either that or your mental health."

"Hey, you're going overboard," Shawn said. "I feel fine. Perfectly fine. I've never felt better. This ossuary and its contents are the most fascinating subject of my career."

Sana suddenly reappeared from the kitchen bearing a candle-covered chocolate cake and singing "Happy Birthday." Shawn and Jack joined in the singing as Sana placed the cake on the side table next to James's chair. As they finished the birthday ditty, they all clapped.

Self-consciously James slipped forward in his chair, causing the bruise-like discolorations on his cheeks to darken. Taking in a big lungful of air, he blew out all the candles in one large sustained puff amid further applause.

As per usual, he didn't let on what he'd wished, if he'd wished; but if he did, Jack had a good idea what it had been.

24

Do you call this parked?" Jack questioned, standing on the curb with his hands on his hips and gazing at the more than two feet that separated James's Range Rover from where he was standing.

"It was the best I could do," James said. "Don't give me a hard time! Just get in. I assure you I can get you home safely."

Both men climbed into the SUV's front seat. Jack made a point of fastening his seat belt. If James's park job was as good as he could do, Jack was mildly concerned. "You haven't had too much wine, have you?"

"As wired as I am, I don't feel like I've had any."

"I could drive," Jack offered. "I had very little."

"I'm fine," James said as he maneuvered out of the tight space.

They drove in silence through the West Village, each digesting the dinner party's edgy conversation.

"Shawn is impossible," James said suddenly, while they waited for a traffic light before getting onto the West Side Highway. "Of course, he's always been impossible."

"He's always been his own person," Jack said.

James glanced in Jack's direction, catching the man's strong profile against the streetlights. "That's rather limp support."

Jack looked over at James, and their eyes caught for a moment before the light changed, and James had to drive ahead. "I'm sorry," Jack said. "And I probably shouldn't say anything at all for fear of making things worse for you. I can certainly tell how passionately you feel, but from my humble perspective, he does seem to have a point."

"You're on his side?" James demanded, with a mixture of surprise and dismay.

"No, I'm not on anyone's side," Jack said. "But last time he invited me to dinner, which I told you about, and we were alone, washing the dishes, we did speak briefly about you and your impressive successes with the Church hierarchy. That stimulated him to tell me a few things that I'd never known. By the time we all came in contact, in college, he was already a lapsed Catholic, but I had never known why."

James cast another quick glance in Jack's direction before returning his attention to the road. "Don't tell me! He wasn't molested himself, was he?"

"No, nothing as dramatic as that, but close."

"This is new material," James said. "What do you mean 'close'?"

"Because I had no experience with religion growing up in an atheist household, I feel at a disadvantage telling his story, but I'll give it a go. Apparently, as a very young teenager, he loved the Church, as did both his parents."

"I'm aware of that," James said.

"Then you know he and his parents were very active in their parish."

"I'm aware of that as well."

"Anyhow," Jack said, "he reached puberty without much preparation, maybe none. As he tells it, it is rather humorous if nothing else. Apparently, he masturbated the first time by accident and utter surprise. He was in the shower, and he was washing his privates such that the cleaner they got, the better it felt, until he had an orgasm, which he described as divine pleasure. For obvious reasons, that episode ushered in a proclivity for taking showers, up to three a day, which made him feel closer to God and all the saints than he ever had previously."

James found himself chuckling despite his general unease. He could clearly see Shawn telling such a story, as he was a gifted raconteur. A moment later he quieted, as he feared how the story was about to unfold.

"Apparently," Jack continued, "it was several blissful weeks later that he came in contact with the teaching of the pope he mentioned tonight."

"You mean Pope Gregory the Great?" James asked.

"I believe that's the one," Jack said. "Was he as negative about sex as Shawn suggested?"

"He was," James admitted.

"Anyway," Jack continued, "Shawn described the collision with the supposed antimasturbation dogma of the Church and his own sense of experiencing the divine as cataclysmic, especially learning that to receive the Eucharist he had to confess every episode of self-gratification and every unclean thought, such as fantasizing about Elaine Smith's ass."

"Was Elaine Smith's ass something to admire?"

"According to Shawn and the number of times he had to confess he'd fantasized about giving it a good look."

"I know this amusing anecdote has to be going somewhere bad, so let's hear it."

"Shawn said he struggled with this epic battle for as much as

six months, trying to regain his chaste life so as to be in accordance
with Church dogma. To do so required him to confess his transgressions week after week, such that to remember what he'd done
when he got into the confessional, he began to keep a very accurate diary of his masturbation episodes, which had moved out of
the shower because, as he said, his skin became too dry. As for his
unclean thoughts, they had expanded to take in more parts of
Elaine Smith's supposedly enchanting anatomy."

"You're dragging this out," James complained.

"Okay," Jack agreed. "Sorry. As I said, this battle went on for
months, with Shawn doing his best to remember everything he did
and confess it each Friday in minute detail."

"And?" James asked impatiently.

"Shawn began to notice that the two priests who normally
heard confessions began to get progressively interested."

"Good Lord, no!" James uttered.

"Don't get upset," Jack warned. "Nothing really happened, at
least overtly."

"Thank God!"

"But no matter how much detail Shawn offered in the confessional, it was never enough, and each week toward the end, he was
asked more and more questions, such as even he, as a newly pu-
bescent teenager, knew that something was wrong. The crowning
moment for Shawn was when one of the priests offered, in the
confessional, to meet with him privately to help him overcome
this soul-endangering habit."

"Did they ever meet?"

"Not according to Shawn. Instead it was at that point, to the
consternation of his parents, that Shawn decided he and the
Church would sever relations, supposedly on a temporary basis but
which has been maintained until today."

"That is an unfortunate happening," James agreed. "It is a pity that he didn't have more knowledgeable priests to help him at such a crucial juncture."

"But isn't that one of Shawn's points? Celibate priests are probably not the best guides for children through the stresses of puberty, just as they are probably not the best guides for young adults starting families. Having children is always much more problematic than people imagine, even in the best of circumstances." Jack couldn't help but think about his own current situation.

"I cannot contest that, and it is an issue I will pray upon. But now I have to concentrate on the problem at hand."

"You mean your hope of talking Shawn out of publishing his findings?"

"Exactly."

"Here's my sentiment. You are fighting an awfully steep uphill battle. Unless Shawn and his wife come up with definitive proof somehow that the bones cannot be the Blessed Virgin's, he is going to publish that they are, even if he cannot prove it. You are not going to talk him out of it. Your switching your attack from talking about his hurting the Church in general to hurting you personally was clever, but even that didn't sway him, especially after he got you to admit you didn't believe yourself that it was inevitable you'd be punished for his errors."

"Unfortunately, I think you are right," James said with resignation. "I'm the last person who should be trying to talk him out of something he truly wants to do and has convinced himself he should do as if he's on a mission from God. When I heard that, I knew I was surely barking up the wrong tree. Thank goodness it's not as messianic as I'd feared when I first heard it."

"Why do you think you are the last person who should be trying to influence him?" Jack questioned. "I think you are the perfect person. He knows you, trusts you, and you have probably the most clerical credibility of anyone in this country."

"We're too good friends," James explained, as he exited from the West Side Highway at 96th Street. "I know he was quite besotted, but he still feels comfortable calling me lardo, which is what he used to call me in college when he was angry, which he knows I detest, probably because it is rather accurate. But such familiarity puts me at a distinct disadvantage."

"If not you, who?" Jack asked. "I hope you're not thinking of me, because I haven't been any more successful than you've been. In fact, I've been completely unsuccessful. Especially compared with you two guys, I know nothing about the Catholic Church."

"Where is it you live again?" James asked, after reassuring Jack he didn't intend to saddle him with the problem of Shawn and Sana. Jack gave him the street and the number.

"So if not me, who?" Jack persisted.

"That's the problem," James said, approaching Jack's home. "I haven't the faintest idea, although I'm beginning to have an idea of the qualities I'd like the person to have."

"Like what?"

"Persuasive, of course, but more important, absolutely and completely devoted to the Blessed Virgin. I mean a young person who has totally dedicated his or her life to the study and veneration of the Virgin Mary."

"That's an idea," Jack said, suddenly sitting up. "A young attractive woman! Or we could find his old friend Elaine Smith, especially if she'd maintained her figure and had become a specialist in Mariology."

"I know you are trying to buoy my spirits by being humorous, but I'm being serious here, my friend. I need to find immediately an incredibly persuasive zealot, tell him or her the story, and force Shawn to put up with him or her for a number of days. That is my last hope. I hadn't thought of such a plan, because I was hoping not to have to tell anyone else the story to avoid anyone besides the four of us from knowing it. Obviously, I've decided it is a risk we have to take."

James pulled over to the side of the road directly opposite the stoop on the front of Jack's house. "Thanks for coming tonight. I really appreciate it. And thank your wife for letting you come, and tell her I'm looking forward to meeting her."

After shaking hands, Jack put his hand on the door opener, then looked back at James. "How are you going to find this person you've described in time? I don't think I've ever met a single person who comes close to fulfilling those narrow requirements."

"Actually, I don't think it will be too difficult. Christianity has never been without its share of fanatics and zealots. Luckily, the early bishops recognized these people and supported them, creating in the process the concept of monasticism, where people could go to commit themselves entirely to God, or later to the Virgin Mary. Monasticism thrived, and it still does. In my archdiocese alone there are probably a hundred or more, some of which the chancery doesn't even know about, and some of which if we did, we would try to shut down. I'm going to start a rapid search of these institutions and find the perfect person."

"Good luck!" Jack said, climbing down from the Range Rover's cab and shutting the door behind him. Then he stood there in the street for a few minutes, waving and watching James's taillights until they reached Columbus Avenue and turned left. Heading up his front steps by twos, Jack was invigorated. He felt like he was a participant in a kind of unfolding real-life mystery-thriller, the denouement of which taxed his creativity to even imagine how it was going to play out. The only thing he sensed was that Shawn was not going to back down easily.

James felt better than he had all day, and specifically better than he had all evening. Plan B had evolved out of nowhere, and he gently chided himself for not thinking of it earlier. As the early monks had helped stabilize the early Church, particularly after Constantine had legalized Christianity and let in the masses, the monks of today would come to the Church's aid. Somehow James was sure of it, and sure that he would find the individual who could do it.

Consciously suppressing his urge to drive too quickly in order to get to the residence, where he intended to begin plan B that very evening, James drove down Central Park West to Columbus Circle. From there he used Central Park South to cross to the East Side and drop off his vehicle at his garage. Then he walked quickly home to the residence, deliberately trying to be noisy when he entered the front door.

It soon became obvious that he'd not been noisy enough, as neither Father Maloney nor Father Karlin appeared. Assuming they were already settled for the night in their small gabled rooms on the fourth floor, James climbed into the residence's small elevator, which he rarely used, and was whisked up to the top floor. Climbing out of the car on the tiny upper hallway, James banged mercilessly on the two doors, calling out that he wanted to see both secretaries in his office ASAP.

With the surprising announcement made and without waiting for a response, James returned into the elevator and descended two floors. Once in his office, he turned on the lights and then settled back behind his desk to await the surprised secretaries. Never before had James disturbed them once they'd retired for the day.

Father Maloney was the first to arrive. He'd merely pulled on his plaid robe over pajamas and to James resembled a scarecrow because of his height, the thinness of his body, and the gauntness of his face. Even his cropped short red hair sticking out in spikes added to the impression, as it looked something like straw.

"Where's Father Karlin?" James demanded, without giving any explanation for such an unprecedented late-night meeting.

"He called out to me through his closed door he'd be here as soon as he could manage . . ." Father Maloney said. His voice trailed off, as he was hoping for an explanation of what was on the archbishop's mind, but nothing was forthcoming.

James impatiently drummed his fingers on his desk. Just when he was about to pick up his phone and call Father Karlin's room, the man walked into the office. In contrast to Father Maloney, he'd assumed the worst—namely, that he'd be up for hours—and had taken the time to fully dress, artificial white clerical collar and all.

"Sorry to interrupt your prayers," James said to begin. He motioned for his two secretaries to sit. Tenting his fingers, he added, "We have what I consider to be an emergency. I'm not going to tell you exactly why, but you two have to find me immediately a person who is charismatic and persuasive and generally alluring in some manner. But most of all, he or she must be fanatically passionate and zealous about the Blessed Virgin Mary, the more the better, and totally committed to the Church with a sense of mission."

The two priests glanced at each other, each hoping the other understood the assignment and how to proceed better than the other. As the senior secretary, Father Maloney spoke: "Where would we find such a person?"

In his excitement, James had little patience for what he interpreted as negativity on his secretaries' part. He rolled his eyes at

Father Maloney's ridiculous question. "I ask you," James said with uncamouflaged frustration, "where ultra-devoted followers of Mary, the Mother of God, might be found?"

"I suppose as members of Roman Catholic Marian movements and societies."

"Very good, Father Maloney," James said with a touch of sarcasm, acting as if he was teaching a Sunday-morning catechism class to preteens. "Starting at the crack of dawn, I want you to begin calling such institutions and talk to their abbots, mother superiors, or bishops, to let them know that I have called this an archdiocesan emergency to find the right person. Let them know it is a serious affair, as this individual will for a week or so work directly under me on a mission of high importance concerning the Blessed Virgin and the Church in general. And make it clear that this is not an award for someone's past labors. It is for the here and now. I'm not looking for an old, distinguished Marian scholar. Actually, I'm looking for a young person filled with youthful zealousness who is mystically capable of expressing his or her zeal to others. Do I have full understanding here?"

Both Father Maloney and Father Karlin quickly nodded. They had never seen their usually in-control boss quite so fervid.

"Now, I would participate myself, but I have Mass to celebrate in the morning with a sermon, which I have yet to outline. I need to trust that you two will not fail me. When I return here to the residence around noon, I want there to be at least one and hopefully several candidates for me to interview. How you get them here, I do not care, nor is cost an issue. As the weather is supposed to be good, a helicopter might be necessary. Again I ask, are both of you on the same page here, or what?"

"You have not told us what this person will be actually doing," Father Maloney said, "and you have specifically said that you would not. But I can see that question coming up from the abbots, mother superiors, and bishops. What should we answer?"

"Answer that it is my judgment that no one, except of course the individual selected, should know the problem the archdiocese is facing."

"Very good," Father Maloney said as he got to his feet and clasped his robe more tightly about his bony slenderness. Father Karlin stood as well.

"That will be all," James said. "And I pray you will be successful."

"Thank you, Your Eminence," Father Maloney said, bowing slighting at the waist before following Father Karlin by backing out the door.

As the two priests climbed the flight of stairs from the second floor to the third, Father Karlin, who was in the lead, called down to Father Maloney, who was just starting up, "This might be the strangest task I've been charged with since my arrival here five years ago."

"I guess I'd have to agree," Father Maloney said.

At the base of the stair run up to the fourth floor, Father Karlin hesitated and waited for his colleague. "How are we going to get the phone numbers of these Marian societies?"

"There are plenty of ways," Father Maloney said, "especially now, with the Internet. Besides, it was clear that the cardinal wants a particularly extreme individual. For that we go to the most radical organization. Maybe, if we're lucky, one call may do the trick."

"Are you aware of the most fanatical organization?"

"I believe I am," Father Maloney said. "A friend of my family contacted me several years ago to try to get their child out of an organization called the Brotherhood of the Slaves of Mary. I had never heard of it, and it's not that far away, literally up in the

Catskill Mountains, although figuratively it's on another planet. Apparently, it's a modern revival of a seventeenth-century fanatical European Marian society, which the then Pope Clement the Tenth felt compelled to outlaw some of the practices of."

"Good grief," Father Karlin voiced. "What kind of practices?"

"Using chains and other enslavement instruments for penance for mankind's sins."

"Dear God," Father Karlin added. "Did you manage to get the child out?"

"I didn't. Multiple phone calls and even a visit were for naught. He apparently loved the place, as it was what he needed. I don't know if he's still there or not. I haven't been in contact with the family, as they were disappointed in my efforts."

"Do you still have the contact numbers?"

"I do. I'll call first thing. Of course, if the cardinal knew the society existed and he visited it, he'd probably close it down."

"That is an irony, especially if we find someone there who fulfills the cardinal's needs."

25

James enjoyed a heady sensation as he left the cathedral redolent
with incense to make his way back to the residence. The cathedral had been packed for the High Mass, with people standing
along the aisles and not a single seat available in the entire nave.
The choir had done an excellent job with nary a mistake, and his
sermon had gone well and had been well received. The previous
evening, after the secretaries had left to return to their gabled
rooms, James had decided to preach that morning about the role
of Mary in the modern Church, both because it was appropriate
for the feast day coming up the next day and because it had been
dominating his mind for several days.

Now, with the stress of the High Mass out of the way, James
was eager to get back to the Shawn, Sana, and the ossuary issue.
He knew that the upcoming week was going to be critical, and he
prayed that his secretaries had made some progress. As he came
up the stair, the first thing he saw was that the wooden bench just
outside his office was occupied by what looked like a fifteen- to
sixteen-year-old towheaded boy with such a beauteous face,

beatific smile, and lustrous, shoulder-length, golden hair that James did a double take, believing he could be having a vision of the Angel Gabriel. The boy was dressed in a black habit with a hood, cinched with a medium-blue cord.

Gathering his wits with some difficulty, James broke off eye contact with the youth and passed into his office. Quickly, he slipped behind his massive oak desk to catch his breath, knowing that Father Maloney would undoubtedly momentarily materialize. The big question in James's mind was whether or not the boy was someone chosen as the possible interventionist. If so, James's immediate impact was off the charts, which was something he was hoping for. Yet as positive as that was, there was a problem. The individual was too young, a mere boy, and James asked himself if he could possibly entrust someone so immature with such an important task.

As James expected, the door opened after a sharp knock, and in stepped the secretary. Carrying a folder, Father Maloney quickly crossed to the desk and handed it to James. "His name is Luke Hester, and yes, he was definitely named after the evangelist Luke."

"He is striking," James said. "I have to commend you on that, but isn't he too young for a theological emergency? There is going to be a need for some innate psychology."

"If you check the rapid biography I've thrown together, you will learn that he is older and therefore hopefully wiser than his youthful, angelic looks suggest. He is twenty-five years old, about to be twenty-six in a matter of months."

"My word," James exclaimed. He placed the folder on his desk and opened the cover and stared at the date of birth. "I never would have guessed."

"There was a kind of mild hormonal problem that had never been investigated," Father Maloney stated. "But that problem has been attended to and his hormones are now in the normal range.

The brothers where he lives had him evaluated and treated a few years ago here in the city."

"I see," James said, rapidly glancing through the biography and learning that Luke was an only child of a devout Catholic mother and lapsed Catholic father. The boy had run away from home to join a Marian society called the Brotherhood of the Slaves of Mary when he turned eighteen.

"Have you spoken with him?"

"I have. I believe he comes the closest to the individual you described last night than anyone I've ever met. *Charismatic* is not a strong enough word. He's also disarmingly intelligent."

"Is he committed to the Virgin Mary?"

"Totally, heart and soul. He is a walking, talking homily to the Blessed Virgin."

"Thank you, Father Maloney. Why don't you have him come in."

A half-hour later, James was as convinced as Father Maloney. From James's perspective, Luke couldn't have been better qualified if he'd been sent from central casting. His relatively short life had not been easy, caught among an alcoholic, abusive father and a victimized, overindulgent mother and a pair of rural priests who had failed him. James hated hearing about the priests, especially having heard a similar story the previous night from Jack about Shawn. But what he did like hearing was Luke's description of finding the Virgin Mary and how she had saved him as well as returned to him his trust in the Church itself.

Once he was convinced that Luke was a good candidate to be the needed savior, James switched the conversation to the problem posed by Shawn and the ossuary, but not before extracting from Luke the solemn oath of secrecy based on his love for the Blessed Virgin.

"Appropriately enough, the problem involves the Mother of God," James said, as soon as Luke had pledged his word. James went on to tell the story of the discovery of the ossuary, his belief that it was fake, its illegal transport to the United States, and its recent opening. He then described Shawn's commitment to damage the reputation of the Virgin by suggesting the bones in the ossuary were hers, and thereby discrediting the infallibility of the pope. "It will be a devastating rebuke to both Mary and the Church," James stated. "And only you will stand between Dr. Daughtry and such an abomination."

"Am I worthy?" Luke questioned, in a deeper voice than one would expect based on his youthful appearance.

"As archbishop, I believe you are worthy and uniquely qualified because of your veneration of the Blessed Virgin. Although it will not be an easy task, as I believe your opponent has the help and attention of Satan, it is imperative you succeed."

"How do you see me accomplishing this task?" Luke asked, in a tone belying his youthful appearance.

James sat back and thought for a moment. In truth, he'd not thought past finding the perfect person, but now that he believed he might have, he tried to think of the details. The first, of course, was to get Luke and Shawn together for an extended period of time. Only then would Luke have the opportunity to convey to Shawn the devastation he personally would suffer if Shawn goes along with his publishing plans.

"What I will do is get you invited as a houseguest at the Daughtrys' home in the Village. That will give you access and time. You were told you'd be here in the city for a week or so, correct?"

"That is correct, but I am concerned about such a long stay, Your Eminence. I have not allowed myself to be in the occasion of sin since I moved in with the brothers."

"You'll be too busy to worry about being in the occasion of sin," James assured him. "As I said, this will not be an easy assignment. In fact, it may not work, but it is imperative that you try your best. I tried, but I have failed. I'm entirely confident, however, that in his heart of hearts, Dr. Daughtry is a devoted Catholic. He just needs to get back in touch with that aspect of himself."

"What if Dr. Daughtry and his wife repudiate me?"

"That's a risk we have to take," James said. "I still have some power with my friend, which I will try to use to advantage to keep him from spurning you. Besides, I'm going to be completely up front with him by telling him exactly why you are there, so there will be no surprises. God has picked you to be the savior of Blessed Mary's reputation and her standing in the Church as being free of sin and therefore worthy to be assumed into heaven body and soul."

"When can I start this mission?" Luke asked, eager to begin.

"I believe you can start later today," James said. "Here's the plan. I will have one of my secretaries take you over to the cathedral, where I would like you to pray for guidance from the Lord for this role you are about to undertake for Mary and the Church's benefit. While you are there, I will go out and prepare your reception. I could do it by phone, but I think in person will be better. If I'm unsuccessful getting you invited to spend the night and hopefully a good portion of the week at the Daughtrys', then you will stay here with us in our guest room. Fair enough?"

"I'm grateful to be given this opportunity, Your Eminence."

"It is I who am grateful," James said, picking up his phone and asking Father Maloney to come in.

Although still not positive this plan B was going to work, James felt better than he had since the arrival of the ossuary. At least he had a plan and was doing something. Returning to his private apartment, James changed back into the civilian clothes he wore the night before at the Daughtrys'. He could even recognize an olfactory reminder of the evening's wood fire on his sweater. It was a pleasant aroma, which reminded him of his retreat at Green Pond.

Without offering any explanation to Father Karlin, who was sitting just outside, James left his office, descended to the first floor, and used the indoor connection between the residence and the cathedral for the third time that day. When it was as cold as it was that day, it was a welcome luxury. Halfway he met up with Father Maloney, who said he'd deposited Luke in the central nave.

"You did fine work finding Luke," James commented. "If what I'm trying to do happens, we will all be in your debt. He is exactly what I had in mind."

"I am pleased to be of service, Your Eminence," Father Maloney said. Lifting his head to make himself slightly taller, he strode away toward the residence.

As James passed through the cathedral, he made it a point to catch a brief glimpse of his new monk warrior. He was, as instructed, kneeling in prayer with his blue eyes closed but with the same beatific smile on his face. As if attracted like flies to honey, a group of people were clustered near him, making James wonder if they'd been drawn to him or he to them.

Emerging incognito from the front of the cathedral directly onto Fifth Avenue, James waved for a cab. Climbing in, he asked for 26th Street and First Avenue. He was pleased not to be recognized coming out of his own church.

With minimum traffic, the cab made good time. En route, he pulled out his cell phone and called Jack. As if pouncing on the call, Jack answered before the first ring had been completed. "That was fast," James said. "Were you waiting for my call?"

"I thought it was going to be my wife, Laurie," Jack said.

"Sorry to disappoint."

"Not at all. In fact, I'm relieved. When I left this morning, our new baby was unhappy. I was concerned I was about to learn it had worsened. What's up?"

"Where are you?"

"I'm with Sana and Shawn here at the OCME DNA building."

"I was hoping that would be the case."

"Why is that?"

"Simply because I'm on my way there as we speak. Ask Shawn if it is okay and if I'm welcome."

Jack went off the line. James could hear him ask Shawn, and he could hear Shawn's enthusiastic acquiescence. "Did you hear that?" Jack asked, coming back.

"I did."

"When will you be here? I'll have to come down to get you through security."

"Rather quickly," James said. "I'm in a taxi on Park Avenue passing Thirty-sixth Street at this very moment."

"I'll start down now," Jack said.

Within five minutes, James's taxi was cruising down 26th Street. James had the driver cross First Avenue and drop him off at the DNA building's pullout. Jack was waiting just inside the glass revolving door.

"Thanks again for giving me a ride home last night," Jack said.

"It was my pleasure," James answered.

After easily passing through security with Jack vouching for James, the two rode up in the elevator.

"I've found my zealot to work on Shawn," James announced as they exited on the eighth floor.

"Really!" Jack commented. He was surprised. "So quick. When you described the kind of person you would be looking for, all I could think of was *Good luck*. I thought it would take months."

"I have resourceful secretaries."

"You must."

They came to the door to the laboratory Sana and Shawn had been assigned, and Jack knocked. Shawn, who was sitting at the center table with his back to the door, leaped up and opened it.

James entered with some trepidation of what he would find, and his fears were quickly validated. In front of him were the bones of the ossuary laid out on the table in anatomical positions. Even though he trusted in his heart they were not the bones of the Blessed Virgin, having them so irreverently displayed seemed to him a sacrilege similar to how he felt when he'd watched Shawn and Sana dump the ossuary into the dirty trunk of the taxi. James found himself trembling.

"What on earth is the matter?" Shawn questioned, sensing James's discomfiture.

"These bones," James managed. "It seems so disrespectful. It's like staring at someone naked."

"Should I cover them with some gowns while you are here?" Shawn questioned.

"It's not necessary," James insisted. "It was just the initial shock." Instead of looking at the bones, James directed his attention to Shawn's work area at the end of the table, where he had the first of the three scrolls immobilized and his Rube Goldberg cold-humidifying device set up along with a stack of glass panes. It was obvious that his unrolling the scroll was proceeding at a snail's pace.

"Are you having trouble?" James asked, bending over to look at the script on the several pages that had been unrolled.

"It's a painstaking process," Shawn agreed.

"It's very beautiful Aramaic script," James commented. "Have you learned any more?"

"After the first two very enlightening pages, the text has devolved to an autobiography of Simon's childhood and his early progress of becoming a magician. It seems that he had very early success."

"How's Sana making out with her mitochondrial DNA work?" James asked. He looked through the glazed door into the gowning room and then through a second glazed door into the laboratory itself. James could see Sana scurrying about with an intent expression on her face.

"If you want to go in, you'll have to gown and glove and put on a hood. She's being very careful about contamination. As far as her progress is concerned, I haven't the faintest idea. When we arrived this morning, she went directly in there after changing into her scrubs. My sense is that she's doing just fine. If not, I'm sure she would have been back in here to complain. Thanks to Jack, she's got a terrific lab to work in, with all the latest equipment."

James rapped loudly on the gowning-room glass door in hopes of attracting Sana's attention. He could tell it was immediately successful, because she suddenly stopped moving and lifted her head as if listening. James rapped on the glass again and caught her attention by waving. She waved back. Then James waved for her to come back into the outer office, which she immediately did.

"Good morning, James," Sana said as she poked her hooded head into the office. "Or is it afternoon already?"

"It's afternoon," James said. "And would you mind joining us for a few moments? I have a proposition to share with you people."

Sana hesitated, realizing she'd have to change her scrubs if she passed beyond the gowning room. Recognizing that was hardly much of an inconvenience, she stepped beyond the door she was holding ajar and let it close behind her.

"What kind of proposition?" Shawn asked warily.

"Yes, what do you have in mind?" Sana questioned, while pulling off her hood.

"First, let me ask how you are doing in there?" James questioned. "I see Shawn is making headway, if not at the speed he'd prefer."

"I'm doing extremely well," Sana said. "The lab is truly

twenty-first-century and conveniently designed to maximize productivity. I'm already going to be at the extraction phase this
afternoon with the centrifuges. Right now my pulp sample is in
the solvents with the detergent to break open the cells and the
proteinases to denature the proteins. At this rate, I could be at the
polymerase chain reaction, or PCR, stage as early as tomorrow."

"No need to fill me in on the details," James said. "It's all Greek
to me!"

Everyone laughed, even James. "Second of all, I'd like to thank
you for such a wonderful evening last night, and say that the food
was out of this world."

"Thank you, Father," Sana said, blushing to a degree.

"I wish I could say the same about the company," James added,
with a chuckle to indicate he was trying to be humorous. "I'm joking, of course, but I was disappointed to learn that my wish for the
Blessed Virgin to be left out of this affair is not going to happen.
At least not at this time. Am I right in this assumption, Shawn?"

"Absolutely. I don't know how to be more clear. Last night I
must confess I was bombed, and for the life of me I cannot remember everything I said. For that I apologize, but I believe I was
quite clear about my intentions in relation to the ossuary and its
contents."

"Clear, indeed," James said. "Clear enough for me to spend a
good amount of time thinking and praying for guidance after leaving your home last night about what I should do to try to change
your mind. First of all, I personally have given up trying to do it
myself. We are too familiar with each other, as evidenced by your
calling me lardo."

"Good God!" Shawn cried, slapping his forehead. "Don't tell me
I called you lardo. How disrespectful. I'm terribly sorry, old friend."

"I'm afraid you did," James said. "But you are forgiven, as I have
done far too little to diminish its sad appropriateness. Going

beyond that, I have decided to allow you both to continue your studies of the ossuary contents, with one caveat."

A small, derisive smile appeared on Shawn's face. "What makes you think you are *allowing* us to do our work? From my perspective, your wishes are relatively irrelevant, although, being a realist, a call from you to Jack's boss might be sufficient to put us out on the street. But if that happens, we will go elsewhere."

"Sometimes I am truly surprised at your naïveté," James said. "First of all, you still don't seem to recognize that ultimately the proof of these bones being those of the Blessed Virgin must rely on Simon Magus telling his assistant, Saturninus, that it was so. From a theological perspective, which is what this is all about, you are basing your argument on the worst possible source. If all Simon wanted to do was trade the bones for Peter's healing powers, there would have been no need to make the extra effort to get the real ones. Any female bones would have sufficed, which is what I believe these bones are. They are the bones of a random first-century female, not the Blessed Virgin's."

"I counter that argument with Saturninus's statement about Simon being disappointed that the bones themselves didn't mystically convey to him the healing power. If they weren't definitely the Virgin's bones, he wouldn't have suspected or hoped that they would have done the trick themselves."

"I've given up debating this affair," James said, holding up his hand. "As I said earlier, I have relinquished trying to change your mind myself. But as for my power to stop you, consider this. Unless you accept the caveat I alluded to, I plan to go to the authorities today. That sounds like a desperate move, but I am desperate for the Church and myself. I will declare the ossuary a hoax and you a thief so that instead of being an accessory, I will more likely be considered a hero for risking myself to expose this faithless attack on the Church."

"You wouldn't do that," Shawn said, but without much confidence. After all, had he been caught in a web similar to James's, he might very well do the same thing. For as much as the ossuary affair was a win-win for him, for James it was clearly a lose-lose.

"I'm going to contact the Pontifical Commission for Sacred Archaeology today, let them know how you abused their original courtesy to you, and let them contact their counterparts in both the Italian and Egyptian governments, who will not take kindly to your antics, and who will demand you be arrested, and you, too, Sana. Whether there will be an extradition, I don't know, but surely the ossuary and its contents will immediately be returned, as will the codex and Saturninus's letter."

"You're extorting me!" Shawn cried.

"How would you characterize what you are doing to me?"

"This is outrageous," Shawn continued.

"What is the caveat you spoke of?" Sana questioned.

"Thankfully, we have one sensible individual as part of the conspiracy," James said. "The caveat is very simple and quite innocuous. I have found a charming, even radiant, young man who has in effect devoted his life to Mary and has been living in a Marian monastery for nearly the last eight years. I want you to hear from him and to feel his passion, and I want you to do it not as two ships passing in the night, which would enable you to close your ears to him and wall up your heart. I want you to spend quality time with him. Being realistic, how much longer do you two think you will need to study the ossuary's contents?"

Shawn looked up at Sana, who responded, "My input in this affair, as I mentioned, is going extremely well. Provided there are no surprises, a total of about a week at most."

"It's harder for me to say," Shawn admitted. "It's all up to how long the unrolling is going to take. My guess and hope is that after one or two more three-hundred-sixty-degree cycles, it will become one hundred percent easier. It's been my experience that the original moisture caused more of a problem with the pages closest to the scroll's surface. With that variable in mind, I'd say anywhere from one week to two months."

"All right, then," James said. "I'll accept you people inviting Luke Hester as a houseguest for one week. But this must be, as I said, quality time. You must engage him and be interested in his life story, which has not been the easiest. The man has suffered but with the help of the Blessed Virgin has overcome his travail and torments. In other words, you must be hospitable to him as a true guest, like the child of one of your closest friends."

"What's being hospitable?" Shawn asked warily. In some ways, this caveat seemed too easy. In other ways, he thought it capable of driving him crazy. Shawn had never been good at small talk, except with attractive women in bars with the aid of alcoholic lubricant.

"I believe that is intuitive," James said.

"How old is this man?" Sana said.

"I'll leave that up to you to determine," James said. "There is a disconnect between his age and his appearance. I found him very easy to speak with, and he is, as I said, quite charming and intelligent. Of course he might have some psychological scars from his difficult childhood, but they were not apparent at all when I interviewed him."

"I hope you're not sticking us with some young, proselytizing born-again Christian," Shawn said. "I'm not sure I could take a week of that."

"I mentioned he is charming," James said. "I meant it. I've also told him the whole story about the ossuary, so you will have plenty to talk about. Now, what I'd like to know is whether we have a clear understanding of what the deal is here. I'm going to give him a mobile phone so he can call me. If he calls and complains that either of you is not engaging him appropriately, the deal is off. Is that understood?" James looked at both Shawn and Sana in turn, making sure he got clear acquiescence from both. The very last thing he wanted was for one of them, after the fact, to claim that they didn't understand the deal. With a threat, the problem was that you had to be willing to carry it out.

"When is this guest week going to begin?" Sana questioned.

"What time will you be getting home tonight?" James asked.

"About five would be my guess," Sana said.

"He'll be waiting at your door," James said.

"Wait a second," Shawn said. He looked at Sana. "We're planning on going out to dinner tonight, as Sana had enough of the kitchen last night."

"That's not a problem," James said. "He's eminently presentable. It will be a good way for you all to get acquainted on neutral ground."

"We've got to take this stranger out to dinner?" Shawn complained.

"Why not? It's a good way to start the relationship. I imagine it's been a long time since he's been taken out to dinner, if he's ever been taken out to dinner. Think of the excitement you'll be adding to this man's life."

"Who's going to pay?" Shawn asked.

"I don't believe you," James said, "but I should. You are as cheap as you were in college."

"That's for sure," Jack said, speaking up for the first time.

"If I have to endure it, I don't think I should have to pay for it," Shawn said, defending himself.

"The archdiocese will cover Mr. Hester's meal tonight, but not yours, big spender. Keep accurate records and receipts if you expect to be reimbursed."

"No problem," Shawn said. "Now, if you don't mind, I'd like to get back to work."

26

Luke Hester had never felt quite so vulnerable as he did standing at the front door to the Daughtrys' wooden house beneath the cone of light from a downward-directed spotlight. He'd just used the door knocker to announce himself, and the harshness and loudness of the clang had surprised him and fanned the fires of his nervousness. Turning, he eyed the vehicle in which he'd been driven down to the Village with the archbishop sitting at the wheel. Self-consciously, he waved. The archbishop waved back and gave him a thumbs-up sign. Luke did the same back, wishing he felt half as confident as the archbishop professed to feel that he, Luke, was going to be successful talking the husband-and-wife team out of publishing articles detrimental to the Blessed Virgin and the Church. What had caused him the most pause was the cardinal's assertion that Dr. Daughtry has the help and attention of Satan. As a consequence, Luke was terrified to face whoever was about to open the door.

Perhaps the biggest reason Luke had not allowed himself to leave the monastery on his own since he'd fled there eight years ago was the fear that he would have to confront Satan, and here he was doing just that. And although he'd been forced during his teenage years to deal with Satan on a daily basis through his godless father, Luke conceded that he was still probably the least capable person to deal with the Prince of Darkness on any level.

Adding to his unease and vulnerability was Luke's apparel. It had been James's idea that wearing his Brotherhood of the Slaves of Mary habit would be too much for Shawn, so Fathers Maloney and Karlin had between the two of them come up with a very casual wardrobe of jeans and shirts, some of which he was wearing at that moment and the rest of which he had stashed in a small roll-on suitcase at his side. Also in the suitcase were toiletries that the two priests had gone out to buy, as Luke had brought nothing of the kind with him from the monastery. Besides clothes and toiletries, the suitcase contained a cell phone, some cash, and a new Rosary blessed by the Holy Father himself as a special gift from the cardinal. If he needed anything, Luke was supposed to call Father Maloney or His Eminence.

Suddenly, the Daughtrys' door was pulled open to its full extent, and Sana and Luke confronted each other. Both froze in total surprise, as neither person came close to matching the other's expectation. Sana was the most surprised, instantly overwhelmed, as James had been, by both Luke's angelic, youthful appearance and virtuous aura but mostly by his soft, imploring eyes that looked to her like bottomless crystal-blue pools and his pouty, vulnerable lips. For his part, Luke had expected an unattractive, threatening male figure like an allegorical image of the devil in a medieval painting.

"Luke?" Sana questioned, as if she was experiencing a vision.

"Mrs. Daughtry?" Luke questioned, as if perhaps he was at the wrong house.

Sana looked around Luke's thin but shapely body and caught sight of James, who had his vehicle's interior light on. She waved to let him know that Luke was safe. James responded with a wave of his own, and then turned the vehicle's interior light off in preparation of leaving.

"Please come in!" Sana said, with an uncertain voice. She was weak-kneed and astounded by Luke's luminosity, particularly the color and shine of his shoulder-length white-blond hair and the perfection of his skin as he passed by her. "Shawn!" she called out. "Our guest's here."

Shawn appeared from the kitchen with a scotch on the rocks in his right hand. With a surprised reaction similar to Sana's, he pulled himself up short and gazed openmouthed at Luke. "Good Lord, boy, how old are you?"

"Twenty-five, sir," Luke said. "About to be twenty-six." He was relieved to a degree. Shawn didn't look quite as formidable or devilish as he had feared.

"You appear much younger," Shawn commented. The boy had such enviably perfect skin, and teeth as white as new fallen snow.

"Many people have said as much," Luke responded.

"You are to be our houseguest for a week," Shawn continued. "Welcome."

"Thank you, sir," Luke responsed. "And I was told you have been openly informed why I am here."

"You have been retained to talk me out of publishing my work."

"Only if it deals with the Blessed Virgin Mary, Mother of the Church, Mother of Christ, Mother of God, my personal savior, who has brought me to Christ, Mary of the Immaculate Conception, Mary Queen of Heaven, Queen of Peace, Stella Maris, and Mother of All Sorrows. It is to her I am devoted and have already begun to pray that you will not denigrate her by suggesting she was not assumed into heaven to reside with God: the Father, the Son, and the Holy Spirit."

"My word," Shawn commented, taken aback by this man-child, whom he already found incomprehensible. "Such an amazing litany. I understand you live in a monastery."

"That is correct. I am a novice with the Brotherhood of the Slaves of Mary."

"Is it true you haven't left for eight years?"

"Almost eight, at least not on my own. I did come here to the city with some of the brothers to have some medical tests a number of years ago, but this is the first time on my own."

Shawn shook his head. "It's hard for me to believe a young person like yourself would be willing to deny your own freedom."

"My freedom I gladly sacrifice to the Holy Mother. Staying within the walls of the monastery gives me more time to pray for her intervention and the peace it brings."

"Intervention for what?"

"To keep me from sin. To keep me close to Christ. To help the brothers in their mission."

"Come on!" Sana said to Luke. "Let's take you up to your guest room."

Luke studied Shawn's face for a moment, then followed Sana up the stairway leading to the upper floors. They passed the second floor, where Sana said Shawn was sleeping, and the third floor, where Sana said she was sleeping, to the fourth floor. It was a room with dormer windows that faced the front of the building.

"Here's where you will be staying," Sana said, standing to the side, letting Luke step into the room dominated by a queen-size, four-poster bed. "Does it look like your room at the monastery?"

"Hardly," Luke said, taking a peek into the bathroom the guest room shared with the second guest room on the floor. He then returned to the roll-on suitcase and unzipped its cover. The first thing he pulled out was a small plastic statue of the Virgin Mary, which he placed on the side table. The second thing was a small, doll-like statue of the infant Jesus, dressed in an elaborate robe and wearing a crown. With tender care he placed the doll next to the Blessed Virgin.

"What's that?" Sana questioned.

"The Infant of Prague," Luke explained. "It was one of my mother's favorite possessions before she passed away."

Next, Luke pulled out his black habit and hung it in the closet.

"Is that your usual attire?" Sana questioned.

"It is," Luke answered, "but the cardinal thought it better that I wear more typical clothes that belong to his secretaries. Luckily, one of the men is close to my size."

"You wear what you like," Sana said. "We will be going out to dinner in a half-hour or so. You do have time to take a shower if you so please. I am about to do so. Otherwise, we'll meet you downstairs in the living room."

Shawn, Sana, and Luke arrived back at the Daughtrys' home in a taxi just before nine-thirty p.m. The dinner at Cipriani Downtown had gone pleasantly enough until Luke had tried to turn the conversation over to his mission. Shawn, with almost as much alcohol on board as he'd had the night before, had used the opportunity to inform Luke that he was facing an impossible task, and the sooner he faced the reality, the better for them all. When Luke persisted, Shawn had gotten angry, and then the atmosphere had steadily disintegrated to where Shawn had refused to talk to Luke, whom he persisted on calling derogatorily "boy."

"Are you retiring for the night?" Shawn asked Sana, avoiding talking with Luke.

"I think I'll stay up for a little while with Luke," Sana whispered. "I don't want to have Luke report back to James that he's not being received hospitably."

"Good idea," Shawn said, reaching out to steady himself with the banister leading up the front stairs. "What time do you want to leave here in the morning to get to the OCME DNA building?"

"How about after nine?" Sana said. "That will give me time to make breakfast for our guest so we get a good report."

"Another good idea," Shawn said, slurring his words. "See you in the morning."

As Shawn slowly rose and disappeared up the stairs, Sana turned toward Luke. "How about a fire in the fireplace?" she suggested.

Luke shrugged. He couldn't remember the last time he'd experienced the pleasure of a fire. In some ways, he was nervous about enjoying himself too much after the disappointing evening, as he was depressed about his chances of overcoming Satan.

"Come on!" Sana said encouragingly. "Let's build the fire together."

Fifteen minutes later the two were sitting on the couch, mesmerized by the crackling fire that was beginning to spread upward from the kindling into the piled logs. Sana had a glass of wine, while Luke had a Coke. It was Sana who broke the silence. "The archbishop told us you've not had an easy life. Do you mind sharing with me your story?"

"Not at all," Luke said. "It is not a secret. I share it with those who will listen, as it is a tribute to the Blessed Virgin."

"We were told you had run away from home at age eighteen to join the monastery. Can I ask why?"

"The immediate cause was my mother's death," Luke explained, "but the long-term cause was a very difficult childhood dominated by a godless father. In sharp contrast with my father, who was an abuser of alcohol and a wife beater, my mother was a very religious person who sincerely believed that she was at fault for my father's behavior and not he. She believed, like Eve, that she had turned away from God by marrying my father and was a sinner to the point that she had convinced me that I was a child born in sin. She was so convinced that she told me that if I expected to salvage my eternal soul, I had to pray to the Virgin and consecrate my life to her, Christ, and the Church."

"My goodness," Sana voiced, feeling strong compassion about Luke's story. Although hardly the same, she had always felt she'd suffered from her father's premature death when she was only eight, even to the point of now wondering if one of the reasons she'd married Shawn was because when she first met him he was, to a large degree, a father figure that she'd missed. "Did focusing on the Church help?" she asked.

Luke gave a short, contemptuous laugh. "Hardly," he said. "One of the priests clearly perceived me as a troubled child and, being troubled himself, proceeded to take advantage of me for over a year."

"Oh, good Lord, no!" Sana said, feeling even more compassion for Luke. She was so taken aback that she had to actively suppress a strong urge to envelope him in her arms for fear of what his reaction might be. He might misinterpret her gesture as being more than empathy. He was, after all, not a child but a man. Besides, there was something rote about Luke's delivery.

"At first I thought it was relatively normal behavior," Luke said wistfully, "as I thought I loved the individual. But as I grew older I came to recognize it was wrong. Not knowing what to do, since the priest was one of the more popular in the parish, I worked up the courage to tell my mother."

"Was she sympathetic?" Sana asked, with concern about where the story was headed, considering what Luke had already said about his mother.

"Absolutely the opposite. Just like with her mixed-up belief she was at fault in regard to my father's abuse, she was totally insistent that I had seduced the priest rather than vice versa, especially when she had asked me why it had lasted for so long and I had admitted that I had liked it, at least in the beginning. It's been only in the last few years that the brothers at the monastery have finally gotten me to understand what really happened, and that I wasn't responsible either for the inappropriate relationship with the priest or for my mother's suicide."

"Oh, good Lord in heaven!" Sana said, as overwhelming compassion lessened her restraint and dissolved any questions about Luke's story being rote, as if a memorized script. Without forethought she enveloped Luke in a sympathetic embrace, at least until she perceived his stiff resistance, at which point she quickly let go. "What a tragic story," she added, with deep sympathy. She gazed at him with tenderness, wishing somehow to help the burden she imagined he suffered in relation to his mother, no matter what he said about the brothers helping him. She also felt distinct anger at the Church for having abused him, which suddenly gave her a better understanding of Shawn's current mind-set.

27

Monday and Tuesday had been good days for everyone, except James, who had to field a call from Luke on both mornings, neither of which provided encouraging news. After Shawn and Sana had left each day for work, Luke had informed the cardinal that the devil was being completely resistant to Luke's attempt at changing Shawn's mind. Instead, Luke had had to report that Shawn was becoming resistant to even discussing the issue. James's response had been to encourage him to pray harder and not to give up, and that James and the Church were counting on him to eventually succeed. He explained that persistence would be key.

"Have you explained to him how much his casting doubt on the Blessed Mother's assumption will affect you?" James had asked, trying to be helpful and encouraging, as he had no plan C.

"As much as he'll allow me," Luke had responded, "although now he immediately changes the subject whenever I bring it up. He's even threatened to ask me to leave."

"How about his wife?"

"She's been most hospitable," Luke had said. "She has made up for him and then some. I'm convinced that if I can change his mind, she will agree as well. She's not nearly as committed as he."

"Please keep trying," James had said. "There's still a good portion of the week left."

Other than making the two calls to James and having little luck with Shawn, Luke had enjoyed himself immensely, despite the continued uneasiness of being out in the world and exposed to sin. Both mornings Sana had awakened early and prepared a sumptuous breakfast for Luke, explaining to him that she loved to cook and was continuously disappointed that Shawn didn't care if they had fast food or gourmet food. Luke had confessed that in contrast to Shawn as well as his brothers, he loved to eat good food and had been rewarded with an outstanding dinner the night before and looked forward to the same that night.

Even more than the food, Luke had enjoyed Sana coming home early on Monday, the day before, saying that she'd made wonderful progress on her DNA studies and had gotten the pulp samples already into the PCR stage, which Luke had not understood at all. Not that it mattered, since Sana had used the free time to take Luke out to buy him clothes that fit instead of wearing Father Karlin's, which didn't.

For Luke shopping had turned out to be a delightful experience, as he had not shopped for clothes for as long as he could remember, and he appreciated Sana's input as he tried things on and struggled over choices. He'd also enjoyed the festive holiday atmosphere with a mere fourteen shopping days left before Christmas. Then to cap the day, Sana and Luke had stayed up after dinner to enjoy another fire, while affording Sana a turn to tell her life story and even her current problems. Luke had been sympathetic when his impressions had been confirmed that Shawn was not treating her as Shawn did when they were first married, particularly in the intimacy realm, as Luke knew that Shawn slept in a guest room on the second floor while Sana slept in the master bedroom on the third floor. Although Luke did not pretend to understand everything Sana said, he had told her that he'd pray for her, and that he couldn't understand why Shawn did not want to sleep with her, because he thought she was beautiful.

"Thank you for the reassurance and the prayers," Sana had said. "But, to be truthful, at this point, I prefer not to sleep with him."

Similar to Sana, Shawn had made real progress as well over the previous two days. He'd reached the stage he'd hoped for, where the unrolling of the first scroll was proceeding much more rapidly. Monday he'd finished only a single page, but that day, Tuesday, he'd done more than two. Taking the time to read the unrolled portion, he was also feeling better about Simon not being quite the ogre he was reputed to have been. Even though he recognized that Simon was writing about himself, Shawn thought the better he came off as a person, the better witness he would be to the identity of the bones.

"Luke!" Sana called up the stairs. She and Shawn had just arrived home. When she heard Luke answer in the distance, she assumed he was saying his afternoon prayers. "We are home!" She then followed Shawn into the kitchen, where she unpacked the groceries they had just bought. While she was busy doing that, Shawn poured himself some scotch as his first cocktail of the evening. Just a few days previously, Sana had gotten disturbed at Shawn's progressive drinking, but not that night. In fact, she wanted him to drink as much as he pleased, as it caused him to retire early. As had been the case the two previous evenings, she was looking forward to spending time with Luke without Shawn's interference or Luke's attempt to bring up the progressively incendiary Virgin Mary issue, which he'd been unflaggingly continuing to do, despite Shawn's increasingly negative response.

It had been two good days for Jack as well, and mainly because it had been good for JJ and Laurie. When Jack had returned home

Monday evening, Laurie had reported that JJ had had the best day he'd had in months, with no crying whatsoever. Jack expected a similar story that evening, because Laurie had called him about three p.m. to say things had been going similarly all day.

Taking the stairs by two or three steps at a time, Jack poked his head into the kitchen. As he assumed would be the case, Laurie was involved with dinner preparations, and JJ was contentedly playing in his playpen. Jack quickly went over to Laurie, gave her a quick peck on the cheek, and looked in on JJ. To Jack's delight, the boy smiled.

"I believe he's going to allow us to have a real dinner tonight," Laurie said.

"Fabulous," Jack replied. "Are you going to feed him and put him to bed beforehand?"

"That's the plan."

"With him as content as he is, I'd like to play basketball for an hour or so."

"I think that's a good idea," Laurie said. Then with a wink she added, "Just don't get yourself too tired."

Jack enjoyed thinking about what she had in mind for the evening as he wasted no time getting into his basketball gear and heading back down the stairs. With JJ apparently feeling as well as he was over the last two days, Jack tried to keep his excitement in check to avoid future even more serious disappointments, but everything was going so well that it was difficult. The previous morning he'd gone back to see Bingham yet again and asked for some time off, not to avoid coming into the office but just from autopsies. As he'd suggested he would, Bingham had agreed immediately, although he'd asked Jack, in return, to at least sign out the murder case where the on-call ME had forgotten to have the hands bagged, so the issue could be put to bed. Jack had been happy to inform him it had already been done.

Freed from additional autopsies, Jack had been able to spend more of both days with Shawn and Sana, where things were also going well as moving along at a rapid pace. Sana expected to do the mitochondrial sequencing the next day, which Jack and James were hoping would tell them where the individual whose bones they were had originated. The question being whether they were from the Middle East, in which case they might still be the Virgin Mary's, or from Rome, where they'd been ultimately buried, meaning they couldn't be the Virgin Mary's. As Jack ran across the street and entered the playground, he thought it ironic that just when he'd found the perfect distraction, JJ was doing better than he had for more than a month. Jack wondered if it would be appropriate with such a change to have JJ's mouse antibody level tested in case they could again start his treatment.

As far as Luke was concerned, the dinner had been equally delicious as it had been the evening before and so different from what he was accustomed to, it was beyond his ability to describe. Unfortunately, what also had been the same was Shawn's behavior. He'd totally refused to talk about the issue with the Virgin Mary and the ossuary, and, with scotch before dinner and wine making him drunk, he'd taken himself up to his room, supposedly for a short rest. By a little after nine, when Sana and Luke had finished the dishes and had come into the living room to stoke the fire and enjoy their Coke and wine, he still hadn't appeared.

"I think I'll check on Shawn," Sana said, putting down her wine and before allowing herself to truly relax.

"He'll be fine," Luke protested, preferring not to see the inebriated and frustrating man again that evening.

"I'm thinking more about us than him," Sana said with a smile while heading for the stairs.

Luke sat on the couch and listened to her footfalls on the stairs and the squeaking of the joists as she went into the room Shawn was using. Luke pondered her comment. He wasn't sure what she meant, so when she returned he asked her.

"I meant I wanted to get up there now before I was settled," Sana said, making herself comfortable with her feet on the coffee table, "and before we were into some interesting conversation." She was eager to hear more of his story than the rote version he'd told her.

"Is he okay?" Luke asked. He couldn't help but remember his father and the violence alcohol engendered.

"He's on the bed and passed out, if that's your definition of okay."

"Since we talked about it last night, I still don't know why he stopped sleeping with you."

"It's simpler now than it was six months ago when it was more his idea than mine. We've grown apart. Have you noticed how little we touch? What I'm talking about is little things, like my putting my arm on his shoulder, like this." Sana was sitting to Luke's right, so she lifted her left arm and casually draped it across Luke's shoulder behind his neck. Then she pulled her arm back and laid it along his leg with her hand on his knee. "Or even just sitting close with my arm on his knee. When we were first married, we both did such little physical things that were no more than an urge to let the other know that we were together, and that we were enjoying being together, like I'm doing to you. But all that stopped, and as I said, at first it was him, but now it is us. At first I thought it had something to do with our large age difference, but now I'm not so sure: I'm afraid it is more."

Luke felt a sudden heat enter his leg and travel up toward his groin. He was infinitely conscious of Sana's arm against his thigh and that her hand was ever so loosely clasped over the top of his knee. It was as if her fingers were on fire.

Sana was completely unaware of the emotional avalanche she'd unwittingly started in Luke's mind, with its backed-up hormonal overload. She'd placed her arm and hand near him in what she thought was a platonic way, but it was also a physical reminder of how close she felt toward him, and she assumed he felt the same way toward her, as they had been trading extremely private thoughts and feelings since he arrived. In fact, Luke was the first person to whom Sana had verbalized the growing problems with her downward-spiraling relationship with Shawn. As a direct consequence, she felt Luke understood something about her hidden life, forming a bond, an attraction like a brother and sister, a special place in her mind, that even though Luke appeared to be a mysterious man-child, he projected an emotional perception older than his apparent years. After all, Sana reasoned, he had seen things on his own about her relationship with Shawn and had commented, and he was only a little more than three years younger than she.

For the moment, Luke wasn't thinking. He was feeling. The heat from Sana's hand was still burning against his knee, and now the length of her arm was doing the same, all the way up to the point of his hip. Each heartbeat he could feel pulsate in his swelling penis while his testicles contracted under him into painful knots. He needed relief. He needed to move, which caused the muscles in his legs and groin to begin to contract in rhythmical spasms.

Sensing Luke's muscular contractions, Sana started. She was sitting directly next to him, and she suddenly spun around to face him, her left hand dragging innocently up his thigh. Seeing perspiration dotting his forehead and his dazed expression, her first horror was that the man-boy was having a heart attack. She stood up at once and tried to get him to lie down. But he fought her, and fought her with overwhelming strength so that the pushing match was short-lived.

"Okay!" she cried. "You're hurting me!" He had grabbed her wrists and was compressing them to the point of shutting off the blood supply to her hands.

As if waking from a kind of seizure or at least a daze, Luke let go of Sana, who immediately recovered her wrists and rubbed them to restore circulation.

"My God, you hurt me," Sana complained, still massaging her wrists.

As if in a postictal state, Luke merely stared at Sana. He didn't try to talk, merely stared at her with a flaccid, shell-shocked face.

"Are you all right?" Sana asked. Even his eyes seemed glazed. His mouth was slack, with lips slightly parted. Although the firelight made his complexion difficult to judge, it seemed to her it was more pale than it had been earlier. "Luke! Are you all right?" Sana repeated. She reached forward with both hands to grip his shoulders and give him a little shake. "Talk to me, Luke! I need to know if you are all right."

Leaning forward, Sana studied Luke's face. His eyes, which had been recently focused on her lips, now slowly rose. She could see that he was returning to the present, wherever he'd been, but it was a disturbing present. Instead of being the happy person he'd been, he was returning angry and censorious. Before he spoke, which Sana could tell he was about to do, it suddenly dawned on her what had happened. She couldn't help but smile, especially because now that she thought about it, she couldn't understand why it had taken so long.

"You had an orgasm, didn't you?" Sana questioned with relief and even humor. "I think I'm right. Well, don't be embarrassed on my part. I think it's terrific. Congratulations. I'll even take it as a compliment. It is reassuring to know that someone finds me sexually attractive, even if my husband doesn't." Sana had carried on in an attempt to forestall embarrassment on Luke's part, as it was her impression that he'd never had sex with a woman, not that what they had done was sex but because his response was certainly dependent on sex. It was her hope that despite the traumas he'd experienced since puberty, there was a chance he could turn out normal.

"Whore!" Luke yelled suddenly.

"Excuse me?" Sana said. She'd heard, but she didn't want to hear such nonsense, certainly not from Luke, her special friend.

"Satan," Luke snapped.

"Oh, really?" Sana questioned contemptuously. "So it's like your mother and father all over again. The victim is at fault. This time it was all up here, my friend," Sana added, while reaching out with her index finger to touch Luke's head.

Luke viciously batted Sana's hand away, causing her to briefly cry out in pain. "Satan's whore," he snapped, in the grittiest voice he could muster.

"Well, that's that," Sana said, babying her hand. "I thought you were doing well on the religious-fanatic chart, but I suppose I was overly hopeful about your progress. As for your welcome here, I have to warn you that it's getting very thin. As for me, I'm going to bed with a locked door, so even if you consider apologizing, I'll hear it tomorrow. Needless to say, I do think it in your best interest to apologize. Good night!"

Sana strode toward the stairs, while behind her she could tell that her mini-lecture had fallen on deaf ears. Luke let out a final "Satan, be damned for all eternity" as Sana started up the old, noisy stairs.

28

By nine-forty-three a.m., James was already in his office clearing his mail and answering e-mail. It amazed him how much of the business of the archdiocese was accomplished by e-mail, and he regularly attributed most of his thirty percent productivity increase to his adaptation to the new technology. What it did magnificently was speed the spread of information and eliminate many otherwise-lengthy telephone calls. For James the latter effect was so crucial.

He'd been up that morning from well before six; he'd already read his Breviary, showered, and shaved while listening to the news. He'd said Mass with his staff and breakfasted with the *Times* before repairing to his study, where he now sat. At ten he was due in the "consulter's" room, where he was to meet with the chancellor and the vicar general, where he was debating possibly dropping the first words about the ossuary problem, when the phone rang. Checking the LED screen, he snapped it up immediately because it said ARCHDIOCESE, which James knew would be Luke Hester.

"Good morning, Your Eminence," Luke said the moment James had said hello. "I believe I have some good news for you."

James rocked forward in his seat, his pulse quickly speeding up. He happily envisioned Gabriel the Archangel on the line. "Has he changed his mind?" James demanded gleefully. From chatting with Luke on the two previous days, James had essentially given up hope on plan B and worried that a plan C did not seem to be in the offing.

"Not yet, but I'm sure he will."

"That is heavenly music to my ears."

"I hope you will always hold me in high esteem for this," Luke said. "This has not been easy."

"I never imagined it would be," James admitted. "Actually, I'm somewhat surprised, considering how made-up his mind was. Yet I always believe, once a faithful Catholic, always a faithful Catholic, and I always believed that about Shawn Daughtry despite his anticlerical bluster. Should I call him to congratulate him?"

"Not until tomorrow or all will be ruined."

"Then I should gladly wait until the morning. What argument did you finally choose?"

"The solution represents less of an argument and more tactics."

"I'm impressed. Will you ultimately tell me?"

"You will certainly be privy to the details."

James smiled. The young man often spoke as if his only contact with the outside world was with the Bible.

"The solution was dependent on more fully comprehending what I was up against."

"I would say that such an aphorism holds true in many conundrums."

"What I had to learn was that Satan is involved with both the husband and the wife, and not just the husband."

"Well, they are working on the same project," James offered.

"It was my mistake, then," Luke said. "I thought they were different people, but both are an occasion of sin."

"Thank you for giving me this update," James said. "I must confess, I was quite close to despair."

"I was glad to have been given this opportunity to serve the Church and, most important, the Blessed Virgin."

Luke disconnected from the archbishop. He was in the kitchen getting himself something simple to eat. Sana had not gotten up early to make him breakfast, nor had he wanted her to do so. He didn't want to confront her that morning, now that he knew who she really was.

Content with his toast and milk, Luke headed back up to his room. There he went into the suitcase and got out the money he'd been given. It was four hundred dollars, a fortune to him, and much more than he needed. After all, it wasn't going to be a long shopping trip, as the house was already perfect.

The temperature outside was seasonable, which was good, since he did not own the warmest coat. Back at the monastery, his work did not require him to go outside, and accordingly, during the winter, he rarely did. That morning, Luke's biggest problem was finding a sizable hardware store where he'd find a good exterior lock. It was his idea to add another to the three that were already on the front door.

It took only a few blocks to reach one of the many commercial areas in the Village, and as soon as he did, he asked for a hardware store. Fifteen minutes later he walked into a good-sized one on Sixth Avenue not too far from Bleecker Street. As far as outdoor locks were concerned, they had many to choose from. As it turned out, Luke's choice was the one the store attendant said would be the easiest to install.

On the way home, Luke stopped in two other stores to get

the last two items on his list. They were easier than the lock, since there was no choice other than the brand, which didn't matter. With everything he needed, he was back at the Daughtrys' before noon.

Sana was having fun. The day was progressing as well as the previous two. That morning, earlier than she had expected, she'd finished up with the polymerase chain reaction steps and had moved over to the 3130XL genetic analyzer system. Now, by the middle of the afternoon she was expecting to not only have the full mitochondrial sequence of the ossuary individual's DNA, but she would also have the sequences of a variety of the test areas, which were used to explore the person's genealogical roots.

Once the automatic sequencer was doing its job, Sana had left the lab and had traveled up to Columbia to make sure all her experiments were being attended to appropriately. She'd been glad to find that everything was now in order. Every one of her four graduate students were now working responsibly, to make up for being lax when Sana had attended the Egyptian conference.

As Sana climbed from the taxi after returning from her lab at the medical school campus, she briefly thought of Luke. She'd thought of him the moment she'd awakened but had decided not to make any snap decisions about the previous evening's incident, like telling Shawn about it. She knew that if she did tell him the man-boy would be out on his ear, and Shawn would be on the phone, complaining to the archbishop that he'd made a poor choice for an emissary. Since that would put them back to square one with the archbishop's threats of closing them down, Sana wanted to let the episode percolate in her mind for a while for three main reasons. The first was because, in retrospect, she blamed herself to an extent. Enjoying his company as much as she did, and recognizing her own needs, she'd admitted she'd been titillated herself to some mild degree. The second reason was that although he had essentially attacked her, to her it was ninety percent a defensive act. The final reason was that she was confident he would apologize after he'd given the episode some thought, even though he'd failed to appear that morning to do so.

With the taxi paid, Sana entered the building, flashed her ID to security, who now knew her, and rode up in the elevator. In the outer part of the lab she found Jack working with Shawn on the translation of the first scroll. The unrolling had been completed that morning, which thrilled Shawn. As the translation progressed Shawn was certain that Simon was about to rehabilitate himself to a degree as a theologian in his own right. Shawn had assured the others that Simon was definitely either the first or among the first Christian Gnostics, combining the story of Jesus of Nazareth with basic Gnostic ideas, such as Jesus' true role as a teacher of enlightenment more than a redeemer of sin.

"Did you guys come across anything particularly interesting while I've been away?" Sana asked as she hung up her outdoor coat in one of the coat lockers.

"We're about to start on scroll two," Jack answered. "We're hoping in that one or the third one to have a mention about the bones."

"Good luck," Sana offered. "I'm going to head into the lab and see what I've got with the mitochondrial DNA. We might have some information in the next few minutes."

"Wouldn't that be nice," Shawn said, preoccupied with what he was doing.

Sana stepped into the gowning room and quickly changed. Even though the sequencer had now completed the process, she wanted no contamination into the room, as she might be running certain samples again, or even a totally new sample, depending on what she found. When she was gloved, gowned, hooded, and bootied, Sana went into the lab proper and walked directly to the sequencer. Taking the stack of pages from the printout, she sought the pages that really counted to her. It took only a few minutes. It turned out there were three, and when she finally isolated them, she glanced at each and then looked again, like a double take. Then she shook her head and looked yet again. She couldn't believe it, but there was no way she was going to sit herself down and compare every one of sixteen thousand four hundred and eighty-four base pairs on all three pages. Feeling suddenly light-headed, Sana sat down just the same. She didn't try to do any comparing herself—that was what computers were good for. Instead, she'd sat down to try to fathom what the results were suggesting, something Sana felt from her experience to be impossible.

The problem was this, and Sana checked again to be certain: The mitochondrial DNA sequence of the pulp of the tooth Sana had pulled from the skull coming from the ossuary matched—base pair for base pair, sixteen thousand four hundred eighty-four—with a contemporary woman, as Sana had ordered the computer to check once it had established the sequence by using the brand-new international mitochondrial library called CODIS 6.0.

Although finding a match in the contemporary world wasn't that abnormal because identical twins matched, the problem, however, in this case was that the woman in the ossuary was more than two thousand years old! As exceptional as this match was, the second match was even more fantastic, and frankly inexplicable to Sana. She looked at it and shook her head. "This cannot be," she said out loud. "This simply cannot be."

Suddenly, Sana leaped to her feet and, running out of the lab and through the gowning room, emerged into the office mildly out of breath. Both Shawn and Jack had been seriously startled. Sana didn't care. Instead she gasped, "The impossible has happened!"

Jack, who had forgiven her startling him faster than Shawn, crowded around her and took the printout page she held out to him. He was eager for an explanation.

"That's the woman in the ossuary's MT-DNA sequence," Sana spat out, hitting the page Jack was holding with the back of her hand. "This is the exact same sequence in a contemporary Palestinian woman," Sana continued, handing the second page to Jack. "And this sequence, which is also the same, is the mitochondrial sequence of Eve!" She gave Jack the final page. She was out of breath from excitement.

Jack looked up quizzically from the pages. "What do you mean the sequence of Eve?"

"It is a sequence that had been determined by a supercomputer running for weeks on end to determine the matrilineal most recent common ancestor, or MRCA," Sana explained. "In other words, it's the sequence of the first female ancestor, taking into account every human permutation of the normal sixteen thousand and something base pairs of the human mitochondrial DNA sequence."

"The statistics of something like that happening would be off the charts," Jack said.

"Exactly. That's why this is impossible."

"What are you two mumbling about?" Shawn asked, coming up behind the others.

Sana gave Shawn the same explanation she'd given Jack. Shawn was equally dismissive.

"Something must have gone wrong with the system," he suggested.

"I don't think so," Sana said. "I've done hundreds if not thousands of these MT sequences. Nothing has ever gone wrong before. Why should something go wrong now?"

"Do you have any more of your sample from the PCR?" Jack asked.

"I do," Sana replied.

"Why don't you just run another sequencing and analysis?"

"Good idea," Sana agreed.

"Wait a second," Shawn said, holding up a hand. "Let me ask you two guys something, and then you tell me I'm crazy and to shut the hell up. Okay?"

"Okay," both Sana and Jack said, nearly simultaneously.

"Okay," Shawn said. "Here's the only way that this statistically impossible situation could have occurred. . . ." Shawn hesitated, looking back and forth from Sana to Jack.

"All right, already. Tell us!" Sana protested. Her pulse was still racing.

"We're all ears," Jack agreed. "Shoot!"

"Are you sure you're ready?" Shawn teased, to good effect.

"I'm going back into the lab to run another sample," Sana said, pushing away from the counter where she'd been leaning.

"Wait!" Shawn said, catching her arm. "I'll tell you, promise!"

"I'll give you five seconds to start or I'm going into the lab," Sana said. She'd had enough. She wasn't going to play Shawn's game any longer. She was too excited.

"For a second forget the Palestinian woman. We have two identical samples: matrilineal Eve and the woman from the ossuary. Other than having the same mitochondrial DNA, what makes them similar?"

Sana glanced at Jack, who returned her stare. "They weren't contemporaries, if that's what you are implying," Sana said. "Matrilineal Eve is projected back many hundreds of thousands of years."

"No, no," Shawn said. "Their similarity is not that. Let me put it another way. My belief, thanks to Saturninus's letter, is that the bones in the ossuary are those of Mary, the Mother of Jesus of Nazareth. Let's assume for a moment they are, which would make them extraordinarily holy objects to many, many people. Do you follow me so far?"

"Of course," Sana said impatiently.

"Now, if we had some bones from matrilineal Eve here as well, how would they be similar, besides having the same mitochondrial DNA sequence?"

"Perhaps they'd have the same nuclear DNA sequence as well," Jack suggested.

"Maybe, but that's not what I want to hear," Shawn said, as impatient as Sana. "Think from a theological perspective!"

Jack shook his head while looking at Sana. She shook her head as well. "You are going to have to tell us what you want to hear."

"Theologically, they were both made directly by God the Father. Remember the Catholic feast James mentioned to us this past Sunday that he celebrated? It was the Feast of the Immaculate Conception, which was about the creation of Mary to be the sinless Mother of Christ. Well, Eve was also sinless at first. As the first female, there was no one else around to create her but God himself. Now, how many recipes, so to speak, do you think God might have for humans? My guess would be one, and in terms of mitochondrial DNA sequence, what we have here is *the one*. He used the same recipe for both Mary and Eve, which makes it interesting they turned out so differently, since they are twins."

For a few moments no one spoke. Each was lost in his own thoughts until Jack broke the silence: "If what you say is the case, you two have inadvertently yet scientifically corroborated the existence of the divine."

Both Sana and Shawn laughed gleefully and then hugged despite Sana's barrier gown, hat, gloves, and booties. "Our journal articles are going to be classics even before their publications," Shawn blurted. He then broke away from Sana. "I have to get to

work! I'm not sure if I'll be able to wait to finish all three scrolls.
I've never been more excited in my life about a couple of papers."

"I'm going to run several more samples, just to be totally sure
of the results," Sana announced.

"And while you guys do that," Jack said, getting to his feet, "I'm
going to head home somewhat early to insist my wife take a break."
Actually, Jack had something more specific in mind. He'd called
the pediatric oncologist that morning who was in charge of the
neuroblastoma protocol at Memorial to ask, in light of JJ's several
good days, if Jack should bring the boy in for blood work to check
his level of mouse antibody.

"Congratulations," Jack called out as he opened the door to the
hall. Both Shawn and Sana waved in response. Sana was at that
moment heading back into the gowning room to regown. Shawn
was back at the painstaking unrolling work. "What time in the
morning?" Jack yelled out.

"Let's say ten," Shawn yelled back. "There may be some celebrating tonight."

"By the way," Jack yelled, "I'd hold off telling James about the
mito DNA until it's confirmed."

"That's probably the merciful thing to do," Shawn agreed.

Jack was about to leave when he thought of something else.
Since yelling from the doorway was potentially disturbing to
others in the lab, he returned to the office and approached
Shawn. Jack could see Sana in the gowning room in the middle
of changing.

"I forgot about the Palestinian woman that also matched," Jack
said. "What on earth does that say?"

"Good question," Shawn said, rolling back his chair. He
quickly stuck his head into the gowning room and asked Sana
her opinion.

"She has to be a direct matrilineal relative of the woman in the ossuary," Sana said. "It's possible, because the half-life for a single nucleotide mutation or SNP for mitochondrial DNA is two thousand years. That would be my guess," Sana said, completing her dressing.

"Did you hear that?" Shawn asked Jack, letting the gowning-room door close.

"I did," Jack said. "It's curious to think about. I wonder if she has any idea, or if anyone had an idea. It even makes me wonder if she's a Christian or a Muslim."

"Maybe one of us should look her up sometime," Shawn said, "although I can't help but have the feeling the less she was told, the better."

"It's a curious idea," Jack said. He then took his leave for the second time. As he rode down in the elevator, another associated thought passed through his mind. One aspect of alternative medicine he had not even touched on was faith healing, and the reason was that he gave it even less chance of being efficacious than some of the other methods. A few times, while idly channel surfing on the television in his old life, he'd briefly watched as TV evangelists put their hands on supposed patients' foreheads, which would cause the people to fall back, limp yet cured. Yet if someone had the same DNA as the Mother of Jesus of Nazareth, Jack couldn't help but wonder if she could heal others.

The elevator reached the first floor, and Jack got off. Almost immediately, thoughts about faith healing evaporated from his mind, replaced by thoughts concerning the antibody levels in JJ's body.

29

Although the last thing Shawn wanted to do was stop at the grocery story to get food for dinner, especially since it meant paying for food for Luke, he did it anyway. He was in that good a mood. Not only had he made a single day's largest progress in his document unraveling, but Sana had already run a second sequencing of the tooth-pulp mitochondrial DNA, and the sequence was exactly the same as the first. Thus, all around it was by far their most successful day in relation to the ossuary, and such progress bode well for papers in the not-too-distant future.

"I had an idea," Sana said, as she and Shawn loaded the groceries into the trunk of a yellow cab.

"Really?" Shawn questioned jokingly. "Such a novel occurrence."

Sana hauled off and smacked Shawn playfully with a package of paper towels.

In such a playful attitude, they arrived home. While Shawn paid the fare, Sana walked to the rear of the taxi to get the groceries. As she lifted them to the curb, she thought about Luke and wondered how he was going to act. She truly had no idea, and her thoughts ranged between anger on one extreme to humor on the other. As for how he had acted in the immediacy of the episode, she felt certain he'd be embarrassed, and she hoped he planned to apologize, as she had strongly suggested, so that the incident could be put behind them. After having thought about his response on and off most of the day, Sana still considered it as over-the-top inappropriate. "Satan's whore," she murmured inaudibly. Such language coming from such an angelic-appearing person seemed shocking to her.

"Do you have the groceries?" Shawn's voice rang out. He'd finished paying the driver.

"I could use a hand," Sana yelled back.

Shawn appeared around the side of the taxi and took the two bags that Sana had already lifted from the trunk. She fished out the third and last and slammed the trunk's lid with her elbow.

As they walked up to the front door, Sana got her circle of keys from her purse. "Fine time for one to be thinking of this now," Shawn commented. "I think we finished the final bottle of wine last night."

"If you want, you can walk over to Sixth Avenue later and get some for tonight," Sana suggested. "Our celebrating that you mentioned to Jack is going to be rather lame unless we get some wine."

"Maybe I'll invite Luke," Shawn said. "It would be good for him to get out of the house."

"That's nice of you," Sana said, and meant it. At the same time she wondered what Shawn would say if she told him that Luke had called her "Satan's whore" the night before. When Shawn was angry, he had a sailor's vocabulary.

Sana got the usual three locks open with their respective keys but then noticed there was another one, which she was certain was new. She was about to ask Shawn about it when she tried the door.

It opened without a problem, and that was the last she thought of it. Instead, she stepped aside to allow Shawn to enter first, as he was carrying the bulk of the groceries.

"Hello, Luke," Sana heard Shawn say as she kicked the door closed behind her. She then reached around and threw the three dead bolts. When she turned again, Shawn was talking with Luke, but it was not sociable talking. Shawn was telling Luke that he was not allowed to smoke in the house under no uncertain terms.

"It's just a cigarette," Luke responded. His tone was not defensive or even apologetic. It was more challenging, as if the house rules were his to determine.

"I'm telling you, there is no smoking in this house," Shawn repeated slowly but definitively.

"Fine," Luke said insouciantly. He stood up from the chair he was in, pushed past Shawn, and made his way to the front door. Instead of opening the door, he locked it more securely with a key, which he pocketed, then headed for the stairs.

"Where on earth are you going?" Shawn questioned when he thought Luke was going upstairs. "Don't make me repeat myself yet again!"

Luke passed the entrance to the stairs, blithely rapping his knuckle on the newel post. He seemed strangely detached, openly ignoring his hosts, who had just come home.

Shawn looked at Sana as if he expected her to have an explanation for such bizarre behavior. The man had a lit cigarette but wasn't smoking it, nor was he getting rid of it. It seemed as if he was on a walking tour of the residence until he came to the door to the cellar, which was under the front stairs. There he stopped, and once he had a hand on the doorknob, he turned back to look directly at Shawn and Sana. Appearing now as breezy as he'd sounded just a few moments earlier, he recited a Hail Mary, at the conclusion of which he snapped open the basement door, threw in the lighted cigarette, and slammed the door closed.

"What the hell!" Shawn yelled near the top of his voice. Without a moment's hesitation, Shawn ditched the groceries he'd been holding onto the couch and bolted for the cellar door. Whether he had felt or heard the throaty *whomp* that issued from the basement no one knew. Sana had felt it more than heard it as it rattled the knick-knacks on the mantel. She did call out to him, but he was not to be deterred. His goal was to get the cigarette just as soon as he could and crush it into harmless cinders. As he got to the door, he threw Luke aside, grabbed the doorknob, ripped open the door, and started down, all in the same motion. Unfortunately, a huge ball of exploding gasoline vapor seeking lower pressure rocketed upward and immediately seared off his eyelashes, eyebrows, and most of his hair. Within seconds the old wooden house with its hundreds upon hundreds of pockets of air within its aged walls was a flaming inferno, and the fact that the only insulation in the building was crumbled period newspaper caused the fire to spread even faster. Seconds later, the heat flux soared over the thirteen-hundred-degree flash point such that objects within the building, including people, spontaneously burst into flame. Sana and Shawn, although on fire, did reach the front door, only to find it impossible to open.

Fifteen minutes later, a neighbor, noticing the glow coming from outside his house, looked out and then frantically called nine-one-one. Eleven minutes later the first fire trucks appeared, but by then the only possible thing to save was the chimney.

Epilogue

Since Jack wasn't doing autopsies for the week, he didn't make it a point to arrive at the OCME particularly early, and today he arrived at seven-forty-nine. On normal days by that time he surely would have already picked out what he considered the best cases and would already be down in the autopsy room with Vinnie Amendola, giving him a hard time or vice versa. Instead, Jack was content to be locking up his bike at the side of one of the intake garages in full view of security. When he was finished, he gave security a wave, comforted by knowing the guys would keep an eye on his bike.

Since Shawn and Sana were not expected in until ten or there-abouts, Jack decided to finish the paperwork on all his outstanding cases if possible, so that when he went back to doing autopsies he'd be starting out with a perfectly clean slate, something he'd not experienced in the thirteen years he'd been there. Wanting to get a coffee as well as a sense of what was generally happening in the morgue that morning, Jack went up to the ID room, where he knew one of the better MEs was on duty for the week, Dr. Riva

Mehta. She had been Laurie's office mate for many years and was a dedicated, intelligent, and hardworking colleague, which was more than Jack could say about too many others on the staff.

He could smell the coffee even before he got there. Although he teased Vinnie mercilessly about most everything else, Jack never teased him about making the coffee. Vinnie had it down to a science, and by not varying his technique, the coffee was not only good for institutional brew, it was also consistent. After a half-hour bike ride, it always hit the spot.

"Anything particularly interesting?" Jack asked Riva, squeezing behind her where she was sitting at the desk to glance over her shoulder before turning his attention to the coffee.

"It's about time, you lazy bum," a husky voice announced.

Jack looked up from the coffee machine to see his old friend Lieutenant Detective Lou Soldano toss Vinnie's *Daily News* aside and struggle to his feet. As usual, when Lou appeared early in the morning, it looked as if he'd been up all night, which he had been, with his tie loosened, his shirt's top button unbuttoned, and his broad cheeks and neck stubbled. To complete the picture, the dark bags under his eyes hung down like a hound dog's to intersect with his tired smile creases, while his closely cropped hair, which was never particularly combed, was standing up on end near his cowlick. It looked like he hadn't been home for a week, not just overnight.

"Lou, old friend," Jack said with true affection. "Just the man I want to see."

"Yeah, how's that?" Lou asked warily, as he sauntered over to join Jack at the coffee machine. They briefly shook hands.

"I never apologized for the ridiculous conversation I forced you to have. Remember? It was about chiropractic."

"Of course I remember. Why do you think you have to apologize?"

"I was on a mini-crusade, and I think I carried it all a little too far for a couple of people, yourself included."

"Bullshit, but if you want to apologize, fine! You're forgiven. Now apologize for coming in here so late. I've been here for forty-five minutes thinkin' you'd be coming through the door any second."

"I'm off autopsies this week."

"Christ! Wouldn't you know! How about letting me know next time?"

"I would have let you know this time if I thought you cared. What's up?"

"It was a busy night last night, besides the usual mayhem. There was an arsonist's fire in the West Village, which burnt up three people, two of whom the archbishop tells me you knew."

"Who?" Jack demanded, although he had a sudden painful feeling he already knew, especially it being the West Village, with the archbishop involved. "Was it on Morton Street?"

"Yeah, it was. Forty Morton Street. How well did you know them?"

"One more than the other," Jack said, catching his breath. He suddenly felt weak-kneed. "Good grief," he added, with a shake of his head. "What happened?"

"We're still piecing it all together. How did you know them?"

Jack handed Lou the coffee he was holding and then poured himself another. "I think we better sit down," he said. When they had, Jack told the story about Shawn and Sana Daughtry, and that he had known both Shawn and the archbishop in college. Until he knew more from Lou, he didn't mention the ossuary. "I was at Forty Morton Street last Saturday night for dinner."

"Lucky you weren't there last night," Lou said. "It was a typical arsonist's blaze. The accelerant was gasoline in the basement, but not a lot of help was needed. The house was an eighteenth-century wood-frame firetrap."

"Have you made IDs on the three victims?"

"Reasonably, but we're hoping for confirmation from the OCME. We're quite sure two of the victims are the owners of the house, but we need to corroborate. Everybody is burnt up to a cinder. The third victim was more difficult to identify. We ended up finding some of his belongings, and he is now the prime arson suspect. His name we believe is Luke Hester, and it turns out he's one of these religious nuts who lives upstate at a monastery with a dubious reputation that is dedicated to the Virgin Mary. By contacting the monastery, we learned he was on some kind of assignment to the archbishop of New York, who we then roused out of bed. From the archbishop we got the story. Apparently, this third victim, who truly is supposed to have been some kind of religious fanatic, was temporarily living with the Daughtrys. It's the archbishop's fear that the religious guy killed both himself and the couple as a kind of martyrdom to keep them from publishing anything negative about the Blessed Mother, Mother of God. Can you believe this? I tell you, only in New York City."

"How was the archbishop when you spoke with him?" Jack asked. He could hardly imagine what James was thinking. Jack was sure he must be devastated.

"He was not a happy camper," Lou admitted. "In fact, he was devastated," he added, as if reading Jack's inner thoughts. "Right after I told him, he couldn't talk for several minutes."

Jack didn't respond but rather just shook his head.

"Well, I came over here to watch you do the posts," Lou said. "Just in case some unexpected information becomes available, which you, in particular, are famous for."

"Who's doing the three burned cases?" Jack called over to Riva.

"I am," Riva answered. "But if you want one or two or all three, just let me know."

"No, thank you!" Jack responded. He had already made up his mind to help James rather than Lou by gathering up all the evidence of the ossuary affair and getting it into James's hands. "There you go, Lou," Jack said to his detective friend. "Dr. Mehta is one of the best. I'm certain you will find her more charming than I, and even a bit faster."

"When are you planning on starting, honey?" Lou called over to Riva. Jack cringed. Riva didn't like to be called "honey" by chauvinistic policemen, as evidenced by her not bothering to answer. With his back toward Riva, Jack stepped between her and Lou and made a motion of drawing his finger beneath his chin as if cutting his throat. "No *honey* or *darling* or anything like that," Jack whispered, for Lou's benefit.

"Gotcha!" Lou voiced with immediate understanding. He rephrased his question and got an immediate response: fifteen minutes.

"I got a last bit of advice," Jack said. "Don't waste a lot of time on this investigation. It's nothing more than a sad, regrettable tragedy in which everyone was doing what they thought they had to do."

"I'd pretty much gotten that impression talking with the archbishop," Lou countered. "The monk had no criminal record whatsoever. The most curious aspect, though, was how professional he behaved, except at the end, getting burnt up himself. Our arson investigators were impressed. Not only did he use an accelerant, gasoline, but he knew how to vaporize it maximally and also how to use trailers in the basement to take the fire to all areas of the cellar in the quickest time. He even axed a few vent holes to make sure the fire rose through the house quicker than it would have done otherwise. The man was a natural arsonist."

"I have my cell phone," Jack said, shaking Lou's hand again.

"Right now I'm going to run over to the archbishop's and console him. He's probably blaming himself, since he's the one who introduced the parties. I can't understand why he didn't call me."

"You're right about him blaming himself," Lou said. "He said as much to me. I'm sure he'd like to hear from you."

"Longer than I'd like to admit," Jack said. Confident he was leaving Lou in terrific hands, Jack reversed his direction and proceeded back down to the basement, on his way to the office of the motor pool. Although he had some mild concern about irritating Calvin after the fact, Jack had it in mind to borrow a white medical examiner's transportation team (METT) van with a driver for thirty to forty minutes. When he walked into the motor pool, he wasn't concerned any longer. All five drivers were sitting around having coffee. Five minutes later, Jack was riding shotgun with Pete Molina driving. Pete had been one of the night drivers with whom Jack had gotten acquainted but who'd recently been moved to the day shift.

They drove quickly up to the OCME DNA building, where Jack had Pete pull into the loading dock and wait. Running inside, Jack had security open the lab the Daughtrys had been using. Locking the door behind him, Jack did not waste any time, lest Lou's investigative team learn of the lab before Jack could remove the relics. Jack had a sudden urge to see that everything went back to its rightful owner, a job best done by James.

Back into the ossuary went everything: bones, scrolls, even the remainder of the samples Sana had been working on within the laboratory itself. When that was all in place, Jack added two more objects: the codex and Saturninus's letter, which Shawn had brought from his office two days previously. Jack then loaded the ossuary onto the cart that Shawn had used to bring up all the glass panes.

After checking a second time to be certain he had everything, Jack pushed the cart back down to the service elevator and then to the loading dock. Luckily, Pete was still exactly where Jack had left him. If a delivery had come in, he would have had to move. After showing his ID to another member of security, Jack carried the ossuary onto the METT van and made sure it was properly secured.

"Okay," Pete said, starting the motor. "Where to?"

"The archbishop of New York's residence," Jack said.

Pete looked at Jack. "Am I supposed to know where that is?"

"Fifty-first and Madison. You can turn left on Fifty-first off Madison and pull over to the curb. You'll be dumping me off. You don't have to wait." Jack didn't elaborate for two reasons. One, he wanted the least number of people to know what he'd done, and two, he was already deep in thought of what he was going to say to James. Jack knew that had the roles been reversed, he would have been feeling cataleptic.

Once Pete had navigated the crosstown traffic and turned onto Madison, the drive up to Saint Patrick's Cathedral was slow but steady. It took a bit less than thirty minutes by the time Pete was able to pull over to the side of the road next to the residence. As soon as they'd come to a stop, Jack hopped out, slid open the van's door, got the ossuary over to the edge, and then lifted it. By then Pete had come around, and he closed the slider.

"I appreciate the help, Pete," Jack said over his shoulder.

"No problem," Pete said, eyeing the stark, gray stone residence.

Jack hauled the ossuary up the front stone steps and, balancing it on a bent knee, gave the receiving bell a good pull. Within he could hear the chimes. Always mindful of possible imminent disasters, Jack could suddenly see himself dropping the awkward ossuary down the stone steps, where it would certainly shatter and dump the bones, scrolls, glass panes, codex, and Saturninus's letter out onto the concrete. As a consequence, Jack gripped the stone more tightly and was even contemplating putting it down when the door was swept open by the same priest who'd welcomed him to lunch.

"Dr. Stapleton," Father Maloney commented. "What can I do for you?"

"It might be nice to invite me in," Jack suggested, with a touch of sarcasm.

"Yes, of course, come in!" Father Maloney stepped back to give room. "Is the cardinal expecting you?"

"He might be, since he knows more about what's been going on than I, but I'm not certain. Why don't I wait where I waited last week?"

"That is a superb idea. The archbishop is meeting now with the vicar general, but I will let him know you are here."

"Very good," Jack said. On his own, he'd already started down the hall, clearly remembering where the small private study was located. Father Maloney sprinted ahead and held the door ajar by the time Jack arrived. The first thing Jack did was place the ossuary on the floor. He was careful not to damage the flawless surface.

"Is there anything I can get you while you wait?"

"If you sense it is going to be a while, a newspaper might be nice."

"Would the *Times* suffice?"

"That would be fine."

Father Maloney closed the door behind him. Jack looked around the ascetic room, noting the same details he had on the previous visit, including the strong but not overbearing odor of cleaning fluid and floor wax. Already starting to get warm, he pulled off his leather jacket and tossed it onto the small club chair. Then he sat down on the mini-couch exactly as he'd done when he'd come for lunch, making him acknowledge how much a creature of habit he was.

Contrary to his concern, he did not have long to wait. Within just a few moments of Father Maloney's departure, the door burst open. Dressed like a simple priest, James stepped into the room.

After closing the door behind him, he rushed over to Jack and mimicked their greeting the week before with a brotherly hug. "Thank you, thank you, for coming right over," James managed. It was then that he caught sight of the ossuary. As if a schoolboy, James let go of Jack and clapped his hands in appreciation. "You already brought the ossuary! Oh, thank you! You have answered a prayer that the ossuary would come back to the Church. Tell me, is everything back into it?" James had his palms pressed together as if in prayer.

"Everything is in it," Jack said. "Bones, samples, all of the scrolls, even Saturninus's letter and the codex it came from. After what has happened, I felt I wanted to get it into your hands as soon as possible."

"What did you think of this tragedy?"

"I was blown away," Jack said. "I learned about it only an hour or so ago. I was told by a friend, Lieutenant Detective Lou Soldano."

"I met him last night," James said. "He was here at the residence."

"He told me," Jack said. "He's a good man."

"I sensed that."

"Why didn't you call me as soon as you learned what had happened?"

"I don't know. I thought about it, but I'm so confused. Jack, I don't know if I'm guilty or not."

Jack looked askance at James. "What are you talking about? What do you think you might be guilty of?"

"Murder," James said. Unable to maintain eye contact with Jack, he looked away. "I don't know if I didn't suspect in the hidden corners of my mind that there was a chance this might happen. When one plays with fire, pardon the pun, one can get burnt. I knew the person I was asking for would be unbalanced, maybe even to the extent of feeling he could use sin to fight what he considered to be a bigger sin. Luke called me yesterday morning to tell me that Shawn was about to change his mind and not publish. He said he was confident of success, and it was more due to tactics than argument. I should have known then that a tragedy was about to unfold, but instead I was so pleased plan B was going to work, I didn't question what Luke meant by the word *tactics*. Obviously, in hindsight he meant this horrid martyrdom."

"James, look at me!" Jack demanded, holding on to both of James's shoulders and giving them a gentle shake. "Look at me!" Jack insisted. James's face was an agony of torment, with injected eyes awash with tears and slack skin. Slowly his brimming, blue eyes came up to meet Jack's. "I was part of this almost from day one," Jack continued. "Never once did you have any wishes of physical injury, much less thoughts of death toward Shawn or Sana. Never! Your goal was to find someone passionate and persuasive about the Virgin Mary, which you did. To go beyond that and scheme of killing someone is something your mind or my mind is not capable of doing. It's only after the fact that we are able to consider it. Please don't magnify the tragedy by trying to take responsibility. The responsibility was in the mind of the perpetrator, which we will never understand. Something set him off. Probably we'll never know what, but something."

"Do you truly believe what you are saying, or are you just trying to mollify me?"

"I believe it one hundred percent."

"Thank you for being supportive. Your thoughts are important to me. You have encouraged me to take some time off to think and pray about this affair. I'm going to ask the Holy Father if I could spend a month or so at a monastery conducive to such contemplation and prayer."

"That sounds like a good, healthy plan."

"But first this awful episode must be cleaned up," James said.

He looked intently up into Jack's face. "I'm afraid I have to ask one more rather large favor from you, my friend."

"And what can that be?"

"The ossuary!" James said. "I need to ask you to help me put it back."

"Put it back where?" Jack questioned, although he already guessed. He guessed because he too thought it was the best solution to the entire unfortunate episode. The ossuary should go back to where Shawn and Sana had found it, under Saint Peter's. "Do you mean take it back to Rome . . . ?" Jack continued, his voice trailing off.

"I knew you would understand," James said, reviving to a degree from his melancholy. "You and I are the only ones who know about the story. I would not be able to do it myself. You must help me, and the sooner, the better."

Jack's immediate thought was Laurie, especially considering JJ and the need to check his antibody level to see if treatment could be restarted. "I'm afraid I have a full schedule these days," Jack said. "When were you thinking of doing this?"

"Tonight," James said matter-of-factly. "I have already made reservations for us late this afternoon. I hope you don't feel aggravated by my presumptuousness assuming you'd agree. The ossuary will be coming with us on the same flight. We'll be in Rome in the morning, and tomorrow night I will make arrangements to put the ossuary back where it came from. Then, if you'd like, you can come back to New York on Saturday. It's taking you all the way to Rome, but you'll be gone for only two nights. Don't make me beg, Jack."

Jack suddenly had a thought that made the idea of flying all the way to Europe seem like an interesting idea above and beyond putting the ossuary back into its burial site. It involved one of the three sheets of computer printouts he'd placed in his inner jacket pocket when he'd been packing everything else back into the ossuary in the lab. Instead of adding the printouts to the other objects, since they had come from the lab, he decided to pocket them with the idea of mulling them over at a later date. One of the pages had the name and an address of a patient seen at the Ein Kerem campus of the Hadassah Medical Center.

"I tell you what," Jack said. "I'll come tonight and help you put back the ossuary under two conditions. Number one, my wife, Laurie, and our four-month-old child come with us, provided I can talk her into it, and two, I can tell my wife the whole story of the ossuary."

"Oh, Jack," James whined. "The reason I need you to help is to avoid telling anyone else."

"Sorry, James, that's my offer. But I can assure you she's as good as I or better when it comes to secrets. Not being able to tell her has been a burden and, frankly, not telling her and going all the way to Rome doesn't sit well with me. Anyway, those are the two conditions if you want me to go tonight."

James thought for a few moments and quickly decided that if he had to risk telling someone else, Jack's wife was probably the best risk.

"All right," James said reluctantly. "What time can you get back to me?"

"If all goes smoothly, within the hour. Should we meet here or at the airport?"

"Meet here. I'll have Father Maloney drive us out to Kennedy in the Range Rover."

Leaving the residence, Jack beat it back to the OCME by taxi and ran directly in to see Bingham. Unfortunately, Bingham was over at City Hall, meeting with the mayor. Instead, Jack ran up to the third floor and ducked into Calvin Washington's office.

Luckily, the deputy director was there, and Jack merely informed him that he was going to be away for a long weekend. Since Jack was already off the autopsy rotation, it didn't make much difference. Still, Jack felt better letting the powers-that-be know he definitely was not going to be in the neighborhood. Jack then went down, unfastened the tangle of locks on his bike, and headed home. He knew he had some serious uphill convincing to accomplish.

By the time Jack picked up his bike and carried it into the foyer, he was excited about the trip. He'd loved Rome the four or five times he'd been there, and he'd never been to Jerusalem. Stashing his bike in its closet, he took off up the stairs. It was now afternoon, which meant there were only three or so hours to get ready. James wanted everyone who was going to be at the residence by three.

"Laurie!" Jack yelled as he reached the kitchen, but Laurie was not to be found.

Passing the kitchen, Jack headed down the hall toward the family room and the living room. Just when he was about to yell again, he almost collided with her coming from the family room, a child-rearing book in hand. She also had an index finger pressed to her lips. "He's sleeping," she whispered forcibly. Jack pulled his head in like a turtle, feeling guilty for yelling out as he had. He knew better than to do such a thing before finding out JJ's status. He apologized effusively with the explanation that he was excited.

"What on earth are you doing home so early?" Laurie questioned. "Is everything okay?"

"It's fine!" Jack said, pronouncing "fine" with emphasis. "In fact, do I have a deal for you."

"For me?" Laurie questioned with a smile. She ducked back into the family room and regained her seat on the couch with her feet on the coffee table. She had a cup of honey tea on the side table. "Not bad, huh. Woman of leisure! JJ's having another good day. This might be the longest nap he's ever had."

"Perfect," Jack said. He sat down on the coffee table to be close when he talked with her. "First, I have to make a mini-confession. I have not told you the full story of this ossuary that my archaeologist friend and his wife had been working on. I have to say, it is fascinating. The reason I hadn't told you was because my archbishop friend pleaded with me not to do so. Anyway, that injunction is no longer valid, and I'm looking forward to telling you the whole story."

"Why the change?"

"That's a story in itself. My archaeologist friend, Shawn, and his wife were both killed last night in a house fire, so that's the end of the ossuary-contents examination."

"Oh, no! I'm so sorry," Laurie said with sincerity. "Was it the house where we visited them?"

"Yes, it was. Once those old wood-frame houses catch on fire, look out. They practically explode in flame."

"What a terrible tragedy," Laurie said. "And to think, you were just there getting reacquainted. Does this mean you are losing another diversion?"

"Not quite."

"No? You just said the deaths have halted the ossuary examination."

"That's true, but the ossuary has to go back to where it came from. I'm afraid my archaeologist friend and his wife actually stole the relic literally out from under Saint Peter's Basilica. It had been buried next to Saint Peter for almost two thousand years. I've promised the archbishop that I would help him take the ossuary back and replace it where it had been so that no one is the wiser. The archbishop and you and I will be the only ones to know of its existence, and you'll have to promise not to tell anyone ever if you want to hear its alleged details.

"Now, here's the deal. The three of us—you, JJ, and I—are going to fly tonight to Rome. Tomorrow night, I help James put the ossuary back. Then Saturday you, JJ, and I are going to fly on to Jerusalem so that we can meet with someone. Sunday we will fly home. What do you think?"

"I think you are nuts," Laurie said, without so much as a moment of thought. "You expect me to fly all night tonight with a sick four-month-old child, to be in a foreign city for not even one full day and then fly on to another city, and then fly all the way home? How long would it take to fly from Jerusalem to New York, anyway?"

"I don't know exactly. Probably quite a while. But that's not the point. I want you to do this for me. I know it sounds crazy and that it will be very difficult, probably more difficult than I can imagine, but I feel it is important for me. I will help with JJ. I'll hold him more than half the time. In Rome, we can hire a nurse to give you a little free time, same in Jerusalem. Also, he's been better for the last three or four days, I've lost count."

"It's been three days he's been better," Laurie clarified.

"Okay, three days! We can do this and be back in four days. I will really help. I'd even breast-feed him if I could."

"Yeah, sure," Laurie scoffed. "That's easy to say. So, on the plane you'll hold him even if he gets antsy and excitable."

"Yes, I will hold him. For the whole flight, if you'd like. Just say yes. You will understand more when I tell you the full story of the ossuary, which I'll do on the plane tonight. Say yes!"

"In order for me to even consider such a nutty idea of flying to Rome and Jerusalem with a sick infant, you are going to have to tell me the full story of the ossuary right this second."

"It will take too long."

"Sorry, buster. That's the deal. At least give me a synopsis."

As quickly as he could, Jack outlined the events over the last number of days beginning with his surprise luncheon visit James's residence and seeing the ossuary for the first time.

Although at first doubtful that she was going to find the story interesting enough to justify what Jack was demanding of her, Laurie became truly fascinated. "Oh, all right, damn you," Laurie said suddenly, before Jack had completed has précis. "I'll probably forget how you talked me into this moment of insanity, but you have yourself a deal, although you don't have to hold him for the whole flight, just your share, and not just when he is sleeping, either. You are going to be holding him when he's fidgeting as well as when he's lying still. Is that understood?"

"Perfectly," Jack said, his face lighting up. He leapt to his feet. "Now, I have some preparations to do and calls to make. We have to be at the archbishop's residence by three."

"You think you have preparations," Laurie said, putting her book aside. "I hope we don't regret this."

In some ways Rome was a disappointment for Jack. On his other visits, which had all been in late spring, summer, and early fall, the weather had been bright, sunny, and warm. On this occasion in December, Rome was overcast, dreary, and damp, with some rain. On top of that, he'd anticipated some cloak-and-dagger intrigue involving sneaking the ossuary into the Vatican and then getting it from where they would be staying into the necropolis. Instead, what he learned was that the Vatican was more or less run like a gigantic club for the benefit of the cardinals. If you were a cardinal, anything but everything was okay.

Since James had used the same carton to take the ossuary back as it had arrived, it was naturally assumed by any handlers that the contents were his personal belongings. There had been no attempt whatsoever even to suggest opening it at the airport either on departure or arrival, or when they entered the Vatican. As James had made arrangements for all of them to stay within the Vatican at Casa di Santa Marta, named after the patron saint of hoteliers, Saint Martin, the ossuary and their checked baggage was there waiting for them when they arrived. After having claimed it all at the airport, it had gone ahead in a Vatican van, while James and his entourage had come into town on what James called, "the more scenic route."

The Casa di Santa Marta was built to house the cardinals during a conclave when they were supposed to be attentive to the business of electing a new pope, so the décor was decidedly ascetic, another mild disappointment for Jack. When James had told them they were all staying within the Vatican, Jack had allowed himself to fantasize about some Renaissance décor.

What had been better than expected had been the night flight and JJ. Not only had JJ slept for a long nap that afternoon, he also slept most of the night on the plane, first in Laurie's arms, then Jack's. Jack had had plenty of time to tell Laurie the details of the ossuary story, which he had glossed over that afternoon.

"Will I get to see it?" Laurie had asked.

"There's no reason why not," Jack had responded.

To eliminate any potential snafus for that night, James arranged a private tour of the necropolis for that afternoon with one of the archaeologists from the Pontifical Commission for Sacred Archaeology. When the time came for the tour to begin, JJ was again conveniently asleep, encouraging Laurie to say, "He's catching up from the last two months." Although Laurie was hesitant, she allowed James to talk her into coming on the tour after James found several nuns willing to stay with JJ, one of whom would come and get Laurie the moment the child awoke.

The visit turned out to be quite helpful. At first they couldn't figure out where it could have been that Shawn and Sana had found the ossuary, and it wasn't until the resident archaeologist pointed out to them that to get to the tunnel entering Peter's tomb, one had to raise one of the panels of the glass tourist deck to get down to the lowest level of the most recent excavation.

Although Jack did feel some tenseness and nervousness prior to his and James's setting out that night after ten with Jack carrying the ossuary and James an enormous ring of keys, it quickly dissipated. Jack had thought they would have to sneak in, but they didn't. James had actually visited the archpriest, also a cardinal, who currently administered the basilica, and told him flat out he wanted to visit Clementine Chapel and Peter's tomb that night, and was given the ring of keys and assured the lights would all be left on.

The walk from Casa di Santa Marta to the northwest apse entrance of Saint Peter's was thankfully short, less than a New York City block. After James unlocked the door, Jack walked into the hushed and darkened basilica through what he later learned was the Porta della Preghiera. To him, entering the basilica was the single most memorable moment of the evening. About a half-hour earlier the clouds outside had parted, at least temporarily, and a gibbous moon had slid into view seemingly for Jack's benefit, which was now sending shafts of moonlight through the windows at the base of Michelangelo's dome. The effect was to emphasize the vastness of the interior of the building.

"Beautiful, isn't it?" James questioned, coming up behind Jack.

"It's enough to make me religious," Jack responded, only half in jest.

James led the way across the transept, crossing to the column of Saint Andrews, one of the four holding up the enormous dome, where he unlocked another door that led below to the crypt.

It took them another twenty minutes to descend all the way down to the lowest level of the excavation and the exact location in the wall of the tunnel leading into Peter's tomb where the ossuary was found. The spot was marked by a sharply defined rectangular opening in the wall. Since the dirt was loose, Jack was able to dig it out with ease and quickly discovered all the lights, buckets, and other paraphernalia that Shawn and Sana had used and then buried.

"We're going to have to haul this stuff away," Jack said. "But it will be easy. We can use the buckets. But first why don't you find me some water? I can make a paste and really seal this up."

"Great idea," James said. "I saw a water source a ways back."

While James was off foraging for the water, Jack got the ossuary back into the wall and started packing the rocks, dirt, and gravel around its sides. By the time James came back, he was ready to do the most exterior part, packing now-wet dirt on the end of the ossuary. When he was finished, it was almost impossible to see where the opening had been. As he was packing the last of the dirt, he thought about one unfortunate legacy of what he was doing hiding the ossuary. Mankind would have to forgo the Gospel of Simon. Jack felt bad about that, and although he'd never had much interest in the history of Christianity, he did now, and he would now always wonder what Simon Magus had really been like. Was he the bad boy he'd always been portrayed as, or had he been something else entirely?

As much as Rome was rainy, gray, and dreary, Israel was crystal clear, with a desert-blue sky, and dazzlingly, even luminously, bright. Jack, Laurie, and JJ came into the country on a noontime Rome–Tel Aviv flight, with Jack's nose pressed against the glass. Once again, JJ surpassed Laurie's best-case scenario. As soon as the plane had gotten to altitude, he'd dropped off to sleep, and he was still sleeping when the wheels touched down with a thump and squeak on arrival.

Waiting for them at the gate was a representative of a tour company called Mabat, who helped them through passport control and baggage formalities and then seamlessly handed them off to a car and driver scheduled to take them to Jerusalem. Jack had gotten the name of the tour company from a seasoned traveler, because he wanted to maximize the short time they were planning on staying in the country. The driver, for his part, took them directly to the King David Hotel, where he handed them off to an expat, Midwesterner-cum knowledgeable-tour-guide by the name of Hillel Kestler.

"I understand you want to go first to the Palestinian village called Tsur Baher," Hillel said with a smile. "Now, I've gotten lots of different personal requests, but this is the first to Tsur Baher. Can I ask why? There's not much to see there, I have to warn you about that."

"I want to meet this woman," Jack said, handing over the name and address that had come out of the computer uploaded with CODIS 6.0 and attached to the 3130XL genetic analyzer.

"Jamilla Mohammod," Hillel read. "Do you know her?"

"Not yet," Jack said. "But I'd like to ask her for a favor, a favor that I'm willing to pay for. Is this something you could help us with? Do you speak Arabic?"

"Not too terribly well," Hillel admitted, "but probably good enough. When would you like to go?"

"We have only today and tomorrow unless we decide to stay longer," Jack said. "If you don't mind, let's go. I assume you have a vehicle for us."

"Most definitely. I have a Volkswagen van."

"Perfect. Let's go, Laurie."

"Are you sure about this?" Laurie asked, not sounding convinced. She'd heard the story of the ossuary and the results of the mitochondrial DNA, but still had misgivings.

"We've come all this way. How long to the village, Hillel?"

"It will take about twenty minutes to get there," the guide said.

"Twenty minutes, that's all," Jack said. He reached for JJ and took him out of Laurie's arms. "Let's give it a whirl. There's nothing to lose."

"All right," Laurie said finally.

Exactly eighteen minutes later, Hillel made a turn into a village with a dirt street and a handful of concrete cube-style houses sprouting rebars for further expansion. There were some shops, including a smoke shop, a small general store, and a spice shop. There was also a school with lots of kids in uniforms.

"The easiest way to do this is to visit the mukhtar," Hillel said over the voices of the children.

"What's a mukhtar?" Jack questioned back.

"It means *chosen* in Arabic," Hillel said. He closed the vehicle's windows so as not to need to shout. "It refers to the head of a village. He will know Jamilla Mohammod for sure."

"Do you know the mukhtar here in Tsur Baher?" Jack asked. He was sitting in the front passenger seat. Laurie was in the back, with JJ in his car-seat carrier.

"No, I don't. But it doesn't matter."

Hillel parked and then ran into the general store. While he was gone, several of the schoolchildren wandered over and stared up at Jack. Jack smiled and waved at them. A few of the children self-consciously waved back. Then a man came out of the store and waved the children away.

A moment later, Hillel reappeared from inside the store. He walked over to Jack's side of the car. Jack lowered the window.

"There's a sitting area in the store," Hillel explained. "It's the local hangout, and conveniently the mukhtar happens to be here. I asked about Jamilla, and he has sent for her. If you want to meet her, you are invited inside."

"Terrific," Jack said. He climbed from the car and opened the sliding door for Laurie and JJ.

The interior of the store was stacked with all manner of goods from floor to ceiling, from groceries to toys, from hardware to computer paper. The sitting area Hillel had mentioned was in the rear, with a single window looking out on a hardscrabble backyard supporting a covey of skinny chickens.

The mukhtar was an elderly man in Arabic dress, with sun-baked leathery skin. He was contentedly puffing on a hookah. He was clearly pleased to have company and quickly ordered tea all around. He was also eager to hear that the Stapletons were from New York City because he had family there and had visited twice. While he was busy explaining which part of Brooklyn he'd visited, Jamilla Mohammod walked in. Like the mukhtar, she too was in Arabic dress. She wasn't completely covered, but her dress was black, as was her knotted scarf. Her exposed skin on her hands and face was also about the same color and consistency as the mukhtar's. Life had been a struggle for both, it was clear.

Unfortunately, Jamilla did not speak English, but since the mukhtar did to a degree, Jack spoke to Jamilla with the mukhtar's kind intervention. He first asked her if she had any experience as a healer. Her answer was some experience but mostly with her own children, of which there were eight, five boys and three girls.

He asked her if she'd ever been sick. Her answer was no, although the year before she'd been hit by a car in Jerusalem and had been in the Hadassah hospital for a week with broken bones and blood loss. Jack then asked her if she would try to cure his child by placing her hand on his head and declaring him cured of his cancer. Jack pulled out several hundred dollars in cash and

placed it on the low table. He said it was consideration for her efforts. Jack then took JJ from Laurie and approached the woman.

For the moment JJ was seemingly pleased to be the center of
attention. He cooed contentedly as Jamilla did as she was asked.
The mukhtar translated as Jamilla said that she wanted all illness
cast from the child's body from that moment on. It was obvious
she was self-conscious and unaccustomed to such a role.

Laurie looked on, she too feeling self-conscious. Jack had told
her what he was planning, and although she thought it somewhat
embarrassing, she also thought it harmless, and if Jack seriously
wanted to go through with it, she wouldn't stand in the way. Now,
as it was actually happening, she truly didn't know what to think.
Jack was the opposite. When he'd thought about doing it, he
wanted to go through with it as a way of leaving no stone un-
turned. There was something mystical about the ossuary, and he
wanted to take advantage of it. Now that the faith healing was
actually being attempted, however, he felt silly, like he was grasping for straws. Well, he was grasping for straws.

"Okay!" Jack said suddenly when he felt the affair had gone on
a bit too long, and he pulled JJ back from Jamilla's touch. "That's
terrific! Thank you very much!" He picked up the money, handed
it to Jamilla, then started for the door. All of a sudden he wanted
to be away, to forget the situation. He knew that his actions were
motivated by desperation, just like that of other desperate patients
forced into the hands of alternative medicine. But the reason Jack
wanted to get back out to the car quickly was because he was
afraid he was about to cry.

A ll right," Dr. Urit Effron said. He was on the full-time staff of
the Hadassah University Hospital in Ein Kerem, Jerusalem.
"Here come the images from the Siemens E-Cam, and we'll have

a better idea why your son's urine yesterday was normal for cat-echolamine metabolites."

Jack and Laurie strained forward. Both were intensely inter-ested. The previous day, leaving the town of Tsur Baher, they'd driven back to Jerusalem, where they decided to go to the emer-gency room at the Hadassah hospital. The episode with the faith healer had started them talking about JJ, especially since he'd been acting so normal. What they had decided to do was see if they could get an antibody level for mouse proteins done while they were on the road so that they could recommence treatment as soon as they got home.

What they learned was that they would have to return to Me-morial in New York City for that test, but the pediatric oncology resident who saw them offered to do the blood tests available to see how active JJ's tumors were in light of his doing so well. To everyone's astonishment, particularly his parents, the results had come back normal. At that point the resident had offered to repeat the definitive test for neuroblastoma called an MIBG scan.

Having learned a significant amount about the test and its risks and benefits when JJ had been diagnosed, both Jack and Laurie were eager to repeat it. They wanted to know where they stood after the first go-round with treatment at Memorial hospital. After the injection of the short-half-life radioactive iodine the day be-fore, they had returned for the scan to be done. At that moment, the first images were coming from the machine.

"Well, there you go," Dr. Effron said, "the homovanillic acid and the vanillylmandelic acid were normal because there are no more tumors."

Jack and Laurie ventured a glance at each other. Neither wanted to speak, lest the trance they were in would burst and they'd be forced back to reality. It seemed JJ had been cured!

"This is very good news indeed," Dr. Effron said, looking up from the screen to make certain the parents had heard. "Three cheers for Memorial. Your son's one of the lucky ones."

"What are you trying to tell us?" Laurie forced herself to ask.

"Neuroblastomas, particularly with very young patients like your son, can be unpredictable. They can just suddenly resolve— cure themselves, if you will. Or they can respond to treatment like this. Were your son's rather extensive or widely spread?"

"Very widely spread," Laurie said, beginning to allow herself to accept what she was seeing, no tumors, and what she was hearing, that JJ was cured. Had it been spontaneous as Dr. Effron suggested, or had it been the mouse antibody from Memorial, or had it been Jamilla, Laurie had no idea, but at the moment she truly didn't care.

Bibliography

During the research for *Intervention* I was fascinated by the rich history of early Christianity and the realities of the alternative-medicine issue. For those who might want to read further about both issues, I recommend the following:

Bausell, R. Barker. *Snake Oil Science*, Oxford, 2007

Chadwick, Henry. *The Early Church*, Penguin, Revised Edition, 1993.

Matkin, J. Michael. *The Complete Idiot's Guide to the Gnostic Gospels*, Alpha, 2005.

Matkin, J. Michael. *The Complete Idiot's Guide to Early Christianity*, Alpha, 2008.

Pagels, Elaine. *The Gnostic Gospels*, Vintage, 1979.

Singh, Simon, and Edzard Ernst, M.D. *Trick or Treatment*, Norton, 2008.

Walsh, John Evangelist. *The Bones of St. Peter*, Doubleday, 1982.

Concerning the issue of sex and the modern Catholic Church, I'd recommend the short but thought-provoking article:

Carroll, James. "From Celibacy to Godliness," *The Boston Globe*, page A19, April 9, 2002.